Everything For Marriage

Forbidden to love, and divided by family feuds—could these couples overcome their past to discover that sometimes it's worth risking everything for marriage?

Everything For Marriage

Laurie Paige

Lindsay McKenna

SILHOUETTE®

*First published in Great Britain 2004
Silhouette Books, Eton House, 18-24 Paradise Road,
Richmond, Surrey TW9 1SR*

EVERYTHING FOR MARRIAGE © Harlequin Books S.A. 2004

The publisher acknowledges the copyright holders of the
individual works as follows:

A River to Cross © Olivia M. Hall 1994
The Cougar © Lindsay McKenna 1998

ISBN 0 373 04963 3

64-0504

*Printed and bound in Spain
by Litografia Rosés S.A., Barcelona*

A River to Cross

LAURIE PAIGE

LAURIE PAIGE

writes: 'Sometimes an idea just catches the imagination and won't let go. That happened eight years ago when I read about a pair of eagles in a nature magazine. I knew right then that I'd write the 'eagle' story someday. Each time I'd come up with a hero and heroine, I'd wonder, 'Is this the eagle story?' It wasn't until I visited the Rogue River that it all came together—the eagle theme, the story ideas (like a lightning storm my husband and I once witnessed there, several stories hit me at once) and the characters. Every part of the river was material for a story—ranches, logging operations, pear orchards, resorts, towns and fishing villages.'

Chapter One

"If you'll sign here...." The lawyer slid a sheet of paper and a pen across the polished surface of the desk. "It basically says you picked up the key from us."

Tina Henderson read the form over carefully. She'd learned long ago not to take things—or people—at face value. When she finished, she wrote her name, Bettina J. Henderson, at the bottom, laid the pen on the desk and picked up the key.

Her heart suddenly kicked into overdrive, beating so hard it nearly shook her whole body. Until that moment, she'd thought she was confident about returning to the Rogue Valley area of southern Oregon. She wasn't. Doubts crowded in and she felt...scared.

She stared at the key. Would it open the door to a new life for her? Or would it lead to new hurt in the town that had rejected her and her mother so long ago?

"You'll join me and my wife for lunch, won't you?"

Jack Norton asked. "Adrianna would never forgive me if I let a famous international TV reporter get away without her getting a chance to ask you all about it."

Tina forced her gaze from the key, which felt hot in her hand, and nodded at the attorney. He was in his early thirties. His manner was brisk and his smile generous. He'd been a great help, handling the details of the inheritance during the past months.

Tina Henderson, Heiress! That should make the headlines of the *Riverton Daily News*.

"Good," he said. "I made reservations at the ski lodge. It's a little out of your way, but I thought you might enjoy seeing the countryside. Then I can drop you off—"

"Thanks, but I have a car." She smiled in satisfaction. Having her own transportation was important. "I'll follow you."

She placed the house key in her purse, then slipped her arms into her warm coat when Jack held it for her. In the outer room she said goodbye to the secretary, who had called her many times at the office in Rome during the months it had taken to settle the estate of Anne Snyder, her godmother.

Outside, she unlocked the door of the shiny blue station wagon she'd bought shortly after returning to the States. Its four-wheel drive would make it easier to get out and about in the mountainous country.

March 28, she thought, turning on the wipers to clear the windshield of the snow that had been falling steadily since she'd arrived. What had happened to spring?

Some welcome home.

Again her heart went into a flurry of beats. She clenched the steering wheel, frightened by things she couldn't put a name to.

Quickly, she brought herself under control. She was twenty-nine years old, for heaven's sake, not eighteen. No one could scare her into leaving the way Shane Macklin had long ago.

She sighed, then smiled ruefully. The Macklins were a law unto themselves. They ruled the town and the county. Shane was the sheriff now. He could run things with the sanctity of the law behind him.

He'd better not tell her to get out of town this time. She knew her rights. She'd tell him where to get off. She laughed at her bravado and ignored the sinking feeling in her middle.

The attorney pulled out of the parking lot. She put the car into gear and followed him. Out on the interstate, she stayed several car lengths behind his black sedan. Their sedate pace gave her an opportunity to study the country around her.

The land was ruggedly beautiful. Medford was only 1300 feet above sea level. At 7533, Mount Ashland, thirty miles distant, was the highest point west of the Cascades. Ski trails meandered through the fir and pine forests on the high slopes. Ironically, she'd learned to ski in France, not Oregon.

It had been a long time since she'd been back to the town—eleven years, to be exact—and twenty years since she'd actually lived there. Without the inheritance, would she have returned?

No. She answered the question truthfully in her own mind. The memories of her visits and of the year she and her mother had lived there after her grandfather's death still hurt.

Lorrie's love child.

She'd overheard her grandmother and grandfather talking about her and her mother more than once. They'd talked in hushed, bitter tones about her father, wondering who he was. She herself had wanted to know the identity of the man who'd been her biological father, but her mother had refused to talk about the past.

Tina sighed. She, too, would put the past behind her. Her grandparents had died long ago. Her mother, who'd once left town in disgrace, had married a wonderful man, a college philosophy teacher who'd adopted Tina and treated her as his own.

At the present, she had a job to do—write a book, based on her coverage of events for CNN, on the effects of war on women and children. She had many chilling, unhappy stories to tell. Maybe the world would wake up before it was too late.

A sheriff's car passed her. Her breath caught in her throat. She glimpsed the driver. It wasn't Shane Macklin.

She relaxed her grip on the steering wheel and pulled the cold air into her lungs. She'd have to face him sometime. She knew that. She just wasn't quite ready to do so on her first day back.

The parking lot at the ski resort was pretty full for a Monday in March. People from the valley up for a day of skiing, Shane Macklin decided, pulling into an empty slot. When he stepped out of the warm patrol truck, the wind hit him full in the face, blowing fiercely down the mountain, bringing more snow.

Just what they needed, he thought with a frown of worry and irritation. There would be a dozen accidents on the county roads and main highway before midnight. He'd already ordered a full crew out on extra duty. That would blow the budget even more.

So what else was new?

The winter had been unusual, with hardly a day without fresh snow falling, even in the valley, which was supposed to have mild winters. Mild, ha! So far, it had been colder than a witch's nose in the Klondike. He smiled as he used his family's version of the saying. His mother had been stern about vulgarisms.

He settled his hat more firmly on his head and leaned into the wind. He had a luncheon meeting with the ski-resort owner about some break-ins on the property. They suspected some squatters on public land. He'd probably have to run them off.

The thought of telling people to leave made him uncomfortable. Years ago, he'd done that to someone. He recalled the unreadable emotion that had flitted through her eyes. Then she'd smiled at him. ''Make me,'' she'd challenged.

At the time, he'd been furious. Looking back, he felt other things. Regret, for one. Over the years, he'd tried to figure that out. After all, he'd been acting in the best interests of his family. He'd had to do something about her.

But those eyes…gray and stormy like clouds. She'd been defiant, foolhardy, as she faced him. And valiant. Even now, he felt a niggling admiration for her spunk.

He shook his head. He'd used the oldest, low-downest trick a man could use on a woman—the threat of physical harm.

The kiss, meant to punish and frighten, had backfired. He'd never forgotten it. He didn't know if it had been the rage or her, but no other kiss had ever stirred him like that one.

He grimaced in disgust. His action had been that of a bully, and she'd repaid him in kind by biting him. He still carried the scars of that ill-advised episode. Anyway, the kiss had worked. She'd left town and hadn't been seen in those parts again. He had no reason to feel guilty about that little gold digger.

Enough of the past. He had other problems. The hassles never let up, it seemed. Maybe he was just getting old. He'd be thirty-six on his next birthday. If a male's life expectancy was seventy-two, he'd have lived half of his at that point.

Now *that* was a depressing thought. He grinned at his own morbid thinking.

After stamping the snow from his boots, he entered the lodge and went upstairs to the restaurant. He paused on the threshold of the attractive room.

The view from the plate-glass windows was magnificent—mountains and conifers, creeks and boulders, all covered over with ice and snow…a fairyland to behold. He liked nothing better than strapping on skis and heading out cross-country over the frozen meadows and streams.

The grandeur. The quiet. The solitude.

God, he missed the solitude. Not much of that in his life anymore. He wondered when things had gotten so complicated.

Since his brother's marriage, for one. And since his brother's separation from his wife, for another. Maybe he'd better try and talk some sense into the two of them. Again.

"Hey, Shane, over here." The voice of his friend, Rafe Barrett, broke into his thoughts.

He hung his coat and hat on a hook and hurried to the table. "Sorry to be late. Another wreck on the interstate." He chose a seat giving him a direct view of the room and its occupants rather than the scene outside.

"You'd think people would slow down a tad in a blizzard,'' Rafe said, shaking his head at the foibles of mankind.

"But they don't," Shane finished.

"Well, I hate to bring more bad news, but we had another case of vandalism over the weekend."

"Windows?"

"Yes. In the cabins this time. Two windows in adjacent A-frames. It's strange. My security chief couldn't detect any attempt at a break-in. In one cabin, the door could have easily been opened from the broken window."

"What's the time frame?"

"Broad daylight. The couples renting the cabins returned from the ski slopes by four in the afternoon in each case."

Shane got out his notebook and wrote down the date and location. "Okay, give me the names of everyone involved," he told his friend. "How much damage was there?"

"Two windows. Less than a hundred dollars."

Shane frowned. This was the third window-breaking case in two weeks, all with no entry. Definitely a pattern there.

When the information was recorded, Rafe signaled the waitress. "I ordered lunch for us. My treat," he said.

"I don't know. That might be construed as bribing an officer of the law."

"That would be the day," Rafe scoffed. "Your integrity is matched only by your stubbornness."

Shane ignored the backhanded compliment. "So what other items are on your agenda?"

They discussed the problems of the resort in particular and county politics in general while waiting for their meal. A couple arrived for a late lunch. Shane automatically looked them over.

He recognized Jack Norton, a lawyer out of Medford. The man's companion wasn't his wife, though. This woman had dark hair, so dark Shane couldn't decide if it was brown or black. It was thick, almost straight, then curled under at her shoulders.

A client, he deduced.

She had her back to him while Jack helped her out of her coat. The lawyer hung the garment on the hook next to the one Shane had used. The sleeve of her coat—an expensive-looking fleece—brushed intimately against the black leather of his jacket.

He felt an instinctive tightening in his gut as she turned toward him. Time crawled in slow motion while he waited to see her face, but he already knew who she was.

When she looked directly at him, his lungs quit working. Out of the jumbled thoughts that buzzed through his mind like a planing saw in a logging mill, he realized one thing—he'd never forgotten those eyes. They were the color of storm clouds.

For a second, Tina was overcome by an awful need to run…just run, anywhere, away from Shane Macklin and the cutting stare he bestowed on her. It didn't take a great intellect to know that he was surprised to see her, nor to deduce his next reaction, which was one of pure rage. A shiver of fear poured over her.

She nodded her head ever so slightly and gave him a deliberately bland smile. She'd die before she let him see he still had the ability to unnerve her with that icy glare from his cold blue eyes. He gave her a caustic once-over. She held the smile with an effort.

While her host hung up his heavy coat, she gazed defiantly at her former nemesis.

Shane Macklin was a couple of inches over six feet, almost a foot taller than her five feet three inches. His hair was a thick shock of tawny blond. It still tumbled over his forehead in a manner that made women want to smooth it into place.

His eyebrows and lashes were dark, an attractive contrast to his blue eyes. The hard angularity of his face seemed even more formidable now than it had years ago when she'd last seen him...when he'd accused her of being a fortune hunter and told her to stay away from his brother. His brother, Ty, had been twenty-one at the time, hardly a babe in swaddling clothes.

Shane, she remembered, had been twenty-four. The wise older sibling, he'd been determined to protect his baby brother from the clutches of an eighteen-year-old vamp.

She noticed he looked as lean as a timber wolf in his lawman's uniform. And about as predictable.

A hand on her arm startled her.

"Our table is ready," Jack Norton said, giving her a curious glance before guiding her across the room.

If she were going to live here, she would have to do better, she thought, chiding herself for her silly reaction. She couldn't let a caustic stare upset her. The Mighty Macklin would just have to get used to seeing her around. She lifted her chin to a stubborn angle and took her place at the table with Jack.

"Adrianna will be late," he said with a husband's knowledge of his mate. "Why don't we order a drink while we wait?"

Tina murmured agreement. "I'll have a glass of white

wine and a cup of coffee, unleaded,'' she told the waitress.

After Jack gave his order and the woman left, Tina realized she could see Shane every time she glanced at Jack. She wished she'd chosen the chair taken by the attorney. That way she'd have had her back to Shane.

"Something bothering you?" Jack asked.

"Not at all." She ignored the withering gaze across the way and turned her head to stare out the window.

Jack twisted around, saw the two men at the other table and waved. The four of them were practically the only ones left in the posh restaurant, besides the waitress and busboy. There were a lot of noisy skiers out on the slopes, however, zipping through the fresh snow and enjoying themselves. Tina tried to remember the last time she'd been happy and carefree like that....

"That's the county sheriff," Jack told her when he turned around. "Shane Macklin. The other one is Rafe Barrett, the owner of the resort. He recently got married."

Her heart lurched, then steadied. "Shane?"

"No, Barrett." Jack perused her face curiously. "You know Macklin?"

She nodded, feeling the heat seep into her face. She hoped she hadn't made an utter fool of herself, jumping to conclusions that way. Not that it mattered to her if he was married.

"I had the impression you'd never lived in the area."

"I did when I was nine. My mother and I came here after my grandfather died in an accident. My grandmother was ill and passed away a few months later. And then there was the summer I stayed with Anne. I was eighteen. She helped me get a scholarship to the state university."

Actually, Tina suspected Anne of providing the money, but the woman had never admitted it. Until that summer, Tina hadn't even realized she had a godmother. Her mother had handed her a letter from a Miss Snyder one day and told her to do what she wanted.

The letter had been an invitation to spend the summer as a paid companion to an elderly lady. The lady had been Anne, her godmother, a woman of immense wisdom. They'd become friends.

A mist blurred the menu for a second before Tina blinked it away. Without Anne's encouraging presence, she didn't know whether she could stay in the town. While her godmother hadn't stipulated that she live there, she had asked Tina to keep the house for one year before deciding to sell it.

So here she was, committed to living in the community for a year, by her own decision, while she wrote her great exposé on the evils of war. And of men, she tacked on, giving Shane Macklin a look in kind when he continued to watch her as if she were a suspect at a crime scene. Maybe he thought she was planning a robbery.

A giggle behind her stopped the visual clash. A pretty, rather breathless woman stopped at the table.

"Hello, you must be Tina Henderson. I'm Adrianna. I suppose Jack told you I'd be late." She laughed again, a sound so jolly that Tina had to smile.

"He did mention it." Tina shook hands with the other woman. Adrianna was in her late twenties and had the rushed air of a busy mother who typically ran an hour behind schedule.

"The baby-sitter was late," Adrianna explained. She gave her husband a kiss, then plopped into the chair with a distracted air, removing her knit hat, shrugging her coat over the back of the chair, finding a place for her purse and generally creating an amusing chaos for several minutes.

Finally her order was given and she settled back with a sigh. "Ah, it feels good to slip those shoes off. I can't stand heels, can you?" she asked Tina, as if they were already old friends.

"No. I rarely wear them."

"Wise thinking. I'm going to stick to flats for the rest of the winter. I nearly fell in the parking lot. There was only one spot left and it was icy. Tell me how you got to be a hardened TV reporter at your delicate age."

Tina instinctively liked the woman. Dashing from one subject to another without a pause, Adrianna was without subterfuge. A person didn't have to wonder what she thought or meant, she'd tell you flat out. Tina admired that quality.

"I went to work as a researcher for a wire service right after college. They sent me to Rome when they realized I was pretty good in Italian. Finally, I was allowed to write some stories—after I threatened the boss time and again with bodily harm."

The Nortons laughed appreciatively at her droll account of some of her escapades. Tina had once been captured by a jealous husband who wanted her to take messages to his estranged wife. Another time it had been more serious. A terrorist had refused to speak to anyone but her after reading her article on the making of a radical. That had catapulted her into television.

The fame had led to an international career. There had even been a TV miniseries about the event, with a famous actress playing her role. She wondered if the local people had seen it. Her glance strayed to the nearby table. She looked away when Shane's gaze shifted to her again.

"So it was easy," she said with a laugh and a shrug as her hostess exclaimed in horror.

By the time they finished the meal, Tina was relaxed. Two glasses of wine and some friendly companions had gone far in easing her nerves…added to the fact that Shane had moved his chair so that their eyes didn't meet every time they looked up. And the fact that he had deliberately avoided glancing her way after those first jolting moments of recognition.

Over coffee and dessert, she, Adrianna and Jack talked about her inheritance.

"Are you going to rent out the house?" Adrianna asked. "I know a couple who are looking for a place."

"No, I'm going to live there, at least for a while."

"How long?"

"Adrianna," Jack warned in a tone that said she was encroaching on other people's business.

"That's okay," Tina interjected. "For a year," she said. A tremor ran along her nerves. She felt committed, she realized.

"Oh, good. Do you play bridge? A group of us meet every two weeks, taking turns at each other's houses. We could use another warm body." Adrianna laughed merrily. "Don't worry about your mind. We're all atrocious players."

"That's because they gossip the whole time," Jack put in.

"Well…maybe," Tina hedged, not sure about plunging into the social stream.

"Oh, do. We'd love to have you," Adrianna told her, ignoring her husband's teasing.

Tina felt herself warming to the woman's natural friendliness. It felt nice to be wanted. Her grandparents had resented her. Her mother had loved her, of course, but even as a child, she knew she'd been a "mistake."

Later, Anne Snyder had made her feel welcome, as if she'd come home…until Shane Macklin had let her know exactly where she stood in his estimation.

"When I get the house in order," she said.

"It's fine," Jack assured her. "The roof has been replaced, and everything has been checked and is in good shape."

Tina wanted very much to go to the house and explore it from top to bottom. Her personal things had arrived a month ago. She had given up the lease on her flat and shipped everything from Italy at that time, traveling with only one suitcase while she visited her parents and half sister in Portland.

Now it was on to her new career….

Shane pushed his chair away from the table. "Well, it's back into the cold, cruel world for me, although I'd like to sit here and watch the snow for the rest of the day."

"Don't work too hard," Rafe advised, not at all sympathetic. He stood when Shane did and glanced at his watch. "Speaking of work, I have an appointment in exactly one minute."

"I'll say hello to Jack on my way out," Shane said. He waved goodbye to his host, then ambled over to the threesome at the nearby table. It was mere curiosity, but he wanted to know what she was doing back in town, looking like a million dollars and more beautiful than she'd been ten…no, eleven years ago.

She wore blue slacks and a sweater of dark gold. Over the sweater she wore a vest of gold, black and deep blue, sort of an Indian design. Her eyes, when she glanced at

him, looked more blue than gray, he noted. It was startling. As if she were someone he didn't know.

Except he did know her. Or her kind. After his mother
died, his father had gotten caught by a fortune hunter. It
had cost the family a lot of money to get rid of her. His
father's health had deteriorated rapidly during the nasty
divorce and he'd died of a heart attack shortly after that.

The following summer a sexy eighteen-year-old had
come to town and nearly caught his brother in the same
trap. Luckily, he'd put a stop to that little scheme. He
looked over the expensive outfit, the trim black boots
hugging her feet, the gold watch on her wrist, and wondered who'd paid for them.

"Hello, Jack, Adrianna," he said. No trace of the
strange tumult he felt inside sounded in his voice. As
sheriff, he couldn't allow personal feelings to interfere
with his duty.

"Hi, Shane," Adrianna said, rushing into conversation
in her usual friendly, energetic way. "Guess who this
is?" She pointed at Tina as if she were a prize out of a
Cracker Jack box.

"Tina Henderson," he said.

Adrianna made a moue of disappointment that lasted
about a half a second, then she grinned. "Right. International reporter and celebrity," she added, to make sure
he understood the importance of their luncheon guest.

He swung his gaze to the woman who'd haunted his
dreams for months after she'd left town all those years
ago. She was quietly composed, not even the flicker of
an eyelash giving away her inner thoughts or feelings at
seeing him again.

"Hardly that," she said, correcting Adrianna's ecstatic
introduction.

"More," Shane contradicted. "The rising star of

nighttime broadcasting, according to the latest edition of
People magazine.''

He suppressed the questions that rose to mind and
forced himself to remain coolly cordial. She was probably passing through the area and hadn't been able to resist
the temptation to drop in and show the locals how well
she was doing.

Meeting her eyes, he realized she recognized the un-
dercurrent of suspicion in him. For a taut second, they
engaged in a visual duel, and he was reminded of the
past, when she'd looked at him with the same insouciant
defiance, a slight smile at the corners of her mouth as if
daring him....

He had dared once. He'd kissed that mouth. He'd
tasted the honey. And he'd never forgotten the feel of
those soft, pouty lips under his. She'd resisted at first,
then her mouth had trembled...and parted...and responded, just for an instant. Then she'd bitten the devil
out of him!

A stirring in his body warned him of the dangers of
the memories. One thing he didn't need at the present
was another problem to contend with. His duties as sheriff, plus those to his family, gave him enough headaches.
He didn't need more.

He'd find out what the hell she was doing here...and
how soon she planned to leave.

A slight frown appeared on Adrianna's face. The attorney's wife sensed the hostility between them, he realized. He forced the anger into abeyance.

''What brings you to these parts?'' he asked. He
glanced out the window as a group of skiers paused below, their laughter pealing out above the sound of the
wind. ''Are you on vacation or just passing through?''

''Neither,'' she answered calmly.

That didn't make any sense. The anger stirred again. She was being deliberately evasive. "So why are you in town?" He sounded sharper than he'd meant to, which earned him surprised glances from Jack and Adrianna. He sighed internally. This was going to be a hard day in more ways than a mere snowstorm could account for.

"Is this an official inquiry?" his antagonist countered.

He frowned in frustration. Antagonist? Hardly. When he'd been twenty-four, she'd driven him right over the edge with the cool challenge in those stormy eyes and the half smile that had lingered on her lips. At thirty-five, he had more control.

Against his will, his gaze flicked to her mouth.

Her lips, as delectable as cream puffs, were outlined in a darker shade of the lipstick she wore. With total recall, he remembered how incredibly soft those lips could be.

His sense of self-preservation had already burned to a crisp in the heat of that kiss when the first punishing touch abruptly changed to something else...something that had been beyond anything he'd ever felt before with a woman.

Remembering that day, he felt his anger flare anew. The spiteful little vixen had bitten him! Otherwise—he drew a deep breath and admitted what he'd known unconsciously for years—otherwise, they would have made love, there by the river....

He realized the Nortons were giving him odd looks. It wasn't fair to involve them in the ancient quarrel. She'd left town the day after that kiss and hadn't returned. Until now.

"No, not official," he finally answered. "Just neighborly interest. It isn't often someone famous drops in."

"I'll be living here for a while," she said softly.

He felt the jolt of disbelief clear down to his boots. "How long?" he demanded, a thousand complications coming to mind—Ty and his problems with his wife; Jonathan, their four-year-old son; and now…this.

"A year. Maybe more."

Shane smiled in relief. "You'll never last that long in a backwater like Riverton," he predicted.

Her smile faltered, then returned. "You're so sure," she murmured. Her lashes dropped lower over her eyes. "The Mighty Macklin has spoken. Who dares dispute him?"

He felt the heat creep into his ears. Damn, but she made him feel like a crass youth.

"Riverton was once my home," she reminded him. She spoke softly. "I was happy here as a child.…"

She let the thought trail away, and for a second she looked wistful. He hardened himself to her allure.

"I loved roaming the woods or standing on a mountain with a wide-open vista, feeling that the world was mine to do with as I pleased," she continued.

He'd felt that way once. Long ago. Before a gold digger had snared his father and another one had tried to nab his brother. He wouldn't be fooled by her "poor, world-weary me" act.

"Well, then, welcome back," he said, resisting the urge to tell her to stay away from his family. He'd keep an eye on her personally and see that she didn't upset the status quo.

"Thanks."

"Tina," Adrianna put in, ending the unspoken battle between the other two, "you must come to the April Fool's Ball Friday night. Do you think we can get an extra ticket?" she asked her husband, clearly expecting him to accomplish this miracle.

He looked doubtful. "Well, I'll ask—"

"I have an extra ticket," Shane said. "If you want to go." It looked like his duties would start immediately.

"No, thanks, I'll be busy."

"Oh, you must," Adrianna insisted. "It will be the perfect time to meet everyone in the county. It's held here at the resort, and the proceeds go to the library fund. We'll pick you up."

"I can do that," he volunteered. "Where are you staying?"

She hesitated, as if she didn't want him to know.

Adrianna had no such qualms. "At the Snyder place. That would be perfect, since it's just across the river from your house."

He blinked in surprise, expecting she'd be staying at one of the motels along the interstate or perhaps at the resort. "The Snyder place," he repeated. "No one has lived there since Anne died last year."

"Tina inher—"

"We need to go, Adrianna," Jack interrupted firmly.

Shane put two and two together. "You inherited it? The Snyder place?"

"Yes." She was as cool as buttermilk.

"Isn't it super?" Adrianna enthused.

"Yeah," he agreed, all his suspicions confirmed. "Just dandy."

Chapter Two

Tina almost expected Shane to be waiting for her when she left the resort and pulled onto the county road. She kept looking in her rearview mirror for a flashing blue light.

She was being silly. No one had any reason to pull her over. No one could order her to leave the country—as one head of state had done when she'd looked too closely into his illegal activities, or as Shane had done when she'd gotten too close to his family.

When she came upon a speed limit sign, she quickly checked to make sure she was driving slowly enough, then laughed at herself. She'd probably imagined all the tension between her and the lawman back at the restaurant. There was no reason for it.

Putting it out of her mind, she drove through Riverton to the edge of town. At the end of a quiet street stood the neat brick house that had belonged to Anne Snyder and was now hers.

She stopped in the driveway. Again she felt a sense of homecoming, as if Anne's gentle spirit were there to welcome her. Anne, who had been wise and comforting, who had urged her to forgive weakness in others and who had made her see her own strengths.

''I'll miss you,'' she said aloud.

Her breath became frosted in the air, and she shivered in her new coat, a Christmas present from her family. Suitcase in hand, she walked up the snow-covered sidewalk to the front door. The lock opened smoothly. She stepped inside.

The house was warm. A lamp was on in the living room. Wood and kindling were laid in the grate, ready for a match to be put to them. The smell of cooking food filled the air.

Tina left her suitcase in the hall and went into the kitchen. A note from Anne's housekeeper, Mrs. Perkins, was stuck on the refrigerator with a souvenir map-of-Oregon magnet. The brief letter welcomed her, told her dinner was in the oven and said the housekeeper would be over the next morning.

Tina opened the oven door and sniffed the delectable aroma of a casserole. She found the refrigerator stocked with milk, orange juice and a large bowl of salad greens. Homemade rolls were there, too, ready to be popped into the oven when she wanted them.

A nostalgic yearning overcame her, as it had those first days in Rome when she'd felt so far from everything dear and familiar.

Homesickness was a strange malady for someone who'd never felt she truly belonged anywhere, she mused. She wondered why it seemed important that she find roots. No answer came to her.

Well, there were things to be done. She couldn't stand around all day thinking about it.

Grabbing her suitcase, she checked out the four rooms to the left of the wide entrance hall. One was a master suite, complete with private bath and a sitting room. Anne had used the sitting room as her office. Tina touched the desk and felt comforted.

You're strong, she could almost hear Anne say. *What you make of your life is up to you. Other people's weaknesses and mistakes don't have to be yours. Overcome them.*

But sometimes that's awfully hard, she wanted to tell her mentor. Sometimes strength felt like loneliness.

She found boxes of her personal belongings stored in the closet. Leaving her suitcase in the master bedroom, she hung her coat on the hall highboy, then peeked into the other two rooms.

One was a comfortable bedroom with its own sitting area complete with coffee table and wicker sofa. The bed was covered with a white chenille spread. The room had been her retreat on that summer visit so many years ago.

The other room was a *solarium,* as Anne had called it. A sun room. The Mexican tiles soaked up the sun's warmth—when the sun made an appearance—and stayed warm far into the winter night.

For several minutes, she watched the snowflakes fall at a slant, driven by the wind from the north. When the flurry let up somewhat, she could see the river, a steel gray ribbon running along the southern edge of the town and the property.

Across the river, she could barely make out the house

that sat on a knoll amidst the pine trees, lording it over the extensive sorting and storage barns of the orchards.

The Macklin home...where she hadn't been welcome.

Restless, she returned to the bedroom and worked for a couple of hours arranging her clothing. When she found her ski parka and warm ski hat, she pulled them on and headed out for a walk.

In a few minutes she was at the town square. It didn't take long to get there. Riverton was tiny, not exactly a one-horse town, but there was one grocery store, one drugstore-gift shop, one hardware store, one farm-supply business and so forth.

Surprisingly, there were two cafés, a tea shop and a posh restaurant. The old yarn store had been enlarged and was a sort of general arts-and-crafts house now. A sign in the window indicated basket weaving classes were beginning next week.

She walked the three main blocks and turned into the park that lined the river all the way back to her new home.

The Macklins had owned the property on both sides of the river. Apparently the town had bought the land to preserve it in its natural state. On the other side of the river, pear orchards stood in dark rows against the snow.

There among the fruit-laden trees of summer was where Shane had confronted her, telling her to leave his brother alone. She'd told him he couldn't tell her what to do. Then she'd challenged him. "Make me," she'd said, a smile of defiance firmly in place.

He had. The kiss had caused her to leave town a week before she'd planned to return home to prepare for college. It had melted her resolve to hate him.

Remembering, she felt anger flare anew at her wild, uncontrollable response to him. In self-defense, she'd bitten him, or else they would have made love, there by the river....

The wind hit her all at once, and she realized she was cold. Turning back to town, she went into the tea shop. The mouth-watering scent of cinnamon tickled her taste-buds.

The woman behind the counter removed a tray of hot raisin buns from an oven. "You're just in time," she called out, smiling and indicating the tray.

"I'll take one," Tina decided, "and a cup of tea."

"What kind?"

There were many varieties to choose from, and gour-met coffee as well, which was ground only as it was needed. Tina made a selection from among the herb teas and sat at a table near the window so she could watch the snow, which was coming down much harder now.

She hung her hat and parka on a coatrack.

"Snow's getting worse," the woman said, bringing the snack.

"Yes. I may have made a mistake, setting out for a walk in this weather. I forgot to change to snow boots."

"Someone will give you a lift home. Where do you live?"

"At the other end of town. The Snyder place." She introduced herself and in turn found out the woman was the owner of the shop.

"I always wanted to try my hand at business," the woman said, "but my husband was against it. I sat around for a couple of years after he died, went to Cal-ifornia for the winter and stayed with my daughter last year. I decided to open this place when I came back. Now I'm too busy to leave."

Tina smiled at the obvious pride the proprietress took in her shop. She stocked tea and coffee from all over the world, plus carried a selection of jams, jellies and candy made by local people.

"I encourage my friends to make things for me to sell," she confided. "It gives them extra money for Christmas and such."

A little women's lib taking place here, Tina thought in approval. Everyone needed a sense of personal worth.

Just as she was feeling comfortable, a large figure appeared at the door. Shane Macklin came in, bringing the cold with him.

Tina hugged herself as the chilled air swished past. The closing of the door stopped the draft.

"I knew you'd be in," the owner said with a satisfied smile.

"Smelled those buns all the way to the interstate." He slapped his black felt hat against his thigh, then hung it on a peg next to Tina's. He did the same with his coat. He'd taken two strides before he noticed who was at the lone occupied table. He stopped abruptly.

"Looks like I'm not the only one with a nose for your cooking, Bess," he drawled.

"This is a new neighbor—"

"I know her," he interrupted.

"Well, have a seat. I'll have your stuff in a minute." Bess bustled about behind the counter.

His eyes questioned Tina as he laid a hand on the chair opposite hers. She nodded, her heart pounding hard as it had earlier when she'd seen him. No need to get nervous, she reminded herself sharply. She was bound to run into him, since he lived in the same community. She just didn't like it.

He pulled out the chair and folded his tall, lean body into it, looking perfectly at home in a tea shop.

Perhaps it was his height that gave him that supreme

air of confidence. The world looked up to tall people. Being rather short, she'd always felt at a disadvantage compared to her male colleagues. She'd learned to use her elbows to get to the front for an impromptu interview with some important person.

Now that wouldn't matter anymore, she realized. She had a contract to write a book and a house to do it in. She wouldn't have to compete for her own space ever again.

"Bad weather to be out," Shane commented.

Tina flicked him a glance, then observed Bess as she measured coffee beans and ground them, placing the fresh grounds in a filter atop a large mug. She poured in hot water and brought the mug to the table along with a plate of warm raisin buns. Two, Tina noted.

"Yes," Bess agreed. She turned to Tina. "Say, here's your ride home. The sheriff can drop you off. She walked down," she explained to Shane.

His eyes, as blue as a summer sky, as cold as an icicle, speared hers. When Bess bustled off, pleased with her Good Samaritan effort, he leaned back in the chair and studied Tina casually. "Didn't take you long to look over your inheritance, did it?"

"No. After all, I stayed with Anne when I was here that summer eleven years ago." Tina waited tensely to see what he would say about that past visit.

He watched her, examining each feature of her face until she felt as if he'd branded her. "Do you have to live here a year to keep the place?"

"No, of course not." She lifted her chin. "I chose to stay."

"Why?"

"Why not?"

"Touché," he said softly, surprising her. "No reason,

I suppose, but I can't help wondering at your motives. Why would an important person like you stay in a hick town like this?''

Because everyone needs a home, a place to belong. She didn't say it. She'd never expose her heart that much. ''The peace and quiet? The warm welcome?'' she suggested, tongue in cheek.

He grinned ruefully. ''Guess I asked for that one.''

She noted the two lines across his forehead and the one between his eyes. He looked like a man with problems. Her natural instinct was to draw him out in sympathy. She suppressed it.

''What about your big television career?''

''I'm on leave for a year.''

He mulled this over, but didn't remark on it. He pushed the hot water through the filter, set the device aside and took a sip of coffee. ''Ah, that warms the heart,'' he murmured.

She doubted it could reach his, but she refrained from saying so. They ate in silence. She was aware of him, she realized. Of his lean, masculine power, of the grace in his movements as he lifted his fork, of the craggy planes of his face.

The admission alarmed her. She *had* moved here for peace and quiet after the hectic pace of the past few years, not to finish that…that strange episode of long ago.

After that kiss, he hadn't said a word. Neither had she. They'd stood there by the riverbank, their chests heaving in unison, their eyes shocked and angry at what had happened.

Then he'd turned and left.

She saw him pause now and look at her, a question in his eyes. She realized she'd been staring at his mouth, at two tiny, almost invisible white lines at the base of his lower lip.

He raised a hand and ran a finger over the scars where her teeth had sunk into the flesh. He was probably recalling that it had taken only one kiss to frighten her away before.

"You won't run me off this time," she said. She immediately wished she could recall the words. They sounded juvenile.

"Did I the other time?"

She took a calming breath. "Yes."

"I'm sorry."

Whatever she'd expected from him, it had never been an apology. "For what? You wanted me gone."

"Yes, but..." He thrust his hand through his hair. "I used my strength against you. I've wanted to apologize for that for a long time. Did Anne tell you I came by the next day?"

"Yes."

"You had already left."

"You'd made it plain I'd better get out of town."

"I know. I thought you wanted my brother for the Macklin name and fortune."

She smiled coolly. "I did."

Tina sat in front of the fire in her gown and robe. She held a note from her benefactress, Anne Snyder, in her hand. She'd found it in the middle drawer of the desk. She opened it with shaking hands.

My dear Tina,

By the time you find this, I will be gone. I can truly say I've had a good life—in fact, a joyous one since I met you. You have no idea how your letters brightened my days. Mrs. Perkins can tell you how often I sent her to check the mail these past months. Each word was treasured.

Thank you for accepting the gift of this house. I'd love to think your family will grow up safe and happy beneath this roof, but that is an old woman's wish, and you're to pay no attention to it. Live where your happiness abides.

From time to time, I have written to you little tidbits of my life that may touch yours. You will find the notes tucked here and there. When you've found them all, I hope you'll be wise enough to understand and strong enough to forgive.

It was signed with Anne's familiar signature.

Tina read it through once more. She didn't understand the cryptic last paragraph, but the rest of the letter was like Anne, making her feel special and welcome. There were no ghosts in this house but gentle ones, Tina reflected.

She hoped she'd be as happy as Anne had been in the sturdy brick house, but she wasn't sure if that was possible, considering her neighbor across the river.

With a sigh, she folded the note and laid it on the lamp table. She was tired after several hours of unpacking boxes and finding places for her books on the shelves in the sitting room. She'd also set up her computer and printer.

That done, she'd taken a shower, then eaten the casserole along with the homemade dinner rolls. As long as she'd been busy, she hadn't had time to think. Idle now, her mind returned to the tea shop where she and Shane had talked.

The tension between them had condensed into an almost tangible substance, like a cloud forming on the peak of a mountain, when she'd admitted she'd wanted Ty for his name and fortune. She'd faced the developing fury in Shane with a fatalistic calm.

"At least you're truthful about it," he'd muttered, his tone low, controlled, but surprised, too.

In long, thoughtful remembrances of that summer during her years abroad, she'd realized it wasn't Tyson Macklin she'd wanted, but the prestige and position that went with the name. She'd wanted to show the town that she could be somebody.

However, from the first time she'd met his older brother, Ty had been safe from any machinations on her part. From that moment all her dreams had been of one man, a man who, with his kiss, had destroyed those young, foolish dreams once and for all.

She'd never forgotten the moment he'd jerked back from her, startled by her defensive attack. The warmth of his blood had mixed with the heat of his kiss on her mouth, while the contempt in his eyes had told her how much he despised her.

How young she'd been, thinking he might love her....

A shaky sigh escaped her. It was annoying that he still had the power to get her emotions in a tangle. She was a mature woman now, not a girl with fantasies dancing in her head.

At the tea shop, she'd managed to laugh and make light of that confrontation so long ago. The mighty Shane Macklin would never know the effort it had taken to do that.

The flames in the grate before her blurred. She blinked rapidly and fought a longing that she couldn't name. She glanced at Anne's note, not sure whether she'd stay the year or not.

One day back, and her resolve was already shaken.

Shane had made sure she knew his younger brother was now a married man and a father. His tone had been fiercely protective when he'd mentioned his nephew. Passing on that news had been his primary reason for joining her, she decided. He'd wanted to make certain she knew his family was still off-limits to her.

For the briefest second, she felt a return of the anguish from that first encounter, when he'd made her feel an outcast, unworthy and unwanted. She pushed the emotion aside impatiently.

When she'd prepared to leave the tea shop, he'd insisted on paying both their tabs, then escorting her to his truck, driving her home through the storm and seeing her safely in the front door.

How gallant, she thought mockingly. He was ever the gentleman…except when he was riled. She wondered how it would be to have someone like him on her side, to be friends rather than enemies.

She didn't need anyone to take up her cause, she reminded herself sharply. While she wasn't an outgoing person who collected people like a dog picked up fleas, she'd always had friends to play with and confide in while growing up.

Of course, there had been the usual mean kid in school who'd taunted her about her lack of a father, but she'd learned to live with that. She no longer cared about the identity of the man who'd abandoned her and her mother so long ago.

When the fire sank into ashes, she went to bed, relatively content. Her first meeting with Shane hadn't been as nerve-racking as she'd thought it might be. On the other hand, it hadn't been as easy as she'd hoped, either.

* * *

The sun on the snow was absolutely breathtaking. Tina sat at the table, sipping a fresh cup of coffee, and admired the scene. The backyard swept down to the river in an unbroken fantasy of pure white. Every shrub and tree wore a fluffy shawl of snow.

She watched a blue jay alight on a twig. Its weight dislodged a chunk of snow. A startled rabbit took off in a mad stampede, probably thinking an owl was about to nab it. She laughed.

The ringing of the doorbell caused her heart to speed up, but the caller was Mrs. Perkins, the housekeeper who had been with Anne for almost twenty years.

"Hello. Come in. Would you like some coffee? I just made a pot," Tina bubbled, glad to see a welcoming face.

"Good morning. I wondered if you'd be up and decided you would. You were an early riser when you visited before," Mrs. Perkins recalled, following her into the kitchen. The woman put her coat and scarf over the back of a chair and sat down.

"I'm so glad to see you." Tina poured coffee into a clean cup, refilled her own and resumed her seat at the table in the breakfast nook of the large, old-fashioned kitchen. "I wanted to thank you for the food you left. Everything was delicious."

"Good." Mrs. Perkins added sugar and milk to her cup. "I wanted to be here in person, but I have a new position now."

"Oh, of course." Tina was relieved. She'd wondered how to tell the housekeeper she couldn't afford to have her every day. She'd been careful with her money and had saved enough to live on for the foreseeable future if she was frugal. Her budget didn't include daily cleaning service.

"The Macklin housekeeper retired last year, and Shane told me to come on over when I needed a new place." Her smile became sad for an instant. "Everyone knew Anne wouldn't last out the year. After I wasn't needed here, I moved over there. That house needed putting in order," she declared on a brighter note.

Tina smiled at the woman's self-satisfied tone. She could imagine that Mrs. Perkins would have things running smoothly in no time.

"A young person like you doesn't need an old biddy like me around, anyway. You probably don't stir up more than a smidgen of dust, little thing like you." The housekeeper gave her a critical once-over, as if she thought Tina's size indicated a lack of proper eating habits.

"I can be pretty messy when I'm working," Tina confessed. "I tend to let the dishes pile up in the sink."

"Hmm, well, I could come over once a week or so."

"That's okay. I'll manage."

"So tell me what you've been doing these past few months. Anne kept me up to date from your letters. She was right proud of you, she was. Said she'd always wanted to go off and see the world herself."

Tina told the friendly housekeeper about the book she was going to work on. They talked for over an hour.

"Lands sakes, I've got to get back," Mrs. Perkins commented, checking the time. "Shane will be home, wanting his lunch before long. Why don't you come join us?"

"Uh, I can't. I still have so much to do."

"You sound like Shane." Mrs. Perkins shook her head, as if despairing over young people and their strange ways. "He works all the time, too."

"Fighting off all the women who throw themselves at him, I'll bet," Tina said dryly.

Mrs. Perkins nodded primly. "There was one woman visiting over at the ski resort who near drove him mad. She called a dozen times a day. He finally had to tell her he wasn't interested, in very plain terms."

A chill crept along Tina's spine. She knew very well just how plainspoken he could be.

"That man never has a minute to himself," the housekeeper lamented. "He's always taking care of some problem in the county or for that brother of his."

"Maybe Shane should let Ty learn to handle his own problems," Tina suggested.

"My feelings exactly. With Ty and his wife separated, it's even worse now than before."

"Ty and his wife are having problems?"

"Yes. Nearly from the moment they married. It's no secret," Mrs. Perkins hastened to add.

The impact of Shane's talk in the restaurant hit Tina. If Ty wasn't happy with his wife, he'd be vulnerable. Shane had been warning her not to interfere between the two. She did a slow burn.

What had she ever done to earn his unjustified mistrust? She'd left when he told her to, hadn't she? She hadn't tried to lure Ty into marriage. In fact, she'd refused the offer when he'd pleaded with her to elope with him. Big Brother didn't know about that, she was willing to bet.

"Shane has all the responsibility of a family with none of the joy," Mrs. Perkins added darkly. She picked up her coffee cup with an indignant gesture. It wasn't hard to discern where her loyalty and sympathy was directed.

"I'm sure if Shane had wanted a family, he could have had one without undue difficulty."

Although, with his overbearing disposition, a woman might think twice about embroiling herself in his life.

He'd probably tell her how many times a minute she should breathe.

The older woman sighed worriedly. "After what he went through with his stepmother, I don't think he'll ever marry."

"I didn't know he had a stepmother." Tina pictured his being sent to bed with nothing but bread and water for some minor offense such as laughing in the house.

"He doesn't now, but he used to. She married his poor father less than a year after the first wife died." Mrs. Perkins leaned forward and spoke in a near whisper. "Caught the poor man when he was out of his mind with grief, don't you know?"

"How terrible," Tina commiserated. "How old was Shane?"

"Twenty-three."

"Oh, after he was grown." Her sympathy evaporated.

Mrs. Perkins bobbed her head up and down. "The marriage lasted less than a year, then the new wife took off for New York. Sued for divorce, she did, and tried to get half of everything poor Mr. Macklin owned. It's said she tried to get the son, too, but I don't know about that."

"Shane?" Tina stared at the housekeeper.

"She was a shameless hussy. But even her fancy lawyer knew they couldn't get all she wanted. Shane worked out a settlement, but his father didn't get to enjoy it for long. He dropped dead of a heart attack a month after the divorce. That woman had been a pure torment for him from the day he brought her home."

Mrs. Perkins sat back with a heavy sigh, as if human nature were too much for her. Tina was quiet, absorbing this information and putting it with the rest of what she knew about Shane.

"Ty was at school during all this ruckus," Mrs. Perkins continued, "and Shane had had to fly up there and get him out of some scrape or other a couple of times. Now Ty and his wife are fighting like two cats. I think they both need a good smack, acting like spoiled kids when they have that little boy to raise."

After Mrs. Perkins left, Tina washed her cereal bowl and spoon and started on her tasks once more. The housekeeper had given her several facts to mull over. It sounded as if Shane had gotten the proverbial stepmother from hell.

With his usual skill, he had vanquished the woman just as he had the eighteen-year-old who'd dared invade his turf.

For a moment, Tina regretted that they hadn't met first, before she and Ty had, before a horrible woman had trampled on his grief for his mother, before all the bad things had happened to make him a hard, distrusting man.

Then she mentally gave herself a shake. Whatever Shane Macklin was, he was no concern of hers.

Besides, she had Friday night to worry about. If she didn't hear from him, she'd call and say she couldn't go to the ball. She'd tell him she was coming down with a cold. Yes, that sounded like a wise decision.

With that off her mind, she got on with settling in. The house made her feel welcome in ways she couldn't express. For the first time, she felt she truly belonged.

Chapter Three

Tina picked up the phone. Tomorrow was Friday, the day of the ball, and she had to reach Shane Macklin. She called the number she found in Anne's desktop directory.

"Hello," a woman's voice answered on the first ring.

Expecting Mrs. Perkins to answer at the Macklin residence, Tina hesitated before greeting the unknown female. The telephone banged down in her ear. Startled, Tina hung up.

She checked the number in the phone book. It was correct. Exasperated with her own timidity, she dialed again. This time she was prepared for the impatient voice on the other end of the line.

"May I speak to Shane, please?" she requested. She felt odd, calling to break an engagement when he had another woman in the house. Well, whoever his guest was, Tina had to speak to him.

There was a long pause. Then the woman demanded, "Who's calling?"

Definitely hostile. Tina gave her name.

"Shane's not here."

Tina wondered what he'd done to anger his paramour so early in the day. She thought about leaving a message, but decided the woman probably wouldn't deliver it. She had another idea. "May I speak to Mrs. Perkins?"

"I'll get her."

This was so grudgingly said and the interval before the housekeeper answered was so long that Tina almost decided to hang up and try later.

"Hello, Tina," Mrs. Perkins finally answered in her cheerful tone. "I've made apple turnovers. Would you like to come over?"

"Uh, no, thank you, Mrs. Perkins. I, uh, called to…that is, could you take a message for Shane from me?"

"Of course. That poor boy was called out at four this morning. Bad wreck on the interstate. He hasn't got back yet."

That explained the girlfriend's ire, Tina decided. She didn't like being left alone, nor being disturbed so early. "He was going to stop by for me tomorrow night for the ball—"

"Why, that's wonderful," Mrs. Perkins broke in. "It's about time he started getting out with a pretty girl."

Tina wondered what his houseguest looked like. Probably ravishing. Her voice had been sultry in spite of the acrimonious tone. Some men liked fiery women.

"Actually, I think I'm coming down with a cold and won't be able to go," she said to the housekeeper. "If you'd tell him for me, I'd really appreciate it."

"I'll do that."

Mrs. Perkins sounded so disappointed that Tina felt the heat rise up her neck at the fib. "Thank you."

Before she could say goodbye, Mrs. Perkins inquired about how she was taking care of herself. "Drink plenty of fluids," she cautioned.

"I will," Tina promised. When she finally hung up, she felt limp with relief. That was one thing off her mind...although she would be sorry not to see Adrianna and Jack.

She made a pot of tea with lots of lemon—following Mrs. Perkins's advice—and turned on the computer. After running some checks to make sure the equipment hadn't been damaged in transit, she started to work.

First she wanted to finish typing in all her notes. By marking key words, she'd be able to get a cross-reference file set up in the computer. That would make the actual writing easier.

At five o'clock, she turned the computer off, stood and stretched wearily. She'd forgotten to go for a walk and get some exercise. It wasn't wise to let herself get lazy.

She looked out the window at the snow-covered landscape and gave a soft exclamation of pleasure. Dusk had painted the shadows on the lawn in shades of lavender. Purple-gray clouds on the horizon were tinged with gold around the edges, while the patches of clear sky were deep indigo.

Between snowy banks, the river flowed like liquid pewter. Glints of gold and lavender danced over its restless surface. She thought of all the land it touched on its way to the ocean and felt somehow linked to the others who lived along its borders.

She drifted out of the sitting room, which was now her office, and into the sun room. From there she could see across to the Macklin house, its brick chimneys jutting from among the pine trees. She noticed smoke coming from one chimney.

A picture came to mind—Shane and his guest curled on a comfortable sofa in front of the fire, enjoying a hot toddy while he told her of his day.

She gripped the windowsill as something hard and achy coursed through her. An unbearable loneliness slowly overtook her normally bright spirit.

The inexorable need of one human for another, she decided, rationalizing her mood. It caused women to accept lovers, to marry under the most appalling conditions of war and danger, to take the risk of having children when the world was falling apart....

She heaved a deep sigh. Enough of that. She'd take a shower, put on warm pajamas and rustle up something for supper.

Going into the master bedroom, she quickly shed her wool slacks and sweater and headed for the bathroom. Fifteen minutes later, she emerged.

She shivered in the chill of the bedroom. Her hair, which she'd blown dry, curled around her bare shoulders. Quickly she pulled on warm lounging pajamas made of cranberry-colored velour. Thick, fuzzy scuffs kept her feet toasty.

Before going into the kitchen, she laid a fire in the living-room grate and turned on the gas jet to get it started. She flicked on the floor lamp by the easy chair, adding a soft glow to the shadowy room. Just as she started out, the doorbell rang.

The two-toned chime pealed through the silent house and died away without an echo. Tina paused, the hair on her neck prickling. The moment seemed portentous.

The chime sounded again.

She chided herself for being silly. Glancing at her casual attire, she decided she was properly covered for answering the door. Probably the paperboy wanting to know if she'd subscribe to the *Daily News*. She'd forgotten to call—

The bell dinged three times in rapid succession. She hurried down the hall. Before opening the door, she peered through the peephole installed in the solid oak.

"Oh," she said. She opened the door.

Shane looked her over, leaving no part unnoticed. She felt heat build inside and sweep outward to every extremity.

"Mrs. Perkins said you were coming down with a cold," he said. "She sent you some onion soup."

Tina saw that he held a large glass jar filled with homemade soup in one hand, a plastic bag was in the other. Before she could say a word, he somehow maneuvered past her and stood in the hall. She closed the door.

He headed for the kitchen as if he lived there, too.

"She needn't have done that," Tina protested, trotting at his heels like a well-trained cocker spaniel.

He opened the plastic bag and removed a loaf of homemade bread and a small plastic jar. "According to Mrs. Perkins, this will knock a cold right out," he told her. "I can vouch for that. It's worked several times for me."

"Really—"

"Go sit in front of the fire. I'll fix a tray."

"Oh, but really—"

"I know where everything is. Unless you've changed things around from where Anne had them."

"Well, no, but—"

"Fine. It'll be ready in ten minutes." He opened a cupboard and removed tea bags from the box.

She stood there, uncertain about allowing this invasion, then left the room in a huff. This was her space. He had no right to barge in and take over. She'd explain that very carefully when he finished his good-neighbor act.

Settled in a large easy chair in front of the fire, she prepared several speeches to tell him exactly what she didn't like about him being in her home.

"Here we go," he said. When he came in, she noted that he'd removed his heavy jacket and hat. He carried a large brass tray that had been hanging on the wall in an attractive grouping. Two quilted place mats were draped over his arm.

He placed the tray on the coffee table, then raised the arm of her chair. Hidden inside was a wooden leaf that came up and over her lap like an airline tray. He spread one of the place mats over it, then put a bowl and a small plate on it.

The vapor of hot onion soup tickled her nose. A stack of toasted bread, golden with melted cheese, tempted her palate.

He took a seat on the sofa. "Ah," he said, like a weary traveler at last arriving home.

She watched in disbelief as he put a place mat on the coffee table and set out another bowl and plate.

"I didn't know you had an invitation to dinner." She cast him a caustic glance to let him know his company wasn't wanted.

"Mrs. Perkins had a meeting tonight. She told me to see that you ate your soup. It seemed easier to eat with you." He bit into a piece of toast.

"What about your guest?"

His eyebrows rose in question.

"When I called earlier, a woman answered the phone."

He frowned, looking definitely irritated. "My sister-in-law, I suppose. She's staying at the house for a while."

Tina took a mouthful of soup and found it delicious. She realized it had been six hours since she'd had a sandwich for lunch. Mulling over his statement, she finished every drop of the soup.

"Don't Ty and his wife live with you?" she asked, picking up a toast wedge and munching on it.

"No." He polished off the last of his supper and stood. "They have their own place." He stacked the dishes on the tray and left the room.

She replaced the chair tray and turned off the gas jet. The logs had caught and now burned cheerily. She returned to the chair and sat with one foot curled under her while she watched the flames.

It seemed strange to eat a meal with the enemy, she mused. Although he was much more domesticated than she'd ever dreamed the Mighty Macklin would be. His presence made her nervous.

When he returned, he again carried the tray. This time there was a ceramic teapot and two cups and saucers on it. He poured the tea and handed her a cup, then took one for himself.

She stared at the pale liquid in the cup. "What is this?" she asked. She detected cinnamon, cloves and lemon. Some kind of liquor, too, she thought.

"Mrs. Perkins's version of a hot toddy. Drink it. It's part of the cold remedy." He gave her a lazy perusal. "You sound better already," he remarked.

She went on the defensive. "I'm not going to the dance," she stated, needing to get her decision out in the open at once.

"Adrianna will be disappointed." His gaze was assessing, as if he evaluated every word she spoke for hidden motives. "She apparently thinks of you as a friend."

He made her feel guilty that she'd even tried to get out of going. "Well, I like her, too, but..."

"But?" he encouraged.

She gave him a level stare. "You hardly had a choice about stopping for me."

"You think Adrianna stampeded me into it?"

Tina nodded.

"I volunteered, remember?" He watched her over the edge of the cup, the rising steam a barrier to his thoughts.

She sipped the aromatic brew. It had a hefty addition of brandy in it, she realized. She drank it more slowly. Her head already felt light.

"Yes, but why?"

He poured another cup of tea for himself and topped her cup. "So I can keep an eye on you."

Anger rampaged through her. Her hand trembled as she brought the cup to her lips, holding it like a shield in front of her face. "Just what do you think I'm going to do?"

He yawned, then rubbed his eyes. She realized he looked tired. "I don't know," he admitted. "I just don't think a sexy woman who happens to be beautiful, rather famous and living alone is a good thing in these parts right now."

"I assure you, I have no designs on the community's virtue," she said hotly. She clinked the cup onto the saucer and plunked both down on the coffee table. Rising, she paced the room in quick, angry strides.

Her nemesis spread his arms over the sofa back and leaned his head into the corner, his narrowed gaze following her every move. "Maybe not, but some of the community might have designs on yours."

If you have any. He didn't say it, but she was sure he was thinking it.

She turned to the fireplace and laid her palms against the mantel. She hated violence, but at that moment she experienced an urge to hit him again and again until he took back his doubts and suspicions about her. Whatever her motives for dating his brother years ago, they certainly didn't apply at the present.

"Thanks for your concern, but I can take care of myself. I've done so for a number of years," she informed him.

"And in places much more dangerous than Riverton, I'm sure," he added. "Don't underestimate a small town. Its residents have all the emotions of the world at large."

She tried to decide if this was a warning for her not to get involved with the townsfolk. It didn't take a genius to see he didn't want her within a hundred miles of *his* territory. Taking the poker, she broke open a log so it would burn evenly and added another to the grate.

Finished, she sat on the raised brick hearth and looked at Shane. He was asleep!

She stared at him, unable to believe he'd go to sleep in her presence. After all, he seemed to consider her one of the more dangerous members of the human species.

He moved, slumping further into the sofa. She checked the teapot and found it still half-full. Leaving the pot and her cup, she took the tray to the kitchen, then returned to the living room.

Shane had shifted again. His feet hung off the end of the sofa. His boots were real working boots, not city-slicker ones with high heels and pointed toes. His uniform fit his tall frame perfectly. She wondered if the cellular phone clipped to his belt bothered him, but decided he wasn't feeling a thing.

She remembered that Mrs. Perkins had said he'd had

a call early that morning. He obviously hadn't rested since then.

A town like Riverton surely didn't have much crime....

However, it was next to the interstate highway. Lots of strangers passing through these days. And the area was growing. It had doubled in size since she'd lived here.

Her gaze was drawn to his belt. She wondered if he ever wore a gun and if he'd ever been shot at. A lawman's job was dangerous. A strange feeling, something like fear, went through her.

She poured another cup of the spicy tea and sipped it, feeling its warmth spreading through her on the inside while the fire warmed her back when she sat on the hearth again.

Shane slept serenely, his head on the sofa arm.

A plink against the window drew her attention. Snow was falling again. She placed the empty cup on the table and sat in the easy chair. The house was quiet. She felt at peace with the world for the first time in years.

Odd. She hadn't even known she'd been in contention with it. She yawned and closed her eyes.

Shane woke slowly, painfully. He was cold. His body ached. Hell, no wonder. He'd fallen asleep on the sofa again.

He rubbed his eyes, which felt as if someone had thrown sand into them, and pushed himself upright. It took a supreme effort. His head felt weighted with lead. Looking around, he realized he wasn't in the den at his place. He was at Anne Snyder's house.

And Tina Henderson was asleep in the easy chair.

He mentally groaned. Just what he needed—a rumor about the sheriff and the famous war correspondent making the rounds. He focused on the clock on the mantel.

Damn, almost two o'clock in the morning. He couldn't believe he'd fallen asleep like that.

If anyone had noticed his truck parked in her driveway until all hours there would be hell to pay. That would really set the gossip mill to grinding. He could imagine the smirking grins of the men at the barber shop, a favorite hangout of the town's geezers, who yakked as much as a bunch of women.

Why the hell had she let him sleep?

Every muscle in his body made itself known as he surged to his feet. He pinched the bridge of his nose in an attempt to hold back the headache that was starting to pound behind his eyes.

Tina shifted in the chair, her head sliding down until it rested on the padded arm, her arms crossed over her chest as she tried to stay warm. The fire had smoldered into ashes long ago.

He cursed again. Edging around the coffee table, he stopped near the big easy chair, intending to shake her awake. He had a thing or two to say to her....

She looked small and defenseless, curled into a ball in the chair. For some reason she reminded him of his nephew, her face young and trusting in sleep. Not at all the way she looked when she was awake, he realized.

When she gazed at a man with those stormy eyes, she was wary, guarded...a woman who gave nothing of her inner self away. Only once had he seen emotion reflected in those translucent gray depths. Even now he wasn't sure what it had been.

Anguish? Had she really been hurt when he'd told her to leave his brother alone, or worse yet, to get out of town?

He doubted it. The heart of a gold digger had no soft

spots. He'd learned that lesson well with his stepmother. He'd better remember it.

Yet watching her sleep gave him strange feelings inside, as if he wanted to hold her...protect her...make her trust him until those inner barriers dropped and he saw the real person.

He cursed again, not silently, but low, under his breath. She heard him.

"What is it?" she asked, startled. She sat up and looked around, as confused as he'd been upon finding himself awakening in a strange place.

When she raised her face to stare at him in bewilderment, a surge of hunger, so strong it caused an ache to settle someplace deep inside, ripped through him.

"Shh," he soothed, bending forward, drawn to the rosy hue of her lips, which looked incredibly soft in the light of the lamp she'd left on.

She pushed the dark swath of hair away from her face. "What time is it?"

"Almost two o'clock in the morning," he told her, controlling the hunger with anger. He stepped back. "Why did you let me fall asleep? Do you have any inkling of the gossip this will stir up in town...hell, in the whole county?"

Her eyes opened in an incredulous expression, then she smiled coolly at him. "What's the matter, Sheriff? Afraid your sterling reputation will be tarnished?"

He suppressed the desire to shake her. If he touched her once, he might not quit until it was too late to stop. "Not mine, honey, yours. The small-town double standard is still alive and kicking in these parts."

"I'm sure it is." Her tone was frankly mocking. "Thanks for your concern."

She uncurled herself from the chair and stretched with

the sensuous grace of a cat. Her breasts were momentarily outlined against the soft material of her outfit. He realized she wore no bra. The blood pounded with a dull roar through his ears—whether in anger or passion, he couldn't tell.

Having a man sleep over didn't seem to bother her, so why the hell was he getting all steamed up about it?

He remembered who her neighbors were and gave a low groan of frustration. "Emma Tall lives next door. She and her husband own the local hardware store. She's the biggest gossip around."

The wind blew with an eerie sound around the house. A flurry of snow hit the window. He watched the sway of very feminine hips while his nemesis, as he was beginning to think of her, walked to the window.

"It's snowing again," she said. "It might be dangerous out on the road. I haven't heard any snowplows come through."

"They'll be over on the interstate, keeping it open." He thrust a hand through his hair and worried about getting stuck in her drive. That would be all he needed—a tow truck coming to pull the sheriff out at—he glanced at the clock—two-fifteen in the morning.

"Umm." She leaned forward, putting her forehead to the window like a kid gazing outside, longing to be in the snow. She yawned, then turned around. "I'm going to bed. Do you want the guest room or a blanket for the sofa?"

He stared at her, feeling more than surprised, almost shocked—the way he had earlier when she'd admitted, as cool as a frosted shake, that she'd been after Ty for his name and fortune.

This woman threw him off balance. He didn't like it.

"It would be warmer to share," he drawled, watching

her closely for a reaction. Hell, maybe she did want him. Maybe she was one of those cosmopolitan women who took their pleasures where they found them.

She moved her shoulders in an impatient gesture. "That wasn't an invitation," she informed him crisply. "But even I'm not heartless enough to throw somebody out in the cold at this hour. The damage has already been done to my reputation, if what you say is true, so you may as well stay until morning. I'll even cook you breakfast." She tossed him a sardonic grin.

Heat burned its way right down his backbone. He tried to think, but it was no use; he didn't see any graceful way out of the situation. And she was right. A few hours more or less wouldn't make a damned bit of difference to the local gossips. Besides, if he stayed until morning, maybe the neighbors would think he'd just arrived, rather than spent the night.

"Bring me a blanket. I'll take the sofa."

When she left the room, he built up the fire until it burned brightly, warming the cold room. He heard the furnace click on. She must have turned up the thermostat.

She returned in a few minutes, carrying a pillow, two flannel sheets and a wool blanket. "Do you think this will be enough?"

"Yeah."

"What time do you need to get up?"

"At six. I'll be awake." He always woke without an alarm.

She nodded, glanced around and walked out. "Good night," she called back softly from the hall.

"'Night," he automatically responded.

He shucked his boots and pants, laying them neatly over the arm of the chair. He glanced at the cellular phone and thought of calling the office, then decided against it. Everything seemed quiet. If he was needed, the dispatcher would call.

After preparing his bed, he put his shirt on the chair and crawled between the covers. His thermals would serve well enough for pajamas. Of course, at home he didn't sleep in anything.

His last thought was of his hostess, a surprising, puzzling woman. He wondered if she slept in the seductive outfit she'd had on....

Tina made breakfast as quietly as she could. She stirred the eggs with a plastic spatula, which made no sound against the skillet. Shane was still asleep.

She grinned. It was almost seven. Apparently, his internal alarm clock had switched off.

The microwave dinged, startling her. She removed the rasher of bacon and placed the strips on a platter. Peeking into the oven, she saw that the biscuits were done to a golden brown. She took them out and dumped them into a cloth-lined basket.

Leaving the kitchen, she crept down the hall and into the living room. Shane was snoozing like a baby. Quietly. He didn't snore. A sense of tenderness came over her as she watched him.

The lines had been smoothed from his forehead. He looked peaceful in the gray light of morning. She hated to wake him.

Glancing out the window at the sky, she sighed. It was still cloudy. The snow had stopped, but the wind blew over the house with a relentless sound. She shivered, thinking of the chill factor for the people who had to be outside in the unfriendly elements.

Screwing up her courage, she looked at her guest, wondering if he woke like a bear or a kitten in the mornings. Well, only one way to find out. "Shane," she said.

He opened his eyes at once. She saw instant awareness in him. He knew where he was, where he'd spent the night. It had bothered her at first, knowing he was merely steps away. It had taken her awhile to fall asleep. She'd woken a few minutes after six, had washed and dressed, then gone to the kitchen.

"Breakfast," she told him and hurried out. Her hand tingled. She'd wanted to sit beside him and brush the tumbling curls off his forehead.

Putting plates on the table, she wondered what it would feel like to wake with him. She sucked in a shaky breath. What was the Linda Ronstadt song? "I Know a Heartache When I See One." Yeah, that was it.

Shane came into the kitchen. He was dressed. She'd noticed his clothing lying on the chair when she'd wakened him. He'd been wearing blue thermal knits. A thermal top, she corrected. She was making assumptions about the bottoms.

He must have washed his face in cold water, for it had a healthy pink glow—along with an enticing stubble. She wondered how rough his beard would feel against her skin early in the morning.

Heat slithered through her. She hastily put the thought aside. "Good morning."

He gave her a sour glance. "It's seven o'clock," he announced, as if this were somehow her fault.

"Yes," she said equably.

"I usually wake up...." He let the thought trail away. "How much snow did we get last night?"

She looked out the window. "Two or three inches."

"Damn."

Well, now she knew—he woke up growling like a

bear. She placed the meal on the table, ignoring the slight tremor she seemed to have developed during the night.

"There won't be any tire tracks. I forgot about that."

She tried to figure that one out, but gave up. She poured two mugs of coffee and put them on the table. "Do you want some orange juice or milk or both?"

His laser glance swept over her, then the table. He sighed and took a seat. "Juice, please."

She prepared it and joined him. "Why are we worried about tire tracks?"

"I thought the neighbors might think I'd dropped by this morning on...um, official business. I could tell the geezers I'd had to warn you about snow tires. By the way, you'll need them if you try to get over the pass on the interstate."

"I have aggressive treads with four-wheel drive," she informed him, proud of her foresight.

"Umm." He frowned heavily and bit into a biscuit. "Well, maybe no one will notice the tracks."

"What tracks?" She gave him an exasperated glance.

"That's the trouble. There *aren't* any." He took another bite of biscuit. "Did Mrs. Perkins send these over?" he asked.

"Of course not. I made them. If there aren't any tracks, how could they be a problem?"

He sighed heavily. "My truck. I can hardly say I came over this morning when there aren't any fresh tracks in the snow behind the blasted truck. That's the first thing Emma Tall will notice."

"Perhaps everyone doesn't have as suspicious a mind as yours," Tina suggested. Heaven forbid that anyone should link the pristine Macklin name with hers, she thought waspishly.

"She does," he assured her. "You won't be able to

make a move without her reporting it to the whole town.''

"I really don't see what difference it makes. I learned long ago that people will think what they want to, no matter what.'' She gave him an insouciant smile. "So I vowed never to let other people's opinions bother me.''

He ate in silence for a few minutes. She noted that he'd eaten two biscuits and was starting on a third. At least her cooking met with his approval.

"You seemed to take mine to heart,'' he said thoughtfully after a while. "When I told you to leave, you looked…hurt.''

He had no idea how she'd felt, she reflected. She'd wanted something from him…approval, kindness, acknowledgment of her as a person…she wasn't sure what. She certainly hadn't gotten it.

She stared at her plate, filled with a strange yearning and a restlessness that bedeviled her soul. When she looked up, he was watching her, waiting for an answer.

"I was angry,'' she informed him, "not hurt.''

He ignored her statement. "Did I get too close to the truth that day? I was right. By your own admission, you were after the Macklin name. If I hadn't sent you packing, you'd have lured Ty into marriage before he knew what hit him.''

She could almost hate him for thinking that of her. He thought he was right, but he didn't know the workings of her heart. Only Anne had seemed to detect the inner feelings she kept so carefully concealed. She suddenly missed the older, wiser woman's counsel.

He looked around the kitchen, then back at her. "Yet Anne must have thought you were pretty special to have left her home to you rather than her niece.''

"Her niece?'' Tina had known there had been a

nephew, deceased, whom Anne hadn't been close to. She hadn't realized Anne had also had a niece.

"You must know," he said, studying her with a narrowed gaze. "Anne's niece—great-niece, actually—is my sister-in-law, Ty's wife." He paused as if to let this sink in, then continued, "This time you got the money without having the bother of a husband along with it."

Chapter Four

Tina considered hitting Shane on the head with a heavy object. Except the object would probably break, and she'd have to clean up the mess.

"I didn't know about your sister-in-law," she said with great calm, given how she felt. "Jack Norton handled everything. He said Anne had few relatives and none she was close to."

Tina couldn't imagine having a relative in the same town and not being close to her, especially someone as wonderful as Anne.

"Hmm," Shane said.

Which could have meant he did or did not believe her, not that it mattered to her.

He buttered a fourth biscuit and reached for the jar of homemade jam. "Did you make this, too?"

"Hardly. I found the jam in the pantry."

He added a generous dollop of jam to the biscuit and

polished off the meal. "That was good," he said when he'd finished.

"Thanks."

"What's wrong?"

"Not a thing," she said with a mendacious smile. "You just barge in, make yourself at home, spend the night, eat my food and accuse me of being an opportunist who robbed your sister-in-law of her inheritance from her only living relative. Nothing to be upset about in that scenario."

He shrugged, picked up his cup and tried the coffee. "Perfect," he murmured. To her surprise, a smile crinkled the hard, attractive planes of his face.

A slight indentation—she wouldn't dare call it a dimple—etched a line at the corner of his mouth. Wary and alert, she watched him, expecting him to say something harsh.

He drained his cup, eyed the pot regretfully and stood. "I've got to go," he told her.

She trailed at his heels down the hall, almost jogging to keep up with his long stride. *"Arf, arf,"* she muttered, irritated by the way he made her feel. He was just so damned confident, doing as he pleased in *her* house.

"What?" He stopped for his jacket and hat, which were hanging next to her coat on the highboy, and gave her a quizzical glance.

"Oh, nothing."

"Are you always a grouch in the mornings?" he inquired.

"Moi, a grouch?" She feigned amazement. "Look who's talking—Mr. Sunshine himself."

He watched her with a thoughtful expression. "Sorry. Things have been…difficult this week."

Things like his sister-in-law? she wondered. How often did the woman stay at his house? Maybe that was the reason he let himself fall asleep here. Maybe he hadn't wanted to go home and listen to a litany of complaints.

And maybe she was getting soft in the head, feeling sorry for Shane Macklin. From her own experience, she knew he had no problem speaking his mind. If he wanted his sister-in-law gone, he'd tell her to leave.

After putting his jacket and hat on, he paused again and studied her. She was aware that she wore no makeup, that her jeans were old and her blue flannel shirt had faded to silvery shades.

The silence built. She noticed the loud ticking of the clock in the kitchen echoing through the hall. Her heart thudded at the same rate, heavy and slow and, for some reason, afraid.

He stared at her lips. She knew he was remembering that other parting years ago. For a moment, she wished… she wished…

The unbearable longing for things she couldn't name rose in her. She pressed a hand to her throat, terrified of feelings she didn't want to acknowledge. A tremor ran through her.

"I've got to go," he muttered. He opened the door and stepped outside into the frigid air. "I'll see you at six-thirty," he said. He bounded off the porch, through the fresh snow and into his utility vehicle. He waved, not at her, but next door.

She looked in time to see the curtain drop on her neighbor's window. She closed the door and watched Shane back out and drive off. His tire tracks were the first ones in the snow that morning.

* * *

Tina hung the sophisticated black-sequined pants outfit back in the closet. What the heck did a person wear to an April Fool's Ball, anyway?

She remembered she had a blue-and-white domino cape. Court jesters—the king's fools—had once worn similar garb. That should be appropriate. She was a fool for going with Shane.

She decided on a blue lace dress lined with beige silk—her one French-designer outfit. It was demure, yet rather provocative at the same time. Her hands shook as she finished dressing.

Really, there was no need to be nervous. A country ball was nothing. She raised her chin and gave herself a stern examination in the mirror. She could handle it.

Six-thirty seemed early for a ball. She paced the living room, wishing she'd told Shane she was *not* going. She'd call—

Too late. He was turning in the drive.

She stared at the expensive sports car, not sure he was inside. A tall, masculine figure climbed out and crunched through the snow on the sidewalk. She'd made a brave-hearted attempt to clear it away that morning, but mostly she'd worked off a lot of tension before giving up partway to the drive.

Her heart gave a gigantic leap as he came up the porch steps into the light. He wore a dinner suit, which looked elegant on his lithe frame. He was handsome and distinguished and mysterious.

She'd never seen him in formal attire. The summer they'd met, he'd worn jeans, and shirts opened halfway—sometimes all the way—down his chest while he worked in the orchards. When she'd put her palms against him to push him away, she'd touched bare flesh, lightly furred with tawny hair across his chest.

Forcing the disturbing image from her mind, she opened the door. He stepped inside, crowding into the hall, invading her space.

"Well, the little beggar girl gets to meet Prince Charming," she said, her voice husky rather than cynical as she'd meant it to be. She dropped into a sweeping curtsy to hide the sudden case of nerves that overtook her.

A hand on her arm pulled her upright, not exactly roughly, but not in a friendly way, either.

"Come on, Cinderella," he said, his tone dry as straw. "Midnight will be here before you know it."

"Oh, I'll know." Then the magic would disappear and she would go back to being the despised intruder in their midst. "But until then…"

She gave him a saucy glance. No matter how many qualms she felt about being with him, she was determined not to let him know. She'd be so cool he'd think he was with an icicle.

He frowned thoughtfully at her from his superior height. "You're in a strange mood tonight."

"Be careful," she warned in a playful whisper. "It's April Fool's Day. All may not be as it seems."

"With women, it rarely is."

"Ah, thus speaks the cynic." She tilted her head to study him. His gaze wasn't cold tonight. It roamed over her with restless energy, then returned to her face. She felt warm and feverish, not like an icicle at all.

"For instance," he went on, ignoring her quip, "you look like an angel—small, adorable…untouched."

His voice cascaded over her like the liquid notes of a gypsy violin. Her heart quivered with each vibrant inflection.

His voice dropped to an intimate level. "But I know there's fire inside, and more of the temptress than the angel,'' he added, giving her a cool assessment as if he'd noted all her charms and found them amusing.

"Gee, thanks." She managed to inject just the right note of sardonic humor in her voice. "Shall I take my warm coat? I have a short cape." She held up the domino.

He reached for her heavy coat. "Wear this in the car. You can wear the cape when we go to the ball. It has a nice dramatic flair. The artsy crowd will love it."

She let him help her into her coat. When she had her purse and the cape in hand, they went out. The air was so cold it made her teeth chatter. In fact, she felt cold clear through.

Clinging to the banister, she walked carefully down the steps. High heels were precarious at the best of times. On an ice-slick surface, they were plain stupid. When her foot skidded, a strong hand caught her elbow.

"You're going to break your neck," Shane said impatiently.

She was swung up into strong arms. She clasped her own arms around his neck instinctively. "Don't," she protested. "I can make it on my own."

"Be still," he ordered. "If I fall, we both might bust our bottoms." He grinned at her, and she recognized a taunting spirit of recklessness in him.

She was enchanted. This close, she was aware of his shaving lotion, of the clean scent of his shampoo, of the fresh-shaved smoothness of his cheeks. She wanted very much to kiss him.

It would be easy. Their mouths were so close. An abrupt stirring inside her had her gritting her teeth and trying to remain as still as possible. It was hard not to melt against him.

The crusted snow broke under their combined weight,

and Shane wavered for a second before regaining his balance. She held on for dear life, her face pressed into his neck.

"Open the door," he murmured near her ear.

She did as he said. He placed her inside the car. Across the yard, she saw the curtain fall into place. On a defiant impulse, she waved to Mrs. Tall. So did Shane.

He was still grinning when he got in his side of the car and started the engine. He'd enjoyed the slight taunt to her nosy neighbor.

It was a delightful side of him, she realized. Playful, but not mean spirited. Endearing. She drew her coat tightly around her, troubled by the feelings that threatened to block her common sense.

"You don't weigh as much as a sack of cotton," he commented. He looked her over before putting the car in gear. "I forget how tiny you are when we're in the midst of a battle."

"I'm not tiny. Short, maybe, but not tiny."

He chuckled at her retort. "And with the heart of a tigress," he tossed at her. "And the teeth."

"The better to bite you with, my dear," she said in a deeper voice, a warning that he'd better not tangle with her.

"Ah, yes." He touched his lower lip.

She was silent, thinking of the past. He'd apologized to her for the punishing kiss. She would have to be as magnanimous about the bite. "I'm sorry for that."

He flicked her a glance as they pulled onto the pavement. "I deserved it."

Her heart went into high speed at the sudden intensity in his gaze. When he looked back at the road, she clasped her hands together. Desire, hot and pungent, poured through her like liquid heat.

It was dangerous to feel like this. She was in over her head and not sure which way was up. She tried to think of some wise words her mentor might have used to guide her, but none came.

Oh, Anne, what am I doing here, riding through the night with my nemesis? This can't be wise, can it?

"We're going to have dinner with friends of mine before we go to the ball," Shane informed her.

"I wondered why we were going so early."

She dreaded meeting his friends. She could imagine the speculation in their eyes. If they knew about him being at her house last night...

"Rafe Barrett's wife was in Europe with the foreign service. You might know her—Genny...um, I forget her maiden name."

"I didn't know many people. I moved around a lot the past five years. I was rarely in one place for very long."

"I see. Pretty exciting life," he commented. "You'll be bored with us local yokels."

"A wise person once told me only boring people are bored, that life is what a person makes of it," she said softly.

"Anne."

"Yes." She watched him in the dim light from the dash and broached a point she'd wondered about. "You knew where things were in her house."

He slowed on a narrow bridge. The road was shiny with ice. "I stopped by to see her occasionally after you left. We got to be friends." He seemed to think about this last statement. "She wouldn't give me your address at college."

"You asked for it?"

He nodded. "I was going to apologize, remember?"

"I wonder why Anne didn't give it to you. I never told

her about us, about what happened.'' Tina stared into the darkness, perplexed at the news.

His laugh held a cynical edge. ''She said I was to leave you alone, that you didn't need me in your life right then.''

''Really?'' Tina was surprised by Anne's attitude.

''She also said you would come back someday. I wonder… Did she tell you she was going to leave you the house? Or did you suggest it?''

''Of course not!'' She curled her hands into fists. ''I would never have accepted the house if I'd known there was a living relative. She wrote that her nephew had died years ago.''

''Yeah. He was a banker in Medford. He had a heart attack on his way to work one morning. Anne said it was a blessing he went quickly, saved his family a lot of trouble.'' Shane smiled. ''She was something, wasn't she? Acerbic and witty, yet she could be kind. She knew how to listen.''

''Sometimes she heard more than a person wanted to tell,'' Tina murmured, remembering how often Anne had seemed to gaze right into her soul. But no one, not even Anne, had known of her feelings after that episode down by the river…nor of the tears she'd shed.

He pulled to a stop at the ski resort. Instead of getting out, he hooked a wrist over the steering wheel and watched her for a long minute. ''She said you hadn't received the richness of life that you deserved.''

Heat flamed in Tina's face. Sometimes she'd suspected Anne had felt sorry for her. She raised her chin. ''That was a long time ago—''

''She said it last September, shortly before she died. I've often wondered what she meant.''

''I'm sure I don't know.''

"Maybe someday we'll find out." He swung out of the car and helped her out. She removed her coat and put the cape around her shoulders. All the way to the door of the lodge, she was aware of his warm clasp on her arm.

Inside, they went to a private dining room down the hall from the restaurant where she'd first seen him.

"Hello. Come in," Rafe Barrett called, crossing the room to meet them at the open door. "Tina Henderson," he said, giving her a warm handshake. "You're as pretty in person as on the tube. I've enjoyed your broadcasts."

She thanked him, then followed as he led her and Shane into the smaller, more intimate room.

Votive candles burned on a table set for six, she noted. A sinking sensation grabbed her middle. While she'd never minded going to the various embassies as a reporter, she stayed away from parties as a rule. She'd seen too many love affairs induced by a common nationality and loneliness to trust the social setting.

The women standing across the room smiled at them as they approached. "My wife," Rafe said. "Genny used to live in Paris."

Genny Barrett welcomed Tina cordially. She was a lovely woman, a bit older than Tina, with dark hair and green eyes. She had a scattering of freckles over her nose and cheeks. Her dress was emerald velvet.

"I saw you once," Tina said, her reporter's instincts aroused. "You were visiting...um, in Egypt, I think. There was an embassy party. You were there with your uncle, an ambassador." She looked at Rafe. "Your father—is he by any chance Ambassador Barrett?"

"Yes," her host replied.

"It's a small world," a masculine voice commented at the door in an amused voice.

Tina whirled. "What are you doing here?" she demanded, her surprise giving way to delight.

Gabe Deveraux came forward, his arm around the waist of a tall redhead in a long black skirt and a white blouse. Her old friend gave her a quick hug.

"Looks like Old Home Week," Shane commented dryly, giving her a sharp glance. He shook hands with Deveraux and said to Tina, "This is Gabe's wife, Whitney. Whitney, Tina Henderson."

"I'm glad to meet you," Tina told the other woman.

The redhead returned the greeting. Her smile was warm and genuine. "We saw you on television. Gabe said he knew you."

While their host was mixing drinks, Tina found a moment to speak to Gabe. "Your wife is lovely. You look happy."

He nodded and let her see the contentment in his eyes. "Marriage," he said. "You should try it."

When she'd known him, there'd been an anger in him that he'd kept carefully under control. She sensed it was gone. A lump came to her throat. She and Gabe had dated some, then remained good friends when things didn't work out, seeing each other occasionally when they were in the same part of the world.

"Gabe and I worked on a couple of cases together," their host commented when they were seated. His gaze flicked to Tina. "How did you two meet?"

When she hesitated, Gabe answered, "Tina and I both happened to be in the wrong place at the wrong time. We were caught in the crossfire between two warring factions."

"He saved my life," Tina put in after his brief explanation.

"He just has to play the hero," Whitney said when he

protested. Her manner was droll, but her eyes were filled
with loving pride. Husband and wife exchanged smiling
glances.

Tina looked away from the happy couple, trying not
to be envious. Maybe someday she'd find bliss, too.

"Ah," Rafe said, "here's our meal."

There was speculation in Shane's steady gaze while
the first course was being served. The meal was French
cuisine and very good. Tina was aware of Shane's
warmth beside her while she chatted with her host and
he talked to their hostess and Whitney. She glanced at
Gabe, her old friend, and smiled.

"What are you planning on doing now that you're one
of our famous residents?" Genny Barrett inquired at one
point.

Everyone looked at Tina.

She felt herself blush. "I'm going to write a book on
war from the perspective of the women and children
caught in it."

"That could be pretty grim," Deveraux said.

"War is grim," Rafe Barrett put in before she could
answer.

Tina saw his wife give him a comforting smile. "Be
sure and notice the decorations tonight," the woman said,
tactfully changing the subject. "They were made by local
elementary-school students."

When the meal was over, they went to the ballroom,
where the dance was already in progress. A table had
been reserved for them.

A troop of actors dressed as jesters pranced among the
crowd, juggling various items and playing jokes on the
guests. Clown cutouts decorated the walls all around the
room. Tina's short cape, which she wore around her

shoulders in the cool room, was noticed at once by the troop.

"One of our own," a jester in yellow-and-purple satin cried.

She was whisked off. They added her to the act by having her toss rings, balls and teacups into the air for them to juggle. When two of them made a saddle by crossing their arms, she was lifted onto it and carried about the room in a great rush while they shouted, "Make way for the queen, the Queen of Fools! Make way!"

Just when she was beginning to wonder if she'd ever get away, Shane appeared. He plucked her from the two jesters and looped an arm around her shoulders. "The queen wishes to dance," he said.

The men staged a mock joust, as if fighting him off. One of them shouted an alarm, "He has stolen the queen! Where are the guards? The mortal has taken the queen!"

His partner laughed. "The more fool he. The queen will turn him into a dancing pig."

Waving their arms like windmills, the jesters ran off into the crowd. Shane lifted Tina's hands to his shoulders. He linked his together behind her back.

The top of her head barely came to his shoulder. He glanced at a couple dancing past, their cheeks pressed together in romantic bliss. "You're too little," he said. His eyes roamed her face, their summery blue shimmering with thoughts that seemed suddenly dark and deep and unreadable.

"I know." Her heart was tripping all over itself. For a moment, she forgot that they were enemies. "It's hard to dance with someone short."

"There are other ways. You're so light, I could lift you right off your feet."

She felt as if she'd float away at the slightest breeze. "To dance?"

He smiled slightly. "Yes."

A wave of giddiness washed over her. She recalled that she'd had two glasses of wine with dinner. Or had it been three?

Shane took a deep breath. She felt a shudder go through him. She leaned her head back and gazed at him, aware of the heat that spread slowly between them. For the space of a heartbeat, she saw the bright flare of hunger in his eyes, then it was gone.

"The jesters were right. You have turned me into a dancing pig...or a fool...." His voice was a deep, soft rumble that mixed pleasantly with the music. "Only a fool would play with fire."

"Yes."

He gazed at her through narrowed eyes. "You feel it, too."

There seemed no point in denying what they both knew. She said nothing. Dreams that had once seemed farfetched suddenly took on new possibilities. She gazed at him, lost in the wonder of the moment, in the music that strummed in her blood.

"You sometimes have such an innocent look," he murmured. "I can't decide if you're a beguiling enchantress who will fill my life with magic or a devil-woman sent to torment me."

She smiled at his plaint and the frustration he experienced trying to figure her out. This was more of himself than he'd ever revealed to her before. "How much wine did you consume?"

"Not enough to make me numb," he muttered.

He pulled her closer, until she had no choice but to rest her head on his chest, her body tucked intimately against his. He moved them in a slow shuffle, dancing in a circle in the same spot.

It was the second time she'd been in his arms. The first time superimposed itself on this one like a double-exposed snapshot. There'd been anger in him then, but not now.

"Relax," he growled into her hair. He rubbed his nose back and forth in the tresses, taking a deep breath as he did. "You smell so damned good. What kind of perfume are you wearing?"

"None. I mean, it's soap and shampoo, not perfume."

"Hmm," he murmured.

Enchantress, he'd called her. She felt they were both caught in a spell. If she didn't watch herself, she'd end up melting at his feet like a candle set too close to a fire.

The next hour passed in a blur of enchantment. Shane introduced her to the mayor, who had a booming voice and a happy manner, and the mayor's wife, who was a calm, smiling woman.

They danced several times and chatted with the resort owner and other couples they met. Everyone made her feel welcome; everyone wanted to hear about her life.

"It isn't as exciting or dangerous as it sounds," she explained modestly. She didn't want to mislead people, but they seemed intent on treating her like a heroine. She met the owners of the local newspaper, the *Riverton Daily News*.

"I write the living, food and social columns," the wife, Dolly Adams, explained the operation of the paper. "Clint does the front page, letters to the editor and the typesetting on the computer."

"We could use some help," Clint told her. "If you want a job, just show up any day at seven a.m."

"He isn't joking," Dolly informed them with an impish grin. "The mayor dropped in one day to talk about an item for the paper. The collator had quit, so Clint, who knew he was a retired airplane mechanic, put him to work fixing it. The poor man didn't get out of the office until seven that night."

"Remind me not to go down there," Shane muttered in an audible aside. The group around them laughed.

Tina drank two glasses of champagne punch, then refused any more. She was already floating on a cloud.

Shane was attentive, but rather quiet. His gaze was warm when he looked at her. After dancing once more, she sighed deeply as they started back to the table. "Tired?" he asked.

"Yes, I think I am."

"We'll say good-night to the others and leave."

They returned to the table and thanked the Barretts. The newspaper owners were there, too.

"Isn't it interesting," Dolly mused, pointing out the Deverauxes on the dance floor, "that Whitney and Gabe both returned to this area because of an inheritance? Rafe recently bought back the ranch his uncle left him, and now here's Tina, who also came back because of an inheritance. I think there's a feature article here—a sort of returning to one's roots."

"Or stealing someone else's," a feminine voice remarked in an acidic purr.

Tina looked around. Behind them stood a couple. She easily recognized Tyson Macklin. His hair was the same tawny shade as his brother's, although his eyes were a lighter blue. He wasn't as large as Shane, nor as broad, but the physical likeness was there.

The woman with him was a lovely blonde of average height whose generous bustline filled a low-cut sequined bodice. Her eyes were blue with gold flecks. Right now, they were shooting venomous looks at Tina. Anne's niece, she deduced. Ty's wife.

"Pull in your claws," Shane advised his sister-in-law in the uncomfortable silence that followed her accusation. "Tina, you remember Ty. This is his wife, Ronda."

"You're lovelier now than eleven years ago," Ty said, taking her hand in his. He looked tired. His smile was tinged with a bitterness that hadn't been present all those years ago.

Tina eased her hand free. She felt sorry for him, she realized. He'd always been at a disadvantage compared to his older brother; now he was apparently trapped in a marriage that wasn't working out. She wondered if he loved his wife.

Watching the blonde speak to the others in the group, Tina saw that Ronda had adopted a brave, silently suffering front. It was an obvious bid for sympathy from her audience and about as real as a three-dollar bill.

She also noticed the lines of discontent around the woman's mouth. A person used to getting her own way, she concluded; one who didn't take kindly to being thwarted. One who flirted her way through life, but kept her nails sharpened for use against anyone who didn't fall for her charm.

A chill crept up Tina's neck and along her scalp.

Glancing at Shane, she found he was also watching his sister-in-law. His gaze had softened, and he looked completely taken in by that poor-brave-me act. Tina was amazed.

Was he in love with Ty's wife?

"Who's with Jonathan?" Shane asked during a pause.

"Mrs. Perkins," Ronda answered.

Shane frowned. "She had a movie planned for tonight."

Ty's wife dropped her gaze flirtatiously and looked petulant. "I was bored. When I mentioned the dance, she kindly volunteered to watch Jonathan so I could come."

Shane looked at his brother.

Ty shrugged. "She called me. I'm always handy as an escort...when she can't get you."

The sardonic statement revealed a lot of animosity, Tina thought. Her heart went out to Ty. His life couldn't have been easy these past few years. Yet he and Shane had been close when she'd first met him. He'd looked up to his older brother then.

Shane let out a deep breath, as if forcing himself to relax. "I'm taking Tina home now. I'll talk to you tomorrow," he said to Ty.

"Sure, Big Brother." Ty strode off toward the bar.

"I think I'd like to leave now, too. May I catch a ride?" Ronda asked. "Ty was so difficult on the way over."

To Tina's shock, there were tears in the woman's eyes. Maybe she'd misjudged Shane's sister-in-law. Maybe she was sincere. But if Anne hadn't cared for her...

"I'll come back for you," Shane offered.

Ronda nodded, managing to look disappointed and eager at the same time. It gave Tina an uneasy feeling. Glancing toward the bar, she saw Ty drink half a glass of liquor in one swallow.

"Don't get mixed up with Ty," Shane advised cooly on the way to his car. "He has enough troubles without the Lolita of his youth returning to tempt him."

Tina stiffened. "I agree. It must be hard to watch your brother cut in on your wife."

Chapter Five

Anger surrounded Shane like a dark aura. Tina waited for the fury to break around her. He didn't speak until they were in the car on the road.

"Just what the hell did you mean by that nasty remark?" he demanded, his hands clenched around the steering wheel in a manner that suggested what he'd do to her neck if he had a chance.

"It's obvious. You take the wife's side against her husband. That's interference, in my book."

"I'm not on anybody's side," he growled, casting her a feral glance before looking back at the ribbon of light cutting through the darkness.

Peering out the window, she saw only patches of stars. Clouds dotted the sky, bringing the threat of more snow. Spring had never felt so far away, and she had never felt so alone.

She decided not to add any more fuel to Shane's flaming temper. She'd keep her mouth shut. After all, what did she know about anyone's life here? She was an outsider.

"I believe in the sanctity of marriage," he informed her after a silent five minutes went by. "I've tried to talk sense into both of them. Neither Ty nor Ronda will listen. Jonathan is caught in the middle of the mess."

"Jonathan is your nephew?"

"Yes." A worried line appeared between his eyes at mention of the child.

"How old is he?"

"Four. The kid needs both his parents, especially now. He hasn't been well lately."

"What's wrong with him?"

"The doctors don't know or won't say. They're running tests." This last was said with an exasperated twist of his lips.

"I see."

She couldn't help the softer note that invaded her tone. It was the one thing she couldn't bear—for children to hurt. In a world at war, whether between parents or countries, children were the losers.

Shane heaved a deep sigh. "That's what I'm telling you—stay away from Ty. He needs to solve the problems he has, not compound them with...complications."

"What about you?" she inquired coolly.

"What about me?"

"You're going back to pick up his wife at the ball. Why not let her husband take her home? Maybe part of the problem is you."

Shane cursed under his breath. "Ty knows I'd never do anything underhanded. I'm trying to help them patch things up."

She knew she should let it drop—after all, she hadn't

come back here to get tangled up in other people's disputes. "It seems to me the best way to do that is to stay out of it."

He pulled into her drive and turned off the engine. In the sudden silence, they could hear the wind moaning through the fir trees. Her neighbor had left an outside light on. It cast long, eerie shadows through the trees. The shadows pitched to and fro in a frantic dance on the snow, driven by the commands of the wind.

"Since when did you become an expert on marriage?" he asked with more than a trace of sarcasm.

"Sometimes an outsider sees things others miss. As long as your sister-in-law can go running to you for sympathy when things go wrong with her husband, she will."

"Thanks for the advice. Now I won't have to write Dear Abby."

Tina had to smile, thinking of Shane sending his problems to an advice columnist. "With your ego, I'm sure you think you should be writing the column for her."

He leaned toward her. In the dim light reflecting off the snow, she could barely make out his features. She didn't have to see him clearly to know how penetrating his direct blue gaze was, nor how it could cut right into a person's heart.

"You said that before…eleven years ago," he said quietly, an odd note in his voice.

"What?" Whatever she'd expected, it hadn't been that he'd recall the past.

"About my ego. You told me that the best thing I could do for Ty was to stay out of his life. You said my ego was so colossal that I thought I could play God…."

His voice trailed off. For a moment, she was thrown back to that day he'd come to her at the river instead of Ty. She'd maintained an outward calm, smiling all the time he told her off. Her insouciance had made him furious.

The touch of a warm, rough finger on her mouth caused her to jump.

"You're remembering," he said.

She pulled away, but he caught her chin and brought her around to face him.

"I've never forgotten your eyes...cloudy eyes that never reveal your thoughts. What are you thinking now?"

"That it's darned cold out here and, as much as I'd like to debate the philosophy of life with you, I really should go in."

She saw the flash of his smile, then it was gone. He leaned closer. She tensed. Her eyelashes felt incredibly heavy. She wanted to close her eyes, but knew she mustn't. That could be taken as an invitation for him to kiss her.

"I remember your fire," he murmured, his gaze dark and searching. "You were soft in my arms...hot... responsive—"

"No, I wasn't. I didn't."

He traced the line of her lips, making them tingle unbearably. She licked the sensation away. Her tongue touched his finger. She heard him draw in a sharp breath while a tremor of undefined longing went through her.

She shouldn't have gone to the dance. She'd known, deep inside, how it would be...dancing with him, being in his arms...feeling his warmth, the strength in his body, the gentleness of his touch. She shouldn't have gone.

"You trembled in my arms that day," he said. His breath fanned over her mouth. "I was shaking, too."

"I was angry," she said, "just as you were."

"That's something I've been wondering about ever

since.'' His lips were closer. His breath deepened, became heavy.

''What?'' she whispered, barely able to speak.

''Was it all in anger?''

''Yes.'' She closed her eyes. ''Yes.''

''Was it?'' His lips touched hers.

It was the softest grazing of flesh on flesh, but it was like a lightning bolt striking. Her breath hung suspended between one eternity and another.

His mouth brushed softly over hers, again and again, then pressed ever so gently, parting her lips. His tongue dipped briefly inside.

''You taste so damned good,'' he said.

''The champagne…''

''No,'' he whispered. ''You.''

He covered her lips possessively, hungrily, and probed slowly, sensuously beyond them, following the line of her teeth, the curve of her mouth, then delving deeply into her while stars swirled madly behind her closed eyelids.

All power of reasoning left her. She knew she shouldn't allow this, but it was too hard to think why. His wonderful stroking of her mouth started an upheaval inside her that spread into faint nervous tremors throughout her entire body.

His arms slipped around her, drawing her as close as possible. It wasn't enough. She clung to his broad shoulders as if he were her only anchor in a world gone berserk.

He shifted, cracking his knee on the gear shift as he did so. When he cursed softly, she drew back from his arms with an effort.

''That's what I get for trying to make out in a parked car,'' he said ruefully, then added in an almost irritated tone, "but that's what you do to me—make me forget things I should remember."

Reason returned. Tina released her grasp on his suit lapels. She hadn't been aware that she'd been holding on. Realizing how foolishly she'd behaved, she pushed against him, wanting to be free from his embrace, but he didn't let her go.

Permitting that kiss to happen had been the height of folly on her part. Her lips still tingled from the effects. She licked them and tasted the faint flavor of the brandy he'd consumed before they left the ball.

"Such as?" She was proud of her cool control.

"Such as—why did you return to this two-bit town when you had the world in your hand?"

His suspicions hurt in ways she couldn't begin to explain. She hated it that he saw her as a fortune hunter out for the main chance, yet her pride wouldn't let her argue with him. What would be the point? He wouldn't believe anything she said.

"I—I need to go in," she said, disturbed at the slight break in her voice that betrayed emotion.

"Yes, else the neighbors will have something new to talk about." A slight smile flicked at the corners of his mouth, then disappeared. He looked harsh and firmly in control of his emotions once more, his breathing calm and easy.

She suppressed the insane desire to see him trembling in her arms from the passion they shared. She wanted him to feel unsure and vulnerable and filled with the same unbearable longing as she, for things she couldn't begin to explain.

That would be the day. Tell this man, with his confidence, his control, his cynical view of life, how she felt so he could laugh at her? Never.

But his heart had pounded hard beneath her palms when they'd kissed. It wouldn't have taken much to propel both of them over the edge…to disaster.

Hastily, she reached for the door. One finger hit the edge of the handle and she felt a nail break in the brittle cold.

"Wait," he ordered, stopping her frantic haste to get away. "I'll help you. The sidewalk is slippery."

She sat still while he got out and came around to her side of the luxury car. She was composed when he opened the door. Then he scooped her into his arms.

"The neighbors will think I've forgotten how to walk," she remarked dryly, resigning herself to the inevitable. She didn't know why he thought he had to carry her. "A helping hand would probably be sufficient."

"You're such a midget, it's easier to carry you."

"I may be a fraction short, but I'm hardly a midget."

"Right. If you weigh a hundred pounds, I'll eat my hat."

"With ketchup or without?" she inquired sweetly. "I weighed a hundred and ten the last time I checked."

He let her slide down his hard length to the porch, which was a step above where he stood. She had to look up only a couple of inches to meet his eyes, had to lean forward and stretch up ever so slightly to meet his lips.

The frown line appeared between his eyes. He caught her to him. "When you look at me like that…"

She turned her face away and stepped back.

His hand tightened on her back, then he slowly released her. That he didn't want to let go was obvious. A thrill ran along her nerves at his reluctance. He followed her to the door, waited while she fumbled with the key and finally opened the door.

The wind rushed through the house. From the back,

they heard a sound like glass shattering. Shane moved her aside and stepped into the hall ahead of her. "Wait here," he ordered in a terse whisper before moving soundlessly to the car.

She started when she saw him return with a pistol in his hand. He moved silently down the hall.

With an effort, Tina closed the front door against the wind, which had gotten steadily stronger during the evening. She tiptoed along the hall, aware of the beat of her heart and the fear she felt for Shane. If a burglar was in the house, he might shoot before Shane had a chance.

"It's okay," he called out just as she reached the kitchen.

When she entered, she saw him studying the window above the sink. Then she saw the glass…and the rock.

"Someone threw a rock through the window?" She stared at the evidence. It seemed a personal affront, as if someone didn't want her there. Which was silly. She'd been in town less than a week.

"Yeah. The wind caused another sliver of glass to fall out when you opened the front door. The back door is still bolted, and I don't see signs of anyone entering."

Tina stopped beside him and stared at the rock and shards of glass lying in the stainless-steel sink. "Why would someone do that?" she wondered aloud, perplexed by the apparently random act of violence.

"Made any enemies since you arrived in town?" he asked.

Only your sister-in-law. "Not that I know of," she said.

He shook his head. "Kids, probably. This place is a good target. It's the last house on the street. With woods on one side and the river behind you, there's a great deal of privacy."

He frowned thoughtfully, his gaze flicking from the window to her. A cold blast came through the broken pane and she shivered, feeling invaded by the vandalism, made vulnerable by it.

"I'll see if I can find something to cover this until you can get it fixed tomorrow." He headed for the door leading down to the old root cellar. "Don't touch anything."

He returned with a piece of heavy cardboard, then sorted through a drawer until he found the masking tape. He cut the cardboard to fit and taped it over the hole.

"Don't go outside," he advised. "In the morning, I'll check for footprints in the yard. It was most likely some kids goofing off. I don't think you'll have any more trouble."

She thought of gangs of wild youths in black leather, sinister and tough, running around looking for trouble. She thought of guns and knives and things that hurt.

"Are you afraid to stay here alone?" Shane asked, a curious note in his voice.

"I...no, of course not." She shook off the images.

He reached out and took her hand. It was icy cold. "You're trembling," he said, his voice deep and quiet, making her shake even more.

She ordered the shaking to stop. "I've never been vandalized before." She glanced at him, then away, afraid of the emotions he stirred to life. It wasn't some unknown prankster she feared, but him and the way he made her feel, she realized.

"Something like this can make a person seem vulnerable."

"Yes." She removed her hand from his warm clasp. "I'm all right. It's late. You'd better go."

"How about a cup of cocoa?" He spoke casually, but she detected a hint of something more—sympathy?—in him. He went to the stove, found a pan and poured in milk to heat.

Tina sat at the table, only then realizing she still had her coat on, her purse and cape clutched in one hand. She took the heavy coat off and laid her stuff on a chair.

"Why don't you change into something comfortable?" he suggested. "The cocoa should be ready when you get back."

"I…all right." It seemed a sensible idea. She went to her bedroom. After a moment's indecision, she put on her thick lounging pajamas and fuzzy house shoes. She clipped the broken nail and washed her face before returning to the kitchen.

"Just in time." Shane put water in the pan and set it back on the stove, then brought two mugs to the table. "You're still trembling," he said when she lifted it to her mouth.

"I always do. It's reaction." She avoided his eyes, embarrassed that he should notice her one weakness.

As a war correspondent, whenever she returned to Rome after witnessing the aftermath of violence, she'd tremble for days.

"You've got to harden yourself," her editor had told her once after a particularly harrowing assignment. "You're an excellent reporter, but you've got to be tough to last in this business."

"People died," she'd said, haunted by visions she couldn't erase. "How do you ever get used to that?"

The nightmares would sometimes stay with her for months. That was the reason she'd returned to Riverton. She hadn't been able to distance herself from other people's suffering. It was a weakness she couldn't seem to overcome.

Shane studied her, a perplexed expression in his eyes.

He listened when the clock began to strike the hour. "Midnight," he said softly when the last *bong* died away. "The ball is officially over, Cinder-girl."

"Totally," she said and sighed. She managed a wan smile. "I guess I'd better clean up the glass before someone gets cut."

"Leave it," he told her. "I'll take care of it. You'd better go on to bed. You look beat."

"Thanks. That's just what every woman loves to hear."

His gaze skimmed along her loose pajama top, which was high necked and long sleeved, then settled on her face. She'd washed the makeup off when she'd changed clothes. She knew her face was pale, her hair disheveled.

Slowly, his perusal changed. His face took on a forbidding moodiness. He looked angry, but she instinctively knew it was more than that. He wanted her, and it bothered him.

Tension hummed between them like electricity on a high-voltage wire. Her breath became tumultuous, difficult. She held herself rigid, unwilling to let this strange, hurting need overtake her common sense.

"I wonder what you're thinking," he mused aloud. "Your eyes don't reveal your thoughts. You're the only person I've never been able to read."

She shrugged and kept her eyes on the steam rising from the chocolate. If he knew what she was thinking now—how she'd like to touch him…how she'd like to snuggle against him…how she'd like to make love with him until time dissolved—he'd probably be shocked.

"I'm a simple soul," she insisted. "You're the one who keeps his cards close to the chest."

His smile was harsh. "I learned to do that a long time ago."

"Because of your stepmother?" she ventured, then wished she hadn't. It was none of her business.

A grimace of distaste appeared and was gone in the blink of an eye. "She was one of the lessons in life I learned well."

"And I'm another," she concluded.

"You I haven't figured out yet. But I will." There was a wealth of meaning in that declaration…and a warning that she didn't miss. He wanted her, but he didn't trust her. He thought she was up to no good, as her grandmother would have said.

He finished the cocoa and took the mug to the sink. "I'll clean up this mess."

"I can do it—"

"There might be a clue," he cut in. He found a plastic bag and secured the stone inside, careful not to touch the smooth granite with his bare hand. Next he cleared the glass away, then washed the pan and the mug he'd used.

"Stone is too porous to hold fingerprints," she pointed out.

"How do you know that?"

"I once dated a man who was an expert," she replied coolly.

"Deveraux," he said, watching her closely. "I thought there was more to you two than a professional relationship."

"He was my friend."

"And lover?"

"My friend," she repeated.

He didn't pursue the matter. Instead, he peered out the window. "Perhaps I should stay over," he muttered, glancing at the clock. "With a reporter's curiosity, you might go out searching for clues and mess up any prints before I see them."

"I won't. You have my word. There's no need for you to stay. I'm fine now." She stood and held out a hand. "See? I'm hardly shaking at all."

He glanced at her hand. "Stay in the house," he ordered. "Keep your doors locked at all times, even during the day. Someone could walk in on you when you're working." He frowned. "I don't like you being here alone. In a small town, word gets around."

"I'll sleep with a brick doorstop under my pillow," she promised in a mock-serious tone, in control once more.

He nodded, making her feel guilty for her flippant reply. People who threw stones could be dangerous. She followed him to the front door. "I'll see you in the morning," he promised.

After he left, she bolted the door, turned on the porch light, which she'd forgotten earlier, and went to bed. It was a long time before she slept.

All her misgivings about living there returned. Shane Macklin stirred up too many controversies inside for her peace of mind. Plus she had a feeling someone didn't want her in town.

Dingdong.

Tina sat straight up in bed, startled out of a sound sleep. She glanced at the clock. Barely six. What had awakened her?

Dingdong. Dingdong.

The impatient two-tone chime of the doorbell answered that question. A neighbor must have an emergency. She leapt from the warm covers and rushed to the front door.

Peering through the tiny spy hole, she saw Shane on

the other side. "Hurry up and open the door," he called. "It's cold out here."

She spared one thought for her appearance, then, with a frown, unlocked and opened the door. She unlatched the storm door and pushed it open with her foot. He hurried inside.

"Breakfast," he announced.

"At six o'clock on a Saturday morning?"

"I came to fix the window."

He headed down the hall. She rolled her eyes to heaven, ran her fingers through her hair to smooth it somewhat and followed at his heels.

He held up the bag he'd brought in. "Cinnamon buns, still warm from the oven, compliments of Mrs. Perkins."

"I didn't think you'd stayed up all night, or what was left of it, baking rolls for breakfast," she told him, not disguising her waspish tone.

"Hmm, you are a grouch in the morning."

She gave him a sour glance and headed for her quarters. There, she washed her face, brushed her teeth and combed her hair before hurrying back to the kitchen. Shane was at the table. The coffee maker gurgled merrily on the counter. She took her seat.

"But you're also beautiful," he remarked. He took a bite of cinnamon roll while he looked her over.

All at once, his teasing good humor disappeared, replaced by something she couldn't name. Then it, too, went away. He looked at her with frank desire. She took a big drink of milk while her insides burned to cinders. They ate in silence.

He looked extraordinarily handsome that morning. He wore a deep blue V-neck sweater over a white shirt, which was opened at the collar. Tawny curling hair was visible at the throat.

"I'd better get to work," he said. His voice was husky.

She looked into his eyes, then away. For a second she felt impossibly young and foolish, like a girl in the throes of her first love...as if she were eighteen again....

"You really don't have to bother," she said coolly. "I can get someone to do it."

"It's no bother. I measured the glass last night and brought a matching pane from an old window in one of the sheds."

There didn't seem to be anything to say to that. When he went out, she tossed the napkins and paper plates in the trash and went to her room.

After a quick shower, she put on soft suede-cloth pants in a rich brown. Over a deep russet sweater, she added a vest that matched the pants. Heavy socks and brown suede oxfords completed the outfit. A russet scarf held her hair away from her face. She added lipstick and a dash of blush before returning to the kitchen.

The cardboard was gone, she saw, and the windowpane replaced. An empty cup was on the counter. The coffee was ready. She poured a cup, sipped it, grimaced, added some tap water and sipped again. Better.

Leaning against the counter, she peered out the window. Shane was studying the ground, walking from the old stable, which held a lawn mower and outdoor furniture, to the side of the house. He bent and held his hand against a track in the snow to measure its length.

Her heart seemed to tighten as she watched him work. Last night she would have made love with him if he'd pressed only the slightest bit. She wanted him with a compelling need that had never changed, not from the first moment she'd met him.

Was there only one person who would make her feel this way? Why did it have to be Shane Macklin? She clenched her hands as confusion washed over her in crashing waves of irony and despair.

She remembered those first years in Rome. In loneliness and desperation, she'd turned to someone—a wonderful man who had accepted it gracefully when she'd told him she'd rather be friends, not lovers. Gabe Deveraux was a rare man and a true friend. She was glad he'd found happiness.

With a sigh that spoke of the loneliness she now felt, she prepared a fresh pot of coffee, then knocked on the window to attract Shane's attention.

When he entered the back door, the cold air swirled in with him, making her shiver all the way down to her comfortable shoes. She hugged the vest around her as his gaze ran over her slacks and the russet sweater. He pulled off his heavy winter jacket and hung it on a peg.

"Find anything?" she asked huskily.

He looked rested, in spite of not getting much sleep. "Some prints, but they're not very clear. He must have dragged his feet. There was only one person."

She was relieved. "A random act of vandalism. It happens everywhere these days."

"Yeah." He poured a cup of coffee into the mug on the counter and took a hearty swallow. "Umm, either my coffee improved a lot upon standing, or you made a fresh pot. What's your secret?"

"Well, I start with cold water and half as many coffee grounds," she suggested.

He grinned and her heart turned over. She quickly looked away. In snug jeans and black boots, he looked solid and powerful.

"You aren't in uniform, so I assume you're not working today. Why didn't you sleep late?"

"My mom used to ask me the same thing. I wake

about the same time each day. It seems to me that when
the sun comes up, it's time to rise and shine. Mrs. Perkins
said you were the same. I thought you would be up." He
looked her over, the way the housekeeper might have,
and seemed to approve of her appearance.

"I see."

A loud *chirr* broke into the conversation. It sounded
like a large cricket. She glanced around for the cause,
and saw Shane pull the portable phone out of his pocket.

He answered, then listened. His brows drew deeper
into a frown. She could detect a feminine voice at the
other end of the line across the kitchen. It sounded angry
and accusing.

"Something came up," he said. "I forgot."

Tina realized he'd forgotten all about returning to the
ball for his sister-in-law last night. So had she.

"There was a, um…an emergency." He glanced over
at Tina, and his eyes seemed to darken with mysterious
thoughts.

Her ears suddenly felt hot as she listened to his end of
the conversation. She was glad the scarf covered them so
he couldn't see her embarrassment.

"I'll be busy all day. Perhaps you should talk to Ty
yourself," he suggested. "Maybe you can work it out
between the two of you."

Tina stared at him in surprise.

He listened for another minute, then said goodbye. After taking his place opposite her at the table, he inquired
with a grave demeanor, "Was that the politically correct
thing to do?"

"Yes." She picked up her cup and took a drink to
hide the shock of his deferral to her suggestion.

"Maybe I'm not as egotistical as you thought," he
suggested.

She wondered if she'd hurt his feelings with her accusation. "Maybe. Thanks for fixing the window. What do I owe you?"

"Nothing."

It felt strange to have him doing things for her. Of course, part of it was in his official capacity, but still...

Stop it, she ordered her too-active imagination. He was doing his job and being a good neighbor. And keeping an eye on her, she added, so she didn't tempt his baby brother into mischief.

For a moment, she thought of trying to see how far she could tempt the tough, hard-edged sheriff himself.

A frisson swept over her like a cold north wind.

"Someone walk over your grave?" he asked.

She looked at him in confusion.

"You shivered."

"Oh. No, I..." She lapsed into silence.

He took a deep breath, then stood. "I've got to go to the office." He grabbed his coat off the peg and let her precede him down the hall.

She stopped at the door and looked up at him. A mistake, she realized at once. His gaze fastened on her mouth.

They watched each other warily, their chests moving as their breathing deepened.

Time wavered and dissolved. She licked her lips and thought she could detect the taste of him, as if he'd just kissed her.

He made a sound deep in his throat and reached for her, pulling her up on her toes. She spread her hands over the warmth of his sweater just as his mouth covered hers. This was no grazing of the lips, but a full-scale, mouth-to-mouth kiss.

His tongue swept inside and demanded a response. She

gave it to him without reserve. The yearning broke free inside her.

She strained upward. His jacket slipped to the floor, and his hands cupped her hips, bringing her completely into the embrace of his thighs. She felt his muscles flex against her as pure, rampant need took control of her senses.

Melting…she was melting.

When she looped her arms around him, he released his grip and let his hands slide up her ribs. His thumbs touched the sides of her breasts. He caressed her there while his tongue played havoc in her mouth.

It was only a few steps from the hallway to her bedroom. She felt him take those steps without breaking the kiss.

The backs of her legs touched the mattress, then she was lowered gently and his lean, hard body came to rest beside her, his thigh capturing both her legs.

"You should have come to *me* all those years ago," he murmured, kissing along her neck. "You should have been mine, not Ty's."

She stiffened as the words penetrated her haze of passion. Shock swept over her at her wanton response. And what he obviously thought of her—that she was available to any Macklin male for the taking.

"Don't," she said when he cupped her breast. Spirals of electricity shot off into her nether regions. "Let me go."

When she struggled, he lifted his head, his eyes narrowed in disbelief. "You don't mean that."

Desperation seized her as he moved slightly away from her. She wanted to snuggle against him, to experience his warmth forever. No, no, no… "Yes, I do. Let me go, Shane."

He pushed up, then stood. He drew a deep breath and closed his eyes briefly. When he opened them, he was in control once more, and his gaze was filled with loathing. "You're right. This would be a mistake of the first magnitude."

Before she could think of a reply, he'd turned and gone. She heard the door close after him. It was like a slap in the face, a reminder of the cold reality of life. She'd not forget again.

Chapter Six

Tina stared at the rain through the swishing windshield wipers. The weather had changed abruptly over the weekend. The cold wind that had been blowing fiercely from the north shifted to the south. The snow turned to a gray, misty rain.

Heading into her drive, she pushed the button on the remote control. The garage door had slid smoothly open by the time she reached it and pulled inside.

The pickup truck that had followed her from the exit to the interstate stopped on the blacktop a few feet behind her.

Through the rain-beaded back window, she identified the face of Ty Macklin at the wheel. She popped the trunk lid and climbed out of the station wagon. Ty also got out and came toward her.

"Hi. Need a hand?" he asked.

Her first inclination was to tell him no, she didn't want

him in the house. Then she realized how ridiculous that was. Whatever he might have become during the years since she'd last seen him, he wasn't an ogre she had to avoid—which would be impossible in a small town, anyway.

"Sure," she said casually.

He hefted two plastic bags of groceries while she carried the third and the gallon of nonfat milk. He swung the lid closed and entered the kitchen after her.

"Shall I make coffee?" she offered. "Or is this an official call?"

"Official?" He gave her a puzzled glance and placed the bags on the counter next to hers.

After putting the milk away, she started a pot of coffee. "I thought you might be the deputy sheriff or something."

"Not me." His snort of laughter was laced with bitterness. "Only Big Brother gets to wear the white hat."

"It was black, last time I saw him in it."

"Black, then," Ty acknowledged. He sat on the stool at the breakfast bar and watched while she put her groceries away. "How have you been?"

"Fine," she said. "Is this a social call?"

"Yeah." He paused, then smiled. A dimple very like his brother's appeared in his cheek. "You weren't quite so suspicious when I came around before."

"You weren't married then," she crisply reminded him.

"Marriage," he said. "Life's a bitch and then you die."

There was just enough caustic humor in the statement to pull at her heartstrings. She saw the disillusionment in his eyes for a second before he laughed again. "Feeling sorry for yourself?" she inquired, but in gentle tones.

A hint of color swept into his ears, a trait he shared with her, she realized. She felt sorry for the young man who'd found out that his older brother couldn't always come to the rescue and make everything right.

"Maybe," he admitted. He blew across the surface of the coffee when she plunked a mug in front of him. He sighed, then smiled, a genuine smile this time. "I just came by to say hello and see how you were doing. Are you glad to be back?"

She thought it over. "Yes, I think so."

"Everyone in town is trying to figure out why you'd come to a dirt-water place like this to live. They think you should have settled in Washington—the capital, not the state."

"I'd been wanting to write this book for about three years. Anne knew about my ambitions to make it as a political writer. I think this house was a way of giving me my chance."

"She told me when you left that you wouldn't return until you were a success. I guess she was right."

Tina absorbed this insight regarding herself and realized it was true. She'd had to feel she could hold her own against Shane Macklin in order to live here.

"Anne knew more than I realized," she murmured.

"You never told me you were leaving," Ty tossed out suddenly, a frown furrowing his forehead. For a moment, he looked tired...and older than his brother, she realized.

"It was best that way. I can't stand drawn-out good-byes," she said, making light of their youthful fling. She wondered how much of Ty's feelings had been defiance of his family.

A lot, she decided.

She'd continued seeing Ty due to pure anger when she'd overheard Shane telling him that she was a fortune hunter, out for what she could get. Shane had made it clear the day Ty had brought her home for a garden party that she was persona non grata at their elegant mansion.

She and her unexpected guest were silent for a moment. She wondered if Ty's memories about that summer were as troubled as hers.

"You make good coffee," he said at last.

"Mrs. Perkins taught me."

"She's with Shane now. Ronda despises the woman. I think that's because Mrs. Perkins wouldn't take over our house."

Tina said nothing. She moved from one foot to the other, ill-at-ease with the conversation.

Ty glanced around the kitchen. "Ronda resents you. She claims you got her inheritance. But she got plenty from her father, and Anne left a healthy trust fund for Jonathan."

"I'm glad," Tina said sincerely.

He studied her for a moment. "I believe you are."

Another doubting Macklin. "I am," she said firmly. "I have work to do." She gestured vaguely to indicate she had scads of chores.

"Here's your hat and what's your hurry?" He set the mug on the counter. "I wonder if our marriage would have been as miserable as the one I have if you'd accepted my offer years ago."

She sucked in a sharp breath at the question. "Don't ever start thinking that," she warned tersely. "I turned you down then. I'd do it again."

"Oh, I know. Once you saw Shane there was no one else in your sights. He might have considered having an affair if you'd offered, but he'd never have married you."

"I don't think this topic is of interest to me." She

didn't need anyone explaining Shane's opinion of her. He did it quite well himself.

Ty sighed. "I'm sorry, Tina. I'm not being a very good neighbor. I really came over to bid you welcome and to say I'm glad to see you again." He walked toward the door, then stopped. His eyes, blue like Shane's, were bleak. "You went off and made something of your life. Don't throw it away here in Riverton." He opened the door, went out through the garage and ran to his truck through the pouring rain.

She'd never felt so sorry for anyone in her life.

Shane lifted his nephew down from the truck. Jonathan loved to ride with him, especially when he turned on the lights and siren. He hadn't needed them on the trip to the barber shop.

It was Wednesday, and as usual, all the old geezers were hanging around, drinking coffee from the tea shop across the street and talking. Doug, the barber, was busy working on the thin fringe of hair that circled over the ears and behind the head of Mr. Tall, who ran the local hardware store.

"Hey, there, young fella," the barber called out to Jonathan. "How about pumping this chair up a notch or two for me?"

Shane watched the boy rush over to push on the pedal that lifted the barber chair a bit higher. His thin leg pumped industriously, and Mr. Tall rose in the air another inch.

"That's fine," the barber said.

Jonathan watched as Mr. Tall got his biweekly trim. He clambered up in the seat when Doug was ready for him. "Uncle Shane said I could get it short on the sides and long in the back," he said proudly.

"He wants a queue," Shane explained with an indulgent smile.

"We're going out for lunch when we finish," Jonathan told the barber, holding still as the drape was tied around his neck.

"I saw that reporter woman go into the tea shop awhile ago," Mr. Tall informed them. "Maybe Ty will be with her."

Shane felt a hot ball of anger collect in his gut. "Why would you think that?" he asked, with just the right amount of interest in his tone.

"He's been over a couple of times…yesterday and the day before, Emma said. Understand they used to see each other right steady back some years ago when the girl was staying with Anne."

"Yes, they were friends," Shane confirmed.

"Too bad about Ty and his wife," one of the other men piped up. "Young people just fly off and get a divorce nowadays and the devil take the hindmost." He gave Jonathan a sympathetic glance.

The gossip had started, Shane realized. He'd learned that Ronda had seen a lawyer over in Medford on Monday. Great. Just what they needed, with the latest test results on Jonathan due by the end of the week.

He sighed. He'd talk to Tina, make her understand that Ty couldn't afford a scandal just now, not when there might be a custody battle looming on the horizon. Next, he'd talk to his brother and Ronda about what they were doing to their son.

Marriage wasn't just for the good times. It was for all time, as far as he was concerned. A couple who had kids had an obligation to raise those kids in a stable environment.

"Next."

He was roused from his introspection and took his seat in the chair. Using the handle, Jonathan let it down so the barber could reach his uncle's hair, which had gotten way too long and unruly.

It had been a hell of a month, Shane reflected, then realized it was only the sixth day of April. The month had barely started.

Tina wished the talkative Bess would hurry her order. Since seeing Shane and a towheaded little boy go into the barber shop across the street, she'd been in a tizzy to rush home.

Running?

Yes. There, she'd admitted it. The way Shane made her feel frightened her. She'd thought, after all this time, that she'd be immune to him. She wasn't.

And there was the complication of Ty. He'd stopped by the house yesterday for a brief chat. She felt a softening within. Ty needed a friend.

She glared at the utility vehicle with the sheriff's decal on the side. Shane should have been the friend Ty went to.

Well, their problems weren't hers. She was *not* going to get mixed up in the affairs of the Macklins.

"Here we are," Bess announced, startling Tina out of her introspection. The tea-shop owner placed the order on the table.

"Thank you. It looks delicious."

"I'll bring you another pot of tea." Bess hurried off.

Tina lifted the sandwich, then paused before she took a bite. Shane and the boy—his nephew, she presumed—were leaving the barber shop. Instead of climbing into the truck, they crossed the street.

She realized they were heading for the tea shop. Just

her luck. Her tummy did a nosedive to her toes as she watched them splash through potholes filled with the rain that had been falling off and on for four days.

The child was thin and winter pale, but she could tell he was going to be tall like the Macklin men. At present, his hair was the cotton blond often found on children, but he would most likely inherit the thick, tawny locks of his father and uncle. He held his uncle's hand and skipped along beside him, chatting all the while and gazing up with adoring eyes the same shade of blue as his father and uncle had.

Shane should have a son of his own.

She laid her sandwich down without tasting it. Wild, hurting sensations ripped through her. Images of Shane walking with a child on his shoulders, holding another by the hand, came to her. She saw them in the meadow by the river, laughing and skipping stones while a woman laid out a picnic lunch, smiling and watching them with all the love she felt reflected in her eyes....

No! Dear God, what was she thinking?

When the door swung open and the little bell jangled merrily to announce their arrival, she kept her eyes on her food, unable to meet the cynical gaze of the man who had shattered her youthful fantasies with his punishing kiss.

"Come in, you two," Bess called out. "I thought you might be by today. I put the stew on early."

"Jonathan and I couldn't come this close, then pass up a chance at your stew, Bess. It's the best." Shane hung his hat and coat on the rack. He helped his nephew with his wrap, then he and the boy walked over to Tina's table.

She was forced to look up and acknowledge them. "Hello."

"May we join you?" he asked.

She nodded warily, forcing all emotion from her mind.

After they were seated, Shane introduced her to Jonathan.

"Hi," the boy said in friendly tones. "What kind of sandwich is that?"

It obviously never occurred to him that his questions might be intrusive or that he might be rebuffed. He was as confident as his uncle in his expectations of life.

"Vegetarian," she said. "It has sprouts and shredded carrots and cranberry sauce. Would you like a taste?"

He glanced at his uncle, who nodded assent. "Please," the child requested politely.

She cut a corner off, laid it on a napkin and placed it in front of him. He ate it with relish.

"Would you like some more?" she asked.

"Um, no," he decided. "I'll wait for the beef stew. Uncle Shane and I always have that. It sticks to a man's ribs."

"That sounds like something your uncle might say." She gave Shane a glance, then picked up her sandwich and tried again. This time she managed to chew and swallow, although her throat was dry.

Bess brought a huge bowl and a cup of stew and set them before the two males. A basket of crackers and homemade bread accompanied the meal, along with two glasses of milk. She brought Tina a new pot of tea.

"How's the work going?" Shane asked her.

"Fine. I'm still putting my notes in order."

"I suppose it's a nuisance when people drop by without an invitation. They tend to do that in a small town. Sometimes you have to tell them not to."

She wondered if he knew of Ty's visits and recalled that Shane had been to the barber shop, where Mr. Tall had gone earlier. She'd been thinking of telling Ty she was too busy to visit, but the subtle warning in Shane's message angered her. Big brother didn't trust her or Ty, it seemed.

Shane ate all of his meal, but Jonathan didn't have much appetite. He ate barely half. She remembered that Shane had said his nephew wasn't well. The child did look pale, and there were lavender shadows under his eyes, as if he didn't sleep well.

Again she felt her heartstrings tugged by a member of the Macklin family. There was a quietness about the child that didn't ring true. His eyes held a bright intelligence. His expression was alert, but he seemed tired.

"Finished?" Shane asked.

She detected the worry in his eyes as he visually measured the amount of food left on his nephew's plate.

"Yes, sir," Jonathan said. "Thank you. It was very good." He wiped his mouth and laid his napkin on the table, neatly tucked under the edge of his plate in a grown-up manner.

"You haven't finished your sandwich," Shane remarked to her.

"I'm like Jonathan. My eyes were bigger than my tummy."

Jonathan laughed at that and asked her what she meant.

"It means I thought I could eat more than I really could." She poured a fresh cup of the aromatic tea, added a small amount of brown sugar and took a sip. She gazed out the window at the mist, which had started falling again.

The buzz of the portable phone interrupted the silence. While Shane answered, two groups arrived for lunch, laughing and talking so that the peaceful shop took on a lively air.

Tina listened while Shane reported in to the dispatcher. She learned there'd been a seven-car pileup on the highway. Shane stood and spoke to Jonathan.

"Come on, sport. I'll take you home. I have an emergency."

"Can't I come, too, Uncle Shane?"

"Not to this one. People are hurt and need help."

Tina could easily imagine the scene. "I'll take him home," she volunteered. "If you don't mind him walking."

Shane flicked his gaze to her, then out the window, then back. "Are you expecting Ty later?"

"No. I meant I'd take him to your house. It isn't that far to the bridge and across the river."

He shook his head before she finished speaking. "Mrs. Perkins isn't in this afternoon. If you can keep him at your place, I'll send a deputy over to pick him up as soon as I can. Would that be too much trouble?"

"Not at all."

He tossed money onto the table to take care of the meal. "I'll get your lunch."

"That's okay. I can—"

"You're doing me a favor," he told her sharply. "It's the least I can do."

She didn't argue.

"Will I see you again?" Jonathan asked his uncle.

"Probably not today. Later this week we'll go for a ride."

The boy brightened up. "Great!"

"Do what Miss Henderson tells you."

"I will."

When Shane had gone, Tina and Jonathan sat there in silence. More people came in. "Shall we go?" she finally asked. "Bess might need our table."

They put on their coats and hats and started down the street in the light mist. When they came to an intersection, she wondered if she should take his hand. The problem was solved when he slipped his hand into hers. Once across, they continued to hold hands the rest of the way to her house.

"What do you like to do, Jonathan?" she asked.

"I don't know."

She tried to think what might entertain a four-year-old. She had no books for his age group. Recalling that he wasn't feeling well, she tried to think of quiet things they could do. Perhaps make something....

"I was going to bake some cookies this afternoon," she said, going up the sidewalk to the front door. "Would you mind helping?"

"No, I'd like that." He gave a happy smile.

So grown-up, she thought. And trusting. He followed her into the house without hesitation. After they'd hung up their outer wear, they headed for the kitchen.

"I saw a cookbook on the shelf here just the other day," Tina mused aloud. She rummaged through the pantry until she found it.

The book flopped open when she laid it on the counter. She saw a note and picked it up. It was in Anne's familiar writing.

My dear Tina,
The recipes in this book have been used by my family for three generations. I'm delighted that you're thinking of trying some. The old-fashioned brownies on this page were favorites of mine when I was a child. I hope you'll like them, too.

Tina gazed at the graceful signature and put the note aside to add to the other letter she'd found. She glanced at Jonathan. "Did you ever visit your Aunt Anne, who lived in this house?"

He nodded. "Uncle Shane used to bring me here. And once I came with my mom, but she and Aunt Anne didn't like each other," he explained with a child's candor.

"Uh, well, I thought we'd try some recipes from this book. It has belonged to your family for…let's see… you'd be the fifth, no, sixth generation. That means your great-great-great-grandmother was the first to use it. I think."

"Wow."

"Yeah, pretty impressive. I have things that belonged to my grandparents, but your folks go back to the first settlers who came over with the wagon trains. Did you know that?"

He shook his head. "With horses and all?"

"Right."

"Were they soldiers?"

"No, they were farmers. They brought fruit-tree seedlings with them all the way from back east." When he looked disappointed, she added, "It was a very hard journey and very important to keep the roots of the tiny trees damp so they wouldn't die. I once read a story about it, about how the son of the first Macklin family worried about the trees when they came over the mountains because it was so cold. He put the seedlings inside his shirt and kept them warm until they reached the valley. He was only a little older than you when he did that."

"Really?" Jonathan's eyes gleamed with pride.

"Really. He was very smart. He helped his father plant the very first orchard in the valley."

"Did he ride a horse?"

"Umm, yes, I'm pretty sure he did. Everyone did in

those days, you know.'' She smiled. Horses were big with him, it seemed.

"My dad's going to get me a horse just as soon as I'm old enough to take care of it myself,'' he told her proudly. "When I'm six, I think.''

"How nice.'' She'd been assembling the ingredients for the brownies while they chatted. She turned the oven on. "Okay, shall we start on these? You stir and I'll drop the stuff in. Can you do that?''

"Sure.''

She positioned a stool so he could reach the bowl and spoon. Soon they had the brownies mixed and poured into a baking pan. She put the pan in the oven.

"There,'' she said, closing the oven door and setting the timer for thirty minutes. "Now we just have to let them bake.''

Jonathan climbed down from the stool and went to the window. "I can see Uncle Shane's house,'' he said in surprise.

"Yes, it's close to mine, but you have to walk down the main street to the bridge to cross the river.''

"I live down the road—down another road—from his house.''

"I see.'' She resisted the urge to question him, although she wondered how often he stayed with his uncle or Mrs. Perkins. Why hadn't Shane taken the child to his mother or father?

"My mom has gone to Medford,'' Jonathan volunteered. "She and my dad had a fight last night. Dad went out.''

"Shall we build a fire in the living room while our brownies are baking? Then we can make hot chocolate to have with them.''

She distracted him from further confidences with a

number of chores until they were at last seated in front of the fire with brownies and cocoa. After eating, she noticed his eyes drooping.

She pulled off his shoes and laid him on the sofa where his uncle had slept. After placing an afghan over him, she washed their cups and resumed her place in the easy chair. She opened a magazine and read until she heard the sound of a vehicle outside the house.

Shane turned off the engine and sat in the truck until Ty's pickup pulled in behind them. Then he got out and waited for his brother. Together they walked toward the house without speaking.

Shane sighed. "Ty," he said, making an attempt at civility. He and his brother had said some harsh things to each other that afternoon. He bit back the frustration he felt. The family was going to hell in a hand basket, one might say.

"Yeah?" Ty asked dully. His face was pasty, the blue of his eyes brilliant against his red-rimmed eyelids.

"About Tina—"

Ty stopped and turned on Shane. "What is it, Big Brother?" he snarled. "More advice?"

"Yes," Shane snapped, his own temper exploding. "Stay away from her. You have enough problems."

"You're damned right about that," his brother agreed on a cynical note. "But she isn't one of them. She's a friend. She listens without judging. You know, sometimes it's nice to have a friend like that." He leapt up the three steps and reached for the door chime. Before he could ring it, the door opened.

Shane, standing on the steps, controlled his anger with an effort. He saw Tina glance from Ty to him.

"What is it?" she said.

"Is Jonathan here?" Ty asked.

"Yes, he's asleep." She pointed toward the living room.

Ty swept past her. She waited with the door open until Shane came up the steps and into the house. In the living room, he heard Jonathan awaken and exclaim, "Daddy!" with a happy squeal.

Shane motioned for Tina to go ahead of them. They went down the hall and into the warm, cheery room. He saw she'd built a fire.

Ty held his son in his arms, his face pressed into the boy's neck. Shane felt his heart constrict in love and pity for the man and the boy. The Macklin men had bad luck in their women, it seemed. Ronda was making threats about keeping the boy away from his father, and Ty's drinking wasn't helping things.

Neither was having Tina acting the sympathetic friend. He'd have to put a stop to that. Since his brother wouldn't listen, he'd have to make her see reason....

"Ready to go home?" Ty asked his son.

"Sure. Dad, guess what? We made brownies that were real old. Tina said my great-grandmothers made 'em too."

"From Anne's grandmother's cookbook," Tina explained. Her smile was spontaneous and sweet. Shane wondered what it would be like to have her look at him in the unguarded, friendly way she did his brother and nephew. Well, she'd dislike him even more when he reminded her again to stay away from his family. This time he'd see that she knew he meant business.

"Yeah, and one of our grandfathers brought the pear trees in his shirt. Did you know that?" Jonathan squirmed out of Ty's embrace and grinned at them. "Did you, Uncle Shane?"

"Yeah," he said. "Remind me to show you some pictures of the first orchard."

"Super."

Ty collected Jonathan's coat and hat. When he'd dressed the boy, he turned to Tina. "Thanks," he said gruffly, "for your help today. Sorry you had to be bothered with a...family problem." He lifted his son in his arms and headed out, nodding to his brother as he passed him.

"It was no trouble. Jonathan was a big help."

"Right. We did lots of things, Dad."

Shane reluctantly smiled as his nephew recounted all the helpful things he'd done for Tina. It seemed she was good with children. That was a surprise.

He sighed and removed his hat. A fine mist clung to the waterproofed felt. He hung it and his coat on the highboy in the hall while she saw the others out. When he glanced up, she was watching him with her opaque gray eyes, not giving any thoughts away. It wasn't the way she'd looked at Jonathan. He'd seen kindness in her gaze.

Hell, she'd *liked* his nephew. She didn't like him.

"Got any coffee?" he asked. He would try to tactfully ease into a conversation about his brother. After all, she had helped him out in a pinch.

"Yes. I made a pot earlier." She went into the kitchen.

He followed and sat at the table. Through the windows he could see the roof of his house over the pine trees. Below the knoll the house sat on, the fruit trees ran in orderly rows right down to the riverbank. On this side of the river, the lawn, still dormant from winter, rolled in gentle swales to the boulders that lined the Rogue River.

Inside, the scent of brownies lingered in the air, mingling with the spicy aroma of cedar boughs lying in a basket and of wood burning in the fireplace.

He'd always liked this house, he reflected. He had come to Anne whenever life got too hectic and he needed a breather, a place of quiet to rethink his direction. She'd been a good listener.

So was the present occupant, according to Ty.

Tina brought the coffee. He noted the pleasant perfume that surrounded her, a sort of clean smell, like soap and talcum powder. Her hair brushed her shoulders, a rich dark brown, very shiny, but without red highlights. He reached out and touched it.

She froze in place.

He looked into her eyes and saw emotion there, but he couldn't read what it was. If there weren't so many other things on his mind, he thought he'd like to know what made her tick, this small woman who didn't betray her inner being to anyone.

Except maybe Anne.

Leave her alone, Shane. She'll come back when she's ready to face you again.

And here she was.

"Have you eaten dinner?" he asked, letting his finger slide down the lock of hair.

"No."

"I'll take you out."

"I made chili earlier. If you'd like some…" She pulled away from him and hooked her hair out of the way behind her ear.

"That would be nice."

"You—you look tired," she ventured, going back to the stove. "So did Ty."

Shane grimaced at the mention of his brother. Things were tough there. "He and Ronda had a fight last night.

He went out and tied one on. One of the deputies brought him home at three this morning. I kept Jonathan while he slept it off.''

''Where was… Never mind, it's none of my business.''

He watched her efficient movements while she heated a pot of chili and set out crackers in a blue bowl. He drank the coffee she'd given him. ''Ronda came over to the house this morning and left Jonathan. She had an appointment with her lawyer in Medford.''

''For a divorce?''

''Yeah, but there isn't going to be one.''

Calm gray eyes studied him for a minute. ''Thus speaks the Mighty Macklin,'' she mocked softly.

He shrugged. ''I had a talk with Ty. I think he'll try to patch things up with Ronda. They need to stay together because of Jonathan.''

She ladled the chili into bowls and brought them to the table. ''That could be worse for him. I mean, if they argue all the time.''

''They won't. They're going to try counseling.''

The heaviness in his spirit was like a weight pulling him downward into hell. He looked at Tina as she sat opposite him at the table. Why had he stayed after Ty left?

Answer—he hadn't wanted to go home to an empty house. Mrs. Perkins was down in Ashland helping her daughter, who was pregnant and had two other children. She'd be gone all week and probably the next as well, she'd called to say. He hadn't felt like rattling around in the gloom by himself.

Certainly he didn't expect sympathy from his hostess for his worries. Why should she care?

''Shane, what's wrong?'' she suddenly asked, looking directly into his eyes.

He wanted to talk to her, he found. He wanted to tell her of his frustration with his family, of his worries about his nephew, who had been ill with colds and flu all winter and had lost weight.

He shook his head slightly, amazed at the idea. When had he ever needed the comfort of a gold digger? he asked cynically. When had he ever needed anyone? He was the family problem solver. He had been for years.

"Nothing," he said.

"Shall we have brownies and coffee in the living room?" she suggested when they finished.

He nodded and helped her clear the table. "I wanted to tell you we caught the vandals. Some kids formed a secret club. The window breaking was part of the initiation. After a lecture and a tour of the jail, they decided to go straight."

She laughed and picked up the plate of brownies and the pot of coffee. He carried the cups. They went into the living room.

While he added fresh logs to the fire, she refilled their mugs. Then, going to a wall unit of shelves and cabinets, she opened a pull-down door and poured brandy into two snifters. She carried these to the coffee table and set them by the mugs.

She chose her favorite chair. "What happened with the accident at lunch? Was anyone hurt?"

He settled on the sofa. "Yes."

"Not...killed?"

"No, but two people were hurt pretty bad. A young girl, no more than sixteen, will be lucky to walk again."

She wrapped her arms across her chest, remembering the shattered bodies she'd seen, the lives wrecked by injuries that couldn't be described. Shane, in his job, saw them, too.

"I used to shake for days after seeing the aftermath of violence," she murmured. "I wondered how people could do that to each other. No cause was that noble...."

"Car wrecks are worse," he said, continuing her thought. "They're not even for a cause. A careless moment, and lives are ruined for no reason, no reason at all."

"Yes." She gave him a sympathetic glance.

He speared her with a hard, determined stare. "That can happen in people's lives, too. Sometimes, in moments of despair or weakness, we do foolish things."

Cold air settled around her like a shroud. "Why don't you just say whatever it is you want to say?" she invited, letting no emotion show on her face.

"I think it would be better if you didn't get involved in the Macklin family problems. It...could be awkward, especially if things end in a divorce and a custody battle." He paused, then finished in a harder tone, "If you don't discourage Ty from dropping by, I'll have to think of a way to do it for you."

Chapter Seven

Tina watched a drop of moisture collect and run down the windowpane. She sighed and turned off the computer. She hadn't gotten any work done that morning. Nor the day before.

Restlessness pervaded her spirit until she couldn't stand to sit still. She'd walked for miles, but that didn't help much, either. Anger churned in her.

Shane had practically accused her of being a home wrecker. As if she had anything to do with Ty's marital problems. According to Mrs. Perkins, the couple had been quarreling since Day One.

If anyone had a problem, it was Shane. She grinned wryly. True to her nature, she'd reminded him of her view of the situation. They'd ended up having a flaming row.

"Why don't you try being a friend to your brother?" she'd demanded. "You might try asking him what he wants from you, rather than telling him what you think he should do.''

She shook her head in exasperation. She was absolutely, positively *not* getting involved—

The ringing of the telephone halted her advice to herself. She answered with a defensive note in her voice, but it wasn't her nemesis.

''Tina? This is Dolly Adams. From the newspaper.''

''Oh, yes. How are you?''

''Not so good. That's what I'm calling about. The dumbest thing happened. I fell and broke my ankle.''

''I'm terribly sorry,'' Tina at once sympathized.

''Well, the problem is—I know this is an imposition— but do you think…would it be possible for you to…Clint is just going to lose his mind.…''

''Dolly, do you need help at the paper?'' Tina asked, smiling.

''Yes,'' the other woman said with a great deal of relief in her voice. ''Do you think you could do the feature articles for a few weeks, just until I get the cast off? I can handle the rest.''

''I'd be glad to do whatever you need.''

''Bless you. I'll tell Clint, so he can stop tearing his hair out. He doesn't have all that much left.''

Tina laughed with Dolly when she heard the man protesting in the background. ''When shall I come in?'' she asked.

''Today wouldn't be too soon, if that's possible. The paper is supposed to go out this afternoon, but we aren't finished.''

''I'll be there in five minutes,'' she promised.

After hanging up, she went to her bedroom and donned a pair of ankle boots. She put on lipstick, then checked her outfit in the mirror. The black wool slacks, black sweater and black, gold and blue vest would do.

With a quickening feeling of excitement, she slipped into a raincoat and, pulling the hood over her hair, hurried out into the mist. She'd covered half of the three blocks to the newspaper office when a horn honked and a truck pulled to the curb beside her.

"Need a lift?" Ty called out.

She hesitated, then climbed in.

"Where to?" he asked.

"The *Riverton Daily News*. I'm their newest reporter." She told him of the accident.

"Tough luck," he said. "I guess that means you can't have lunch with me?"

She shook her head. "Ty, you need a friend, but that person isn't me. Why don't you talk to Shane?"

"Why? So he can lecture me on family duties and all that?"

"So you can stop feeling sorry for yourself. Maybe it's time you started taking charge of your life. You have a wife and a darling little boy. How is he, by the way?"

Ty shrugged, his jaw set in the stubborn mode of the Macklin males. "The doctors have decided he's just run down. They've put him on iron and vitamins."

"Oh, good. Well, here we are." She was relieved that they'd arrived at the newspaper building. She opened the door and climbed out. "You have a family," she said softly, "something I've always wanted. Your son adores you. Your brother loves you. Make peace with your wife. Be happy." She smiled. "End of lecture."

He smiled, too. There was a sardonic twist to his lips, but it was still a smile. "I take it this is the goodbye you forgot to say all those years ago?"

She nodded. The Macklins didn't need her. They had

each other. She hoped Shane would be happy when he learned she'd decided to do as he'd requested. Ha, he'd probably wonder what she was up to now.

"Goodbye," she said softly and closed the door.

Ty waved and drove off.

She watched the pickup disappear into the parking lot next to the ranch-supply store. She felt a nostalgic fondness for Ty. It had been like a dream come true when he'd asked her for a date that first time. Funny, she couldn't remember if he'd ever kissed her.

Surely he had, she mused, heading toward the door. But after meeting Shane, all she could recall was the older brother's suspicious attitude toward her, his frosty greeting when Ty had taken her to the garden party and introduced her…and finally, that kiss under the pear trees that had melted her defiance and sent her scurrying for safety.

Why wasn't she running now? After that episode in her bedroom last Saturday, she should take off and not look back. Until she'd protested, he'd seemed to think she was his for the taking.

She lifted her chin. She belonged to nobody but herself. She wouldn't run from anyone, ever again. She had a right to live where she pleased.

Anyway, all that was behind her. She would put the Macklin family out of her life. In the future, she'd avoid the whole bunch of them like poison bananas. Satisfied with this decision, she went inside to start her new job.

"Well, that's it," Clint Adams said in satisfaction. The paper had been run through the presses, collated, folded, labeled and tied into bundles. The driver and his helper were at the loading dock, tossing the bundles into the truck for transportation to the post office or the delivery people.

Tina, smiling, placed her hands in the small of her back and stretched. "I'm going home."

It was Friday, a week since she'd come on board. She was so tired she could hardly stand. She'd never realized what a labor of love it was to put out a small-town paper with a staff of six, one of whom was the secretary-receptionist-typist and another of whom was the maintenance man, who kept the computer-controlled printing presses running as smooth as a greased track.

Besides herself and the Adamses, there was one other reporter, a recent college graduate who covered the local sports news, accidents and police reports. Together they'd put out sixteen pages of articles, feature stories, advertisements and lots of pictures of local doings. The comics page came from a national service, thank goodness.

"Wait," Dolly requested. She sat at her desk with her injured foot propped on a cushioned stool. She'd missed only half a day of work with her injury.

Tina hooked her hair behind her ear and sat on the corner of the desk. "Don't tell me we have a weekend story to cover?"

"Well..." Dolly clapped her hands together, something she did when she was particularly excited about an idea. "I've had this brilliant idea to do a series. Clint likes it, too."

"A series?" That sounded interesting. "On what?"

"A day in the life of the mayor, the local pediatrician, the police chief." Dolly smiled excitedly as her idea took hold. "We could do the sheriff, too—sort of contrast his day to that of the local police."

Tina felt her interest dim, then brighten. She could start

with the mayor. By the time they were ready for the sheriff, Dolly would be well, and she could gracefully retire.

She glanced around the cramped, noisy office. She'd missed working. She liked being with people more than she'd realized. She liked interviewing the local politicians and sniffing out stories, from accusation of graft in the school system to photographing the beauty queen in the spring pageant.

Dolly and Clint had made her welcome as a valued member of their team. They'd praised her stories and her style until she'd laughingly threatened to quit if they didn't stop. They made her feel wanted and worthy of their trust.

"I'll start Monday," she promised.

The paper came out weekly, on Friday. Other than special events, they had the weekends off. She used that time for her own project and for housekeeping. Not that she did a lot of that.

Dolly nodded. "Go home and nurse that cold. We can't have you coming down sick."

"I will." Her nose was stuffy, her voice croaky.

She left the office and walked down the street in the rosy twilight. On an impulse, she headed for the river. She'd stroll through the park to her house.

There was a haze of green on the ground, she noted, and on the pear trees across the river. The buds were swelling, ready to pop into bloom after the late winter.

The air was chilly with the departing of the sun. She zipped her jacket up to her throat when she felt the wind pick up. Earlier she'd been outside without even a jacket on, the day had been so warm.

Spring at last.

It brought a strange, painful joy to her heart. Hope reborn, she thought, after the starkness of winter.

She hadn't seen any of the Macklin family that week, thank heavens. That was probably why she felt so chipper. She'd had time to get her equilibrium back. With Dolly and Clint, she had all the friendship she needed, plus work she loved.

The shadows were deeper along the tree-shaded path. Usually she met a jogger or two, but there were none today. It was as if she were the only person in the world.

Nearing her house, the park narrowed until it came to an end at her property line. Here the path ran along the fence that divided the yards of the other houses on her street from the park.

At the end of the path, she easily climbed the wooden rails and jumped lightly down on her own land.

Instead of going inside, she lingered on the banks of the Rogue and watched the sunset darken the water to pewter. The rain last week, as well as the melting snow on the mountains, had turned the river to a torrent that cascaded over the boulders, throwing up white plumes.

"Hi, Tina," a young voice called.

She glanced across the river. Jonathan stood on the opposite side, upstream from her. She noticed that the bank had been eaten away by the rushing water. The child stood on a thin ledge. He waved and jumped up and down to get her attention.

"Jonathan, get back," she called.

Too late. The water-soaked earth began to crumble. Jonathan scrambled backwards, but the landslide moved faster, as if determined to trap the human who had dared venture too close.

He fell into the water with a cry.

Tina looked around wildly. There was no help anywhere. The boy's head bobbed to the surface, disappeared, then came up again. He thrashed against the churning water.

"Look out!" she screamed as he was hurled toward a boulder. "Grab hold. The rock. Hold on!"

He managed to turn toward the huge block of granite. With arms outspread, he was swept up onto it, the force of the water holding him against the stone. He pulled himself up higher and clung with all his strength. Even from there, she could see the terror on his young face.

"I'm coming," she called. "Hold on. I'll be there."

She dropped her purse and kicked off her shoes. In a second, she was out of her coat. Judging the force of the water, she leapt over the fence and ran upstream so she would be carried down to Jonathan. She dived in and came up fighting for breath.

The water was shockingly cold. She sucked in air, got her bearings and struck out in a strong crawl as the current bore her irresistibly down river.

Her knee hit a submerged rock. The pain raced along her leg. She ignored it and forced herself to kick harder. She was coming up on the boulder where Jonathan lay, his strength spent.

Unable to stop, she slapped into him, clutched for the boulder and was torn away like a leaf by the current. She got hold of the child's shoulder and brought him with her.

He roused himself and wrapped his arms around her, locking them behind her neck. She turned on her back so his face was above water. "Hold on. I'm going to swim for shore. Warn me if I'm about to hit anything."

He nodded. His face was chalk white.

A short way downstream, the river curved. She didn't fight the flow, but let it carry her. By kicking and using her arms, she angled them so that they would wash up on the sandbar in the bend.

When she felt the rough edge of a hidden ledge with her hand, she gave a cry of thanksgiving. Turning, she pushed them upright out of the water and stood. The water tugged at her waist, but she kept her balance. Carefully feeling her way, she managed to reach the bank and pull them to safety.

For a while she lay there, breathing hard, clutching Jonathan to her fiercely as if the river might snatch him away again.

She became aware of the cold again when she heard his teeth chattering and felt his thin body shaking. She got them both upright and looked him over.

He'd lost his shoes in the torrent. His pants, shirt and windbreaker were soaked. His lips were blue.

"Come on. We have to get inside." She lifted him into her arms. He dropped his head against her shoulder as if exhausted. She started walking, aware of the chills coursing through her own body.

It seemed forever before she saw the elegant veranda of the Macklin mansion facing the river. Like Jonathan, she couldn't stop shivering now. Fortunately, her feet were numb. She no longer felt the sharp imprint of rocks on her soles.

The house was dark. She crossed the smooth paving stones of the veranda and tried the door. Locked. She knocked on the glass panels, but there was no answer.

"Jonathan, where do you live? Look up! Where do you live?"

He raised his head and peered into the growing dark. The trees were silhouettes against the sky, the shadows beneath their branches deep. He pointed toward the east.

The wind hit her like a solid wall when she stepped

off the veranda. Her legs were made of lead, so heavy she could hardly lift one, then the other. She pushed on. Finally, she saw lights ahead of them.

"Jonathan, is that your house?"

He didn't answer. She peered down at him, but could only detect the pale oval of his face nestled against her throat. He'd stopped shaking. She knew that was a bad sign.

His legs no longer gripped her waist, but hung limply, hitting against her thighs with each step.

Don't let him die. Please, don't let him die.

She leaned into the wind and concentrated on putting one foot in front of the other. Hypothermia. It could kill....

At last they reached the lawn, crossed it.... At the front door, she tried the handle and found it locked. She put her finger on the bell and kept it there. Inside, she could hear the musical tones chiming over and over.

Finally, the door opened.

"What's going on?" Ty's wife demanded. She stared as if she didn't recognize either of them.

"J-Jonathan f-fell in the r-river." Tina couldn't keep her teeth from chattering. "He n-needs h-help."

The irritated scowl changed to shock, then worry. Ronda snatched the boy from Tina's arms and rushed toward the stairs, leaving Tina standing in the open door.

She stepped inside and closed the door. Her legs buckled. She caught at a table, steadied herself and went up the steps. The floor heaved up and down under her feet.

In the upper hallway, she heard Ronda's voice, talking in strident tones to someone...paramedics, Tina thought.

"Hurry. He's unconscious. What should I do?" Ronda demanded. "Yes, I will. Yes. Yes. Hurry."

Tina heard the bang of a telephone being hung up. Help was coming. They'd save Jonathan....

She leaned against the banister, then slipped downward. Her head ached terribly. Annoying black spots danced in front of her eyes, then clumped together, becoming thicker and thicker. Finally, they obscured her vision entirely. Fortunately, she could still hear.

"Wake up, Jonathan. Mommy wants you to wake up. Jonathan, wake up!"

A sound like a slap reached Tina. *Don't hit him. It was an accident.* Tina's tongue wouldn't form the words. She needed to get home. A warm shower. Yes.

Holding on to the railing, she scooted down the steps on her rear. Her legs wouldn't cooperate. At the bottom, she managed to stand up. She realized she'd stopped shivering.

She wished someone would turn the lights on. It was so dark, she couldn't see a thing.

The wail of a siren became louder. An accident. She needed to get there...to cover it. Her job...to see...oh, God, she didn't want to see...blood...blood everywhere when people got hurt.

"What the hell is going on?" someone asked.

She couldn't see the man, but she thought she knew the voice. It was coming from a great distance, though.

"Need help," she said. Was that her? That hoarse croak? Her lips wouldn't work right. So stiff...but not cold...not anymore.

"God, you're wet and chilled through. I thought it was Jonathan. Ronda said he was unconscious."

She opened her eyes. Shane's face wavered into view, then disappeared. The world tipped. Hands touched her. She was lifted into strong arms.

"You're a block of ice," he said.

"Jonathan," she tried to explain. "River."

"Shane! Thank God! Jonathan needs help. Come here. Put her down and come here."

The sharp commands roused Tina again. She tried to straighten up, but she no longer felt her body at all. She realized she was free of it…free and floating. It was marvelous.…

"Be still," a masculine voice growled near her ear.

She felt movement, then heard the man and the angry woman talking, but their words kept fading out, even though she tried to pay attention. More voices joined them.

"Let's take their temperatures," someone suggested.

She felt herself lowered onto something soft. She whimpered and clung to the warm arms that held her.

"It's okay," the man soothed. "I'll be right here."

"Don't leave."

"I won't."

The darkness came over her completely.

Shane stood aside while the medic checked Tina over. The man had already seen to Jonathan, who was on his way to the hospital, his body in shock from the drop in temperature.

Shane unclenched his hands and took a calming breath. He had a lot of questions, but no one to answer them. He deduced that both Tina and Jonathan had somehow fallen in the river. Why and how remained to be determined.

Ronda had been hysterical and unable to explain why her son was outside at twilight, playing near the river. She'd said she thought he was resting. She'd been on the phone and hadn't heard him go out. Then "that woman" had shown up with him. Ronda had accused Tina of trying to drown her son.

Shane shook his head. If she'd been trying to drown him, she wouldn't have walked a half mile in the near-freezing wind to bring him home. He stared at her lips, which were blue like his nephew's. She, too, was in shock.

He'd stripped her wet clothes from her and had put her under the covers until the medics could look her over. She was a small woman, but perfectly formed. He grimaced ruefully. He'd often thought of having her in bed, but not like this.

"She'll be okay," the medic announced. "Her temperature hasn't dropped into the danger zone. She needs to be kept warm, though. We'd better take her to the hospital for observation."

"No." The dark fan of lashes on her pale cheeks lifted. She looked at the medic, then at Shane. "No hospital."

The appeal in her eyes was something he couldn't deny. He forced a smile to assure her he'd take care of her. "I'll keep an eye on her, if that's what she needs."

The medic shrugged. "Give her lots of hot drinks until her temperature is normal." He packed up his bag.

"Jonathan?" she whispered.

"He's going to be fine," the medic answered. "So are you. Better rest for a couple of days before you decide to take a dip in the river again, though," he advised half-facetiously.

She smiled.

Shane's heart contracted. "What happened? Do you remember?"

She frowned as she obviously tried to recall. "The bank gave way. Jonathan fell. So frightened. I thought he was going to die. So awful…when children die.…"

He took her hand. "Shh, it's okay. You saved him."

She glanced at him. "Did I? He stopped shivering. I thought—I thought…"

She closed her eyes and started to cry, silent sobs shaking her body as tears seeped into her hair at her temples. He stood there for ten seconds, then, when the medic moved aside, he sat on the bed and slipped his arms under her shoulders, holding her while she wept.

It gave him a strange feeling, to know she could cry.

Chapter Eight

Tina felt Shane's fingers smoothing away the tears from her temples. She stiffened as she realized what was happening. She was in the arms of her enemy, crying like one of those wimpy females she detested. Moreover, he hadn't said a word when his sister-in-law had accused Tina of trying to drown her son.

She pulled away, holding the sheet self-consciously over her breasts when she realized she was naked. She refused to think about how she'd gotten out of her clothing.

"I want to go home." She sounded pathetic rather than strong, as she'd intended. "Where are my clothes?"

Shane frowned, then nodded. "You're right. You can't stay here. I'll take you home."

She sniffed. He handed her a tissue. She wiped her eyes and blew her nose. "My clothes—"

"They're wet. I'll find you something." He left her.

In less than a minute, he was back. He held a thick, fleecy robe for her to put on.

The color was champagne pink. She shied away from using anything of Ronda's, but didn't have a choice. Stretching one arm out from under the covers, she touched the soft material.

Shane had no thought for her modesty. He slipped the robe over her arm, pulled it behind her, pushed her other arm into the sleeve and swept the sheet aside in one easy motion.

Paying no attention to her glare, he lifted her as if she were no bigger than his nephew, set her on her feet and fastened the buttons down the front. He dropped to one knee and tugged on her foot.

"Lift," he ordered.

He slipped fleece-lined moccasins on one foot, then the other. She hugged her arms across her chest and started shivering again. He frowned at her before sweeping her into his arms. Instinctively, she flung an arm around his neck.

He grabbed a blanket from the bed and tossed it over her before hurrying down the stairs. Outside, he put her in the patrol truck, jumped in and took off. He turned in at the blacktop drive to his house. There he killed the engine, leapt out and came around for her.

"W-wait," she said, confused. Her teeth were chattering again. "I want to go h-home."

He paid no attention to her protests, but carried her inside and upstairs to a suite of rooms facing the river. He efficiently pulled back the covers on the bed, took the blanket away from her, then, as if he had every right, started unfastening the robe.

"D-don't," she ordered. She couldn't seem to stop his hands. They were everywhere—on the buttons...at her

shoulders…down her arms as the robe slipped free…
lifting her to the bed…yanking the moccasins
off…pushing her under the sheet.

"Lie still," he said, forcefully holding the cover over
her. "You're going to stay here where I can watch you.
I'll be right back." He walked out.

She tried to sit upright, intending to grab the robe and
get out of there before her captor returned. Her head spun
dizzily, and she moaned as a wave of weakness ran
through her. She lay down again abruptly.

The shivering grew worse. She huddled under the sheet
and a thermal blanket and tried to will herself to stop
shaking. She couldn't.

When Shane returned, she closed her eyes and pretended she wasn't there.

"Here," he said.

He slipped the covers down and urged her to sit up.
Then he put a pajama top—his, she realized—on her. It
was incredibly warm. He put thick socks on her feet.

"I warmed them in the clothes dryer," he told her,
evidently proud of this idea. He covered her again and
added the blanket he'd wrapped around her earlier.
"You're still shivering."

"Reaction," she managed to say without stuttering.
She forced her eyes open.

Shane stood by the bed, watching her with a worried
frown between his eyes. "Was it like this when you were
covering a story for CNN?"

"Afterward. When I returned to Rome. It's just reaction—"

"It's more than that. Your body temperature was way
down. It still isn't up to normal. I have tea brewing." He
left the room once more.

She hugged the warm cotton of the pajama top to her.

It reached almost to her knees when she smoothed it into place. The shivers came in waves now, but she could at least control the chattering of her teeth.

When Shane returned, he carried a large thermal mug of the type made for commuters to use on their way to work. He sat on the side of the bed, his hip against the curve of her waist.

"Sit up," he coaxed. He stuffed two pillows behind her back so she could rest against them and brought the mug to her mouth.

She was forced to swallow. A drop ran down her chin, but he caught it on a finger and sucked it off.

"Too hot?" he asked.

"No." She removed one arm from the blankets and took the mug, determined not to let him see her totally helpless. She hated being vulnerable in front of anyone, but especially him.

He linked his hands together over one knee and leaned back to watch while she drank the sweet, hot tea. She felt the warmth flow all the way down her throat and into her stomach. As soon as she finished, he brought her another mug, just as hot, just as sweet. The cloying taste began to get to her, and she protested.

"You need it," he said, pushing the mug toward her mouth with one hand under the bottom of it.

Giving him an irritated glance, she drank the contents down, then set the mug on the table. She sank into the pillows with a sigh. The shivers had lessened to an occasional series of tremors.

"I'm all right now," she muttered sleepily. "You can leave. I don't need anybody."

Shane called the night dispatcher to check on things, then phoned the hospital. He talked to his brother, who had joined Ronda at the hospital from the Friday-night poker game at the feed store, which he, as sheriff, wasn't supposed to know about. He'd sent a deputy to the store for Ty after he'd gotten the hysterical call from Ronda and had called for an ambulance. Then he'd headed out himself.

It had been a shock to find Tina at his brother's house, wet clear through and semiconscious. He still hadn't found out how the accident had happened. Or why Ronda thought Tina would have a reason to drown her son.

His lips tightened. It was one thing for him to protect his family from a possible fortune hunter. It was another for Ronda to make wild accusations against her.

He returned to his room and sat by the sleeping woman in his bed. She had a surprising fierceness where children were concerned that reminded him of a lioness protecting her cubs.

Against his hip, he felt the shivers that still ran through her periodically. He realized he, too, was cold. His clothing was damp from where he'd carried her to the bed at Ty's house.

He went to a bureau and got out the bottoms of his pajamas and a long-sleeved sweatshirt. Glancing at his bed, he saw that Tina was resting still, her eyes closed. It stirred some emotion inside him to see her so pale. Even her lips—usually pink and plump as rosebuds—were colorless.

He changed clothes and put on a pair of sports socks to pad around in, then went down to heat some soup for supper. He'd fix some for her, too.

When he returned, he found her asleep, but restless. "Jonathan, don't!" she said. Her voice was hoarse. "Get back," she ordered. Her words became a mumble that he couldn't understand.

"Tina?" He called her name twice before she responded.

She opened her eyes and stared at him in fright. He knew the moment she recognized him and felt a flare of triumph. The fear left her, and she sighed in relief. Whatever else she might feel about him, she knew he wouldn't hurt her. She trusted him.

"Soup," he said. "Not as good as yours. It's out of a can."

"That's okay." She pushed upright and fixed the pillows.

He worried about her. She was definitely coming down with a cold or laryngitis. She must have been sick before she leapt into the river. He placed a tray across her knees.

With one hand, he pulled a chair close and sat down with his tray on his lap. "Can you tell me what happened tonight?"

"I walked along the river on my way home." She cleared her throat and gave a painful grimace. "Jonathan saw me and yelled hello. He was on the other side."

She paused, then continued the tale. Shane experienced a painful clenching inside as he envisioned the danger to both of them. The river was flowing at better than twenty knots with the recent rain and the spring snowmelt. A half mile farther, it dropped into a steep canyon, from which rescue would have been impossible. They could have died.

He tried to analyze the deep wrench that caused him, but couldn't sort it out. He had a sense of his life becoming more and more entangled with the woman who lay in his bed.

Maybe with her in his house—at his mercy, so to speak—he'd find out why she'd returned to the area.

He didn't really believe she'd heard of Ty's problems

and decided to try to win him again. After all, she was a celebrity. If she were after money, she'd surely met wealthier people abroad than any she'd find in Riverton. The pear orchards made money, but not enough to put the Macklins among the country's richest families.

He watched his mysterious guest while she ate the hot soup. He wondered if she'd heard Ronda's wild demand that he arrest her for attempted murder.

Sighing, he shook his head. Things were not becoming clearer where Tina was concerned. They were getting more and more muddled.

Passion was part of the problem, he thought. He couldn't see her without becoming restless with needs he'd ignored for a long time. It had been two years, almost three, since he'd been intimately involved with anyone.

When the woman had demanded a commitment, he'd been unable to make it. His past experiences had crept between them. Hell, he knew better than to trust women, and that was a fact.

Against his will, his gaze was drawn to the delicate-looking female wearing his pajama top and sitting in his bed. She'd risked her life for a boy she barely knew. She trembled in reaction to emotional trauma when others got hurt. That didn't jibe with his view of her as a female predator after the main chance.

He could no longer put her in the same category with his stepmother—an out-and-out fortune hunter. Tina didn't fit neatly into any niche that he could find. So where exactly did she fit?

At last he gave up trying to figure her out and watched while she delicately sipped a spoonful of soup. Her lips, which had always fascinated him, pursed in a way that made him think of other things besides food. His body stirred in lustful need.

It would be a joy to make love to her, he thought, and was amazed at the idea. He'd never connected sex and happiness before.

"Through?" he asked when she laid the spoon down.

She nodded and glanced around. "I, um, need—"

"In there." He pointed toward the bathroom. Gathering the dishes, he started to carry them down to the kitchen. He noticed she didn't leave the bed until he was out of the room.

He smiled, his mood becoming cynical as he headed down the stairs.

She needn't be modest with him. He knew exactly what she looked like with nothing on. He knew how her breasts came to a rounded point, pert as a puppy's nose; how they stood out against the slenderness of her rib cage. He knew how she responded to his touch, thrusting upward to meet his hand. He knew every nuance of love-making he wanted to experience...with her.

Only with her.

Damn.

Tina was woken by her own cry, lashing out in her nightmare against fears she couldn't control or explain. She sat up abruptly and stared around the strange bed-room.

The walls were painted a soft shade of creamy white. One wall was decorated with several landscape paint-ings. Baskets, a copper pot holding a fern, plus ceramic pots with exotic palms lined the floor beneath the pic-tures. A reading table with a forest green cloth and two padded chairs formed a grouping at one end of the room. Built-in shelves and drawers occupied the other end. In the center of the room the huge bed backed against a side wall.

Shane was asleep in one of the chairs, his neck crooked at an awkward angle that Tina knew would make it sore when he awoke.

She realized where she was: in Shane's house…in his bed…. She couldn't remember how she'd gotten there…with nothing on but his pajama top and a pair of socks.

Oh…the river. Yes. She remembered the fright. Shane's nephew. She'd had to save him.

Shane's eyes flicked open. He sat up, grimaced, then rubbed his neck. He gave a low groan.

"Why are you sleeping in a chair?" she asked.

"Damned if I know."

He rose, stretched, then rolled his head in a slow circle to work the kinks out. Covering a yawn, he came to the bed and sat beside her. He took her hand in his and studied it thoughtfully. "Bad dreams?" he asked.

She realized she was trembling. She nodded.

"What about?"

Pulling her hand from his, she combed her fingers through her hair, then clasped her hands together to control the tremors. "I don't know. It's all mixed up. I always think someone is dying and needs me, but I can't get to them…."

"You saved Jonathan."

She looked away from his probing gaze. "It was… I just happened to be there. If he hadn't been trying to attract my attention, he might not have fallen in."

Shane enfolded both her hands in his and chaffed them, restoring the warmth. "Or he might have, and no one would have seen him until it was too late."

Again Tina tried to pull her hands from his, but he

wouldn't let her go. She glanced up into his eyes, then down again. There were things in her she didn't want him to see. His touch was affecting her. It stirred feelings she didn't want to admit.

"Why did you do it? Why didn't you just scream for help?" His eyes, so darkly suspicious of her every motive, roamed over her face. "Did you think you could insinuate yourself into the Macklin family by acting the heroine?"

The haunting loneliness she'd experienced for the last eleven years came over her. She fought it, but like the trembling, she couldn't make it go away.

"Did it work?" she inquired with a mocking smile. The smile wouldn't stay on her mouth.

"Not with Ronda." His eyes crinkled pleasantly at the corners when he smiled, but the smile was without mirth. "Maybe it did with me...."

His hands moved up her arms, stroking slowly and gently. A violent shiver raced through her. He rubbed her shoulders, leaning forward until their faces were no more than a few inches apart.

She closed her eyes and tried the relaxing techniques taught to her by a doctor who'd treated patients with post-traumatic-stress syndrome. Nothing seemed to work.

The problem was, she wasn't sure if the shaking was caused by her dreams or by Shane's shattering presence.

"Feeling better?" he asked in a husky tone.

Slowly she opened her eyes, knowing she shouldn't, knowing she'd be lost to all reason if she gave in to desire.

"I should go," she said, her voice a thread of sound in the quiet room. She wanted to stay.

"You need someone to watch you."

She pulled her resolve together. "I can watch after myself."

He frowned slightly, studying her with a puzzled light in his eyes. "So stubbornly independent," he murmured. "Not a normal trait for a gold digger."

"Right. It's a ploy to confuse you." Her mocking laugh came out as a croak. Her throat ached.

His smile, genuine this time, was accompanied by a sigh of resignation. "You do that just by being here, just by *being*." He smoothed her hair back from her temple.

She felt his breath blow lightly across her ear while he continued to lean over her. Gradually, in spite of his distrust, his presence became comforting to her, then arousing.

Her heart speeded up. She glanced at his lips, a hand span from hers, then away. She swallowed, fighting the desire to throw her arms around his neck and cling to his powerful frame.

He seemed so big, so strong, able to crush her with his hands, yet he stroked her temple as gently as a father would his child. It was unnerving.

She trembled again.

"Are you cold?" he questioned. Without waiting for an answer, he slipped down on the bed, the covers between them, and partially covered her with his body.

Heat rushed from him to her, warming all the cold, secret places of her heart, places she'd never known existed until now. Her bodily rhythms were troubled by his closeness.

First she breathed too fast, taking in great gulps of air that made her dizzy. When she tried to breathe slowly and evenly, she felt light-headed, as if she weren't getting enough oxygen.

She realized his lips were no longer a hand's width

from her lips, but had somehow moved closer while she was trying to breathe. She lay very still, but she was aware...oh, yes, she was aware of him in every cell.

His fingers tunneled into her hair. Very slowly, he turned her to face him. Holding her head like a chalice, he moved ever so slightly closer, then sipped from her lips as if tasting a rare wine.

He drew back and paused. She tried to speak, but her throat would emit no sound beyond a raspy breath. He kissed her again, the merest touch of his lips.

"Kiss me back," he ordered in a low rumble, the need evident in the thickening of his voice.

"I...we shouldn't..."

Stay alert, she ordered, but a rosy haze seemed to shroud her thoughts. A loud hum invaded in her ears, but she couldn't tell if it was from within or without.

"I've wanted you here, like this, for years." He pressed his face against her neck and delicately stroked the flesh there with his tongue, leaving a moist, burning trail. "I wondered, after you left, what would have happened if you'd stayed...if you hadn't run from me...."

"I didn't run." She couldn't let him think he'd scared her away—even though he had. Years ago, she'd learned it was better to face your enemies than to run, to smile rather than to fight. It drove them crazy. "I'm not afraid of anyone."

She smiled at him with an effort, to confuse him further. He chuckled, the sound a caress against her breasts as his chest moved. How had she become locked in his arms?

He laid two fingers on a pulse point in her neck. "Why is your heart beating so hard?"

"Why is yours?" she challenged.

"Because I want you like hell...and you're in my

bed…and I can't think of one good reason to stop.'' He dipped his head and kissed along her collarbone, the heat of his mouth penetrating the cotton of the pajama top.

She caught her breath. Her heart felt jumpy, like a newly broken filly on her first ride outside the paddock.

''It might be a trap,'' she warned hoarsely.

That brought his head up. His eyes went as hard as Oregon granite. ''Not for me,'' he informed her. ''I don't play those games. Any woman who gets mixed up with me knows the rules.''

''Do you make her sign a contract?'' She turned her head and sneezed twice before she could stop. ''Oh,'' she groaned, the spasm causing her throat to hurt unbearably.

Shane sat up and handed her a tissue from the night table by the bed. She used it and looked around helplessly. He tossed it into a nearby wastebasket, which he moved within reach.

To her surprise, he laid a hand on her forehead. ''No fever that I can detect. But you'd better get some rest.''

She was wary of this considerate Shane. It would be so easy to think he cared.…

He pulled the comfortable chair to the bed and sank into it. He propped one foot on the quilt and crossed the other over it at the ankle. ''Go to sleep,'' he advised with a sardonic twinkle in his eyes. ''If you dare.…''

There was some message in that statement, but she couldn't figure out what it was. Just before she drifted back to sleep, she remembered something she'd read once.

Be careful when a rogue is being charming. That's when he's the most dangerous.

She opened her eyes a crack. Shane had his eyes

closed. She let her lashes drift down again. If she stayed in Riverton, they would make love. It was as inevitable as the sunrise.

Tina couldn't remember feeling worse. Her head ached. Her lungs burned. Her throat felt like raw meat. She had a cold.

It was Saturday morning. She'd awakened at six, when Shane had unfolded his long, powerful body from the chair and gone into the bathroom. Then she'd heard the shower come on.

He'd come out wearing a towel around his waist, and she'd quickly closed her eyes and pretended to be asleep when he'd glanced her way. She'd heard him moving around as he dressed.

Once, she'd opened her eyes and gotten a glimpse of him as he pulled on white cotton briefs. She'd clamped her eyelids shut tightly, but she knew she would forever remember the purity of his masculine form in the early morning light…the long, lean lines of his hips and thighs, the strong curve of his back as he'd bent down, the flex of muscles like smooth steel cables under his skin.

As soon as he'd left the room, she'd gone to the bathroom. It had been shockingly erotic to step into the shower, which was still damp and steamy from his use, and know he'd been there only minutes before. She'd never taken a shower with a man.

She'd washed quickly. The steam had helped open her sinuses. After drying, she'd put the blue-striped pajama top back on and the sports socks that came to her knees. She'd dried her hair, using his brush to turn the ends under, and brushed her teeth with toothpaste on a washcloth. Then she'd hurried back to bed, her heart pounding when she'd heard whistling from below.

She fluffed up the two fat pillows behind her and stared

out the window as the sun peeked over the hill, changing the world from shades of gray to shades of gold. The earth reborn, she thought.

The clank of crockery drew her eyes to the door. Shane entered the bedroom. "Breakfast," he announced.

He was incredibly handsome in gray cords with a white T-shirt tucked into them. Over the T-shirt he wore a deep blue corduroy shirt, open down the front, the sleeves rolled back on his forearms. The color matched the blue of his eyes.

"Keep looking at me that way and I'll think you'd rather have me than breakfast," he murmured, giving her a deliciously wicked sideways glance as he bent over the bed.

"You'd be too tough," she said in a hoarse whisper. "I'd probably ruin my teeth trying to get through your hide."

Laughing, he released one tray—she saw he had two—on the bed, placed the other over her knees, removed his own plate and cup to the spare tray and took a seat in the chair.

"You could soften me up with a few nibbles," he suggested. He picked up his fork and began eating his over-easy eggs and sausage. He'd made himself four slices of toast to her two.

She noted he'd prepared her a poached egg, toast, oatmeal and juice. For some strange reason, his thoughtfulness touched her. Her eyes smarted, and she had to blink several times until she was in control once more.

It wouldn't do to let his care get to her, she reminded herself sternly. The situation between them was precarious at best. He made no secret of his hunger for her. And he knew she wanted him, too.

Could she risk her heart in an affair?

After it was over, then what? Like her mother, would she feel compelled to leave town in disgrace, knowing that everyone would be aware he'd tossed her aside when the newness wore off?

"Eat," he said, his tone lower and huskier than before.

She met his gaze. There was blatant desire in the fathomless blue depths. His eyes invited her to share it with him.

A storm of need broke over her. She quickly picked up her spoon and began on the oatmeal. Its heat soothed her throat and helped belay the nervous excitement that coursed through her.

When she finished eating, he took the dishes downstairs and returned with an insulated container of coffee. They drank in companionable silence. "It looks warm out today," she ventured.

He flicked a glance out the window, then returned to a steady contemplation of her. Strange little thrills ran along her skin.

"It's supposed to get up into the high fifties. But there might be a freeze later in the week."

"Would that hurt the fruit trees?"

"Yes." He seemed surprised at her question. "They're budding out now. A freeze could kill this year's crop."

"What do you do to prevent it?"

"We have heaters that we put around the perimeter of the orchards, plus wind jets to keep the air moving. Cold air settles into the low places."

"The whole valley is a low place," she murmured, watching the fruit trees sway in the morning breeze. She could feel the fitful longing deep inside her, growing and swelling like a bud on a tree. She knew the danger in that.

Holding her cup close to her mouth, she inhaled the

rich aroma of the coffee and felt the steam soothe her throat as she tried to think of what she should do.

Go home.

She ignored the advice. She wanted to stay....

When Shane stood and prowled the room, she recognized the restlessness in him as well. He drank deeply from his cup and set it on the table.

"Either your coffee is better than the last time, or my tastebuds are completely useless," she said, forcing a light note.

"I followed your instructions," he told her. He stopped by the bed. After watching her for a minute, he sat on the side, his hip against hers before she scooted over.

"Then it's the coffee," she croaked, trying not to notice the way his gaze—dark and moody, almost resentful—ran over her.

"Why?" he asked in a low growl. "Why do I look at you and think of a thousand delights?"

"I—I don't know," she answered helplessly.

"You look so soft and innocent, and I want you so much, more than I've ever wanted anything...*anything.*" He repeated the word with a perplexed frown.

His breath became deeper, ragged with need he didn't bother to hide. He lowered his lips to hers. She turned her head at the last minute.

"I have a cold," she reminded him. "You'll catch it."

"I already have a fever," he murmured, his breath warm, coffee-scented, fanning over her temple and stirring the tendrils there.

His finger under her chin turned her face to his. All her muscles clenched in tormented longing and anticipation as his mouth hovered above hers. She licked her lips.

''The hunger grows.'' His breath touched her mouth. ''I wonder if a kiss will be enough to satisfy it.''

He paused and looked at her, waiting for her response....

Chapter Nine

Tina trembled when he moved his hand. His fingers brushed the tips of her breasts, which became taut and heavy at the same time. He watched her, his eyes delving into hers as if trying to probe into her soul. She stayed very still.

"I want to arouse you," he said, his eyes going dark with hunger. "I want to see you helpless in my arms, your body flushed with the passion I know I've kindled in you. I want your eyes—such stormy eyes, capable of hiding every thought—to gleam with desire...for me... only for me."

"Shane..." She couldn't say more. Currents like stray bolts of lightning ran randomly through her. She pressed her hands against the white T-shirt, intending to push him away. She *had* to push him away or else...

She didn't.

Of their own volition, her hands spread over his broad

chest. She stared at their pale flesh color splayed against the white cotton. She pressed and felt the muscles contract, then relax under her palms.

"Yes, touch me like that," he encouraged. He lifted his hands to the headboard and leaned toward her.

Was that a plea in his voice? She looked at him. His eyes were closed, as if he were enraptured with her caress. The need was stark on his face. It enthralled her— captured her as nothing else would have—to have him need her.

She stroked him for a minute, then that wasn't enough. She wanted the feel of his flesh. Tugging at the material, she freed his T-shirt from his cords and ran her hands up under it.

He gave a throaty groan that echoed through her, stirring the hunger she tried to suppress. She knew she should stop before this madness carried them both too far....

Slowly, his eyes opened. He gazed deeply into hers. The moment became an eternity.

He lowered his head, his mouth opening as he touched her lips. He caressed her with his tongue, sipping and licking as if he couldn't get enough of her taste, going so slowly and carefully she never thought of holding back after that moment.

He touched her breasts again, the backs of his fingers brushing back and forth across the sensitive tips, first one, then the other until all her being seemed concentrated there.

She caught his hands and pressed them to her.

Shane felt her nipples beaded hard and tight against his palms and felt he was coming apart at the seams. She was so responsive, so *hot* when he got past that cool facade she showed the world. He shifted, raising his head to look at her.

Her eyes opened, and his breath stuck in his throat. They were gray and shining…molten silver…helpless and shocked and filled with desire so strong it drove him wild.

"It's all right," he assured her.

He didn't want to hurt her, only to love her until they both melted in the cataclysmic explosion their lovemaking would produce. He didn't even know how he knew that was the way it would be for them, he just did.

With strong, massaging motions, he caressed her breasts. She closed her eyes and arched upward to meet him. Her arms came around his neck, pulling him closer.

"Want you," she whispered. "So long…so terribly."

"Yes. A lifetime. I've waited for you. Anne said you would come back. I've waited.…"

He heard the words, but they made no sense. The blood roared through his body, drowning out all thoughts that weren't of this moment, part of this magic.

Standing, ignoring her throaty cry of disappointment, he flung the covers aside. With hands that shook, he threw off his shirt and drew the T-shirt over his head. He kicked off the loafers. His hands went to his belt. He paused and observed her, waiting for her refusal.

None came.

Relief washed over him when she smiled at him. Her gaze was restless. Her eyes seemed dark now, the charcoal gray of storm clouds when the storm grew dangerous. The air crackled between them as he shucked his clothing.

When she moved over, he lay down beside her. Her hands caressed his chest, his sides, his hips, running over his flesh as if she couldn't get enough of him.

Dipping his head, he took her breast in his mouth. She writhed against him. He laid a hand at her waist and slipped one leg over her. She opened her own legs, letting him slide between the silky softness of her thighs.

At last, he thought hazily. *At last.*

It was the truth, he realized. He'd waited a lifetime for her to touch him like this. It was worth the wait.

Tina couldn't stop the whimpering sounds of need that escaped from her as Shane ran his hand over her stomach and caressed the thatch of curls at the apex of her legs. The pajama top had somehow climbed to her waist.

"If I touched you, you'd fly apart right in my hands," he whispered hotly. "So would I...if you touched me."

She heard the need and marveled that this man...this strong, confident man...needed *her.* "Shall I?" she asked. She let her fingers glide over his hips, hesitated, then reached between their tense bodies. She touched the masculine staff and found it warm and smooth, hard but not threatening.

He groaned and kissed her deeply, moving his lips restlessly over hers, his tongue thrusting in passionate play until hers answered the demand.

Against her hand, his body throbbed in wild passion that thrilled her beyond words. Slowly, he moved against her in the rhythm of life. He touched her intimately, causing every muscle in her body to tighten in shock and pleasure.

The kiss intensified as their hands brought primitive delight to their senses. He shuddered against her as she gained courage and explored his body more thoroughly. He gasped at one point and caught her hand in his.

"Enough," he whispered, trailing wet kisses along her cheek and temple. He drew both her hands above her head and held them there while he ravaged her breasts with his mouth.

"Shane, I—I..."

Shane raised his head and studied her face, giving them time to come down a bit. He was too close to the edge.

She opened her eyes, and he felt as if he were being drawn into those stormy depths. He realized dimly that he didn't care if he were. It was almost shocking...to want to be that deep in someone else....

He raised himself on an elbow and quickly opened the drawer of the bedside table. He didn't trust himself beyond this point. When he touched her again, he would go for the finish with her, both of them together, riding a wave of pure pleasure.

"One second," he murmured, his voice almost as hoarse as hers. He held out the packet. "Do you want to do the honors?"

Without hesitation, Tina took it from him. She realized he assumed she was much more experienced than she actually was. She removed the condom and spread it over him. When she proved a bit awkward, he helped her complete the job.

He kissed her again, long, drugging kisses, while his hands brought her back to the peak. Then he moved over her.

Slowly and carefully, he merged his body with hers. Sensation spiraled inside her. She moved, spreading her legs wider, taking him deeply into her, loving the feel of their joining.

Whatever else was wrong between them, this was right. She knew it instinctively, the way a salmon knows its river and the way to the spawning grounds. She knew...and it was right.

She moved slightly and the joining was complete, their

bodies so tightly, so warmly nestled into each other that there was no empty space remaining to be filled. Happiness washed over her.

"Shane," she breathed. "Shane."

"Shh," he whispered in a deep, almost reverent tone. "I know. I know."

Looking into his eyes, she knew he, too, felt the magic. She moved her hips against him, wanting more.

"Easy," he cautioned. A smile flickered over his lips. "I want this to last."

It pleased her to know she affected him as strongly as he did her. When he began to move, the world condensed until there was just the two of them. When he slipped his hand between them to caress her intimately, it became even smaller, contracting to that point where they merged into one.

Stars seemed to spin out of control behind her tightly closed eyes. She gasped and cried out his name...again... and again.

"Yes, darling," she heard him say. "Yes. Yes. Yes."

The roaring filled her ears. She lifted toward him, needing him in ways she couldn't begin to comprehend, and he was there for her...holding her...giving her his hands, his mouth, his body, so that she was sated.

She clung to him, feeling his deep thrusts gradually slow as the powerful climax played itself out. When he was still, they lay entwined, their hearts and lungs working in unison as their senses expanded past each other to the bed, the room, the silent house that seemed to sigh in happiness at their union.

Shane lay without thinking for long, long moments, adrift in a sensual fog so thick nothing could penetrate it, except the woman nestled so snugly beneath his body. He held his weight on his arms, careful of her slenderness—this small woman whose passion had matched his own.

Caution returned slowly. He didn't welcome it.

He lifted himself from her, a new awareness washing over him. He'd wanted to see her locked in the passion he'd induced, but he'd been too caught up in it himself to observe her reactions. It was the first time he'd ever been totally lost in lovemaking.

He moved to lie beside her, his energy spent, his body slick with perspiration from their searing contact. So was hers.

Running a hand over her torso, he felt her shiver. Rising to an elbow, he gazed down at her, worried now that the burning hunger was assuaged...for the moment. He knew, as surely as the sun rose in the east each morning, that he'd want her again and again.

At some time during those tumultuous moments, he'd unfastened the pajama top. It opened to each side of her, damp and wrinkled from their lovemaking. Her breath rasped through her throat.

Guilt hit him. She was ill. He'd taken advantage.... No, she'd wanted him as much as he'd wanted her.

The strangest feeling swept over him, something like the way he felt about his nephew at times: tender, protective, loving.

He frowned grimly. He wouldn't be caught in that trap. His feelings were natural—and mutual, he realized, looking into her eyes—and were the result of that incredible climax. Who wouldn't feel tender toward a partner who shattered the world and rebuilt it with magic? It had been the same for both of them.

Pride infused him, along with a sense of triumph, as if he'd just climbed a previously unconquered mountain. Energy flowed through his muscles, and he felt reborn.

There was danger in that kind of thinking, he reminded himself ruthlessly. Sex had been known to make men do foolish things.

He ignored the warning that rang through him. Sliding from the bed, he headed for the bathroom, then turned back.

Tina saw the doubts flicker in his eyes before he smiled at her. "Do you want to join me in a quick shower? Or maybe it will be a slow one," he added with a wicked grin.

She hesitated, wanting to go with him, but not sure.

"I promise not to splash too much."

She wasn't very experienced at love play. When she'd first lived in Europe, she'd been desperately lonely and had gotten involved in a brief affair that had proven very unsatisfactory. She'd found intimacy rather embarrassing.

Strong arms slipped under her. She was lifted from the bed and carried to the bathroom. There he set her on her feet, turned on the water and adjusted its temperature. Then he turned back to her. She shivered when he removed her top and the socks.

Helping her into the shower, he washed her quickly and gently, but without a word. He seemed introspective now. She wondered what he was thinking.

He probably was worried that she was going to try to trap him into marriage in spite of his warnings. The days were long past when women expected gallantry from men, she wanted to tell him.

When he finished with her, he washed himself while she leaned against the shower wall and inhaled the steam. It opened her nose and soothed her throat, so she felt much better when he turned off the water and wrapped a towel around each of them.

He dried her hair and brushed it into shining smoothness before taking care of himself. His consideration made her want to weep. "There," he said when they were both dry.

He let her use his deodorant and powder. He gave her a new toothbrush, and they brushed their teeth side by side at the twin sinks. This felt more intimate than making love...like they were an old married couple, used to sharing.

He pulled on black sweats, the top printed with a mountain lion, its golden eyes staring out at the viewer in lordly disdain. "I should have gone to your house and gotten a gown for you," he said. "I have your key—"

"My purse!" It was the first time she'd thought of it.

"I had a deputy pick it up from the riverbank. Also your coat and shoes."

He studied her as if looking for clues to her motive for rescuing his nephew. His distrust surfacing again, she realized. Her spirits dropped several notches. "Thank you."

He shrugged her gratitude aside. "He took your coat to the cleaners. I washed your wet things. They're in the dryer." A smile flitted over his face. "They're probably done by now."

"Probably," she murmured in the same wry tone he'd used. She wasn't going to let a little thing like the most incredible experience of her life daunt her. She could be as cool as he was. "I'd like to get dressed. I need to go home. I have work to do."

"No," he said, his tone becoming low and fierce.

She was taken aback. "Really, I—"

"Stay here, at least for the weekend," he requested. "I'd feel better if I could keep an eye on you...to see that your cold doesn't take a turn for the worse."

"I see," she said slowly. If she stayed, she knew what

would happen. Meeting his intent gaze, she realized she didn't want to give up the magic, not just yet. Neither did he.

In the bedroom, he opened a drawer and pulled out a blue T-shirt whose message had long faded. He gave it to her to put on. Going to the bed, he yanked off the sheets.

Turning her back to him, she let the towel drop and slipped into the T-shirt. It came to her knees. Then she watched Shane—the Mighty Macklin!—change the bed and put on fresh sheets as efficiently as a housemaid.

"If you ever need another job, I can recommend you for nursing care," she commented, trying for a light touch. She wasn't sure of the protocol between lovers.

"Thanks, I'll remember that." He smoothed the blanket, then flapped a sheet over it and tucked it in. He put another blanket at the foot of the bed. Not the one from Ronda's home, she was glad to see. The robe and moccasins had disappeared, too.

"Okay," he said, straightening and looking at her.

She hesitated. Either she insisted on going home or she stayed and... It was too late. They were already involved.

She went to the bed. He held the covers while she climbed in. She leaned against the thick pillows he'd fashioned for a backrest.

"There doesn't have to be sex," he said quietly, acknowledging her qualms about them. "I brought you here to rest, not to force you into a situation you'd rather not be in."

"You didn't force me," she admitted.

He observed her for a long minute. "Maybe not, but you're ill. You've had a fright, and you've been in thermal shock, not to mention the emotional one. You were vulnerable.''

She thought this over. ''I think you were, too.''

Surprise flickered through his eyes. ''I've wanted you for years,'' he admitted. ''I realized it the moment I saw you again.''

She nodded, understanding how he felt. It had been the same with her, no matter how much she'd tried to deny it. ''Perhaps that's why I returned,'' she murmured, half to herself. ''Because of that old, unfinished passion.'' She looked up at him, troubled. ''Are we done with it now?''

''God, I wish I knew.'' He ran a hand through his tawny hair, mussing up the smooth effect he'd achieved by brushing. He looked as worried about them and their affair as she felt.

A noise below interrupted the moment of revelation. ''Shane?'' Ty called out. They heard his footsteps on the stairs.

''Damn,'' Shane muttered, whirling about.

It was too late. Ty stopped at the bedroom door. Tina saw his gaze take in her position in the bed, Shane standing a couple of feet away, then, finally, the wrinkled sheets on the floor.

Fury swept into his face. ''You bastard,'' he said, crossing the room in three strides. He swung a fist at his brother's face.

Shane ducked, sidestepped the punch and grabbed Ty's wrist, twisting his arm behind him. ''Cool down,'' he ordered.

Ty struggled, almost managing to slip from Shane's hold. Tina watched them in despair. She'd become another complication in their dealings with each other.

''Please,'' she said, her throat aching as she tried to raise her voice above the curses both brothers were muttering as they became locked in combat. "Oh, please! Don't!"

Shane managed to get a choke hold on Ty. "Stop it," he snarled. "You're scaring her."

Ty stopped in midcurse. Both men looked at her. Shane dropped his hold and went over to her.

"See what you've done?" he said to his brother. "You've made her cry." He pulled a tissue from the box and wiped the tears from her eyes.

"What *I've* done?" Ty scoffed. "What about you?"

"We'll talk about it downstairs." Shane shot him a warning glance that said nothing was to be discussed in her presence.

"You mustn't fight," she told them. She couldn't speak louder than a whisper after that hoarse cry.

"You're sick," Ty declared, with a strident glance at his brother. He stepped in front of Shane and sat on the side of the bed, taking her hand as he did. "Are you all right?" he asked.

She nodded, unable to speak for a moment. She squeezed his hand to show her gratitude, then tugged her hand away and pulled the sheet up to her neck, suddenly too tired to cope with the two quarrelsome men.

"If you want to go home, I'll take you," Ty promised, his jaw taking on a stubborn tilt.

Silence descended on the room. She glanced up at Shane. He watched her without a word, his face like a carved statue. She looked at Ty. He was angry and concerned. She thought she saw pity in his eyes.

She looked out the window. The sun was well above the horizon. Nine o'clock. It seemed an eternity since sunrise. "I'll stay," she said in a croaky whisper.

When she glanced at Shane, she felt seared by the flames that danced in his eyes for a second; then he spoke coolly to his brother. "If you can tear yourself away, we'll talk downstairs. Tina needs to rest." He calmly gathered the sheets and towels.

Ty's mouth tightened. He turned to her.

"Please, go on. I'm fine. Truly."

"All right, but if you ever need me…" He cast a hard glance at his brother. "I'll never be able to repay you for saving my son. He's the one thing that makes life worth living nowadays," he told her in a low, tortured voice.

Her heart went out to him. "He's a fine boy, brave and…" To her consternation, her eyes filled with tears again. She was turning into a drippy faucet.

"Call me," Ty said. "Anytime you need me, just call."

"I will." She dabbed at her eyes with the sheet.

Shane snorted from the door, where he waited for the scene to be over. Ty got up and walked out of the bedroom, while Shane lingered for another moment. He looked at her without smiling, his gaze filled with thoughts she couldn't read, but so penetrating she felt he was trying to see into her soul. Then he followed Ty down the steps.

She relaxed against the pillows, her heart sounding loud in her ears. She wasn't sure of anything anymore. All her logical reasons for returning to Oregon seemed a lie, yet she couldn't have returned just for…for *this*.

Gazing around the bedroom, she fought an inner panic. She wouldn't be anyone's kept woman. Not that she was, she assured herself. She had her own home and money enough to live on for a few years. She was still her own person. But she had a sense of her life becoming hopelessly entangled with the Macklin family.

"What are you going to do about her?"

Shane studied his brother, refraining from telling him

it was none of his business. Ty obviously didn't see it that way. He had developed a protective-big-brother attitude toward Tina.

"We'll have to work it out," he said. "We haven't talked—"

"I noticed." Ty cast an enraged glance at the washer, where the used sheets and towels swished around in soapy water.

Shane removed Tina's clothes from the dryer and neatly folded them. Her underwear was pale green, the color of sea foam. It was sheer and dainty, reminding him of the delicate curves of her body. In spite of her fragile stature, she'd held her own with him, answering hunger with hunger, matching need with need.

A sensual pang bit into him. It had been the experience of a lifetime...hot and wild and incredibly arousing, as wonderful as he'd somehow known it would be. Nothing and no one could make him give her up. Except the lady herself.

It would kill him if she said no....

"If you're trying to run her off like you did before, I don't think it will work this time," Ty informed him.

"How did you—" Shane stopped, but it was too late.

"How did I know? Emma Tall lives right across the river from us and next to the Snyder place. When Anne said Tina had left, I had a talk with Miss Em. I figured if anyone knew anything, she would. And she did, Big Brother. Did it make you feel like a hero to scare a young girl into running away by nearly raping her?"

"It didn't go that far," Shane muttered. He touched the tiny scars on his lower lip.

"I know how you got those." Ty grinned suddenly. "I think you've met your match this time, Brother. I can't tell you how much that pleases me. You'd better watch it, or you'll be housebroken in no time.''

With a harsh laugh, he walked out, leaving Shane standing in the kitchen.

Shane looked at the female clothing in his hands and uttered a curse on brothers, small towns and gossiping neighbors, including the geezers at the barber shop. They were going to make his life hell when word got out, as it invariably would, about the sheriff and the town's resident celebrity.

''Just one more shot.'' Clint Adams moved to another angle, bent one knee and snapped the photo.

Tina blinked as the flashbulb went off. Clint had taken several pictures of her on the sofa in the living room of the Macklin home. She had insisted on getting up and dressing when the media deluge began. One television crew had already been there.

''So when nobody was home at Shane's house, you walked on up the road to Ty's place, carrying Jonathan, right?'' Dolly asked.

The newspaperwoman sat opposite Tina, her leg propped on a footstool while she went over her notes for the second time. She and her husband had decided to publish a Sunday edition. They didn't want the local paper to be scooped by the ''big city'' papers in Medford and Ashland.

''Yes, that's right,'' Tina answered in a barely audible voice.

''Then…how did you get back here?'' Dolly wanted to know.

''When she insisted she was fine and refused to go to the hospital, I brought her here to keep an eye on her,'' Shane answered tersely.

Dolly beamed with delight. "What a wonderful story—Sheriff Plays Nursemaid to Local Heroine!"

Shane grimaced good-naturedly. "You have the story. Tina needs to rest now."

Dolly put her notes away while her husband packed up their gear. "Maybe you'll be well enough to do A Day in the Life of the Sheriff for next week. That would be the perfect follow-up to this story." She smiled happily at the idea.

"Well, maybe," Tina temporized.

Shane escorted them outside and helped Dolly into the car. They'd barely gotten out of the drive when the news crew of another TV station pulled in and spilled out of a van.

Tina heard Shane refuse admittance to the brash young reporter who was trying to push his way into the house. "How would you like to be arrested for breaking and entering," he asked in a dangerous tone.

"Who are you?" the reporter demanded.

"I'm the sheriff, and this is my house," Shane explained, his tone that of a grizzly about to attack.

Tina sighed wearily and went to the door. "It's okay," she murmured. "I'll talk to them."

Shane stepped aside and let the reporter and cameraman into the house. He made sure she was comfortable on the sofa, a cup of hot lemon tea by her side, before the interview began.

"How did you happen to see the boy fall in?" the reporter asked, while the cameraman beamed a spotlight at her.

But her voice had gone. Nothing came out but a wheeze of sound. Shane answered most of the questions for her, since he'd heard the story three times that morning.

When the reporter wanted her to return to the river and point out the spot where she'd first noticed Jonathan, Shane put his foot down. In less than twenty minutes, the crew had its interview and were out of the house.

Tina closed her eyes and leaned her head back on the sofa. She ached all over. She heard the door close firmly and the lock snick into place. Then Shane returned.

Opening her eyes, she gazed into his. He bent and scooped her into his arms. "Insolent pup," he growled. "Next thing, he'd be wanting a reenactment of the whole damned scene."

She looped her arms around his neck and laid her head on his shoulder. Against her breasts, she could feel the steady pounding of his heart. Her weariness seemed to decrease as her own heart picked up its tempo.

In the bedroom, he set her on her feet. His hands went to the buttons of her blouse. Before she thought, her hands covered his, stopping him.

They looked at each other for a long minute.

She dropped her hands, allowing him to continue. She didn't know why she'd had a sudden attack of modesty. He'd done much more than undress her in the past twelve hours.

Heat ran along her skin as she recalled his hands on her, rough with passion but gentle...so gentle.

"I feel the same," he said.

"How do you know..." The words trailed away when she met his eyes. She thought perhaps he did know how she felt.

He deftly removed her clothing. "T-shirt or pajama top?" he asked. Both were clean and neatly folded on one of the chairs.

"The T-shirt, please." She held her arms up while he slipped it over her head. "Thank you."

When she was in bed, he sat beside her and held her hand. A frisson slithered down her back. She wondered if he would lie down with her. When he looked at her…

"Rest now," he advised, smoothing her hair back from her face. "I need to answer some messages from the dispatcher, then maybe I'll join you for a nap. Okay?"

His concern made her feel fragile inside, as if she might break at a sharp word or look. She nodded, then let him pull the covers up to her chin. She closed her eyes, infinitely weary, and felt him move away. When he left the room, she dropped the facade of calm that had carried her through the morning.

The future loomed dark and uncertain before her. In giving in to the passion, she seemed to have lost her way in life. She was no longer sure what she should do.

Leave? That was a possibility.

An ache vibrated through her chest. She didn't want to leave yet. There was still so much to discover between her and Shane.

Although she tried to suppress them, little bubbles of hope kept surfacing within her. She swallowed, causing her throat to hurt. But it was nothing compared to the pain in her heart as she admitted the whole truth—she was totally, hopelessly in love with Shane Macklin.

Chapter Ten

Tina woke to the sound of Shane's voice. He was on the telephone, a frown on his face. When he hung up, he glanced at her and saw she was awake. He turned the lamp on. "I have to go out," he said. "Do you need anything before I go?"

"No, I'm fine. Is it an emergency?" Her voice was audible, but she still sounded like a foghorn.

He nodded. "A robbery at a gas station over by the highway."

"Was anyone hurt?"

"No, just scared." He pulled on a pair of boots, then fastened the black belt with the lethal-looking weapon stuck in the holster. He checked his gun with quick, efficient movements and was ready to leave in a matter of minutes. "You look rested."

"I feel much better." She smiled to show him.

He came over to the bed. "We haven't talked."

"A-about what?" She hated the telltale break in her voice.

"Us. About what happened…and where we go from here," he said bluntly. "I haven't the time now, but later, when I get back, we'll figure it out." He sat beside her, his gaze questioning.

She saw the doubts in his eyes and felt her own wariness return. Recalling his warning, she managed a sardonic smile. "That's all right. I remember the rules."

He frowned. "What rules?"

"Yours. One, you don't play games," she recounted. "And two, don't expect anything permanent in an involvement with you, or something like that. I agree completely."

"Do you?" he inquired, giving her a narrow-eyed scrutiny that made him look dangerous.

"Of course. Actually, neither of us has time for a serious relationship. You have important duties, and I have a book to finish. I think I might travel after that."

Shane frowned. He didn't like having his words tossed back in his face, especially by her. "What about your job at the newspaper?"

"That's temporary. I'm helping out until Dolly is well."

He watched her for a minute. She wore that defiant little smile that hid her emotions so well, and he had no time to delve beneath the surface. He had work to do and a responsibility to the citizens of the county to restore law and order. Personal problems would have to wait their turn.

"You'd better go," she reminded him.

She looked so calm and cool there in his bed wearing his T-shirt, yet he'd seen her tremble with aftershock, he'd seen her weep, he'd held her while passion burned them both to a cinder. Someday he'd discover what thoughts and emotions roiled under that unruffled manner. But not today.

"Do I get a goodbye kiss before I venture into the cold, cruel world?" he asked.

He didn't wait for an answer, but bent to her and took the kiss before she could refuse. He felt her hesitate, then her mouth opened beneath his. His body surged with need as she responded. He ran his hands over her in a hungry caress.

"I'll be home as soon as I can," he murmured when he could take no more of the kiss without taking everything.

"Be careful," she said, releasing him.

He nodded, grabbed his hat and coat and headed outside. It gave him an odd sensation inside his chest to know she was worried about him. He started the truck and drove down the driveway. Glancing up at the lighted window in his bedroom before he turned onto the road, he felt a flood of warmth hit him.

She'd be there when he returned, he realized, waiting for him. That was something to look forward to. He'd lived alone so long he'd forgotten what it felt like to have someone waiting, just for him, at the end of the day. They'd talk and sort things out then.

Tina snuggled in the warm bed, Shane's pillow hugged against her so she could inhale his scent with each breath. She watched the sky darken into twilight. She'd slept most of the afternoon. Now she was restless, wanting him to return.

Heat radiated from deep inside her. With a start, she realized she was happy. If she hadn't been so miserable from the cold, she'd have jumped up and danced around the room like one of those whirling dervishes she'd read of but never seen.

She tossed the covers aside and sat up against the pillows. She didn't want to talk. She wanted him to make love to her again.

She sighed deeply. There was more than physical attraction between them. She was certain of it. No one could make love as they had and not be affected by the depths of it. She wanted to see where that shattering intimacy would take them....

Downstairs, a door slammed. Tina glanced at the clock, her heart beating wildly. He'd been gone only an hour.

But it wasn't his step on the stair. It was too light. "Mrs. Perkins?" she called.

"No." Ronda appeared in the doorway.

Ty's wife was dressed exquisitely in black leather pants and a white silk blouse that dipped low to show her generous cleavage. The lacy bra she wore was alternately visible and invisible through the thin silk as she moved. A sequined belt emphasized her small waist and flaring hips.

"Oh," Tina said, startled. Alarm speared through her. For no apparent reason, she felt threatened by the woman.

Ronda put her hands on her hips and gave Tina a look of utter disdain. "Well, I guess the gossips are right for once. I heard you were here...that you'd been here all night." Her lips lifted in a cruel smile.

"Yes," Tina said. She could hardly deny the story, since she'd sat through three interviews in the house that day. "Shane was kind enough to take care of me after the accident."

Her own smile was carefully neutral. She had no quarrel with Shane's sister-in-law. She'd do her best not to invoke one.

"Kind?" The smile turned to mocking laughter as Ronda advanced further into the room. "Yes, Shane is kind. When I begged him to save my marriage from a home wrecker, he said he would. He swore he would stop you from seeing Ty."

Tina couldn't speak. She wanted to deny the charge, but all Shane's earlier warnings for her to stay away came flooding back.

No, she didn't believe Ronda. These were the spiteful words of a spiteful woman. Not even Shane would go that far....

He might. He'd told her he would think of something if she didn't tell Ty to stop coming by. Apparently he didn't know that she had done as he requested.

All the warm anticipation seeped out of her, leaving her empty and cold as she realized exactly how making love to her would put a barrier between her and his brother. By claiming her as his woman, Shane had built a wall around her so solid that no man in the community would dare broach it.

She smoothed the sheet over her legs, then drew her knees to her chest, wrapping her arms around them. She was drawing inward, she realized—closing herself off from hurt as she had in the past.

Ronda seemed to think Tina's silence was a victory for her. One perfectly formed eyebrow rose haughtily. "I admit I never thought he'd go to such drastic measures."

"And very pleasant measures they were," Tina commented with a droll grin, as if she found the conversation quite amusing.

Red flags of fury highlighted Ronda's face.

Score one for my side, Tina thought. The blonde was

one of those women who had to have all men in her
domain at her feet. To have Shane even temporarily involved with someone else, even for a cause she endorsed,
enraged her possessive nature.

"You won't hold him for long," Ronda declared with
a venomous glare. "His last affair lasted little more than
a year."

"Just long enough," Tina declared. "A year is all I
intend to stay in this charming little…town." Her pause
was calculated to offend, as if she were censoring her
real opinion of the town and its residents. She changed
the subject. "How is Jonathan?"

Ronda's eyes, thick with mascara, narrowed sharply.
"Stay away from my son. I don't know what happened,
but I don't believe you tried to save him. He's an excellent swimmer."

"I would never harm a child," Tina said, refusing to
be daunted by the other woman's suspicions.

She didn't know why, but she knew Shane's sister-in-
law was a very real enemy. She wondered what she'd
done to earn such hatred from a person she didn't know.

"The stupid doctors are running more tests," Ronda
finally replied. She walked over to the door. "They're
after the Macklin money…just like you. If you think
Shane will ever marry you, you'd better think again. He's
not a marrying man."

With that barb, she walked out. A minute later, Tina
heard the door slam, then the sound of a motor cranking.
She watched out the window as a sleek luxury car headed
for the house a quarter mile up the road, then she drew
a shaky breath.

She could see the roof of her snug brick house across
the river. *It's past midnight, Cinderella,* she reminded

herself with cynical humor. *No use hanging around waiting for the prince.*

She rose and dressed in the slacks and blouse she'd worn so blithely to work on Friday. Her shoes were in the closet, dry and polished to a high shine, but there were no stockings. They'd been ruined by the rocks in the river. Her coat was at the cleaners, she recalled.

She made up the bed and put the T-shirt in the bathroom hamper. Picking up her purse, she went through it. Her keys were inside. She turned out the lamp by the bed, casting the room into deep shadows.

It was almost dark. She'd have to hurry.

Borrowing a warm hunting jacket of Shane's she went into the garage. She hit the button that opened the garage door. Hitting it again, she ducked and rushed out before the door could come down on top of her.

On the fifteen-minute walk to the bridge, she had time to think about Ronda's statements and accusations.

She couldn't bring herself to believe Shane had made love to her just to stop any friendship between her and his brother, yet...

It was a possibility. There was an undeniable attraction between her and Shane. That, compounded by his very protective attitude toward his family and the aftermath of worry about his nephew, could have overcome his scruples.

He also seemed convinced that she was a troublemaker, if not an out-and-out fortune hunter. From what Mrs. Perkins had told her, she knew his stepmother had made him suspicious of women, but why did he assume she was cast in the same mold?

She stopped on the bridge and watched the rush of water, which looked black and dangerous in the dark of evening. The devil-may-care facade she'd kept up in front of Ronda dissolved. Depression hit her. She shook it off. She'd learned long ago not to wish things were different. They weren't.

For long minutes, she stood there. It seemed as if the river carried her dreams with it…right out to sea. When she continued her journey, all her shields were in place. She crossed the bridge and turned up the street that ran along the woods by the river.

The house was dark when she arrived, but it was warm. She was glad to be home. She felt safer there.…

She hung Shane's coat on the hall highboy and went to the kitchen, stopping to turn on the lights as she did. She made hot tea and a sandwich, then took them with her into the office.

Sitting at the familiar desk, she ate her solitary meal. The summer she'd visited Anne, she'd read randomly through the books of poetry on the shelves. Spying a tome with a piece of paper sticking in it as a bookmark, she retrieved it, returned to the chair and opened it to the marked page.

The passage was one of Wordsworth's poems—his "Ode." She skimmed its stanzas. Closing the book, she reflected on two lines that seemed to have been written for her: "Though nothing can bring back the hour/ Of splendor in the grass, of glory in the flower."

Well, she'd had her hour. She hugged the book to her chest as a tremor rippled through her. Like the poet, she refused to grieve for what was past. But, she admitted, it was hard not to.

Once, all her dreams had been of Shane. She'd gotten over them. She'd get over this, too. If he came by, she'd tell him she'd decided not to see any of the Macklin men. Having made this decision, she read until the clock struck eleven.

Idly, she picked up the piece of paper that had been Anne's bookmark and unfolded it. It was a note from Anne.

My dear Tina,
I have often thought that poetry was the music of the lonely soul. I noticed that you chose poetry to read when you were quiet and introspective, thus I can guess at your mood now. There isn't anything I can do for your loneliness except wish you a true and lasting love. Be patient. I think it will come to you.

In the meantime, a treasure hunt will lift your spirits. Here is the code: 32,23,20. When you find the treasure, remember this: it is a gift from my heart to yours, a connection to the future through you and your children as it was a connection to my past through my mother and hers. Enjoy it as I have.

Tina closed her eyes and waited for the painful surge of emotion to subside. The letter sounded so final. Anne, unafraid to face anything, must have known the end was near.

Glancing again at the number, she realized a possibility. They were surely the—

The chime of the doorbell stopped her speculation. She stuck the note in the book and left it on the desk. The bell dinged again, impatiently. Her heart started kicking. There was only one person it could be.

She turned on the porch light and peered through the peephole. Yes, it was Shane. She opened the door.

He glared at her, pushed the door open farther and came inside. "Damn, it's getting cold again. I hope the bridges don't ice over." He hung his hat and coat on the highboy next to his green hunting jacket. "Why did you leave?" he asked, swinging around to face her. He looked grim.

"I was feeling better, so I thought I'd come home." She'd had that answer ready for the past hour.

"Got any coffee?" He caught her hand and escorted her into the big, homey kitchen.

"I can make some," she said wryly. *Keep it light.*

"Do that. I'm frozen. We had to track one of the holdup men through the woods." He chuckled. "You should have seen it—a real chase scene, just like in the movies. He abandoned his car on a washed-out country road and tried to make it on foot. We caught up with him about a mile out and brought him in."

"He didn't give you any trouble?" She fixed a sandwich after she put the coffee on. She would ease into telling him not to come back, that she didn't have time to see him....

"No. How did you get home?" he asked, suddenly looking like a tough lawman determined to ferret out the truth.

"I, uh, walked."

"Why?"

"Well, it wasn't all that far."

"I meant, why didn't you wait until I got back, so we could talk about it? You were supposed to stay the weekend."

"I didn't agree to that." She spoke calmly, though her heart was beating at a frenzied rate. She had no reason to be nervous, she chided herself. She'd done nothing wrong.

"Dammit!"

The explosive curse startled her. She dropped the knife she was using to spread mayonnaise on the whole-wheat bread. He crossed the room in three quick strides and took her by the shoulders. She stared, expecting him to shake her.

"Don't look so scared," he muttered. "I'm not going to beat you with a rubber hose...yet. Tell me why you decided to run off in the dark of night without a word."

She tried to think of something plausible, something that he would believe.

"Did Ronda come over?" he asked softly, changing tactics.

She glanced away, then back, but it was too late. She'd already given herself away. If she denied it now, he'd know she was lying. "Yes. She said Jonathan was having more tests. Is he ill from the dip in the river?"

The anger left him like a dust devil settling, leaving no trace in the air. His eyes darkened, but his hold on her eased. "No." He let one hand fall to her waist while the other slipped behind her neck. He pulled her to him, surprising her, and laid his cheek on top of her head. "They think he may have leukemia."

"Oh, Shane." She wrapped her arms around his waist and hugged him hard, feeling his pain as if it were her own. "I'm so sorry."

After that, there was nothing to say. She held him, offering him the comfort of her arms, and postponed telling him of her decision not to see him again.

When he shifted, she eased from his arms and picked up the knife. "Go sit down. I'll have your food in a minute."

He nodded, his face so grim and weary it made her want to weep for him. She served the tuna-salad sandwich with sliced fresh vegetables and corn chips. When the coffee was ready, she poured two mugs and joined him at the table.

The outdoor lights at his house were on, but she couldn't see any lights on in the house. "Did you go home?" she asked.

"Yes."

"You didn't turn any lights on."

Shane glanced out the window and studied the dark outline of his roof among the pines. He looked at her. "I didn't need any. No one was there."

He'd been eager to return home, to see her, he admitted to himself. Not that he'd tell her such a thing. The power she held over him was already troubling. When he'd turned in the drive, he'd looked up at the bedroom window, expecting to see a light there.

The entire house had been dark. He'd stopped in front and gone in and found…nothing. No lights, no warmth, no welcome.

And no small, incredibly sexy woman in his bed, waiting for him with her tempting smile and her stormy eyes that saw so much and disclosed so little.

The sensation he'd experienced had been like a rabbit punch to the ribs, quick and painful and possibly lethal.

He'd slammed the door, climbed in the truck and headed over to her house, where the lights gleamed softly from the windows.

It occurred to him that he'd always liked visiting here when Anne had been alive, and now, with Tina. His own house had always been just that—a house, a place to stay when he had nowhere else to go.

Until today. Then he'd been eager to get back.

But it wasn't the house itself that had attracted him, he finally realized. It was the person in it.

He watched his hostess while he ate the food she'd prepared for him. Everything tasted good, and he ate hungrily, aware of other hungers that weren't yet satisfied.

Warmth seeped deep into him, thawing a spot that had been frozen for a long time.

Danger, some sixth sense warned him.

Maybe, but what better way to keep an eye on her? If they were lovers, no other males would come around. She'd be marked as his. A lightness entered his soul, and for the briefest moment, he felt something akin to happiness.

He frowned. He wouldn't be caught in her spell. His motives were simple. By playing the ardent lover, he'd be protecting his family. God knew, he had enough to worry about there. His heart clenched painfully as he thought of his nephew. He'd give his life for the boy....

A small, delicate hand touched his forehead. "You look so fierce," she said.

"Sorry, I was thinking." He smiled at her. Finished with the meal, he captured her hand in his. Flames licked inside him. He wanted to grab her and rush to the bedroom. There, he would strip the hindering clothes from them and bury himself in her until he forgot everything but the bliss of that joining.

He lifted her hand and kissed the back of it, wryly amused at his own wild desires. A man had to show some finesse. Maybe a wife would understand such needs, but an independent woman who kept her thoughts and dreams as carefully hidden as this one did would have to be wooed more gently.

She stood and came to him. He felt a jolt of pleased surprise when she pulled his head against her breasts. Her lips caressed his hair as she bent over him, her hands moving over his shoulders, massaging away the tension of the chase and other worries.

"Come to bed," she whispered.

He knew he should express a token resistance just to

prove that he could. He didn't. Instead, he wrapped his arms around her hips and stood, holding her high in the air.

She smiled at him, and her face was filled with sympathy. A fierceness washed over him. He wanted more than that from her.

Tina was completely aware of Shane in every part of her. Her body was languid, soft, warm…ready for his caresses. He carried her swiftly to the bedroom. With great care, he set her on the rug beside the old-fashioned four-poster.

When he started on his buttons, she undressed, too. They worked in unison, each piece of clothing floating away so that they revealed themselves to each other as if their actions were choreographed. The last items fell to the floor. He gazed at her and let her see the hunger.

His body was ready, hard and erect, and hers answered in its own way, becoming soft and welcoming. However, there was more than physical desire between them, wonderful as that was. In the other room, she'd sensed a need in him, one that was strong, elemental and primitive, that spoke to her soul. That was what she'd answered by taking him to her breast.

She wondered if he had an empty place inside that only she could fill. That was the way it had been for her when they'd made love—fulfillment so sweet, it had stolen her breath away.

A shudder went through him. He moved swiftly, tossing the covers into a careless heap at the foot of the bed, then lifting her onto the high mattress. He stood there, looking down at her, his face pensive, almost moody.

"This scares me," he said in a low, husky voice.

"What?" She could hardly speak above the drumbeats of her heart, which seemed to be lodged in her throat.

"Wanting you. It makes a man...vulnerable."

"It does the same to a woman."

"Does it?" He lay down beside her, leaning over her, his weight on one arm. He placed his hand on her abdomen and splayed his fingers wide. The tip of his thumb and little finger almost spanned the distance between her hipbones.

His confession made her want to open her heart to him. "I've often wondered..." She stopped, unsure of exposing herself this much to him. What if he laughed at her idle fantasy?

"What?" He moved his hand upward until he touched the bottom side of her breast. Her breath became jerky.

"If things would have been different between us if we'd met before—before other things got in the way." She traced the line of his eyebrows, then ran her fingers into his hair.

He lost his moody introspection and stared intently into her eyes as if determined to read her every thought. "When I was still a wide-eyed romantic?" He laughed. "I was never that."

"Me, neither," she said, closing the lid on any further confidences. Life had never let her indulge in dreams for very long. It snatched them away almost as soon as they formed.

He ran a finger lightly over her mouth. "You have the most kissable mouth. The first time we kissed, your mouth trembled under mine. And then you opened your lips and kissed me back. I've never forgotten how exciting that was."

"Before I remembered you were my enemy," she whispered through an aching throat, wanting his kiss now.

"Am I your enemy now?" He bent nearer, his lips but a breath from hers. He waited for her answer.

"Sometimes…"

"No," he growled, denying it.

His mouth took hers. For a second, she felt only the demand and none of the gentleness.

"Kiss me," he ordered. "Dammit, you've stolen my soul, my dreams and my every waking moment, now give me something back."

She opened her lips to him and allowed the tactile plunder of his tongue against hers. But love and desire and a strange, aching pity swirled into one undefined mix of hunger and need that matched his. Wrapping her arms and legs around him, she molded herself to his broad frame and let him reach inside to the very depths.

He kissed her eyes, her nose, her ears, her chin, returned again and again to her lips, and then, with his mouth, he taught her new ways to be intimate.

She moaned when he moved away from her, down to her breasts, which throbbed from his caresses. He rolled his tongue over the sensitive tip, around and around, until she writhed against him.

"Shane," she gasped, loving the wild things his touch did to her. "Oh, love, yes…"

He suckled and nipped until she could stand it no more, then he moved down her abdomen. He paused at her navel and thrust seductively into it. She hadn't realized the erotic potential there until he showed her.

When he slipped between her thighs, she was even less prepared for the overpowering sensations that burst through her. She closed her eyes tightly and clutched the sheet, her movements beyond her control now. She was entirely his.

When the world was in danger of flying apart, he

raised his head. His eyes seared over her, twin flames of passionate blue, so intense she was almost frightened.

He gathered her close, cradling her against his heaving chest. "When you respond like that, it drives me to the edge. One touch and I'd explode. I wouldn't even have to be in you."

"It's you," she protested. "You—you make the world go away so that there's only you...me...and this moment."

She burrowed against him, loving the caress of his chest hair against her breasts, the rougher feel of his body against her smoothness. Spreading her legs, she trapped his hard staff between her thighs and moved slightly against him.

He caught her hips in his hands and stilled her soft thrusts. "Don't rub against me like that," he murmured in a hoarse whisper. "It arouses me beyond endurance."

"I'm glad," she said simply. "Because that's the way you make me feel."

He hugged her to him in a harsh embrace. She responded just as fiercely, needing him in ways she couldn't describe.

"Wait," he said at last, raising his mouth from its devastation of hers. "We have to...take care of things." He gasped for breath and pulled out of her arms.

I wouldn't care if we had a baby. But she didn't say the words aloud. They revealed too much....

She waited while he fumbled through his pockets, then smiled at the string of curses he muttered when he couldn't at once find what he needed. Finally, he returned to her side.

He quickly prepared himself. "I wouldn't be able to take those nervous, fluttery touches from you tonight," he said in apology.

"Shall I get on top?" she asked. She wanted to pleasure him as he'd done for her.

"Only if you don't move," he grumbled. But he rolled
onto his back and, putting his hands on her waist, lifted
her onto him.

They came together easily, naturally, she found. He
gasped and held her still.

"It's been years since I've felt like this…if ever," he
told her. "The first time we kissed, we didn't get this far.
Yesterday we went too fast. Today I want it to last."

She lay over him. He seemed to take her weight easily.
With a new confidence, she took his lower lip between
her teeth. He held his breath. She ran her tongue back
and forth over the captured lip, careful of her hold. His
breath fanned over her mouth in a throaty chuckle.

A reckless passion invaded her, and her spirit soared
as she realized she could excite him as much as he did
her. It was a wild, heady sensation. Yet it was coupled
with a tenderness of feeling so profound that she was as
acutely conscious of his needs as she was of her own.

"Shane," she whispered as emotion and passion
melded.

His mouth took the soft plea from her. He parted her
lips and gave her his tongue, while his hands took her
breasts. She uttered a wild, smothered cry and surged
recklessly against him.

"Don't, love," he cautioned. "Too late."

He grasped her hips and moved her in rhythm with
him. He showed her how to slide her body against his so
that she felt the intense pleasure. She closed her eyes and
welcomed the final plunge as the pulsating climax took
over her senses. Inside her, his body responded in tune
to hers.

They went over the edge together.

When she collapsed onto him, he held her close and stroked her back until she quit trembling. Then he turned so that she rested beside him. They were quiet for a long time.

Finally, he kissed her cheek. "It's hard to believe a frame of such delicate proportions can hold that much passion. You're the answer to every fantasy I've ever had."

She was too spent to reply. Instead, she snuggled close and planted a kiss on his damp chest. The hair tickled her nose. She rubbed the tickle away, laid her cheek against him and slid gently down toward sleep.

This might be a fantasy, but she wanted it to last....

Chapter Eleven

Tina woke to a kiss. When she opened her eyes, Shane stood beside the bed. "Wake up, sleepyhead. I've got to go to work."

Disappointment wafted over her. "Are you leaving now?" She glanced at the clock. It was six-thirty.

"No. Breakfast is ready. If you want to eat with me," he added, a note of uncertainty in his husky baritone.

She smiled, feeling tender toward him. "Yes." She pushed the covers back and realized she wore no pajamas. Heat climbed in her face. "I, uh, need to dress."

He laughed. "I like you as you are. Hurry. The toast is getting cold."

When he left, she dashed for the bathroom and washed up, then yanked on her cranberry velour slacks and top. After pulling a comb through her tangles, she rushed to the kitchen. Shane was at the table, waiting for her.

She took her seat. When she started eating, he did, too.

He'd prepared hot oatmeal again, which felt good on her healing throat.

"You sound better."

"I think the worst is over." She looked out the window, unable to stand his concerned regard without melting right at his feet. "But the weather doesn't seem to be improving. It looks like more rain is coming."

"Yeah." He studied the clouds. "The creeks are close to flood level all over the county. There will probably be some washouts along the gravel roads, plus a mud slide or two...and a few wrecks to liven things up." He recounted the expected disasters with stoic humor.

She grinned at him in sympathy. Finished with the meal, she pushed the dishes aside and sipped the hot coffee.

"Here, you haven't seen the paper yet." He handed her the front page of the *Riverton Daily News*.

Her picture figured prominently on the front page. Another showed the river splashing over the boulders behind her house. A picture of Jonathan and his father fishing along the river at a happier time also accompanied the piece.

"Very touching," she said when she finished reading.

Dolly had used every known trick to dramatize the event so that Tina sounded like a heroine of Olympic proportions. The story cited two authorities on the temperature and velocity of the river, and the danger of being battered against the rocks or swept down the gorge. The effects of hypothermia were explained, making it seem like a miracle that Tina had managed to walk a half mile in the near-freezing wind after courageously fighting her way through the water, all the while carrying the boy.

Last but not least, there was a revealing shot of Shane refilling her cup of hot lemon tea when her voice gave out during the interview. The caption under the photo read "Sheriff Macklin plays nursemaid to heroine."

Tina felt heat pool deep within her. The way he was looking at her... His eyes... Surely anyone looking at the photograph would know they were lovers.

"Dolly was determined to get the nursemaid quip into the story, wasn't she?" Shane smiled good-naturedly.

Tina let out an uneasy sigh. She thought the feisty newswoman had just made life a little more unpleasant for her. When Shane's sister-in-law read the article, she'd be furious.

"Rather domestic, isn't it?" He tapped the photo, his words echoing her worries about the homey little scene.

"Yes."

He touched her temple with his fingertips, drawing her gaze to his. "Does it bother you?"

"What?" She was acutely aware of his fingers trailing down her cheek, then touching her earlobe.

"That people know about us...that we're lovers."

"I don't know," she answered truthfully.

The moment hung suspended between them while he probed her eyes, searching and questioning. She didn't know what he was looking for, but she felt his reservation concerning her as if it were a blow to the heart.

He released her and sighed, his expression thoughtful. "I need to check on a few things today. Do you feel up to taking a ride? I thought we'd stop for lunch at the ski lodge."

She weighed spending the day alone in the house to being with him. Being with him won. "I'll go."

"Wear comfortable clothes and boots."

When they left an hour later, she saw her neighbors, the Talls, backing out of the adjacent drive. They ate breakfast out on Sundays. During the week, Mr. Tall opened the hardware store at seven and his wife usually went down around nine, when she finished with her housework, Tina had learned.

It must be nice to work with your mate, she thought. But then, it would be nice to come home after a hard day and have that special someone there.

Her body warmed as she remembered Shane's arrival last night. The bliss of being in his arms, of knowing he'd wanted her enough to come to her house, revived old dreams that she'd locked away years ago.

A foolish thing to let happen. When the passion was played out between them, she'd leave Riverton. Next time, she'd stay away.

"Not as bad as I'd feared," Shane remarked.

She came out of her reverie and attended to the present. They were at the junction of the Rogue River and one of the many creeks that ran into it. The creek was full right to the top of its banks, the water frothy and brown with silt.

He put the truck in gear and drove along a narrow, paved road. They wound their way up the mountain. The snow under the trees became thicker as they went higher.

Approaching a narrow bend, they came upon a scattering of rocks over the road. Shane turned on the flashing lights of the patrol truck and stopped.

"Dangerous place here," he commented. "There has already been some slippage." He indicated the fallen rocks.

Tina leaned forward and peered at the high bank next to the road. The rock was fractured into irregular pieces, from pea gravel to boulders. The land seemed to tilt in every direction and looked unstable even to her untrained eyes.

"Do you think there will be more?"

"Maybe." He looked worried. "If we have a lot of rain or a fast warming spell that melts the snow, it could cause problems."

"I see."

"I'll have to call the road department." He picked up the phone and dialed.

She listened while he talked to the supervisor in charge of county roads. The man informed Shane a truck had gone through a guardrail and down an embankment. He'd put a crew on it, but it would take two days minimum to repair. A deputy sheriff was on the scene.

Shane told his deputy to route a detour around the area and asked the supervisor to get the job done in one day, if possible.

"Will do," the two men replied and rang off.

"I didn't realize your job entailed so many tasks," she said.

He grinned. "Sometimes I think I'm dogcatcher, nanny and the nursemaid to the entire county."

She laughed. His laughter joined hers. She realized it was the first time they'd ever laughed together. "It's your nature," she told him. "You take responsibility for others."

"The big-brother syndrome?" he mused. "Maybe. You feel like moving some rocks?"

She got out of the truck with him and together they tossed the largest stones off the roadway.

With a push broom, he cleared the rest. "There. That's safe enough for now. A couple of young guys who work for a logging outfit take these curves at max speed. Maybe they won't spin out and lose it on this one."

They returned to the main road and surveyed several other side roads off it. He seemed to know everyone in the county and who lived on what road. He kept her amused with stories about the local residents while she observed him at his work. It was after one when they stopped for lunch at the posh ski resort.

Up there on the mountain there were no signs of spring. Snow still covered the ground in solid white. Skiers zipped along the trails through the woods like brightly plumed, exotic birds.

"Do you ski?" he asked.

"Yes. I learned in France." She shaded her eyes with one hand as she watched a group ski down to the chair lift. "I've never been skiing in the States."

"We'll have to fix that. When you're well, we'll come up during the week one day. The slopes are less crowded then."

"That sounds like fun."

It made her feel odd to be planning an event in the future for them. She felt that each day they were together was on its own, a time out of time that might not come again.

Shane took her hand to steady her as they walked over the snowy path to the lodge steps. Inside, the air was warm. She and Shane pulled off their jackets and went up to the restaurant on the second floor. Rafe Barrett was at a table by the window.

He stood and motioned them over. "Join me for lunch," he invited. "Genny will be here soon. She's translating a book by some French writer."

They were soon settled. When Genny arrived, they ordered, then talked about the ski season.

"With the late snows, the season should go right into May," Rafe explained.

"Unless we have a really warm spell," Genny added. "How are you doing on your book?"

"Great, so far," Tina answered. "I'm getting my notes

in order and using the computer to set up a cross-reference file.''

"How did anyone ever get any work done before computers?'' Genny exclaimed.

"Looks like our women have gone high tech on us,'' Rafe said in an amused tone to Shane.

Tina froze at the casual mention of ''our women.'' She glanced at Shane to gauge his reaction. He seemed totally relaxed. One arm rested on the back of her chair. He idly plucked at a strand of her hair and smoothed his fingers down it.

"Modern times,'' Shane said regretfully. ''Tina only made me a sandwich for supper, while *I* fixed a hot breakfast for her.''

She could have curled up in embarrassment. Nothing like broadcasting their involvement, she thought hotly. Her eyes met Genny's across the table. To her surprise, the other woman beamed in approval.

"Yeah, Genny makes me cook even when we have guests. Of course, I am much better than she is in the kitchen,'' Rafe said with no trace of modesty, while his wife huffed.

"Liar,'' she snarled, nuzzling him with her nose, then biting him on the neck.

Shane rubbed the tiny twin scars on his lip. ''Watch out,'' he warned his friend. ''Women have been known to bite.''

"Hmm, methinks there's a story here,'' Rafe deduced.

"No, there isn't,'' Tina quickly put in.

Everyone laughed, while she turned beet red at giving herself away. Shane tugged at her hair. ''Eat up. We have a couple more chores to do today.''

They discussed the conditions of the roads, the water levels in the creeks, the account of Tina's rescue of Jonathan. When Genny asked, Shane admitted things didn't look good for the boy, but he didn't go into details.

Tina kept quiet, her compassion for both Macklins a vague ache inside. Like yesterday, she wanted to clasp Shane in her arms and comfort him. She didn't think he'd gotten much of that in his adult life.

People needed someone special to share things with, she thought, looking at the affection between Rafe and his wife. They were discussing the wildlife hikes Genny led through the woods twice a week and how popular they were with the visitors.

When they finished, Shane insisted on paying for their share of the bill. "I have to maintain my integrity," he explained.

Rafe scoffed. "You're the only totally honest cop I've ever known."

"Oh, I can be had," Shane quipped, standing and moving his chair so Tina could get out. "You just have to know the price." His gaze on her indicated she was it.

Ignoring him, she said goodbye and told the Barretts that she'd enjoyed the lunch. In spite of its disconcerting moments, she added mentally. Shane seemed determined to claim her as his.

Her heart stopped, skipped a beat, then raced like mad. Was he…could he be falling in love, too?

A delirious joy leapt over her like electric tingles. If they were both in love, the possibilities were endless. Love could conquer anything!

Spoken like a true romantic, she chided. Though she longed to tell him of her love, she didn't. Caution learned long ago kept her silent. She was afraid to expose her heart so completely to him, she realized. If he didn't love her…

"Ready?"

She looked up into his eyes and nodded.

"Let's have lunch later this week," Genny invited Tina. "Come join me on Thursday. Rafe will be out, and we can do girl talk without the men bothering us."

"I'd like that," Tina said. She felt she and Genny were destined to be friends. She'd like to get to know Gabe's wife, too. She'd have the two of them to her place one day soon, she decided.

And Adrianna, her attorney's wife, too. Friends were nice things to have, and she missed her best friend, who was still in Italy, teaching English as a second language.

Saying goodbye once more to the Barretts, she and Shane left the stone, wood and glass lodge, with its view of the mountains and of the town snuggled into a bend of the river.

"You're quiet," he said, driving down the snowbank-lined road.

"Just thinking," she murmured. "Your friends make a lovely couple. I like them."

"You and Genny get along well."

"Yes."

"Does this mean you might change your mind and stay in the area after you finish your book?"

She looked at the question from every angle, but she couldn't tell from it or his inflection if he wanted that or not. "I might," she said noncommittally. "Would you mind?"

He stopped at the main road and looked at her, his gaze dark and unreadable. "As you once pointed out— it's a free country," he finally said. He checked for traffic and pulled onto the road.

They were both being cautious, she realized. With good reason. They'd learned it the hard way—he because of his stepmother and, perhaps, her; she because she'd learned early that people could be cruel, even though the circumstances of her birth had been no fault of hers.

They arrived back in town in late afternoon.

"I need to stop by the office a minute. Would you like the twenty-five-cent tour?"

"Sure. I've always wondered what a sheriff's office looked like," she quipped, matching the light mood she'd maintained all afternoon.

He checked with the dispatcher and with the sergeant at the main desk, discussed some items with them, then gave her a quick run-through of the building, which was busy even on Sunday. She was aware of the speculation behind the polite greetings of the law officers she met.

Shane's office was on the second floor, in a corner room that overlooked the town center and had a terrific view of the river a block away.

"Wow," she commented. "Windows on two walls. That puts you way up on the ladder of success."

"Does it?" He didn't seem interested.

Well, when one had always had money and position, the perks probably seemed one's normal due. "According to all the business magazines."

"Come here," he murmured. He sat on the side of his desk and opened his arms to her.

She went to him.

He enclosed her in a warm hug. "I've wanted to hold you all day. At lunch I could hardly concentrate on the conversation, I was so aware of you beside me."

She beamed a smile of pure happiness at him, surprised and pleased at this revelation.

He opened his legs and pulled her closer. She felt as if his entire body embraced hers. She let herself snuggle to her heart's content. Just to be held by him was wonderful. To make love was simply mind-blowing.

Feelings rose in her, so strong her body felt too small to contain all of them. Tonight, she thought hazily, tonight she'd tell him of her love.

His lips drifted over her forehead in the gentlest of kisses. She closed her eyes and sighed.

"I need to go down to the hospital in Medford and check on Jonathan. Do you feel like coming?"

"Do you think I should? I mean, with my cold?" She leaned her head back and looked at him anxiously.

"Would you mind staying in the waiting room? He probably can't have anyone but immediate family in to see him."

"Oh, of course. No, I don't mind waiting."

He rubbed the back of his knuckles over her cheek. She turned his hand and pressed his palm to her lips.

"I could take you home, if you're too tired. You sound so much better, I forget you've been ill as well as dunked in an icy river in the past two days."

"I'd rather stay with you."

She felt his chest rise in a deeply drawn breath. It gave her a fluttery feeling inside to know how he wanted her with him.

During the short drive down Interstate 5, she watched the scenery whip past. Neither of them spoke much. A worried frown slashed a deep groove between his eyes. She knew his thoughts were on his nephew.

He stopped at a shopping center. "What do you think a kid would like?" he asked, leading the way to the toy department of a large department store.

Tina was enchanted with this vision of Shane. She watched him try out different items with the concentration of a scientist conducting a vital experiment. Finally, she suggested a couple of storybooks, a coloring book with a marker pen set or a monkey that could do loops between two sticks when manipulated by strings.

He agreed and purchased everything she mentioned.

"I can see what kind of parent you'd be," she told him on the way to the truck.

"What kind?" he demanded, giving her a threatening glance.

"Indulgent."

"If you mean I'd spoil the kids, you're probably right." He grinned. After putting the package in the back, he opened the door and helped her step up into the truck. "I'd probably spoil my wife, too," he murmured.

Her heart nearly beat its way out of her chest.

He slammed the door, walked around the front of the vehicle and climbed in his side. The sultry teasing left his face, and she knew his thoughts were on more serious matters. Her heart returned to its normal rate, and she, too, turned grave.

At the hospital, she settled on the vinyl sofa in the waiting room while Shane went to visit, his presents in hand. She picked up a magazine and began reading an article on parental discipline.

When she finished, she put it down and stared out the window at the gray clouds forming over the mountain peaks. The sun had broken through that afternoon, but now the sky looked threatening again. She sighed worriedly. Shane had enough on his mind.

When he reappeared, she stood, ready to leave.

"Jonathan wants to see you," he said. "Would you mind?"

"Of course not." She followed him down the corridor.

Jonathan was in a private room. His gifts from Shane were piled at the foot of his bed. When he saw Tina, he held out his arms. She went to him and received a big hug. She hugged him back, choked up with emotion.

"Dad said I was to thank you for saving my life," he told her. "Thank you."

"It was my pleasure," she said sincerely.

"Did you see our pictures in the paper?"

"Yes. Dolly wrote a nice article to go with it."

"Yeah. Dad read it to me. I liked the part where they told about me and him catching a big fish right where I fell in. If Dad had been there, you'd have had to save him, too."

"I'm sure he could have gotten out without help," she assured her young friend.

"Look at this neat monkey Uncle Shane gave me. It works like this." He showed her how to make the monkey turn a flip. "Now you can try it," he offered generously.

For several minutes, she stood by the bed and played with Jonathan. They both giggled when she flipped the monkey backwards by accident. They were still laughing when the door was pushed open from its half-closed position and Ronda entered the room.

The other woman's mouth tightened when she saw Tina with her son. Tina determinedly kept the smile on her face. "Hello," she said. "Jonathan is teaching me how this thing works. He's a good instructor, but I'm a slow student."

"She made it go backwards, Mom," he explained, giggling again.

"Who let you in?" Ronda demanded sharply, glaring at Tina. Jonathan's laughter disappeared.

"I did," Shane announced.

Ronda peered around the door, which had hid him from her view. "Oh, Shane, I didn't see you." Her voice was a purr. ''I'm surprised the doctor let an outsider visit. He's been so strict.''

''Jonathan wanted to see her. I didn't think it would hurt.''

''Of course. I wanted to thank you for helping Jonathan,'' she said graciously.

Shane made a little sound, rather like a snort. Both women waited for him to speak. When he didn't, Tina picked up her purse from the bed, smiled brightly at Jonathan and announced she'd wait down the hall for Shane. She headed out.

In the waiting room, she breathed a sigh of relief. Ronda's dislike was so puzzling. Tina didn't believe the lovely blonde was jealous of her and Ty. That left her and Shane.

Did Ronda regret marrying the younger brother and wish she'd waited for the older one?

Not a very pretty triangle, if true. It could turn the two brothers bitterly against each other. However, Shane showed no more than brotherly interest in his sister-in-law.

Tina hugged herself as a shiver chased over her. Whatever was between her and Shane, it was no one's business but theirs. If Ronda butted in, Shane wouldn't mince words telling her to butt out.

Leaning against the windowsill, she watched the traffic rush along the street. It seemed busy for late Sunday afternoon. Her thoughts drifted, and she pondered over the day with Shane.

He had paraded her all over the county that morning and afternoon. Had he simply wanted her company, or was he marking her off-limits to the rest of the males in town, telling them they were a couple? It didn't sound so bad...to belong to each other.

When he returned to the waiting room, he stopped behind her, his chest touching her back. She sensed his worry and slipped her hand into his, quietly offering the comfort of her touch. They stood there for several minutes without speaking.

"It's time to go." He kept her hand in his as they walked outside. "Jonathan looked lively, didn't he?" he asked once they were on their way.

"Yes, he did." She spoke as reassuringly as she could.

"It would kill Ty..." He stopped and took a long breath. "Shall we go out for dinner? It's almost six."

"It looks like rain. I think I'd rather go home."

"Yes, of course. You must be tired. I've kept you out all day." He laid a hand on the back of her neck and massaged gently.

The rain had started by the time they arrived at her house. They dashed up the sidewalk and onto the porch through a fine mist that shifted like veils in the air. She quickly unlocked the door, and they went inside to the warmth.

"I love this house. It seems to welcome me each time I return," she said when they paused to hang up their coats.

He pulled her to him. "I used to think that, but now I know the truth."

"What?" she demanded, smiling up at him.

"It's the person who lives here." He kissed her.

The kiss heated her blood and warmed her clear down to her toes. She strained upward, reaching for him. He lifted her and guided her legs around his waist, then linked his hands under her bottom.

"I've never made love standing up, have you?"

She shook her head.

He chuckled seductively. "Let's see, we've done it

with me on top and with you on top.'' He whispered several scandalous suggestions in her ear until she was blushing and laughing helplessly.

"No one could do that,'' she said at one point.

"But it would be interesting to try.'' He lifted her until he could nibble at her breast.

"Dinner,'' she gasped. "We haven't had dinner.''

He let her slide down him, but continued holding her while he walked down the hall to the kitchen. "Okay, dinner,'' he agreed. "My mom always insisted dessert was last, so I guess I'll wait.''

She pushed out of his arms and went to the refrigerator, smoothing her hair and clothing into a semblance of order. She couldn't keep a smile from blooming on her face.

There were serious problems in the world—and in Riverton— but when she and Shane were alone like this, it was possible to leave the worries outside the door for a little while and just be happy together. That was what love was all about.

Oh, yes.

"Chinese?'' she asked.

"What?''

She saw his mind wasn't on food. "Stir-fry veggies with popcorn shrimp?''

"That'll be fine.'' His gaze was hot, so hot, as he watched her, those hungry flames burning deep in his eyes. They licked at her soul and her self-control.

Tonight she'd tell him of her love. She knew now she'd always loved him...and that love was the reason she'd returned. Anne must have known....

Oh, Anne, thank you!

The meal was easy and quick. After she put instant rice in the microwave oven, she dumped frozen vegetables, already sliced, into a skillet, added low-salt soy sauce, one tablespoon each of sesame-seed oil and slivered almonds, and finally tossed in a handful of popcorn shrimp. Last, she sprinkled in garlic powder and pepper, stirred until the mixture was steaming, then served it over the rice.

"Very impressive," he said when she handed him a plate.

With wine and rolls, the meal was plenty for them. They ate, their eyes often meeting across the table. Hers would skitter away as the emotions became too much.

He laughed once and chucked her under her chin. "You make life new and exciting," he murmured, which touched her deeply. "And making love a wonder...."

He let his voice trail off seductively. Eddies of lightning flashed along her skin, burning her alive and leaving her feeling gloriously, foolishly happy.

Tonight…

They ate, then cleaned the kitchen together. Together they drifted down the hall. She paused at the living-room door. He took her hand and guided her into the bedroom. Smiling, she went with him, completely willing.

"The treasure is in here," he murmured.

"Oh, I just remembered. I found some numbers. I think they're a combination. Did Anne ever mention a safe to you?"

"No, I don't think so."

Tina went past him into the sitting room. He followed. She picked up the note and read the numbers.

"Hmm," he said. "Perhaps a wall safe. Have you looked?"

She shook her head.

He glanced around the room, then went to a small picture on a side wall. Nothing. He checked another. Nothing. There was an unused fireplace in the room. A huge mirror held pride of place over it. He tugged at it, then ran his fingers along one edge.

"Eureka," he said.

The mirror swung open. Tina gasped.

"See if the numbers work."

She flicked the knob on the safe in a standard pattern, clockwise first, then back past the first number to the second, then clockwise again for the third. She grasped the handle and turned. The safe opened.

She peered inside and spied two large hinged boxes. They reminded her of jewelry boxes. She pulled one out and opened it.

"It is," she said, stunned. "It is jewelry."

The pieces were obviously heirloom quality. There were rings, pendants, earrings, bracelets—all set with the most exquisite rubies, diamonds, emeralds and other gems she couldn't identify.

"Well," Shane said in a coolly amused voice. "Looks like you hit pay dirt after all."

"What?" She frowned as she turned to stare at him. She saw the cynical amusement in his smile...and the suspicious assessment in his eyes. "What do you mean?" she asked levelly.

He touched a pair of earrings made of diamonds and rubies. "You might not have known about Anne's niece, but you had to have known about the jewels. They were family heirlooms. Anne wore them often. Ronda wondered what had happened to them."

His distrust hovered in the air between them. Tina thought of showing him the letter. It would have dispelled the doubts.

For the moment. Until the next time something questionable came up about her.

A shiver cascaded through her. This time she couldn't put on her words-can-never-hurt-me facade. This time she couldn't smile and pretend it didn't hurt.

''Get out,'' she said. ''Damn you, get out of my house. I never want to see you again…ever!''

Long after the front door slammed behind him, she stood there, shaking and furious—with Anne for not explaining why she would leave a fortune in a wall safe, with him for his suspicions and doubts, and most of all with herself for believing that desire was love and love would make everything right.

Chapter Twelve

Jack Norton lifted a necklace. Its gems gleamed in the lights of the attorney's office. He whistled in admiration.

"They were in a wall safe in the sitting room, the room she used for an office," Tina explained, still not able to believe it. "Could she have forgotten about them? Was she senile at the end?"

Jack gave Tina a sharp glance, then put the necklace back in the hinged velvet box. "No. Anne Snyder had one of the best minds I've ever encountered, right up until the day she died."

"Then why did she leave a fortune in the house?" Tina asked.

"A gift to you, as her letter explained."

She frowned at the lawyer. He was no help at all.

"What are you going to do with them?" He stacked one box on top of the other and pushed them across his desk to her.

She looked at him in exasperation. "Do with them? Why, give them back, of course."

He listed his eyebrows in a quizzical manner. "To whom?"

"Her niece." Tina looked down at her clenched hands and forced herself to relax. She sat back in the comfortable chair and took a deep breath. "I'll give them to Ronda Macklin."

Jack shook his head. "The will stated you were to get the contents of the house."

"But…she didn't leave her niece anything."

He shrugged.

A tense silence filled the room. "Why?" Tina asked at last. "Why would she leave me so much and nothing for her blood kin?"

"You were her goddaughter. Besides, she left Jonathan a trust fund. Her will was very specific, I might add. My father wrote it. He didn't leave any loopholes, I can assure you." He grinned. "There was also a penalty if anyone tried to break the will."

"Anne fixed it so that her niece couldn't contest it?"

"That's right."

"But how? What did Ronda have to lose?" Tina stared at the lawyer, who in turn observed her closely. "There's a mystery here. I'm going to find out what it is."

"Are you?" He leaned forward. "Do you really want to know?"

Fear clutched her by the throat at his portentous words. "Yes." She nodded decisively. "I want to know."

"Anne said you were smart, inquisitive and courageous," he told her with a smile. He stood and went to a locked file.

When he started opening it, Tina's heart gave a gigantic leap. She wasn't sure she wanted to solve this mystery, after all.

"There's only one mystery in my life," she said slowly. "Does this concern my parentage?"

She couldn't bring herself to ask if Anne knew something about her father. All the older woman had ever admitted was that she'd promised Tina's grandmother—an "old and dear friend"—that she would keep an eye on her grandchild.

"I declared myself your godmother," Anne had explained.

Tina swallowed as Jack sorted through file folders and withdrew one. He removed a letter and brought it to Tina.

She took it with trepidation. The letter was sealed and addressed to her. She looked at Jack, puzzled.

"Anne said there was information in here that could hurt you," he said gently. "She said that if you ever asked, I was to give it to you, but if you didn't seem interested in knowing, then I was to destroy it after a certain length of time."

Tina nodded, but her mind was awhirl with confusion.

"Why don't you use my conference room?" he suggested. "You'll have privacy there. When you're ready to talk, we will."

She stood and went into the adjoining room. He closed the door behind her. She noted there were coffee and cups on an oak credenza, along with a box of tissues.

The crying room? she wondered, and determined not to cry no matter what information the letter contained. She lifted her chin, took a seat and slit open the letter.

My dearest Tina,
You have come seeking the truth, and I know you are strong enough to take it. I hope you're also strong enough to forgive.

I know who your father was. My nephew fell in love with your mother the year he graduated from Harvard. Like you, she was lovely, intelligent and a joy. But he had a very deep sense of family responsibility.

Our family started the first bank in the valley. Associated with that is a certain pioneer pride. Sometimes such pride may cause a person to do foolish things.

The bank was in difficulties, you see. It needed an infusion of money to keep it going during a difficult period. My nephew was the key. He was engaged to a woman from a very wealthy family that had agreed to invest in the bank. Then he met your mother, fresh and young and full of life when his life was in a rut of duty and responsibility.

He made a terrible mistake, one he regretted his entire life, I can assure you. He chose duty over love. He chose the bank over your mother and you. Yes, he knew about you. Your mother left town, and my nephew spent his life trying to be a good husband and father to his wife and daughter. But it was a hard life for him. I pray you will understand and forgive.

You are my niece, my dearly beloved kin. You never received your due from your father. He tried to find you after his first heart attack, not to make amends—he knew he could never make up for what he had denied you—but because he'd never forgotten his first—his only—love and the child they'd conceived. He wanted to give you half of his wealth to insure that if you had dreams, you might be free to pursue them as he felt he could not himself all those years ago. But it was too late. He died before he could trace you.

I didn't learn all this until he was on his deathbed. After he died, I took up the search and found you. I want you to have what little in life I have accumulated, including the family jewels I inherited. You mustn't feel you have to give them up. They rightfully belong to you. My nephew's family received their share from his father, who was my brother.

May your days be filled with love and peace, my dearest niece. (It feels so wonderful to be able to say those words.) I hope you achieve all the wishes of your heart.

With love,
Aunt Anne

When Tina finished, she held the letter against her chest and stared out the windows at the mountains for long, long minutes, too stunned to think.

She read it again.

Her father was Anne's nephew, John Franklin Snyder. That meant Ronda was…oh, God, her half sister!

And *she* was aunt to Jonathan, Shane's nephew!

She wanted to laugh or cry hysterically, but she'd learned long ago to control her emotions and show nothing to the world.

Later, she knew, it would catch up with her, when she was alone and no one could see. Then she'd tremble until the emotions were spent. She read the letter through once more, then folded it and put it in her purse. She stood and left the room.

Jack was on the telephone when she returned to his

office. He finished and hung up. "Any questions?" he asked.

She shook her head. "It all becomes clear," she intoned with a faint smile. "Hard to believe, but clear."

"Anne was so afraid of hurting you."

"She didn't. I'm glad to know. I assume you know what was in the letter?"

"Not exactly, but I saw a picture of Anne's mother once. You look very much like her. I put two and two together. John Snyder was my father's friend." Jack glanced at her.

"He was my father."

"I thought so."

She sighed. "I don't know where to go from here. Home, I suppose, to think things over...figure out what I'll do."

"Some advice?" he asked. When she nodded, he said, "Don't do anything. Leave things the way they are."

"Keep the jewels and the house?"

"Yes. They're yours."

"I don't know." She rubbed her forehead as weariness descended. There were too many things to think about. "I'm not sure what's right...."

"Well, one thing's for sure—Ronda doesn't lack for material possessions," he said dryly. "Let things stand, at least for now. Stay for the year as you'd planned. Anne deserves that much. She thought the world of you."

Tina fought the press of tears. "I know. I loved her, too." She rose. "Well, thanks for seeing me on such short notice. I didn't know who else to call about the situation."

"I'm sure Shane would advise you to do the same," the attorney told her with a smile.

It seemed everyone in Medford, as well as Riverton, knew of her involvement with Shane.

"By the way, I think you should get those jewel cases into a safety deposit box right away. Don't leave them at the house."

"I will. Thank you for your help." She folded the letter and put it in her purse along with the jewel cases.

He laid Anne's folder on his desk. "This can go into the archives as a closed file," he said with obvious satisfaction.

On the way home—after putting the jewels in the bank as advised—she thought over his words. It might be a closed file for him, but Anne's letter had opened up serious questions for her.

She'd been uncertain about her rights to keep the house when she'd learned there was a living relative. With the discovery of the jewels, she'd been positive she should return everything. But now...well, she just didn't know.

John Franklin Snyder. Bettina J. Snyder. A rush of disloyalty toward her adoptive father came over her. He was the father of her heart, but to know her real father— her biological father—and to know she had relatives...

Anne, her aunt! It was almost more than she could take in. However, she also had Ronda as a half sister. She grimaced.

Her half sister in Portland was wonderful. Tina had been present when Lucy was born and felt a special love for her little sister, who was now eighteen and a freshman in college.

A horn beeped impatiently behind her. She jumped, then realized the light had turned green. She went through the intersection and stopped at the second traffic light.

Her gaze went to the sheriff's office. To her consternation, Shane came out just then. He was talking to another officer. Maybe he wouldn't see her.

No such luck. He walked to his truck and glanced toward the vehicles at the light. His eyes met hers.

For an eternity, they gazed at each other. Neither smiled. The same horn sounded again. Tina looked at the light. She tromped on the pedal and drove off.

In another minute, she was home. She went into the sun room from the garage, hung up her coat in the hall, then went to the kitchen. She made coffee, more as a reflex than because she wanted any.

When she sat at the table, cup in hand, she watched the river for a long time, her mind carefully blank. She closed her eyes as a picture of Shane came to her. She wanted to go to him, thrust the letter under his nose and say, "See, I belong here as much as you, as much as anyone. I have a right to an inheritance."

"I have a right," she murmured aloud. But it was one she'd never tell anyone about, she realized. What would be the use? It would only stir up old gossip better left buried.

She wondered if she should call her mother and tell her. But her mother already knew the circumstances of her birth. It might hurt too much to have the past opened again.

Tina remembered how poor they had been, how hard her mother had struggled to learn shorthand at night school so she could move up to secretary from clerk-typist. Finally, she'd gotten a degree in business and had gone into personnel management.

She and her mother had been close during those years of struggle. Never had her mother made her feel she was an unwanted child. Then there had been her wonderful stepfather, who'd claimed her along with her mother.

Ronda had been brought up in wealth, but what had life been like for her in a loveless household?

Tina couldn't help but think she'd had the better deal. For now, she decided, she'd accept Anne's gifts for what they were—symbols of the deep affection and kindness the older woman had felt toward her. The rest of the past would stay closed, just like Jack Norton's file.

She sighed and went to call Dolly at the newspaper office, to tell her she would be well enough to work the next day.

"Well, you're looking better than you did Friday, in spite of your dip in the river," Dolly greeted her on Tuesday morning when she arrived at the office, ready for work.

Tina breathed in the scent of stale coffee, musty paper and dusty equipment. It felt like home. She thought she might talk to Dolly and Clint about a permanent job. Perhaps a part-time position while she worked on her book.

"It's good to be back," she said, patting at a yawn. "What's on the agenda today?"

"A day in the life of Sheriff Macklin," Dolly reminded her. "The follow-up to the rescue story, remember? Be sure and get an update on Jonathan. He's still in the hospital. Did he catch pneumonia or something?"

Tina realized the community at large didn't know of the boy's illness. Shane had told her, but no one else. "No. I'll check it out," she said. She wouldn't betray his confidence. If the family wanted the news known, they'd have to tell it.

One thing she knew how to be—a professional. No matter how she'd felt, she'd covered her news stories the best she could…no matter how she might react afterward. She'd do the same here.

Going to her desk, she settled at it and picked up the phone. "This is Tina Henderson at the *Daily News*. I'd like to speak to Sheriff Macklin, please."

"I'll transfer you to his office."

"Thank you." She clenched the telephone in a panicky grip. She hadn't expected him to be in.

"Macklin," he said in a throaty baritone growl.

"Shane, this is Tina. Dolly has asked me to do a story on you as sheriff. I'd like to follow you around this week—"

"I'm doing mostly paperwork. It isn't very exciting."

"Oh. Are you refusing then?"

There was a lengthy pause.

"Of course not," he said. "The sheriff's office is always glad to cooperate with the media. Tell me what you want to do." He had changed to the smooth politician.

"How about lunch? My treat. I'll interview you on background—how you got to be sheriff and all that."

"I was appointed by the county commission."

"I'll get it all down at lunch. Shall we meet at…" She didn't want to go to the tea shop or the ski lodge, where they might be joined by friends. "Land's End down by the river?"

"Fine. What time?"

"One-thirty, after the crowd thins out?"

"Good. I'll see you then." He hung up.

Tina replaced the receiver and huffed a sigh of relief. She could handle this, she assured her quaking heart. What did it matter what the Mighty Macklin thought of her? She was strong. She was tough. She could do it.

She wished she didn't have to.

* * *

He was late. Tina looked at her watch. If he stood her up... No, there he was, coming down the street. Like her, he'd opted to walk the short block to the posh river restaurant. It was so pleasant out, a person didn't need a coat. The spring day was warm with sunshine, the air clear after the recent rains.

As she'd expected, the dining room was filled mostly with tourists and businessmen on expense accounts. This should be on the paper's account, but she'd decided she would absorb the cost, since she'd chosen the most expensive place in town.

She watched him come closer, his long, confident stride covering the ground effortlessly. He wore a formidable frown.

A dart of pain arced through her. She ignored it. She wasn't going to let Shane's opinion bother her. Lifting her chin, she prepared to meet him...her lover, her enemy...with equanimity.

He spotted her by the window. When he entered the restaurant, he came immediately to the table. She smiled coolly when his eyes met hers. His narrowed slightly, then relaxed.

"Sorry, I got tied up at the last minute," he said.

"No problem."

He took the chair opposite her and laid his hat on the one next to him. She noticed he hadn't worn his gun or two-way radio. Only a pager was clipped to his belt.

They studied the menus, then ordered. When he chose coffee, she did the same, although she thought of ordering a bottle of wine to see if she couldn't get him to loosen up and talk freely.

Ha, that would be the day! Shane would say exactly what he wanted her to know—no more, no less.

"Fire away," he invited when they were alone. His

tone was neutral, but she detected the underlying anger. He was convinced beyond a shadow of a doubt that she was a fortune hunter who'd managed the ultimate scam.

"What made you decide to seek the office of sheriff?" she asked, getting her notebook out. She put a tiny tape recorder on the table between them. "Do you mind the recorder?" she inquired automatically. No one ever did.

"Yes."

She was taken aback. She met his hard gaze with a glare of her own. He didn't blink. She gritted her teeth, shut the machine off and stuck it back in her purse. "The sheriff's office," she said to remind him of the question.

"I didn't seek it. They came to me."

"Who?" she asked.

"The county commission."

"What were their reasons?"

"They said I was known for my integrity."

"Are you?" She leveled a challenging glance at him. "Do you consider yourself an honorable person?"

His chest lifted in a slow, deliberate breath, as if he wanted her to know he was controlling his temper with an effort. "Yes."

"A lawman of few words," she mocked.

One way to break a difficult interview open was to make the person angry. Another was to ask an easy question that had nothing to do with the topic at hand. Barbara Walters's tactic was to ask, "What's your favorite color?" Tina liked to go for anger.

He raised one dark eyebrow. A sardonic smile appeared at the corners of his mouth. He didn't reply.

The stubbornness that had gotten her through more than one tough situation in life reared its head. She was going to get information from him or die trying.

"What's the hardest part of your job?"

His smile widened. "Dealing with the press."

She glanced at her notepad. "Touché," she said softly. She'd heard complaints about the press from those in the public eye on many other occasions.

He inclined his head, acknowledging her concession of a point to him in their ongoing battle.

All's fair in... She broke off the thought without completing it. There was no love between them.

She continued to look at him, captured by the deep blue of his eyes, the hard, sculptured planes of his face, the softer cast of his lips. She wished things could be different....

So did the rest of the world, she mocked.

His expression subtly altered, becoming introspective as he studied her. She saw the hunger deep inside him, a longing that matched hers, she realized. It came to her that he was a lonely man in spite of having family and friends all around him.

Everyone needed someone special, even the Mighty Macklin.

"Why haven't you married?" she asked.

He blinked. She'd taken him by surprise with that question. Score one for my side, she thought, briefly triumphant.

"No one ever asked me."

She bit back the anger. He was determined not to give her a damned thing she could use. "Why did you take the job of sheriff?"

He became serious. "I felt an obligation to the town. The former sheriff had been indicted for graft, along with malfeasance, misfeasance and nonfeasance of office. He'd given his friends jobs in high places. He was blackmailing one of the commissioners. The town needed cleaning up."

"Ah, yes," she murmured, "The Mighty Macklin to the rescue."

He stood. "I don't have time to take a lot of crap right now. Unlike my predecessor, I try to do the job. If you want to see what I do, then come to the office at seven in the morning and we'll start. You can spend the entire day learning the sheriff's duties." He picked up his hat and walked out.

Tina sat there, silently furious…with him and with herself. She had been baiting him, she admitted, but on a personal level rather than a professional one. She could do better.

She smiled grimly. When the story was finished, she'd tell him she'd been walked out on by heads of states. It didn't bother her at all. She dropped enough money on the table to pay for the two uneaten meals and headed back to the office. She'd do some digging in the old files.

Tina saw there was one other person in the tea shop when she stopped by late that evening, ravenous after having had no lunch or dinner. "Hello, Mrs. Tall," she said after speaking to Bess.

Mrs. Tall looked delighted to see her. "Come join me," she invited, moving her knitting from the other chair at her table.

Tina walked over slowly. She didn't want to hurt her nosy neighbor's feelings, but she didn't feel like talking.

"Isn't the sunshine nice? My hip bothers me in rainy weather, so it's good to see the sun." Mrs. Tall's chatter filled the silence while Tina took the chair.

"Yes," she agreed. She ordered a sandwich and helped herself to French roast coffee.

When the shop owner answered the telephone in an office off the main room, Mrs. Tall confided, "Bess is doing right well here. Surprised us all, she did. She just opened the tea shop without asking anyone how to do it. Her husband probably turned over in his grave more than once, watching her spend their life savings that way.''

"Would you like your coffee warmed?" Tina asked politely. When Mrs. Tall nodded, she refilled the cup and returned the pot to the counter. "Do you take anything in yours?"

"Just a little sugar," the woman said. "I've learned to do without cream since it's supposed to be bad for a person. My father had cream, *real* cream, with his coffee every day of his life, and he ate two eggs and sausage for breakfast every morning. Lived to be ninety-three, he did."

"Makes you wonder if we're living right, doesn't it?" Tina said in sympathy. She joined the older woman at the table, and laid several packages of sugar in the middle.

"It does," Mrs. Tall agreed. Her soft, fluffy white curls bounced up and down as she nodded. "That was a good piece you did on the school administration staff decorating their offices with money that was supposed to buy textbooks. Huh, ten thousand dollars for a bronze horse! Mighty fancy decorations for a small town, it seems to me. How did you happen to catch on to it?"

"I recognized the name of the artist and knew the prices he gets for his pieces," Tina explained patiently. "I'm working on a story about Shane Macklin now. 'A Day in the Life of the Sheriff' is what it'll be called. Tomorrow I'll spend the day with him."

"That sounds nice."

"Right now I'm gathering information about him. I saw in the old newspaper files that he was president of his class in high school and in college."

"Yes, I believe he was. He was good in sports, too. We used to never miss a game until my arthritis got to acting up. I can't sit on those hard benches anymore, don't you see?"

Tina nodded in sympathy. Bess brought her sandwich, then bustled off to put a batch of cinnamon rolls in the oven.

After a moment of silence, Mrs. Tall started talking again. She related incidents of Shane's past. He'd fallen in the river once when he was a kid, she said.

Like uncle, like nephew, Tina thought with a tenderness she didn't want to feel. She would use the information in her article.

"That stepmother." Mrs. Tall shook her head in disgust. She ate the rest of her pastry. "Well, there's no fool like an old fool, they say. I guess it proved true for Johnny Macklin. I thought he had better sense."

She related the gossip about the stepmother and her demands on the family. Tina felt slightly guilty for gathering old gossip on Shane, but defended it as being part of her job.

"I saw her myself, hanging onto Shane and trying to kiss him one day down by the pear-sorting shed. Poor boy, he couldn't get away fast enough." Mrs. Tall grinned, reminding Tina of a jolly old elf with a mischievous bent. "Not the way it was with you two that day over by the river...the summer you stayed with Anne," she added, as if Tina might have forgotten.

Tina hadn't realized anyone had seen them. Heat flowed up her neck to her ears. "Oh," she said faintly.

"I'm glad you're getting back together again. I don't think he ever forgot you. Although," Mrs. Tall added truthfully, "I did think there was a woman over in Medford who was going to get him to the altar, but they broke up two or three years ago."

"He's had no serious relationships since then?"

Mrs. Tall shook her head. "He hasn't time, what with taking care of the town and refereeing the fights between his brother and that Snyder girl from Medford. Uppity, she is, don't you know?"

"Umm," Tina said noncommittally.

"Isn't it terrible about the boy?"

"Jonathan?"

"That's right. Milly Smith over at the hospital says he's real sick. Leukemia, it is. The doctors don't give him more than six months."

Tina gasped. "Are you sure?"

"Yes, some fancy doctor gave the word yesterday, according to Milly. She's head of the children's ward, so she would know."

Tina set her coffee cup down. She'd been so awful to Shane at lunch. She remembered how grieved he'd been the other night at her house, when he'd told her they suspected the disease. She'd held him against her breast, wanting to comfort him.

She wanted to hold him now. She wanted to be held. Jonathan was her nephew, too, a bright, laughing child with the confidence of spirit that his uncle had. The world would be a lesser place if that spirit were snuffed out.

Mrs. Tall continued to talk, relating tales of other tragedies concerning children that had happened over the years in the area.

Tina hardly listened. She was restless. She needed to walk and think. Staring out the window, she felt pity for Shane and Ty, and for Ronda. For all their money, life hadn't been particularly happy for any of them, it seemed, and now this....

It was another thirty minutes before Mrs. Tall left. She was going to the store to stay with her husband while he closed up.

Tina paid for her meal, slipped into her jacket and headed for the river park. She walked along the trail, her thoughts and emotions in turmoil.

There was a terrible compulsion inside her, a desire to go to Shane and apologize. And, she admitted, she simply wanted to be there for him if he needed someone.

Upon nearing her place a bit later, she saw his truck on the drive to his house. The house itself was dark.

By contrast, her house—where a lamp came on automatically at dusk—looked bright and welcoming in the deepening twilight. She leapt over the fence and went to one of the boulders that lined the river. She sat there and watched the last golden light fade from the sunset.

When she glanced across the river, she started. A tall masculine figure stood on the other side.

His eyes met hers, and for a moment she saw the stark need in him. Then it was gone. He turned and walked up the knoll to his large, empty house.

She sat there until the night wind chilled her, forcing her to go inside. If he'd come to her, she wouldn't have refused to take him in.

Chapter Thirteen

To Tina's surprise, Shane wasn't in uniform when she arrived at his office promptly at seven. In fact, he looked very much the successful tycoon in a blue pin-striped suit.

"I'll be with you in a minute," he said. "There's coffee and bagels on the table. Help yourself."

He picked up the telephone, punched a button where a call was on hold and spoke for several minutes to the mayor of Medford about a patrol for an upcoming event at the county fairgrounds.

"I can put on five extra men if you can pick up the cost," he told the man.

Tina prepared a cup of coffee, then sat quietly as Shane and the mayor worked out the details of their problem. She noted that the lines on Shane's face seemed deeper. He looked tired.

She pulled her gaze away and hardened her heart. She

wouldn't be swayed by pity. She, too, was worried about Jonathan.

Blowing gently at the steam rising from the coffee, she marveled again at her own kinship to the child. It wasn't until she'd learned about her father's family that she realized how much she'd missed that connection to her past.

She glanced at Shane, then away, as he concluded his conversation with the mayor. "Ready?" he asked, standing.

"Yes. For what?" She rose, notepad and pen in hand.

"Staff meeting. After that, the schedule for next month, then we go to the resort for the Chamber of Commerce luncheon."

"A busy day," she remarked wryly. She glanced down at her outfit. She wore black slacks with a gold silk blouse and a gold cardigan. Her black loafers were rather informal.

"You look okay," Shane assured her.

His gaze slid over her like a heat wave. She felt flushed and nervous all at once. "Good."

She sat through the meeting, faithfully jotting down the problems and noting Shane's efficient handling of details. What surprised her was his skill with the staff who reported to him.

He was patient, understanding and very clear in what he expected from each individual. He treated failure as a problem to be solved, not as a chance to place blame. She was impressed.

Later, when she sat through the review of the next month's schedule, she noted he made sure each request for specific time off by his deputies was honored.

While he was on the telephone, returning calls before they went to lunch, her mind drifted into its own musing.

She wondered why he gave everyone but her the benefit of the doubt. He'd been wonderfully understanding of his staff. Why did he regard her every move with suspicion?

"Ready for lunch?" he asked, putting the phone down.

She focused on the present. "Yes."

"Are you getting enough information?" He held the door open for her. They went out to the patrol truck.

"Yes." She settled in the seat while he closed the door and went around to his side. In a minute, they were on the road to the ski lodge. "You're very good with the people under your command," she commented.

"Am I?" He sounded skeptical.

"Yes."

They rode in silence for a while. It wasn't until they were pulling into the resort parking lot that he spoke again. "You're different today. Quieter."

He turned the engine off, removed the keys, then studied her for a long minute. She looked at him without speaking.

"I expected anger and that little mocking smile you wear when you're hurt, but instead you've become... quiet. It's unnerving." He shook his head, then gave a snort of laughter. "I've been trying to figure you out since you returned, but what man ever understands a woman?" he asked philosophically.

"Why would you want to?" she returned in the same vein. She opened the door and jumped to the ground.

They went into the lodge and upstairs to the private dining room. Her arm burned where he held her, guiding her through the throng of merchants to a table. They joined Whitney Deveraux and Rafe Barrett, plus several others. She recognized her neighbor.

"Well," Mr. Tall commented, "looks like there's a

twosome here. Those wedding bells going to be ringing soon?''

"One never knows," Shane replied smoothly.

Tina gritted her teeth and smiled perfunctorily. She and her involvement with Shane would always be a subject of speculation in Riverton. Gossip could drag on for years in a small town. She knew that from personal experience.

She'd stay for a year—just to show people she couldn't be run off—then she'd sell out and leave, she decided. That would give her time to finish the book and seek a new direction.

With that decision made, she sat back and listened to the flow of conversation about her, feeling isolated, an island that nothing could touch. Life was better this way, she'd found.

Once, when Shane sent her a curious glance, she smiled in her old manner—defiant, a tad mocking, revealing nothing.

"Keeping up with the latest in medicine is the hardest," Dr. Payne admitted. "It's difficult for a regular physician to evaluate new procedures. Some are no better than the old methods. Some are worse. There are fads in medicine just as there are in everything else."

"I see." Tina brushed a strand of hair away from her face. She was tired. She'd been up almost all night while the harried doctor had handled two emergencies, one involving surgery at three that morning. He'd let her observe the operation.

Today was the last day she would follow the family doctor on his myriad rounds. She had to get the final copy ready tomorrow for the paper on Friday.

She had successfully written up the sheriff's ''day'' last week, and Dolly was ecstatic over the comments from local citizens on the story. This week Tina was doing the doctor, since the mayor was out of town at a convention.

Dr. Payne put the patient's folder on his desk and sat back with his fingers linked behind his head. He looked weary, as if his soul were burdened by the hurts of others.

"The Macklin case," he murmured.

Her heart speeded up. "How is Jonathan?"

He shook his head. "Not good. He's on chemotherapy. The specialist wants him transferred from the local hospital to Seattle while they try to find a bone-marrow donor."

"A donor?" she repeated. "What about his family? I thought there had to be a strong genetic link."

"That's where we looked first, but none of his immediate kin has the same blood factors."

"Was Shane tested?"

"Yes, but he's A negative. Jonathan is O negative—the universal donor—which means he can accept blood only from other O negatives." The doctor rubbed his eyes, then yawned.

Little bolts of current shot along her nerves as Tina digested the news. She was also O negative, having neither the A, B, nor the Rh factor in her blood. She and Jonathan were the same. There was a possibility, a strong possibility, that she and the child were compatible.

"I'm O negative," she said.

The doctor dropped his hands to the arms of the chair and looked at her with interest. "There's a slim chance," he mused aloud. "You might be a match. Would you volunteer to be a donor if you were?"

"Yes," she said without hesitation.

"It can be painful," he warned. "Any intrusive procedure, any time a person goes under anesthesia, has a potential—''

''It doesn't matter,'' she interrupted. ''A child's life is at stake. Even if he weren't…'' She stopped before she revealed her connection to Jonathan. ''Children have hard lives in many ways,'' she said when Dr. Payne gave her a thoughtful scrutiny. ''If I can help one child to a happier future, then I want to do it.''

''We'll have to move fast,'' he told her. ''Jonathan's illness is of a particularly virulent form. When could you be ready if you pass the test?''

''I'm ready now.''

''All your…affairs in order?''

She smiled at the delicate phrasing. ''Yes. I have no dependents, no responsibility to anyone but myself. I'll let my parents know, of course. My will is already made, if that's what you're asking,'' she assured him with a wry smile.

He smiled, too. ''Well, let's set up a schedule.''

Tina wrote her feature articles during the next few weeks. She helped get the paper out each Friday. The rest of the time she walked for miles, too restless to stay still while waiting for the results of the many tests being done on her and Jonathan.

Monday, a month after the tests began, they would know the results. Dr. Payne had called to tell her that last Friday.

The doctor had told her the procedure was simple for Jonathan. He would receive an injection of cells. The marrow cells would migrate to his own bone marrow, where they belonged, and start making good cells for Jonathan. If all went well, he would be cured.

Simple, she thought. As simple as life and death. She

waited by the telephone Monday morning. When it rang, she jumped, almost afraid to pick it up, afraid she wasn't a match....

"Hello?"

"You're it," Dr. Payne said in an elated voice. "An almost perfect match. It couldn't be closer if you were his twin."

Relief rushed through her. "Thank God," she breathed. "When do we do the transplant?"

"Can you report in to the hospital Thursday?"

"Yes."

She made the arrangements with the doctor, then picked up her purse and headed downtown. She had to talk to Clint and Dolly. She had an idea she thought she could handle in the short week. Whitney Deveraux's bed-and-breakfast would make an interesting article.

After she explained her plan, the newspaper couple agreed wholeheartedly. "Here's another feature," Dolly exclaimed. "You donating bone marrow to Jonathan, saving him twice—"

"No, please, I'd rather the news not get out," Tina protested. "It's a private thing."

"Now, now. Don't be so modest. It isn't often we get one heroine, much less two...or rather, one who's a heroine twice." She cast an appealing eye at her husband. "Help me out."

"Dolly's right. This isn't news that you're going to be able to hide. All the wire services will pick it up. Give us an exclusive and that will save you from the rest." Clint grinned.

Tina knew when to give in gracefully. "Okay, but can't it wait until we know whether the transplant is a success?"

"The TV people will want it on the news tomorrow

night. It might be better if you have an official spokesman to feed them details, such as the surgeon. Or Shane. He could handle it,'' Dolly suggested.

Shane paced the narrow corridor in front of the double swinging doors where he wasn't allowed to enter, not even as sheriff. Only doctors, nurses and hospital staff could go into the inner sanctum of the operating wing. Today was the big day.

They had found a donor for Jonathan. An anonymous donor.

It worried him that he didn't know who the person was. He'd wanted to run a thorough check to make sure the donor wasn't a drug addict or something like that.

Old Doc Payne had laughed and assured him that wasn't the case. The physician, who'd been doctor to both Shane and Ty since they'd been born, had screened the person, he'd told Shane. He'd said he knew her personally.

Her. A female. Shane wondered who it was and how the doctor had found her on such short notice. He had a gut feeling....

A nearby door opened and his sister-in-law came out into the hallway. ''Let's get some coffee,'' she said irritably.

The strain of hospital life was showing on her, Shane noted. Ronda didn't handle crises well. In fact, she'd been a bitch, at times demanding more sympathy than she deserved. After all, it was the child who was ill.

They walked down the hall toward the coffee machine set up in a small room next to the nurses' station. The surgeon and Dr. Payne stood in the doorway of the room. They were talking to someone he couldn't see.

''We'll keep you overnight for observation. The marrow is taken from the hip. You'll be sore for a few days. You understand the risks?'' the surgeon asked.

''Yes, Dr. Payne spelled them out,'' a familiar voice said.

''What the hell is going on?'' Shane demanded.

The two doctors turned and looked at him in surprise. Beyond them, he saw a small, dark-haired woman.

''No,'' Ronda said, pushing past him. ''Not her. I won't allow it.'' She grabbed Dr. Payne's sleeve and shook it furiously. ''Is she the donor for Jonathan? She can't be! We have to find someone else, someone more suitable.''

Shane put a hand on Ronda's shoulder. ''Easy,'' he cautioned. He felt as stunned as his sister-in-law. However, he wasn't angry, only perplexed. ''Is she the donor?'' he asked.

Dr. Payne nodded. The surgeon looked annoyed.

''How?'' Shane asked, unable to accept the fact that the woman who haunted his nights was again coming to his nephew's rescue. ''I mean, is she really that close?''

''She was tested for six blood-antigen factors. She and Jonathan are compatible on all of them,'' Dr. Payne explained.

''No,'' Ronda insisted. ''I don't believe you.''

A page sounded. The surgeon walked off a few paces. ''I'm due in surgery. I'd appreciate it if you'd solve this problem and let me know the outcome. I'll be ready for Miss Henderson right after lunch.'' He walked toward the swinging doors.

Ronda turned on the other woman. ''You're not wanted here. No one wants you. My father didn't want you or your mother when you were born. No one wants you now. We'll find someone else.''

Shane felt as if the blood had drained from his body.

He knew the circumstances of Tina's birth. He'd checked her out eleven years ago when she'd had Ty in her clutches.

Now the truth hit him. Tina was the illegitimate daughter of John Franklin Snyder. Half sister to Ronda. Aunt to Jonathan.

Looking at her still form, her white face, he realized she knew. He thought of all the things he'd said to her, accused her of, and felt a sickening wrench of guilt inside.

When Ronda made a move toward Tina, he grabbed her arms, not sure of her intent. Tina turned whiter, if possible.

"I'll be in the waiting room when you're ready for me," she said quietly to the doctor as she walked past them, disappearing into a room down the corridor.

Shane noticed several nurses staring at them. This would be all over town before nightfall.

"The match is perfect," Dr. Payne said coldly. "Your son's life depends on Miss Henderson. I'd suggest you treat her with more respect. She doesn't have to do this. She volunteered."

He, too, walked off and left them. Shane pushed Ronda into the coffee room. "How long have you known Tina was your sister?" he asked, fury mounting in him.

"She isn't," Ronda cried. "The detective lied to my father, saying he'd found the long-lost child. I destroyed the report. No one could have known. But Aunt Anne found out—" She broke off her hysterical tirade and stared at him.

The hatred in Ronda's voice chilled Shane. Things fell into place. He realized Ronda had known of Tina, of her father's desire to find his lost daughter, and had destroyed the evidence. Anne had somehow found out and be-friended the girl.

Tina...Anne's niece. Ronda's half sister. Jonathan's aunt.

The perfect match for the child's needs. The perfect match for anyone....

"You got everything from your father," he said slowly. "She got nothing, because of you."

Ronda threw herself against his chest, her tears wetting his shirtfront. "I had to do it. I couldn't have her here. It would have been a disgrace. He wanted to give half... *half!*...of everything to a—a bastard."

Shane felt an acute dislike for her, this selfish, conniving woman who put her jealousy and hatred ahead of her son's life. He pushed her away. "Control yourself," he snapped. "You have a sick child. Try to think of him for once."

"Well, well," Ty said, "hasn't it been written—that you can fool all the people some of the time, and some of the people all the time, but..." He let the words trail off.

Shane met his brother's eyes. They exchanged a glance so full of understanding it nearly made him weep. He'd blamed Ty for a lot of things that might not have been his fault, at least not entirely. It took two to make a marriage.

He swallowed hard as he thought of his own failures. He'd blamed Tina for things that hadn't been her fault. He'd cast her in the same mold as his stepmother that summer they'd met, and, in spite of evidence to the contrary, he'd kept her there upon her return to the area, afraid to believe the prompting of his heart.

A hard pain hit him in the middle of his chest. He had

to talk to her. "Excuse me," he said as he hurried down the hall.

She was gone.

He searched the corridors and the main lobby, but Tina wasn't in any of them. He returned to the nurses' station. He found out she had been admitted and was in her room. She'd requested that no visitors be permitted.

"It's important that she doesn't get upset, Shane," the head nurse told him sternly. "She has surgery at one."

"Will you let me know the moment she's back in her room?"

The woman softened toward him. "Of course."

He returned to the waiting room. The noon hour crept by. Ty joined him while Ronda sat with Jonathan. Another hour crept past. It was almost two o'clock when an alarm sounded over the hospital paging system.

He and Ty leapt to their feet and stood in the doorway while several doctors and nurses ran for the double doors and disappeared inside. The surgeon they'd met earlier came down the hall, stripping out of his white coat as he went. A nurse met him at the swinging doors and started filling him in. They, too, disappeared.

"It might not be her," Ty said, laying a hand in brief comfort on his brother's shoulder.

"Yeah," Shane agreed, but he knew something was wrong.

"You're in love with her," Ty continued after a moment.

There was nothing to say to this.

"She loves you, too. She did from the first. I asked her to elope, but she turned me down. After she saw you—"

"I hurt her," Shane said, doubling his fist and bringing it down quietly against the wall. "I doubted her. Every time there was a chance for us, I blew it by doubting her.''

"So?'' Ty challenged. "When has a Macklin ever let a little setback stop him? You'll just have to convince her that you've seen the light.'' His smile was tinged with bitterness and resignation. "I wish I had it so good. You know there's going to be a divorce, don't you?''

Shane nodded. "I'm sorry, Ty, for not understanding sooner. I thought, because Ronda came from money and had money of her own, that she…well, I was wrong.''

Ty shrugged. "They're going to do the transfer later today if everything checks out okay. I think I'll go to lunch, then relieve Ronda with Jonathan.''

After his brother left, Shane paced the hall from the waiting room to the swinging doors. He glared at the No Admittance sign.

He knew something was wrong with Tina, knew it gut deep, the way a bird knows to fly south, the way a whale knows to migrate to its mating grounds. When he saw the surgeon come out in wrinkled green surgical clothes, he rushed to him.

"How is she?''

"You are?'' the man asked.

"Her fiancé,'' Shane replied in no-nonsense tones. A giggle behind him made him turn his head. Milly Smith, one of the nurses, had evidently heard his declaration. She gave him a big smile.

"She had a reaction to an injection, but she's resting now. She'll be fine.''

"Can I see her?'' He heard the desperation in his voice, but there was no help for it. He was desperate.

The doctor thought it over. "Yes. She'll be moved to Room 307 in about ten minutes.''

Shane hurried to the room. He saw it was ready for

her, the bed made, the water jug filled and her clothing neatly tucked into the closet. He hung his jacket and hat there. Then he waited.

Tina woke for the second time feeling like she'd been run over by a truck. No one had mentioned this terrible, aching soreness. Nausea swept over her, making her weak. She clamped a hand over her mouth and retched helplessly.

A basin appeared under her chin as if by magic. A soothing hand slipped behind her neck as she pushed upright.

She got a fleeting glimpse of Shane before she was wrenchingly sick. She fought illness and embarrassment in equal parts until the episode was over. Lying exhausted against the pillow, she flinched as a cool cloth was drawn over her face. She realized she wasn't in the recovery room this time, but in her room again.

"Rinse your mouth," a deep baritone suggested.

She sipped through a straw that touched her lips, then spat into the basin, which had been emptied.

"Would you like to try some soda?" Shane asked.

She shook her head. If she kept her eyes closed, maybe he would go away. Maybe this whole thing was a bad dream.

The cloth brushed gently over her face again, then stayed on her eyes. She lifted it so she could look at him.

As usual, he was incredibly handsome in gray flannel slacks and a red chamois shirt with a white T-shirt under it. His hair fell over his forehead in a thick, tawny wave.

"I told them I didn't want visitors," she said.

"I'm not a visitor," he murmured. He smoothed her hair back from her face.

She was weak and helpless, and she hated it. She was

going to cry in front of him again, and she couldn't bear it.

"Go away," she said, not sounding firm at all.

"Never."

She put the damp cloth back over her eyes so she wouldn't have to look at him...so he wouldn't see her cry. She breathed slowly and deeply until she was in control once more.

"Well, look at the lovebirds," a cheery voice exclaimed. A nurse bustled into the room, placing vases of flowers on the table and windowsill. "Look at these red roses! Aren't they the prettiest things you ever saw?"

She stuck a thermometer in Tina's mouth and took her pulse. Then she raised the bed so that Tina was sitting almost upright. "I have some broth heating for you. It'll make your tummy feel better. Are you nauseated?"

"She threw up," Shane answered.

Tina tossed him a glare. "I'd like to be alone," she told the friendly nurse, who looked capable of evicting Shane from the room.

"Don't worry about how you look. Shane thinks you're beautiful," Milly teased. "Here, you should read your cards. People from all over are sending cards and flowers to you and Jonathan. Clint Adams was on TV news at noon telling all about it. Here's the card from the roses."

Tina smiled faintly. Clint had appointed himself official spokesman, it seemed. She opened the envelope Milly had thrust into her hand. There were only two lines, both in a bold hand she instinctively knew was Shane's.

"Roses are red... I'll tell you the rest in person," the note said.

She tried to make sense of it. There were lots of endings to the old Valentine verse. "Roses are red, violets are blue,'' she said aloud. ''Get out of town, before I arrest you?''

It took an effort, but she managed to smile, a wry, mocking smile meant to throw Shane off balance.

The tiny indentation that she didn't dare call a dimple deepened in his cheek. He nodded.

''What's my crime?'' she demanded, insouciant to the end.

''Breaking and entering,'' he said in the strangest voice she'd ever heard from him. ''Stealing.''

She had to look at him then. When she did, her breath nearly stopped. He looked so solemn, so serious…so sad?

''Jonathan?'' she said in alarm.

''Shh, he's fine.'' He smoothed the hair from her temple. ''Rest now. I'll see what I can find out.''

She waited restlessly for his return. Milly brought the broth and stayed until Tina drank it down, then left.

Tina couldn't keep her gaze from straying to the tall vase of red roses. Red roses meant ''I love you'' in the language of flowers.

Her heart beat so hard it caused an ache in her chest. She pressed a hand to it and waited for Shane.

Ty came back with his older brother. He came to the bed and gathered her into his arms. He kissed her on the mouth, a closed-mouth kiss, but one full of tenderness and warmth.

''Ahem,'' Shane finally said.

Ty raised his head. ''Don't get jealous,'' he advised his brother. ''This is probably the last time I'll ever get to hold her. You know how I feel, don't you?'' he asked Tina.

She nodded and patted his lean jaw with deep affection.

''Words aren't enough to thank you for my son's life,''

he continued. "The doctor is pretty sure it's going to work. Jonathan isn't showing one adverse sign, not even a rise in temperature. It's like the bone marrow came from himself. Or a close relative." He paused. "Are you his aunt?"

"I...yes."

She and Ty talked while Shane stood by and listened. Under Ty's prodding, she told them the whole story, or what she knew of it from Anne's letters. She faltered when it came to disclosing that Ronda had destroyed the first report from the detective. She didn't want to tell Ty that.

"It's okay," he assured her. "I know about it. Ronda and I had a little talk while you were in surgery. The truth will out, as someone once said. In fact, it's all over town. Everyone in the hospital heard the little scene in the hall."

"Everyone knows about me—who my father was?"

He nodded. "Don't let it bother you," he advised. "None of it was your fault."

Tina sighed. A curtain of darkness settled over her soul. "I'll leave," she said. "It'll all blow over—"

"No," Shane cut in. "You won't leave."

He gave her such a fierce look, she forgot to tell him that he couldn't tell her what to do and instead wondered why he seemed so miserable.

Shane stayed with her the rest of the day. Clint came in to take some pictures of her smiling bravely from her hospital bed. He loved the fact that she'd had a reaction and nearly died...but didn't.

"What a story!" he said. "Dolly is thrilled."

"I didn't nearly die," she contradicted.

"You could have," Shane told her in a low growl.

As if he blamed her for staging the reaction just to

alarm everyone. She gave him a hard glance, then ignored him.

That night, when she fell asleep, he was still there.

The real problem started the next morning. When it came time for her to go home, Shane was there. So were several reporters and cameras. She resigned herself to being gracious.

Until they were in the car and on the way. When he passed the turnoff to her house, she protested. "I want to go home," she said.

"You are," he said calmly, ignoring her anger as he turned into his driveway. "Mrs. Perkins is back. She'll take care of you until you're feeling better."

"I hate you," she said, her voice quavery.

"I know." He stopped the car and looked at her quietly. "I know."

Chapter Fourteen

Mrs. Perkins was angry with her.

Tina watched the housekeeper move about the bedroom, dusting the furniture and picking up the newspapers on the floor.

The mess wasn't hers, but Shane's. He'd had breakfast with her each morning for the four days she'd been imprisoned there.

Mrs. Perkins disapproved of Tina's coolness to the mighty Macklin. She also thought Tina was an ingrate for wanting to go to her own home.

When the other woman left the room, Tina grimaced and forced herself out of bed. Her body still felt like it had been run over by a truck.

She showered and dried off, then wrapped the towel around her and returned to the bedroom—a guest room this time.

Memories of that other visit stuck in her mind. She

vividly recalled sleeping next to Shane, her body tucked close to his. Worse, she remembered every caress they'd shared during that time.

Dropping the towel, she pulled on her clothing. It still hurt her hip when she bent forward or put any weight on her right leg.

A knock sounded on the door, then Shane entered. He looked her over in a quick survey that left her feeling warm and filled with yearning. "You seem to be better," he said.

She licked her lips nervously. Her hands trembled as she buttoned the blouse she'd worn to the hospital and hadn't had on since. "I am." She took her courage in her hands. "I'd like to go home...today...now."

Lifting her chin, she looked at him resolutely.

He nodded.

Her mouth dropped open in surprise.

A smile touched the corners of his mouth, then was gone. She watched him curiously. Since leaving the hospital, he'd been very quiet, sort of...sad. There seemed to be a mocking bitterness in him, directed at himself or life or something, but not at her.

She didn't understand him at all.

"Jonathan sent you a message," Shane told her. "He says he feels much better already and is glad that you're his aunt."

She nodded. "Dr. Payne called earlier. He says it looks good so far. I'm glad for Jonathan. I hope...do you think Ronda would let me see him once in a while?"

"Ty will. He's going for joint custody."

She couldn't think of anything else to say. "Well, I'm ready," she said brightly, picking up her purse and retrieving her jacket from the closet. She glanced at him.

"Shane, what's wrong?" she asked. "Is there something you're not telling me?"

His smile was definitely sardonic. "I don't think it's anything you'd want to hear."

She sat in one of the comfortable chairs by the window, placed her purse and coat on the table and invited, "Try me."

He walked toward her slowly. Fear crawled through her. She couldn't begin to imagine what awful thing he was going to tell her.

He dropped to the floor and sat at her feet, startling her into drawing back. "Don't worry. I'm not going to touch you."

She leaned toward him. "What's wrong?"

"Me. I'm what's wrong."

"I don't understand." She couldn't bear for him to look so sad and sort of lost...and vulnerable. Something terrible must have happened to shake his confidence this way.

"I met a girl once," he murmured, almost as if talking to himself. "She was brave...and honest...and good. Only I didn't know it at the time. I got her confused with another woman, who had made my life miserable for a couple of years."

"Your stepmother," Tina guessed.

He nodded. "I was wrong about you eleven years ago. I was wrong about you when you returned. I looked at you and saw someone after the main chance. I couldn't figure out how you'd wheedled the house and jewelry from a sharp old gal like Anne. I was wrong," he ended. He looked at her.

Something that had been closed and hard within her softened at his admission. "I...that's all right. It doesn't matter now."

"Doesn't it?"

She couldn't bear the brief glimpse of misery she saw in his eyes before he sighed and shut it away. "Not to me," she said quickly. "Actually, I had a happy life, taken as a whole. I think I was luckier than Ronda. My parents loved each other. And they loved me. They still do."

"Everyone who knows you comes to love you," he said softly.

"Not everyone."

"Oh, yes, everyone. Including me. Only I was too busy being the Mighty Macklin to see it. It made me furious when you called me that. I thought I had to protect my family from you and keep Ty's marriage from falling apart." He shook his head. "Stupid, that's what it was."

"Shane..." She didn't know what to say. She wasn't sure what he was telling her.

"So I deserve your hatred. But I wish you felt the flip side of that coin." He paused and looked at her, letting her see inside him, into his soul.

She explored the depths of him. She felt the powerful forces of his emotions as he let her delve further and further into his heart. She felt dizzy, faint....

Fleeting impressions of hope bubbled within her. Yet she was afraid. She'd been wrong about them too often in the past.

"Shane?" She didn't know what she was asking.

He took her hand. Suddenly, he was pressing against her knees, opening a space for him between her thighs. His mouth was close to hers. He pressed her hand to his chest. She could feel the rapid beating of his heart.

"Shane?"

"Yes," he said. "Yes, to whatever you're asking. If

you want to know if I love you...I do. If you want to know if I want you to stay with me, to live with me, to marry me...I do.''

Tina wasn't sure if she could believe her ears.

Shane closed his eyes briefly, then looked directly into her eyes. ''Ty thinks you love me. If you do, then tell me. I need the words. I can't take anything for granted where you're concerned.''

She was enchanted. Any moment now, the fairy would wave her magic wand and Tina would wake up, the fairy tale over....

He sighed and let go of her hand. ''It's too late. I've destroyed anything we might have had—''

''No!'' She caught his hand and, following his lead, pressed it against her heart. ''No. I—I...''

The words were incredibly hard to say.

''I love you,'' he coaxed. ''Say it. Please.'' He looked so desperate.

''I—I love you.''

Before she could blink or smile or anything, she was caught up in a bear hug that nearly shut off her breath. Next, kisses rained over her face like a summer storm. Finally, she was lifted and planted firmly in his lap while he took her place in the chair.

''God, I never thought I'd hear those words from you,'' he whispered raggedly. He kissed her, passionately, possessively, as if he'd never let her go.

When he let her up for air, she stared at him.

''I love you,'' he told her. ''I think I have for years. I think Anne knew. She kept me informed of your whereabouts and let me read your letters. I wouldn't let myself believe in your kindness and affection for an old lady. I told myself you were probably trying to get something out of her.''

Tina gave him a reproving glance.

"I know. I was wrong, so wrong." He hugged her close, making her wince. "I'm sorry, darling. I want you so damned much, but I'll try to be patient until you're completely well. When can we be married?"

"Well, I need to tell my folks. And have you meet them," she said, still dazed. "I...why can't we make love now?"

"Do you want to?" His eyes blazed with desire.

"Oh, yes."

He looked at her for a long minute, then lifted her into his arms. She wrapped her arms around his neck. The light of love shone in his eyes. His step was light and confident. She smiled and snuggled against him.

This time...this time there would be no parting.

"Happy birthday to you, happy birthday to you..."

Tina smiled as the children sang the song to six-year-old Jonathan, who was taking a deep breath in preparation for blowing out his candles. He gave a huge *whoosh* and...made it.

Everyone cheered.

Across the lawn, her eyes met Ty's. He winked at her and made motions in the air with his hands, then pointed to her. She grinned and nodded.

He had outlined a pregnant female's figure, asking if she were expecting. She had replied in the affirmative. She'd seen Dr. Payne yesterday to have her suspicions confirmed. Now her favorite brother-in-law—as he'd entitled himself—laughed, clasped both hands in a victory signal, then loped off to bring Jonathan's surprise birthday present from the shed.

Shane wrapped an arm around Tina's waist and held her close. She leaned her head against him. He'd been ecstatic at the news and had made the most incredibly tender love to her.

"Tired?" he asked.

"A little."

"We'll take a nap after the surprise is over."

Ty returned while Mrs. Perkins was cutting the cake and dishing up the ice cream. He led a brown-and-white spotted pony by a halter.

"My horse!" Jonathan screeched at the top of his lungs.

He was doing well in spirit and body, she thought. There were no signs of the leukemia a year and a half after the injection of the marrow cells. He lived with Ty and attended the local school. His mother lived in New York and traveled extensively with her new, very rich husband. Jonathan spent vacations with her for short periods. It seemed his new stepfather had little patience with children. The little boy took the arrangements well.

"Look, Aunt Tina, look!" he called. "I told you! I told you I'd get a horse when I was six!"

"I remember. He's a beauty." She watched as Ty lifted his son into the saddle. Jonathan took the reins and clicked his tongue, not at all afraid. The Macklin confidence.

She laid a hand over her abdomen, thinking of the child she carried.

Shane's hand covered hers. "Life is good," he said, surprising her with the husky emotion in his voice. "Life is good."

"Yes," she said. "It is."

* * * * *

The Cougar

LINDSAY McKENNA

LINDSAY McKENNA

is a practising homoeopath and emergency medical technician on the Navajo Reservation in Arizona. She comes from an Eastern Cherokee medicine family and is a member of the Wolf Clan. Dividing her energies between alternative medicine and writing, she feels books on and about love are the greatest positive healing force in the world. She lives with her husband, David, at La Casa de Madre Tierra, near Sedona.

To my cyberfriends:
Melissa Weaver, Carla Rowan,
Maria Theresa Bohle and Carol B Willis.

Chapter One

"This wasn't a very good idea, Rachel Donovan." The words rang out briefly in the interior of the brand-new car that Rachel was driving. Huge, fat snowflakes were falling faster and faster. It was early December. Why shouldn't it be snowing in Oak Creek Canyon, which lay just south of Flagstaff, near Sedona? Her fingers tightened around the steering wheel. Tiredness pulled at her. A nine-hour flight from London, and then another six hours to get to Denver, Colorado, was taking its toll on her. As a homeopathic practitioner, she was no stranger to the effects of sleep deprivation.

Rubbing her watering eyes, she decided that the Rachel of her youth, some thirty years ago, was at play this morning. Normally, she wasn't this spontaneous, but in her haste to see her sisters as soon as possible, she'd changed her travel plans. Instead of flying into Phoenix, renting a car and driving up to Sedona, she'd flown into Denver and taken a commuter flight to Flagstaff, which was only an hour away from her home, the Donovan Ranch.

Home… The word made her heart expand with warm feelings. Yes, she was coming home—for good. Her older sister, Kate, had asked Rachel and their younger sister, Jessica, to come home and help save the ranch, which was teetering on the edge of bankruptcy. A fierce kind of sweetness welled up through Rachel. She couldn't wait to be living on the ranch with her sisters once again.

Glancing at her watch, she saw it was 7:00 a.m. She knew at this time of year the highways were often icy in the world famous canyon. There was a foot of snow on the ground already—and it was coming down at an even faster rate as she drove carefully down the twisting, two-lane asphalt highway. On one side the canyon walls towered thousands of feet above her. On the other lay a five-hundred-foot-plus drop-off into Oak Creek, which flowed at the bottom of the canyon.

How many times had she driven 89A from Sedona to Flag? Rachel had lost count. Her eyes watered again from fatigue and she took a swipe at them with the back of her hand. Kate and Jessica were expecting her home at noon. If she got down the canyon in one piece, she would be home at 9:00 a.m. and would surprise them. A smile tugged at the corners of her full mouth. Oh, how she longed to see her sisters! She'd missed them so very much after leaving to work in England as a homeopath.

The best news was that Kate was going to marry her high school sweetheart, Sam McGuire. And Jessica had found the love of her life, Dan Black, a horse wrangler who worked at the ranch. Both were going to be married seven days from now, and Rachel was going to be their maid of honor. Yes, things were finally looking up for those two. The good Lord knew, Kate and Jessica deserved to be happy. Their childhood with their alcoholic father, Kelly Donovan, had been a disaster. As each daughter turned eighteen, she had fled from the ranch. Kate had become a rebel, working for environmental causes. Jessica had moved to Canada to pursue her love of flower essences. And Rachel—well, she'd fled the farthest away—to England.

Rachel felt the car slide. Instantly, she lifted her foot off the accelerator. She was only going thirty miles an hour, but black ice was a well-known problem here in this part of Arizona. It killed a lot of people and she didn't want to be the next victim. As she drove down the narrow, steep, road, dark green Douglas firs surrounded her. Ordinarily, Rachel would be enthralled with the beauty and majesty of the landscape—this remarkable canyon reminded her of a miniature Grand Canyon in many respects. But she scarcely noticed now. In half an hour, she would be home.

Her hands tightened on the wheel as she spotted

a yellow, diamond-shaped sign that read 15 mph. A sharp hairpin curve was coming up. She knew this curve well. She glanced once again at the jagged, unforgiving face of a yellow-and-white limestone cliff soaring thousands of feet above her and disappearing into the heavily falling snow. Gently she tested her brakes on the invisible, dangerous black ice. The only thing between her and the cliff that plunged into the canyon was a guardrail.

Suddenly, Rachel gasped. Was she seeing things? Without thinking, she slammed on the brakes. Directly in front of her, looming out of nowhere, was a huge black-and-gold cat. Her eyes widened enormously and a cry tore from her lips as the car swung drunkenly. The tires screeched as she tried to correct the skid. Impossible! Everything started to whirl around her. Out of the corner of her eye, she saw the black-and-gold cat, as large as a cougar, jump out of the way. Slamming violently against the cliff face, Rachel screamed. The steering wheel slipped out of her hands. A split second later, she watched in horror as the guardrail roared up at her.

The next moment there was a grinding impact. Throwing up her hands to protect her face, she felt the car become airborne. Everything seemed to suddenly move into slow motion. The car was twisting around in midair. She heard the glass crack as her head smashed against the side window. The snow, the dark shapes of the fir trees, all rushed at her. The nose of the car spiraled down—down into the jagged

limestone wall well below the guardrail. Oh, no! She
was going to die!

A thousand thoughts jammed through her mind in
those milliseconds. What had been up on that highway? It wasn't a cougar. What *was* it? Had she hallucinated? Rachel knew better than to slam on
brakes on black ice! How stupid could she be! But
if she hadn't hit the brakes, she'd have struck that
jaguar. Had there been a jaguar at all? Was it possible? She had to be seeing things! Now she was
going to die!

Everything went black in front of Rachel. The last
thing she recalled was the motion of her car as it
arched down like a shot fired from a cannon, before
hitting the side of the cliff. The last sound she heard
was her own scream of absolute terror ringing
through the air.

Warm liquid was flowing across Rachel's parted
lips. She heard voices that seemed very far away.
As she slowly became conscious, the voices grew
stronger—and closer. Forcing open her eyes, she at
first saw only white. Groggily, she looked closer and
realized it was snow on part of the windshield. The
other half of the windshield was torn away, the
white flakes lazily drifting into the passenger's side
of the car.

The accident came back to her as the pain in her
head and left foot throbbed in unison. Suddenly she
realized she was sitting at an angle, the car twisted
around the trunk of a huge Douglas fir.

Again she heard a voice. A man's voice. It was closer this time. Blinking slowly, Rachel lifted her right arm. At least *it* worked. The seat belt bit deeply into her shoulder and neck. The airbag, deflated now, had stopped her from being thrown through the windshield. A branch must have gouged out the right half of the windshield. If anyone had been sitting there, they'd be dead.

It was cold with the wind and snow blowing into the car. Shivering, Rachel closed her eyes. The image of the jaguar standing in the middle of that icy, snow-covered highway came back to her. How stupid could she have been? She knew not to slam on brakes like that. Where had the jaguar come from? Jaguars didn't exist in Arizona! Her head pounded as she tried to make sense of everything. She was in trouble. Serious trouble.

Again, a man's voice, deep and commanding, drifted into her semiconscious state. Help. She needed medical help. If only she could get to her homeopathic kit in the back seat. Arnica was what she needed for tissue trauma. Her head throbbed. She was sure she'd have a goose egg. Arnica would reduce the swelling and the pain.

The snowflakes were falling more thickly and at a faster rate now. How long had she been unconscious? Looking at her watch, Rachel groaned. It was 8:00 a.m. She'd been down here an hour? She had to get out! Rachel tried to move, but her seat belt was tightly constricting. She hung at a slight angle toward the passenger side of the car. Struggling weakly, she tried to find the seat belt latch, but her fingers were cold and numb.

"Hey! Are you all right?"

Rachel slowly lifted her head. Her vision was blurred for a moment, and when it cleared she noticed her side window was gone, smashed out, she guessed, in the crash. A man—a very tall, lean man with dark, short hair and intense blue eyes, wearing a navy blue jacket and pants—anchored himself against the car. He was looking at her, assessing her sharply. Rachel saw the patch on his jacket: EMT. And then she saw another patch: Sedona Fire Department.

"No…no…I'm not all right," she whispered, giving up on trying to find the seat belt latch.

"Okay…just hold on. Help's here. My name is Jim. We're from the Sedona Fire Department. We got a 911 call that an auto had flipped off the highway. Hold on while I get my buddies down here."

Rachel sank back, feeling relief. This man… Jim…radiated confidence. Somehow she knew she'd be okay with him. She watched through half-closed eyes as he lifted the radio to his strong-looking mouth and talked to someone far above them. The snow was thickening. The gray morning light accentuated his oval face, his strong nose and that mouth. He looked Indian. Rachel briefly wondered what kind. With his high cheekbones and dark hair, he could be Navajo, Hopi or from one of many other tribal nations.

Something about him made her feel safe. That

was good. Rachel knew that he could get her out of this mess. She watched as he snapped the radio onto his belt and returned his full attention to her, trying to hide his worry.

"Helluva way to see Arizona," he joked. "The car is wrapped around this big Douglas fir here, so it and you aren't going anywhere. My buddies are bringing down a stretcher and some auto-extrication equipment. My job is to take care of you." He smiled a little as he reached in the window. "What's your name?"

"Rachel…" she whispered.

"Rachel, I'm going to do a quick exam of you. Do you hurt anywhere?"

She closed her eyes as he touched her shoulder. "Yes…my head and my foot. I—I think I've got a bump on my head."

His touch was immediately soothing to her, though he wore latex gloves. But then, so did she when she had to examine a patient. With AIDS, HIV and hepatitis B all being transmissible via blood and fluids, medical people had to protect themselves accordingly. As he moved his hands gently across her head, she could feel him searching for injury. Something in her relaxed completely beneath his ministrations. She felt his warm, moist breath, his face inches from hers as he carefully examined her scalp.

"Beautiful hair," he murmured, "but you're right—you've got a nice goose egg on the left side of your head."

One corner of her mouth turned up as she lay

against the car seat. "If that's all, I'm lucky. I hate going to hospitals."

Chuckling, Jim eased a white gauze dressing against her hair and then quickly placed a bandage around her head. "Yeah, well, you'll be going to Cottonwood Hospital anyway. If nothing more than to make sure you're okay."

Groaning, Rachel barely opened her eyes. She saw that he'd unzipped his jacket and it hung open, revealing a gold bar over the left top pocket of his dark blue shirt that read J. Cunningham. *Cunningham.* Frowning, she looked up at him as he moved his hands in a gentle motion down her neck, searching for more trauma.

"Cunningham's your last name?" she asked, her voice sounding faint even to her.

"Yeah, Jim Cunningham." He glanced down at her. She was pasty, her forest green eyes dull looking. Jim knew she was in shock. He quickly pressed his fingertips against her collarbone, noticing her pale pink angora sweater and dark gray wool slacks. Under any other circumstance, she would turn a man's head. "Why?" he teased, "has my reputation preceded me?" He quickly felt her arms for broken bones or signs of bleeding. There were some minor cuts due to flying glass from the windshield, but otherwise, so far, so good. He tried not to show his worry.

"Of the Bar C?" she asked softly, shutting her eyes as he leaned over her and pressed firmly on her rib cage to see if she had any broken ribs. How close he was! Yet his presence was utterly comforting to Rachel.

"Yes...how did you know?" Jim eased his hands down over her hips, applying gentle pressure. If she had any hip or pelvic injuries, they would show up now. He watched her expression closely. Her eyes were closed, her thick, dark lashes standing out against her pale skin. She'd had a nosebleed, but it had ceased. Her lips parted, but she didn't answer his question. Looking down and pushing aside the deflated airbag, he saw that her left foot was caught in the wreckage. *Damn.* That wasn't a good sign. His mind whirled with possibilities. He needed to get a cuff around her upper arm and check her blood pressure. What if her foot was mangled? What if an artery was severed? She could be losing a lot of blood. She could die on them.

He had to keep her talking. Easing out of the car window, he reached into his bright orange EMT bag. Looking up, he saw his partner, Larry, coming down, along with four other firefighters bringing the stretcher and ropes as well as auto-extrication equipment.

"Well," Jim prodded, as he pushed up her sleeve and slipped the blood-pressure cuff around her upper left arm, "am I a wanted desperado?"

Rachel needed his stabilizing touch and absorbed it hungrily. Consciousness kept escaping her. For some reason she would slip away, only to be brought back by his deep, teasing voice. "Uh, no...."

"You sound like you know me. Do you?" He quickly put the stethoscope to her arm and pumped up the cuff. His gaze was focused on the needle, watching it closely as he bled off the air.

Rachel rallied. Opened her eyes slightly, she saw the worry in Jim's face. The intensity in his expression shook her. "You don't remember me, do you?" she said, trying to tease back. Her voice sounded very faraway. What was going on? Why wasn't she able to remain coherent?

Damn! Jim kept his expression neutral. Her blood pressure wasn't good. Either she had a serious head injury or she was bleeding somewhere. He left the cuff on her arm and removed the stethoscope from his ears. She lay against the seat, her eyes closed, her body limp. Her breathing was slowly becoming weaker and weaker. His medical training told him she was losing a lot of blood. Where? It *had* to be that foot that was jammed in the wreckage.

He *had* to keep her talking. "I'm sorry," he apologized, "I don't remember you. I wish I did, though." And that was the truth. She was a beautiful woman. *Stunning* was a word Jim would use with her. Her dark brown hair was thick and long, like a dark cape across her proud shoulders.

"Listen, I'm going to try and get this door open." Jim made a signal to Larry to hurry even faster down the slippery incline. Studying the jagged cliff, Jim realized that if the car hadn't wrapped itself around this fir tree, it would have plunged another three hundred feet. More than likely, Rachel would be dead.

Larry hurried forward. He was a big man, over six feet tall, and built like a proverbial bull.

"Yeah, Cougar, what are the stats?" He dropped his bag and moved gingerly up to Jim.

Scowling, Jim lowered his voice so no one but his partner would hear. "She's dumping on us. I think she's hemorrhaging from her left foot, which is trapped beneath the dash of the car. Help me get this door open. I need to get a cuff on her upper leg. It'll have to act like a tourniquet. Then those extrication guys can get in here and cut that metal away so we can get her foot free to examine it."

"Right, pard."

Rachel heard another male voice, but it was Jim's voice she clung to. Her vision was growing dim. What was wrong with her? She heard the door protest and creak loudly as it was pulled opened in a series of hard, jerking motions. In moments, she heard Jim's voice very close to her ear. Forcing open her eyes, she saw that he was kneeling on the side of the car where the door was now open. She felt his hand moving down her left leg, below her knee.

"Can you feel that?" he demanded.

"Feel what?" Rachel asked.

"Or this?"

"No...nothing. I feel nothing, Jim."

Jim threw Larry a sharp look. "Hand me your blood-pressure cuff. We're going to apply a tourniquet." In the gray light of the canyon, with snowflakes twirling lazily around them, Jim saw that her left foot and ankle had been twisted and trapped in the metal upon impact. With Larry's help, he affixed the cuff around her slim calf and then inflated it enough to halt the blood flow in that extremity.

Four other firefighters arrived on scene. Larry put a warm, protective blanket across Rachel. He then got into the back seat and held her head straight while Jim carefully placed a stabilizing cervical collar around her neck, in case she had an undetected spinal injury. He was worried. She kept slipping in and out of consciousness.

As he settled into the passenger seat beside her, and the firefighters worked to remove the metal that trapped her leg, Jim tried to draw her out of her semiconscious state.

"Rachel," he called, "it's Jim. Can you hear me?"

She barely moved her lips. "Yes…"

He told her what the firefighters were going to do, and that there would be a lot of noise and not to get upset by it. All the while, he kept his hand on hers. She responded valiantly to his touch, to his voice, but Jim saw Larry shake his head doubtfully angle as he continued to gently hold her head and neck.

"You said you heard of me," Jim teased. He watched her lashes move upward to reveal her incredible eyes. Her pupils were wide and dilated, black with a crescent of green around them. "Well? Am I on a wanted poster somewhere?" he asked with a smile.

Jim's smile went straight to Rachel's heart. It was boyish, teasing, and yet he was so male that it made her heart beat a little harder in her chest. She tried to smile back and realized it was a poor attempt. "No…not a wanted poster. I remember you from high school. I'm Rachel Donovan. You know the Donovan Ranch?"

Stunned, Jim stared. "Rachel Donovan?" His head whirled with shock. That was right! He recalled Jessica Donovan telling him over a month ago that Rachel, the middle daughter, was moving home from England to live at the ranch.

"That's me," Rachel joked softly. She forced her eyes open a little more and held his gaze. "You used to pull my braids in junior high, but I don't think you remember that, do you?"

Jim forced a grin he didn't feel at all. "I do now." And he did. Little Rachel Donovan had been such a thin stick of a girl in junior high. She had worn her long, dark brown flowing mane of hair in braids back then, like her mother, Odula, an Eastern Cherokee medicine woman. Rachel was the spitting image of her. Jim recalled the crush he'd had on little Rachel Donovan. She'd always run from him. The only way he'd get her attention was to sneak up, tweak one of her braids and then run away himself. It was his way of saying he liked her, for at that age, Jim had been too shy to tell her. Besides, there were other problems that prevented him from openly showing his affection for her.

"You were always teasing me, Jim Cunningham,'' Rachel said weakly. Her mouth was dry and she was thirsty. The noise of machinery filled the car. If it hadn't been for Jim's steadying hand on her shoulder, the sound would have scared her witless.

''Hey, Cougar, we're gonna have to take the rest of this windshield out. Gotta pull the steering wheel up and away from her.''

Jim nodded to Captain Cord Ramsey of the extrication team. ''Okay.'' He rose up on his knees and took a second blanket into his hands.

''Rachel,'' he said as he leaned directly over her, ''I'm going to place a blanket over us. The firefighters have to pull the rest of the window out. There's going to be glass everywhere, but the blanket will protect you.''

Everything went dark before Rachel's eyes. Jim Cunningham had literally placed his body like a wall between her and the firefighters who were working feverishly to free her. She felt the heat of his body as he pulled the blanket over their heads. How close he was! She was overwhelmed by the care he showed toward her. It was wonderful.

When he spoke, his voice was barely an inch from her ear.

''Okay, they're going to pull that windshield any moment now. You'll hear some noise and feel the car move a bit. It's nothing to be concerned about.''

''You're wonderful at what you do,'' Rachel whispered weakly. ''You really make a person feel safe…that everything's going to be okay even if it isn't.…''

Worried, Jim said, "Rachel, do you know what blood type you are?"

"AB positive."

His heart sank. He struggled to keep the disappointment out of his voice. "That's a rare blood type."

She smiled a little. "Like me, I guess."

He chuckled. "I have AB positive blood, too. How about that? Two rare birds, eh?"

Rachel heard the windshield crack. There was one brief, sharp movement. As Jim eased back and removed the blanket, she looked up at him. His face was hard and expressionless until he looked down to make sure she was all right. Then his features became very readable. She saw concern banked in his eyes.

"Listen, Jim, in the back seat there's a kit. A homeopathic kit. It's important you get to it. There's a remedy in there. It's called Arnica Montana. I know I'm bleeding. It will help stop it. Can you get it for me? Pour some pellets into my mouth?"

He frowned and looked in the back seat. There was a black physician's bag there on the eat next to Larry. "You a doctor?"

"No, a homeopath."

"I've vaguely heard about it. An alternative medicine, right?" He reached over the back seat and brought the leather case up front, resting it against his thigh as he opened it. He found a small plastic box inside along with a lot of other medical equipment. "This box?" he asked, holding it up for her to look at.

"Yes...that's the one. I'll need two pills."

Opening it, Jim located the bottle marked Arnica. He unscrewed the cap and put a couple of white pellets into her mouth.

"Thanks...." Rachel said. The sweetness of the small pellets tasted good to her. "It will help stop the shock and the bleeding."

Jim put the bag aside. Worriedly, he took another blood-pressure reading. She was no longer dumping as before. He suspected the tourniquet on her lower leg had halted most of the bleeding, and that was good news.

"Did I hear someone call you Cougar?"

Distracted because the extrication team was finally prying the metal away from her foot, Jim nodded. "Yeah, that's my nickname."

"H-how did you get it?" Rachel felt the power of the homeopathic remedy begin to work on her immediately. "Listen, this remedy I took will probably make me look like I'm unconscious, but I'm not. It's just working to stabilize me, so don't panic, okay?"

Jim nodded and placed himself in front of Rachel to protect her again as the extrication equipment began to remove the metal from around her foot. "Okay, sweetheart, I won't panic." He watched her lashes drift down as he shielded her with his body. Her color was no longer as pasty, and that was promising. Still, her blood pressure was low. Too low.

Looking up at Larry, Jim said, "As soon as we get her out of here, have Ramsey call the hospital and see if they've got AB positive blood standing by. We're going to need it."

"Right."

Rachel savored Jim's nearness. She heard the screech of metal as it was being torn away to release her foot. She hoped her injury wasn't bad. She had a wedding to attend in a week. Her foot couldn't be broken!

"What's the frown for?" Jim asked. Her face was inches from his. He saw the soft upturn of the corners of her mouth. What a lovely mouth Rachel had. The spindly shadow of a girl he'd known was now a mature swan of indescribable beauty.

"Oh...the weddings—Katie and Jessica. I'm supposed to be their maid of honor. My foot...I'm worried about my foot. What if I broke it?"

"We'll know in just a little while," he soothed. Instinctively, he placed his hand on her left shoulder. The last of the metal was torn away.

"Cougar?"

"Yeah?" Jim twisted his head toward Captain Ramsey.

"She's all yours. Better come and take a look."

Rachel felt Jim leave her side. Larry's hands remained firm against her head and neck, however.

Cunningham climbed carefully around the car. The temperature was dropping, and the wind was picking up. Blizzard conditions were developing fast. Jim noted the captain's wrinkled brow as he made his way to the driver's side. Getting down on his hands and knees, squinting in the poor light, he got his first look at Rachel's foot.

He'd been right about loss of blood. He saw where an artery on the top of her foot had been sliced open. Quickly examining it, he placed a dressing there. Turning, he looked up at the captain.

"Get the hospital on the horn right away. We're definitely going to need a blood transfusion for her. AB positive." Rachel had lost a lot of blood, there was no doubt. If he hadn't put that blood-pressure cuff on her lower leg when he did, she would have bled to death right in front of him. Shaken, Jim eased to his feet.

"Okay, let's get her out of the car and onto a spine board." When he looked up to check on Rachel, he saw that she had lost consciousness again. So many memories flooded back through Jim in those moments. Good ones. Painful ones. Ones of yearning. Of unrequited love that was never fulfilled. Little Rachel Donovan. He'd had a crush on her all through school.

As Jim quickly positioned the spine board beneath Rachel with the help of the firefighters, he suddenly felt hope for the first time in a long time. Maybe, just maybe, life was giving him a second chance with Rachel. And then he laughed at himself. The hundred-year-old feud between the Cunninghams and Donovans was famous in this part of the country. Still he wondered if Rachel had ever had any feelings for him?

Right now, Jim couldn't even think about the past. His concern was for Rachel's loss of blood and her shock. The clock on the car had stopped at 7:00 a.m. That was when the accident had probably occurred. And it had taken them an hour to get here. Whether he wanted to admit it or not, her life hung in a precarious balance right now.

"Hey," Ramsey said, getting off the radio, "bad news, Cougar."

"What?" Jim eased Rachel onto the spine board and made her as comfortable as possible.

"No AB positive blood at Cottonwood."

Damn! "Try Flagstaff."

Ramsey shook his head. "None anywhere."

Placing another blanket across Rachel, Jim glanced up at his partner. "You tell Cottonwood to stand by for a blood transfusion, then," he told the captain. "I've got AB positive blood. She needs at *least* a pint or we aren't going to be able to save her."

"Roger," Ramsey grunted, and got on the radio again to the hospital.

Chapter Two

The first thing Rachel was aware of was a hand gently caressing her hair. It was a nurturing touch, almost tender as it brushed across her crown. Unfamiliar noises leaked into her groggy consciousness, along with the smell of antiseptic. Where was she? Her head ached. Whoever was caressing her hair soothed the pain with each touch. Voices. There were so many unfamiliar voices all around her. Struggling to open her eyes, she heard a man's voice, very low and nearby.

"It's okay, Rachel. You're safe and you're going to be okay. Don't try so hard. Just lay back and take it easy. You've been through a lot."

Who was that? The voice was oddly familiar, and yet it wasn't. The touch of his hand on her head was magical. Rachel tried to focus on the gentle caress. Each time he followed the curve of her skull, the pain went away, only to return when he lifted his hand. Who was this man who had such a powerful touch? Rachel was no stranger to hands-on healing. Her mother, Odula, used to lay her hands on each of them when they were sick with fever or chills. And amazingly, each time, their aches and pains had disappeared.

The antiseptic smell awakened her even more— the smell of a hospital. She knew the scent well, having tended many patients at the homeopathic hospital in London. Her mind was fuzzy, so she continued to focus on the man's hand and his nearness. She felt his other hand resting on her upper arm, as if to give her an anchor in the whirling world of gold-and-white light beneath her lids.

Gathering all her strength, Rachel forced her lashes to lift. At first all she saw was a dark green curtain in front of her. And then she heard a low chuckle to her right, where the man was standing— the one who caressed her as if she were a very beloved, cherished woman. His warm touch was undeniable. Her heart opened of its own accord and Rachel felt a rush of feelings she thought had died a long time ago. Confused by the sights and sounds, she looked up, up at the man who stood protectively at her side.

Jim's mouth pulled slightly. "Welcome back to the real world, Rachel." He saw her cloudy, forest green eyes rest on him. There was confusion in their depths. Nudging a few strands of long, dark brown hair away from her cheek, he said in a low, soothing tone, "You're at the Flagstaff Hospital. We brought you here about an hour ago. You had a wreck up on 89A coming out of Flag earlier this morning. Do you remember?"

Rachel was mesmerized by him, by his low tone, which seemed to penetrate every cell of her being like a lover's caress. He had stilled his hand, resting it against her hair. His smile was kind. She liked the tenderness burning in his eyes as he regarded her. Who was he? His face looked familiar, and yet no name would come. Her mouth felt gummy. Her foot ached. She looked to the left, at her surroundings.

"You're in ER, the emergency room, in a cubical," Jim told her. "The doc just got done looking at you. He just stitched up your foot where you severed a small artery. You took a pint of whole blood, and he said the bump on your head is going to hurt like hell, but it's not a concussion."

Bits and pieces of memory kept striking her. The jaguar. The jaguar standing in the middle of that ice-covered highway. Rachel frowned and closed her eyes.

"The cat…it was in the middle of the road," she began, her voice scratchy. "I slammed on the brakes. I didn't want to hit it…. The last thing I remember is spinning out of control."

Jim tightened his hand slightly on her upper arm. He could see she was struggling to remember. "A cat? You mean a cougar?"

Everything was jumbled up. Rachel closed her eyes. She felt terribly weak—far weaker than she wanted to feel. "My kit...where is it?"

Jim saw a dull flush of color starting to come back to her very pale cheeks. The blood transfusion had halted her shock. He'd made sure she was covered with extra blankets and he'd remained with her in ER throughout the time, not wanting her to wake up alone and confused.

"Kit?"

"Yes..." She moved her lips, the words sticking in her dry mouth. "My homeopathic kit...in my car. I need it...."

He raised his brows. "Oh...your black bag. Yeah, I brought it in with me. Hold on, I'll be right back."

Rachel almost cried when he left her side. The strong, caring warmth of his hand on her arm was very stabilizing. The noise in ER was like a drum inside her head. She heard the plaintive cry of a baby, someone else was groaning in pain—familiar sounds to her as a homeopath. She wished she could get up, go dispense a remedy to each of them to ease their pain and discomfort. She wasn't in England any longer, though; she was in the U.S. Suddenly she felt disoriented.

Her ears picked up the sound of a curtain being drawn aside. She opened her eyes. He was back, with her black leather physician's bag.

"Got it," he said with a smile, placing the bag close to her blanketed leg.

As he opened it, Rachel tried to think clearly.

"Who are you? I feel like I know you…but I'm not remembering names too well right now."

His mouth curved in a grin as he opened the bag. "Jim Cunningham. I'm the EMT who worked with you out at the accident scene." He pulled out the white, plastic box and held it where she could see it.

"Oh…"

Chuckling, he said, "Man, have I made a good impression on you. Here you are, the prettiest woman I've seen in a long time, and you forget my name."

His teasing warmth fell across her. Rachel tried to smile, but the pain in her head wouldn't let her. There was no denying that Jim Cunningham was a very good-looking man. He was tall, around six foot two, and lean, like a lithe cougar with a kind of boneless grace that told her he was in superb physical condition. The dark blue, long-sleeved shirt and matching pants he wore couldn't hide his athletic build. The silver badge on his left pocket, the gold nameplate above it and all the patches on the shoulders of his shirt gave him a decided air of authority.

Wrinkling her nose a little, she croaked, "Don't take it personally. I'm feeling like I have cotton stuffed between my ears." She lifted her hand and found it shaky.

"Just tell me which one you want," he said gently. "You're pretty weak yet. In another couple of hours you'll feel a lot better than you do right now."

Alarmed at her weakness, Rachel whispered, "Get me the Arnica."

"Ah, the same one you used out at the accident site. Okay." He hunted around. There were fifty black-capped, amber bottles arranged by alphabetical order in the small case. Finding Arnica, he uncapped it.

"Now what?"

"My mouth. Drop a couple of pellets in it."

Jim carefully put two pellets on her tongue. "Okay, you're set." He capped the amber bottle. "What is this stuff, anyway? The ER doc wanted to know if it had side effects or if it would cause any problems with prescription drugs."

The pellets were sugary sweet. Rachel closed her eyes. She knew the magic of homeopathy. In a few minutes, her headache would be gone. And in a few more after that, she'd start feeling more human again.

"That's okay," Jim murmured as he replaced the vial into the case, "you don't have to answer the questions right now." He glanced up. "I called your family. I talked to Kate." He put the box back into Rachel's bag and set it on a chair nearby. "They're all waiting out in the visitors' lounge. Hold on, I'll get them for you."

Rachel watched through half-closed eyes as Jim opened the green curtain and disappeared. She liked him. A lot. What wasn't there to like? she asked herself. He was warm, nurturing, charming—not to mention terribly handsome. He had matured since she'd known him in school. He'd been a tall, gangly, shy kid with acne on his face. She remembered he was half-Apache and half-Anglo and that they'd always had that common bond—being half-Indian.

So many memories of her past—of growing up here in Sedona, of the pain of her father's alcoholism and her mother's endless suffering with the situation—flooded back through her. They weren't pleasant memories. And many of them she wanted to forget.

Jim Cunningham… In school she'd avoided him like the plague because Old Man Cunningham and her father had huge adjoining ranches. The two men had fought endlessly over the land, the often-broken fence line and the problems that occurred when each other's cattle wandered onto the other's property. They'd hated one another. Rachel had learned to avoid the three Cunningham boys as a result.

Funny how a hit on the head pried loose some very old memories. A crooked smile pulled at Rachel's mouth. And who had saved her? None other than one of the Cunninghams. What kind of karma did she have? She almost laughed, and realized the pain in her head was lessening quickly; her thoughts were rapidly clearing. Thanks to homeopathy. And Jim Cunningham.

"Rachel!"

She opened her eyes in time to see Jessica come flying through the curtains. Her younger sister's eyes were huge, her face stricken with anxiety. Reaching out with her right hand, Rachel gave her a weak smile.

"Hi, Jess. I'm okay…really, I am.…"

Then Rachel saw Kate, much taller and dressed in Levi's and a plaid wool coat, come through the curtains. Her serious features were set with worry, too.

Jessica gripped Rachel's hand. "Oh, Rachel! Jim called us, bless him! He didn't have to do that. He told us everything. You could have died out there!" She gave a sob, then quickly wiped the tears from her eyes. Leaning down, she kissed Rachel's cheek in welcome.

Kate smiled brokenly. "Helluva welcome to Sedona, isn't it?"

Grinning weakly, Rachel felt Kate's work-worn hand fall over hers. "Yes, I guess it is."

Kate frowned. "I thought you were flying into Phoenix, renting a car and driving up from there?"

Making a frustrated sound, Rachel said, "I was going to surprise you two. I got an earlier flight out of Denver directly into Flag. I was going to be at the ranch hours earlier that way." She gave Kate a long, warm look. "I really wanted to get home."

"Yeah," Kate whispered, suddenly choked up as she gripped her sister's fingers, "I guess you did."

Sniffing, Jessica wiped her eyes. "Are you okay, Rachel? What did the doctor say?"

Rachel saw the curtains part. It was Jim Cunningham. Her heart skipped a beat. She saw how drawn his face was and his eyes seemed darker than she recalled. He came and stood at the foot of the gurney where she was lying.

"Dr. Forbush said she had eight stitches in her foot for a torn artery, and a bump on the head," he told them. He held Rachel's gaze. She seemed far more alert now, and that was good. When he'd stepped into the cubicle, he'd noticed that her cheeks were flushed. Pointing to her left foot, he said, "She lost a pint of blood out there at the wreck. She got that replaced and the doc is releasing her to your care." And then he smiled teasingly down at Rachel. "That is, unless you want to spend a night here in the hospital for observation?"

Rachel grimaced. "Not on your life," she muttered defiantly. "I work in them, I don't stay in them."

Chuckling, Jim nodded. He looked at the three Donovan sisters. "I gotta get going, but the head nurse, Sue Young, will take care of getting you out of this place." He studied Rachel's face and felt a stirring in his heart. "Stay out of trouble, you hear?"

"Wait!" Rachel said, her voice cracking. She saw surprise written on his features when he turned to tell her again. "Wait," she pleaded. "I want to thank you...." Then she smiled when she saw deviltry in his eyes as he stood there, considering her plea.

"You serious about that?"

"Sure."

"Good. Then when you get well, have lunch with me?"

Stunned, Rachel leaned back onto the bed. She saw Jessica's face blossom in a huge smile. And Kate frowned. Rachel knew what her older sister was thinking. He was a Cunningham, their enemy for as long as any of them could recall.

"Well…"

Jim raised his hand, realizing he'd overstepped his bounds. "Hey, I was just teasing. I'll see you around. Take care of yourself.…"

"I'll be right back," Kate murmured to her sisters, and she quickly followed after him.

Jim was headed toward the small office in the back of ER where EMTs filled out their accident report forms when he heard Kate Donovan's husky voice.

"Jim?"

Turning, he saw her moving in his direction. Stepping out of the ER traffic, he waited for her. The serious look on her face put him on guard. She was the oldest of the three Donovan daughters and the owner of a ranch, which was teetering precariously on the edge of bankruptcy. He knew she had worked hard since assuming the responsibilities of the ranch after Kelly died in an auto accident earlier in the year. Because of that, Jim also knew she had more reason to hate a Cunningham than any of the sisters. Inwardly, he tried to steel himself against anything she had to say. His father, unfortunately, had launched a lawsuit against Kate's ranch right now.

There was nothing Jim could do about it, even though he'd tried to talk his father into dropping the stupid suit. Driven by the forty-year vendetta against Kelly Donovan, he'd refused to. It made no difference to him that the daughters were coming home to try and save their family ranch. The old man couldn't have cared less.

With such bad blood running between the two families, Jim was trying to mend fences where he could. His two older brothers weren't helping things, however. They derived just as much joy and pleasure out of hurting people, especially the Donovans, as their old man. Jim was considered the black sheep of the family, probably because he was the only Cunningham who wasn't into bad blood or revenge. No, he'd come home to try and fix things. And in the months since he'd been home, Jim had found himself living in hell. He found his escape when he was on duty for the fire department. But the rest of the time he was a cowboy on the family ranch, helping to hold it together and run it. Ordinarily, he'd loved the life of a rancher, but not anymore. These days his father was even more embittered toward the Donovans, and now he had Bo and Chet on his side to wage a continued war against them.

As Kate Donovan approached him, Jim understood how she felt toward him. It wasn't anything personal; it was just ancient history that was still alive and injuring all parties concerned. Even him. The darkness in her eyes, the serious set of her mouth, put him on guard. He studied her as she halted a few feet away from him, jamming her hands into the deep pockets of the plaid wool jacket she wore.

"I want to thank you," Kate rasped, the words coming out strained.

Reeling, Jim couldn't believe his ears. He'd expected to catch hell from Kate for suggesting lunch with Rachel. He knew she had a lot of her father in her and could be mule headed, holding grudges for a long time, too.

"You didn't have to call us," Kate continued. "You could have left that to a nurse here in ER, I know." Then she looked up at him. "I found out from the nurse before I went in to see Rachel that you saved her life—literally."

Shrugging shyly, Jim said, "I did what I could, Kate. I'd do it for anyone." He didn't want her to think that he'd done something special for Rachel that he wouldn't do for others. In his business as an EMT, his job was to try and save lives.

"Damn, this is hard," Kate muttered, scowling and looking down at her booted feet. Lifting her head, she pinned him with a dark look. "I understand you just gave her a pint of your blood. Is that true?"

He nodded. "Rachel's blood type is a rare one." Looking around the busy hospital area, he continued, "This is a backwoods hospital, Kate. They can't always have every rare blood type on hand. Especially in the middle of Arizona, out in the wilds.'' He tried to ease her hard expression with his teasing reply.

Kate wasn't deterred in the least. ''And your partner, Larry, who I just talked to out at the ambulance, said you'd stopped Rachel from losing even more blood by putting a tourniquet on her leg?''

''I put a blood-pressure cuff around Rachel's lower leg to try and stop most of the bleeding, yes.'' Inwardly, Jim remained on guard. He never knew if Kate Donovan was going to pat him on the head or rip out his jugular. Usually it was the latter. He saw her expression go from anger to confusion and then frustration, and he almost expected her to curse him out for volunteering his own blood to help save Rachel's life. After all, it was Cunningham blood—the blood of her arch enemy. The enemy that her father had fought against all his life.

Kate pulled her hand out of her pocket and suddenly thrust it toward him. ''Then,'' she quavered, suddenly emotional, ''I owe you a debt I can't begin to pay back.''

Staring at her proffered hand, Jim realized what it took for Kate to do that. He gripped her hand warmly. The tears in her eyes touched him deeply. ''I'm glad it was me. I'm glad I was there, Kate. No regrets, okay?''

She shook his hand firmly and then released it. ''Okay,'' she rasped nervously, clearing her throat. ''I just wanted you to know that I know what really happened.''

He gave her a slight smile. ''And there's nothing

to pay back here. You understand?'' He wanted both families to release the revenge, the aggressive acts against one another. Kelly Donovan was dead, though Jim's father was still alive and still stirring up trouble against their closest neighbors. Kate was struggling to keep the ranch afloat, and Jim admired her more than he could ever say. But if he told her that she wouldn't believe him, because he was a Cunningham—bad blood.

Nodding, she wiped her eyes free of tears. ''You sure know how to balance ledgers, don't you?''

Scrutinizing her closely, Jim said quietly, ''I assume you're talking about the ledger between our two families?''

''Yes.'' she stared up at him. ''I can't figure you out—yet.''

''There's nothing to figure out, Kate.''

''Yes,'' she growled, ''there is.''

His mouth curved ruefully. ''I came home like you did—to try and fix things.''

''Then why does your old man have that damned lawsuit against us?''

Kate's frustration paralleled his own. Opening his hands, Jim rasped, ''I'm trying to get him to drop the suit, Kate. It has no merit. It's just that same old revenge crap from long ago, that's all.''

She glared at him. ''We are hitting rock bottom financially and you and everyone else knows it. Rachel came home to try and make money to help us pay the bills to keep our ranch afloat. If I have to hire a lawyer and pay all the court costs, that's just one more monetary hemorrhage. Can't *you* do anything to make him stop it?''

''I'm doing what I can.''

She looked away, her mouth set. ''It's not enough.''

Wearily, Jim nodded. ''Kate, I want peace between our families. Not bloodshed or lawsuits. My father has diabetes and often refuses to take his meds, so he exhibits some bizarre behavior.''

''Like this stupid lawsuit?''

''Exactly.'' Glancing around, Jim pulled Kate into the office, which was vacant at the moment. Shutting the door, he leaned against it as he held her stormy gaze. ''Let's bury the hatchet between us, okay? I did not come home to start another round of battles with you or anyone else at the Donovan Ranch.''

''You left home right after high school,'' Kate said in a low voice. ''So why did you come back now?''

''I never approved of my father's tactics against you or your family. Yes, I left when I was eighteen. I became a hotshot firefighter with the forest service. I didn't want to be a part of how my father was acting or behaving. I didn't approve of it then and I don't now. I'm doing what I can, Kate. But I've got a father who rants and raves, who's out of his head half the time. Then he stirs up my two brothers, who believe he's a tin god and would do anything he told them to do. They don't stop to think about the consequences of their actions.''

Kate wrapped her arms against her body and

stared at him, the silence thickening. "Since you've come back, things have gotten worse, not better."

Releasing a sigh, Jim rested against the edge of the desk. "Do you know what happens when a diabetic doesn't watch his diet or doesn't take his meds?" he asked in a calm tone.

"No," she muttered defensively. "Are you going to blame your old man's lawsuit and everything else on the fact that he's sick and won't take the drugs he's supposed to take?"

"In part, yes," Jim said. "I'm trying to get my brothers to work with me, not against me, on my father taking his medication daily. I'm trying to get our cook to make meals that balance my father's blood sugar and not spike it up so he has to be peeled off the ceiling every night when I get home."

Kate nodded. "If you think I feel sorry for you, I don't."

"I'm not telling you this to get your sympathy, Kate," he said slowly. "I'm trying to communicate with you and tell you what's going on. The more you understand, the less, I hope, you'll get angry about it."

"Your father is sick, all right," Kate rattled. "He hasn't changed one iota from when I was a kid growing up."

"I'm trying to change that, but it takes time." Jim held her defiant gaze. "If I can keep channels of communication open between us, maybe I can put out some brushfires before they explode into a wildfire. I'd like to be able to talk with you at times if I can.''

Snorting, Kate let her arms fall to her sides. ''You just saved Rachel's life. Your blood is in her body. I might be pigheaded, Cunningham, but I'm not stupid. I owe you for her life. If all you want in return is a little chat every once in a while, then I can deal with that.''

Frustration curdled Jim's innards. He'd actually given one and a half pints of blood and he was feeling light-headed, on top of being stressed out from the rescue. But he held on to his deteriorating emotions. ''I told you, Kate—no one owes me for helping to save Rachel's life.''

''I just wonder what your father is going to say. This ought to make his day. Not only did you save a Donovan's neck, you gave her your blood, too. Frankly,'' Kate muttered, moving to the door and opening it, ''I don't envy you at all when you go home tonight. You're going to have to scrape that bitter old man of yours off the ceiling but good this time.''

Jim nodded. ''Yeah, he'll probably think I've thrown in with the enemy.'' He said it in jest, but he could tell as Kate's knuckles whitened around the doorknob, she had taken the comment the wrong way.

''Bad blood,'' she rasped. ''And it always will be.''

Suddenly he felt exhausted. ''I hope Rachel doesn't take it that way even if you do.'' There was nothing he could do to change Kate's mind about his last name, Cunningham. As her deceased father had, she chose to associate all the wrongdoings of the past with each individual Cunningham, whether involved in it or not. And in Jim's case, he was as much the victim here as were the Donovan sisters. He'd never condoned or supported what his father had done to Kelly Donovan over the years, or how he'd tried to destroy the Donovan Ranch and then buy it up himself. But Kate didn't see it—or him— as separate from those acts of his father. She never would, Jim thought tiredly.

"Rachel's a big girl," Kate muttered defiantly. "I'm not going to brainwash her one way or another about you Cunninghams."

"Right now, Rachel needs peace and quiet," Jim answered. "She was in pretty deep shock out there. If you could give her two or three days of rest without all this agitation, it would help her a lot."

Kate nodded. "I'll make sure she gets the rest."

The office turned silent after Kate Donovan left. Sighing, Jim rubbed his brow. What a helluva morning! His thoughts moved back to Rachel. Old feelings he'd believed had died a long time ago stirred in his chest. She was so beautiful. He wondered if she had Kate's bitterness toward the Cunninghams. Jim cared more about that than he wanted to admit.

First things first. Because he'd given more than a pint of blood, he'd been taken off duty by the fire chief, and another EMT had been called in to replace him on the duty roster. Well, he'd fill out the accident report on Rachel and then go home. As he sat down at the desk and pulled out the pertinent form, Jim wondered if news of this event would precede him home. He hoped not—right now, he was too exhausted to deal with his father's ire. What he felt was a soul tiredness, though, more than just physical tiredness. He'd been home almost a year now, and as Kate had said, not much had changed.

Pen in hand, the report staring up at him, Jim tried to order his thoughts, but all he could see was Rachel's pale face and those glorious, dark green eyes of hers. What kind of woman had she grown into after she'd left Sedona? He'd heard she'd moved to England and spent most of her adult life there. Jim understood her desire to escape from Kelly Donovan's drunken, abusive behavior, just as he'd taken flight from his own father and his erratic, emotional moods. Jim's fingers tightened around the pen. Dammit, he was drawn to Rachel—right or wrong. And in Kate Donovan's eyes, he was dead wrong in desiring Rachel.

With a shake of his head, he began to fill out the form. Why the hell had he asked Rachel out to lunch? The invitation had been as much a surprise to him as it had been to the Donovan women. Kate was the one who'd reacted the most to it. Jessica was too embroiled in worry for Rachel to even hear his teasing rejoinder. And Rachel? Well, he'd seen surprise in her green eyes, and then something else.... His heart stirred again—this time with good, warm feelings. He wondered at the fleeting look in

Rachel's eyes when he'd made his sudden invitation.

Would she consider going to lunch with him? Was he crazy enough to hold on to that thought? With a snort, Jim forced his attention back to his paperwork. Right now, what he had to look forward to was going back to the Bar C and hoping his father hadn't heard what had happened. If he had, Jim knew there would be a blisteringly high price to pay on his hide tonight.

Chapter Three

"I heard you gave blood to one of those Donovan bitches."

Jim's hand tightened on the door as he stepped into the Cunningham ranch house. Frank Cunningham's gravelly voice landed like a hot branding iron on him, causing anger to surge through Jim. Slowly shutting the door, he saw his father in his wheelchair sitting next to the flagstone fireplace. The old man was glaring at him from beneath those bushy white eyebrows, his gray eyes flat and hard. Demanding.

Jim told himself that he was a grown man, that his gut shouldn't be clenching as it was now. He was over thirty years old, yet he was having a little boy's reaction to a raging father. Girding himself internally, Jim forced himself to switch to his EMT mode. Shrugging out of his heavy jacket, he placed it on a hook beside the door.

"Looks like news travels fast," he said as lightly as possible. Judging from the wild look in his father's eyes, he guessed he hadn't taken diabetes medication.

"Bad news always does, dammit!" Frank punched a finger at Jim as he sauntered between the leather couch and chair. "What are you doing, boy? Ruining our good name? How could you?"

Halting in front of him, Jim placed his hands on his hips. He was tired and drained. Ordinarily, giving blood didn't knock him down like this. It was different knowing who the accident victim was, though. He was still reeling from the fact that it was little Rachel Donovan, the girl he'd had a mad crush on so long ago.

"Have you taken your pill for your sugar problem?" Jim asked quietly.

Cursing richly, Frank Cunningham snarled, "You answer my questions, boy! Who the *hell* do you think you are, giving blood to—"

"You call her a bitch one more time and it will be the last time," Jim rasped, locking gazes with his angry father. "Rachel doesn't deserve that from you or anyone. She could have died out there early this morning."

Gripping the arms of his wheelchair with swollen, arthritic fingers, Frank glared at him. "You don't threaten me, boy."

The word *boy* grated on Jim's sensitized nerves.

He reminded himself one more time that he'd come home to try and pull his family together. To try and stop all the hatred, the anger and fighting that the Cunninghams were known for across two counties. Maybe he'd been a little too idealistic. After all, no one had even invited him back. It was one thing to be called home. It was quite another to wonder every day whether he'd have a home to come back to. Frank Cunningham had thrown him out when he was eighteen and Jim had never returned, except for Christmas. Even then, the holidays became a battleground of sniping and snarling, of dealing with the manipulations of his two brothers.

"Look, Father," Jim began in a strained toned, "I'm a little out of sorts right now. I need to lie down for a while and rest. Did you take your medicine this morning at breakfast? Did Louisa give it to you?"

Snorting, Frank glared at the open fireplace, where a fire crackled and snapped. "Yes, she gave it to me," he muttered irritably.

A tired smile tugged at the corners of Jim's mouth. "Did you take it?"

"No!"

In some ways, at seventy-five, Frank was a pale ghost of his former self. Jim recalled growing up with a strapping, six-foot-five cowboy who was tougher than the drought they were presently enduring. Frank had made this ranch what it was: the largest and most prosperous in the state of Arizona. Jim was proud of his heritage, and like his father, he loved being a cowboy, sitting on a good horse, working ceaselessly during calving season and struggling through all the other demanding jobs of ranching life.

Pulling himself out of his reverie, Jim walked out to the kitchen. There on the table were two tiny blue tablets, one for diabetes and one for high blood pressure. He picked them up and got a glass of water.

He knew his father's mood was based directly on his blood sugar level. If it was too high, he was an irritable son of a bitch. If it was too low, he would go into insulin shock, keel over unconscious and fall out of his wheelchair. Jim had lost track of how many times he'd had to pull his father out of insulin shock. He could never get it through Frank's head that he might die from it. His father didn't seem to care. Frank's desire to live, Jim realized, had left when their mother died.

Jim walked back out into the living room. It was a huge, expansive room with a cathedral ceiling and the stuffed heads of elk, deer, peccary and cougar on the cedar walls. The aged hardwood floor gleamed a burnished gold color. A large Navajo rug of red, black and gray lay in the center of the room, which was filled with several dark leather couches and chairs set around a rectangular office table.

"Here, Dad, take it now," Jim urged gently.

"Damn stuff."

"I know."

"I *hate* taking pills! Don't like leaning on anything or anyone! That's all these are—crutches," he said, glaring down at the blue pill in his large, callused palm.

Jim patiently handed him the glass of water. Neither of his brothers would ensure that Frank took his medicine. If they even saw the pills on the kitchen table, they ignored them. Jim had once heard Bo say that it would be just that much sooner that the ranch would be given to him.

As he stood there watching his father take the second pill, Jim felt his heart wrench. Frank was so thin now. His flesh, once darkly tanned and hard as saddle leather, was washed out and almost translucent looking. Jim could see the large, prominent veins in his father's crippled hands, which shook as he handed the glass back to him.

"Thanks. Now hit the hay. You look like hell, son."

Jim smiled a little. Such gruff warmth from his father was a rare gift and he absorbed it greedily. There were moments when Frank was human and compassionate. Not many, but Jim lived for them. "Okay, Dad. If you need anything, just come and get me."

Rubbing his hand through his thick silver hair, Frank grunted. "I got work to do in the office. I'll be fine."

"Okay...."

Jim was sitting on his bed and had pushed off his black boots when he heard someone coming down the hardwood hall. By the sound of the heavy footsteps, he knew it was Bo. Looking up, he saw his tall, lean brother standing in the doorway. By the state of his muddied Levi's and snow-dampened sheepskin coat, Bo had been out working. Taking off his black Stetson hat, he scowled at Jim.

"What's this I hear about you giving blood to one of those Donovan girls? Is that true? I was over at the hay and feed store and that was all they were talkin' about."

With a shake of his head, Jim stretched out on top of his double bed, which was covered with a brightly colored, Pendleton wool blanket. Placing his hands behind his head, he looked up at the ceiling.

"Gossip travels faster than anything else on earth," he commented.

Bo stepped inside the room. His dark brows drew down. "It's true, then?"

"Yeah, so what if it is?"

Settling the hat back on his head, Bo glared down at him. "Don'tcha think your goody two-shoes routine is a little out of control?"

Smarting at Bo's drawled criticisms, Jim sat up. "I know you wish I'd crawl back under a rock and disappear from this ranch, Bo, but it isn't going to happen."

Bo's full lips curved into a cutting smile. "Comin' home to save all sinners is a little presumptuous, don't you think?"

Tiredness washed across Jim, but he held on to

his deteriorating patience. "Someone needs to save this place."

"So you gave blood to Rachel Donovan. Isn't that a neat trick. You think by doing that, you'll stop the war between us?"

Anger lapped at him. "Bo, get the hell out of here. I'm beat. If you want to talk about this later, we'll do it then."

Chuckling indulgently, Bo reached for the doorknob. "Okay, little bro. I'll see you later."

Once the door shut, Jim sighed and lay back down. Closing his eyes, he let his arm fall across his face. The image of Rachel Donovan hovered beneath his eyelids. Instantly, he felt warmth flow through his tense body, washing away his irritation with his father, his anger toward his younger brother. She had the most incredible dark green eyes he'd ever seen. Jim recalled being mesmerized by them as a young, painfully shy boy in junior high. He'd wanted to stare into them and see how many gold flecks he could find among the deep, forest green depths.

Rachel had been awkward and skinny then. Now she was tall, elegant looking and incredibly beautiful. The prettiest, he felt, of the three sisters. She had Odula's face—high cheekbones, golden skin, dark brown hair that hung thick and heavy around her shoulders. Finely arched brows and large, compassionate eyes. Her nose was fine and thin; her mouth—the most delectable part of her—was full and expressive. Jim found himself wondering what it would be like to kiss that mouth.

At that thought, he removed his arm and opened his eyes. What the hell was he doing? His father would have a stroke if he suspected Jim liked Rachel Donovan. Frank Cunningham would blow his top, as usual, and spout vehemently, "That's like marrying the plague!" or something like that. Donovan blood, as far as Frank was concerned, was contaminated filth of the worst kind. Jim knew that to admit his interest in Rachel would do nothing but create the worst kind of stress in this household. His older brothers would ride roughshod over him, too. He was sure Frank would disown him—again—as he had when Jim was eighteen.

Jim closed his eyes once more and felt the tension in his body. Why the hell had he come home? Was Bo right? Was he out to "save" everyone? Right now, he was trying to juggle his part-time job as an EMT and work full time at the ranch as a cowboy. Jim didn't want his father's money, though Bo had accused him of coming home because their father was slowly dying from diabetes. Bo thought Jim was hoping to be written back into the will. When Jim had left home, Frank had told him that the entire ranch would be given to Bo and Chet.

Hell, Jim couldn't care less about who was in the will or who got what. That didn't matter to him. What did matter was family. His family. Ever since his mother had died, the males in the family had become lost and the cohesiveness destroyed. His mother, a full-blooded Apache, had been the strong, guiding central core of their family. The backbiting, the manipulation and power games that Bo and Chet played with their father wouldn't exist, Jim felt, if she were still alive. No, ever since his mother's death when he was six years old, the family unit had begun to rot—from the inside out.

Jim felt the tension bleeding out of him as he dwelled on his family's history. He felt the grief over losing her mother at such a young, vulnerable age. She had been a big woman, built like a squash, her black, flashing eyes, her copper skin and her playful smile so much a part of her. She'd brought joy and laughter to the ranch. When she died, so had the happiness. No one had laughed much after that. His father had changed drastically. In the year following his mother's death, Jim saw what loving and losing a person did to a man. Frank had turned to alcohol and his rages became known county wide. He'd gotten into bar fights. Lawsuits. He'd fought with Kelly Donovan on almost a daily basis. Frank Cunningham had gone berserk over his wife's passing. Maybe that's why Jim was gun-shy of committing to a relationship. Or maybe Rachel Donovan had stolen his heart at such a young age that he wanted no one but her—whether he could ever have her or not.

All Jim could do back then, was try to hold the rest of his suffering, grieving family together. He hadn't had time for his own grief and loss as he'd tried to help Bo and Chet. Even though he was the youngest, he was always the responsible one. The family burden had shifted to Jim whenever their father would disappear for days at a time. Frank would eventually return, unshaven and dirty, with the reek of alcohol on his breath. The weight of the world had been thrust upon Jim at a young age. Then, at eighteen, right after high school graduation, Jim had decided he had to escape. And he did—but the price had been high.

Slowly, ever so slowly, Rachel's face formed before his closed eyes again. Jim felt all his stress dissolve before the vision. She had such a peaceful look about her. Even out there at the accident site, she hadn't panicked. He admired her courage under the circumstances.

Suddenly, anger rose within him. Dammit, he *wanted* to see her again. How could he? If Frank knew, he'd hit the ceiling in a rage. Yet Jim refused to live his life knowing what his father's knee-jerk reaction would be. Still, it was hell having to come back to the ranch and take a gutfull of Frank's verbal attacks. But if Jim moved to his own place in Sedona, which was what he wanted to do, who would make sure his father took his meds?

Feeling trapped, he turned on his side. He felt the fingers of sleep encroaching on his worry and his desires. The last thing he saw as he drifted off was Rachel trying to smile gamely up at him in the ER when she regained consciousness. He recalled how thick and silky her hair had felt when he'd touched it. And he'd seen how his touch had affected her. In those moments, he'd felt so clean and hopeful again—two things he hadn't felt in a long, long time. Somehow, some way, he was going to find a way to see her again. He *had* to.

Rachel absorbed the warmth of the goose-down quilt lying over her. She was in her old bed, in the room she'd had as a child. She was back at the Donovan Ranch. Gloomy midafternoon light filtered through the flowery curtains at the window. Outside, snowflakes were falling slowly, like butterflies. The winter storm of this morning had passed on through.

Her foot ached a little, so she struggled to sit up. On the bedstand was her homeopathic kit. Opening it, she found the Arnica and took another dose.

"You awake?"

Rachel heard Jessica's hopeful voice at her door before her younger sister smiled tentatively and entered the room. Jessica's gold hair was in two braids and the oversize, plaid flannel shirt she wore highlighted her flushed cheeks.

"Come on in," Rachel whispered.

Pushing a few strands of hair off her face, Jessica sat down at the bottom of the bed and faced Rachel. "I thought you might be awake."

"I slept long and hard," Rachel assured her as she placed the kit back on the bed table. She put a couple of pillows behind her and then pushed the quilt down to her waist. The flannel nightgown she wore was covering enough in the cool room. There was no central heating in the huge, main ranch

house. Only the fireplace in the living room pro-
vided heat throughout the winter. Rachel didn't
mind the coolness, though.

Jessica nodded and surveyed her. "How's your
foot?"

"Okay. I just took another round of Arnica."

"What does that do for it?"

Rachel smiled, enjoying her sister's company.
Jessica was so open, idealistic and trusting. Nothing
like Kate, who distrusted everyone, always questioning their motives. "It reduces the swelling of the
soft tissue. The pain will go away in about five
minutes."

"Good." Jessica rubbed her hands down her
Levi's. "I was just out checking on my girls—my
orchids. The temperature is staying just fine out
there in the greenhouse. This is the first big snow
we've had and I was a little worried about them."

Rachel nodded. "Where's Kate?"

"Oh, she and Sam and Dan are out driving the
fence line. Earlier today, she got a call from Bo
Cunningham who said that some of our cattle were
on their property—again."

Groaning, Rachel said, "Life doesn't change at
all, does it, Jess?"

Giggling, Jessica shook her head. "No, it doesn't
seem to, does it? Don't you feel like you're a teenager again? We had the same problems with the
Cunninghams then as we do now." She sighed and
opened her hands. "I wish they wouldn't be so nasty
toward us. Frank Cunningham hates us."

"He hates everything," Rachel murmured.

"So how did Jim turn out to be so nice?"

"I don't know." Rachel picked absently at the bedcover. "He *is* nice, Jess. You should have seen him out there with me, at the accident. I was in bad shape. He was so gentle and soothing. I had such faith in him. I knew I'd be okay."

"He's been home almost a year now, and he's trying to mend a lot of fences."

"Are you saying he was nice to me because of the feud between our families?"

Jessica shook her head. "No, Jim is a nice guy. Somehow, he didn't get Frank's nasty genes like the other two boys did." She laughed. "I think he has his mother's, instead."

Rachel smiled. "I know one thing. I owe Jim my life."

"You owe him more than that," Jessica said primly as she tucked her hands in her lap. "Did he tell you he gave a pint of *his* blood to you?"

"What?" Rachel's eyes grew wide.

"Yeah, the blood transfusion. You lost a lot from the cut across your foot," she said, pointing to Rachel's foot beneath the cover. "I found out about it from the head nurse in ER when we came in to see how you were. Jim had called us from hospital and told us what had happened. Well," she murmured, "he was selective in what he told us. He really downplayed his part in saving you. He's so humble that way, you know? Anyway, I was asking the nurse what all had been done for you, because we don't have medical insurance and I knew Kate would be worrying about the bill. I figured I'd do some investigating for her and get the info so she wouldn't have to do it later.'' Clasping her hands together, she continued, ''You have a rare type of blood. They didn't have any on hand at the hospital, nor did they have any in Cottonwood. So I guess Jim volunteered his on the spot. He has the same blood type as you do.'' She smiled gently. ''Wasn't that sweet of him? I mean, talk about a symbolic thing happening between our two families.''

Rachel sat there, digesting her sister's explanation. Jim's blood was circulating in her body. It felt right. And good. ''I—see....'' Moistening her lips, she searched Jessica's small, open face. She loved her fiercely for her compassion and understanding. ''How do you feel about that?''

''Oh, I think it's wonderful!''

''And Kate?'' Tension nagged at Rachel's stomach over the thought of her older sister's reaction. Kate held grudges like their father did.

Jessica gazed up at the ceiling and then at her. ''Well, you know Kate. She wasn't exactly happy about it, but like she said, you're alive and that's what counts.''

''I'm glad she took the high road on this,'' Rachel murmured, chuckling.

Jessica nodded. ''We owe Jim so much. Kate knows that and so do I. I think he's wonderful. He's trying so hard to patch things up between the two families.''

"That's a tall order," Rachel said. She reached for the water pitcher on the bed stand. Pouring herself a glassful, she sipped it.

"I have faith in him," Jessica said simply. "His integrity, his morals and values are like sunshine compared to the darkness of the Cunningham ranch in general. "I believe he can change his father and two brothers."

"You're being overidealistic," Rachel cautioned.

"Maybe," she said. Reaching out, she ran her hand along Rachel's blanketed shin. "We're all wondering *what* made you skid off 89A. You know that road like the back of your hand. And you're used to driving in snow and ice."

Setting the glass on the bed table, Rachel frowned. "You're probably going to think I'm crazy."

Laughing, Jessica sat up. "Me? The metaphysical brat of the three of us? Nooo, I don't think so, Rachel." Leaning forward, her eyes animated, she whispered, "So tell me what happened!"

Groaning, Rachel muttered, "I saw a jaguar standing in the middle of 89A as I rounded that last hairpin curve."

Jessica's eyes widened enormously. "A jaguar? You saw a jaguar?"

Rachel grimaced. "I told you you'd think I was crazy."

Leaping up from the bed, her sister whispered, "Oh, gosh! This is *really* important, Rachel." Typical of Jessica, when she got excited she had to move around. She quickly rounded the bed, her hands flying in the air. "It was a jaguar? You're positive?"

"I know what I saw," Rachel said a bit defensively. "I know I was tired and I had jet lag, but I've never hallucinated in my life. No, it *was* a jaguar. Not a cougar, because I've seen the cougars that live all around us up here. It was a jaguar, with a black-and-gold coat and had huge yellow eyes. It was looking right at me. I was never so startled, Jess. I slammed on the brakes. I know I shouldn't have—but I did. If I hadn't, I'd have hit that cat."

"Oh, gosh, this is *wonderful!*" Jessica cried. She clapped her hands together, coming to a sudden halt at the end of Rachel's bed.

"Really? What's so wonderful about it? If this story ever gets out, I'll be the laughingstock of Sedona. There're no jaguars in Arizona."

Excitedly, Jessica whispered, "My friend Moyra, who is from Peru, lived near me for two years up in Canada. She helped me get my flower essence business going, and tended my orchid girls with me. What a mysterious woman she was! She was very metaphysical, very spiritual. Over the two years I knew her, she told me that she was a member of a very ancient order called the Jaguar Clan. She told me that she took her training in the jungles of Peru with some very, very old teachers who possessed jaguar medicine."

Rachel opened her mouth to reply, but Jessica gripped her hand, her words tumbling out in a torrent. "No, no, just listen to me, okay? Don't interrupt. Moyra told me that members of the Jaguar Clan came from around the world. They didn't have to be born in South America to belong. I guess it has something to do with one's genes. Anyway, I saw some very strange things with Moyra over the two years she was with me."

"Strange?"

"Well," she said, "Moyra could read minds. She could also use mental telepathy. There were so many times I'd start to ask her a question and she'd answer before I got it out of my mouth! Or…" Jessica paused, her expression less animated "…when Carl, my ex-husband, was stalking me and trying to find out where I was hiding, Moyra told me that she'd guard me and make sure he never got to me. I remember four different times when she warned me he was close and protected me from being found by him."

"You mean," Rachel murmured, "she *sensed* his presence?"

"Something like that, but it was more, much more. She had these heightened senses. And—" Jessica held her gaze "—I saw her do it one day."

"Do what?"

Jessica sighed and held up her right hand. "I *swear* I'm telling you the truth on this, Rachel. I was taking a walk in the woods, like I always did in the afternoon when I was done watering my girls in the greenhouse. It was a warm summer day and I wanted to go stick my feet in the creek about half a mile from where we lived. As I approached the creek, I froze. You won't believe this, but one minute I saw Moyra standing in the middle of the creek and in the next I saw a jaguar! Well, I just stood there in shock, my mouth dropping open. Then suddenly the jaguar turned back into Moyra. She turned around and looked right at me. I blinked. Gosh, I thought I was going crazy or something. I thought I was seeing things.''

Jessica patted her sister's hand and released it. "There were two other times that I saw Moyra change into a jaguar. I don't think she meant for me to see it—it just happened.''

"A woman who turns into a jaguar?" Rachel demanded.

"I know, I know," Jessica said. "It sounds crazy, but listen to this!" She sat down on the edge of the bed and faced Rachel. "I got up enough courage to ask Moyra about what I'd seen. She didn't say much, but she said that because she was a member of this clan, her spirit guide was a male jaguar. Every clan member has one. And that this spirit guide is her teacher, her protector, and she could send it out to help others or protect others if necessary." Excitedly, Jessica whispered, "Rachel, the last thing Moyra told me before I drove down here to live was that if I ever needed help, she would be there!''

Stymied, Rachel said, "That jaguar I saw was Moyra—or Moyra's spirit guardian?" Rachel had no trouble believing in spirit guardians, because

Odula, their mother, had taught them from a very early age that all people had such guides from the invisible realms. They were protectors, teachers and helpers if the person allowed them to be.

"It must have been one or the other!" Jessica exclaimed in awe.

"Because," Kate Donovan said, walking through the door and taking off her damp wool coat, "about half a mile down 89A from where you crashed, there was a fuel-oil tanker that collided with a pickup truck." She halted and smiled down at Jessica, placing her coat on a chair. "What you don't know, Rachel, is that five minutes after you spun out on that corner, that pickup truck slid into that tanker carrying fuel oil. There was an explosion, and everyone died."

Stunned, Rachel looked at Jessica. "And if I hadn't spun out on that corner..."

Kate brought the chair over and sat down near her bed. "Yep, *you* would have been killed in that explosion, too."

"My God," Rachel whispered. She frowned.

Jessica gave them both a wide-eyed look. "Then that jaguar showing up saved your life. It really did!"

Kate combed her fingers through her long, dark hair, which was mussed from wearing a cowboy hat all day. "I heard you two talking as I came down the hall. So you think it was your friend's jaguar that showed up?"

Jessica nodded. "I have no question about it.

Even now, about once a month, I have this dream that's not a dream, about Moyra. She comes and visits me. We talk over what's happening in our lives. Stuff like that. She's down at a place called the Village of the Clouds, and she said she's in training. She didn't say for what. She's very mysterious about that.''

"So, your friend comes in the dream state and visits with you?" Rachel asked. Odula had placed great weight and importance on dreaming, especially lucid dreaming, which was a technique embraced wholeheartedly by the Eastern Cherokee people.

"Yes," Jessica said in awe. "Wow…isn't that something?" She looked up at Kate. "How did you find this out?"

"At the ER desk as I was signing Rachel out. Once they had you extricated from your rental car," Kate told Rachel, "Jim's ambulance had to drive up to Flagstaff to get you ER care because of that mess down on 89A. There was no way they could get through to the Cottonwood Hospital. There were fire trucks all over the place putting out the fire from that wreck."

Rachel studied her two sisters. Kate looked drawn and tired in her pink flannel shirt, Levi's and cowboy boots. She worked herself to the bone for this ranch. "Once upon a time, jaguars lived in the Southwest," Rachel told them.

"Yeah," Kate muttered, "until the good ol' white man killed them all off. I hear, though, they're coming back. There're jaguars living just over the border in Mexico. It wouldn't surprise me if they've already reached here.'' She rubbed her face. ''And this Rim country where we live is ideal habitat for them.'' She smiled a little. ''Maybe what you saw wasn't from the spirit world, after all. Maybe it was a live one. The first jaguar back in the States?''

''Oh,'' Jessica said with a sigh, ''that would be neat, too!''

They all laughed. Rachel reached out and gripped Kate's work-worn hand. ''It's so good to be home. It feels like old times, doesn't it? The three of us in one or the other's bedroom, chatting and laughing?''

''Yeah,'' Kate whispered, suddenly emotional as she gripped Rachel's hand. ''It's nice to have you both here. Welcome home, sis.''

Home. The word sent a tide of undeniable warmth through Rachel. She saw tears in Jessica's eyes and felt them in her own.

''If it wasn't for Jim Cunningham,'' Rachel quavered, ''I wouldn't be here at all. We owe him a lot.''

Kate nodded grimly. ''Yes, we do.''

''Tomorrow I want to see him and thank him personally,'' Rachel told them. ''Jessica, can you find out if he's going to be at the fire department in Sedona?''

''Sure, no problem.'' She eased off the bed and wiped the tears from her eyes. ''He's the sweetest guy.''

Kate snorted. ''He's a Cunningham. What's the old saying? A tiger can't change his stripes?''

Rachel grinned at her older sister's sour reaction. "Who knows, Kate? Jim may not be a tiger at all. He may be a jaguar in disguise."

"You know his nickname and his Apache name are both Cougar," Jessica said excitedly.

"Close enough for me," Rachel said with a smile.

Chapter Four

"Hey, Cunningham, you got a visitor!"

Jim lifted his head as his name was shouted through the cavernous area where the fire trucks and ambulance sat waiting for another call. The bay doors were open and bright winter sunlight poured inside the ambulance where Jim sat, repacking some of the shelves with necessary items.

Who could it be? Probably one of his brothers wanting to borrow some money from him as usual. With a grunt he eased out of the ambulance and swung around the corner.

His eyes widened and he came to an abrupt halt. Rachel Donovan! Swallowing his surprise, he stood watching as she slowly walked toward him. Noontime sunlight cascaded down, burnishing her long dark hair with hints of red and gold. She wore conservative, light gray woolen slacks and a camel-colored overcoat.

Struck by her beauty, her quiet presence as she met and held his gaze, he watched her lips lift into a smile. Heat sheeted through him as he stood there. Like a greedy beggar, he absorbed her warm gaze. Her green eyes sparkled with such life that he felt his breath momentarily hitch. This wasn't the woman he'd met at the car accident. Not in the least. Amazed that she seemed perfectly fine three days after nearly losing her life, Jim managed a shy grin of welcome.

"Hey, you look pretty good," he exclaimed, meeting her halfway across the bay.

Rachel felt heat sting her cheeks. She was blushing again! Her old childhood response always seemed to show up at the most embarrassing times. She studied the man before her; he was dressed in his usual dark blue pants and shirt, the patches for the fire department adorning the sleeves. When he offered his hand to her, she was struck by the symbolic gesture. A Donovan and a Cunningham meeting not in anger, but in friendship. As far as she knew it was a first, and Rachel welcomed it.

As she slid her hand into his big square one she felt the calluses and strength of it. Yet she could feel by his grip that he was carefully monitoring that strength. But what Rachel noticed most of all was the incredible warmth and joy in his eyes. It stunned her. He was a Cunningham, she, a Donovan. Nearly a century-old feud stood between them, and a lot of bad blood.

"I should hope I look better," Rachel replied with a low, husky laugh. "I'm not a homeopath for nothing."

Jim forced himself to release Rachel's long, thin fingers. She had the hands of a doctor, a surgeon, maybe. There was such a fluid grace about her as she moved. Suddenly he remembered that she could have bled to death the other day if they hadn't arrived on scene to help her when they had, and he was shaken deeply once again.

"I'm just finishing up my shift." He glanced at his watch. "I have to do some repacking in the ambulance. Come on back and keep me company?"

She touched her cheek, knowing the heat in it was obvious. "I didn't want to bother you—"

"You're not a bother, believe me," he confided sincerely as he slid his hand beneath her elbow and guided her between the gargantuan fire trucks to the boxy ambulance that sat at the rear.

As Rachel allowed him to guide her, she saw a number of men and women firefighters, most of them watching television in the room off the main hangar. Yet she hardly noticed them. So many emotions were flowing through her as Jim cupped her elbow. What she recalled of him from junior high was a painfully shy teenager who couldn't look anyone directly in the eye. Of course, she understood that; she hadn't exactly been the homecoming queen type herself. Two shadows thrown together by life circumstance, Rachel thought, musing about their recent meeting.

Once they reached the back of the ambulance, Jim urged her to climb in. "You can sit in the hot seat," he joked, and pointed to the right of the gurney, where the next patient would lie.

Rachel carefully climbed in. She sat down and looked around. "Is this the one I was in?"

Jim smiled a little and opened up a box of rolled bandages. He counted out six and then stepped up into the ambulance. "Yes, it was," he said, sliding the plastic door on one of the shelves to one side to arrange the bandages. "We call her Ginger."

"I like that. You named your truck."

"Actually, my partner, Larry, named her." Jim made a motion toward the front of the ambulance. "All the fire trucks are ladies and they all have names, too." He studied Rachel as he crouched by one of the panels. "You look like your accident never happened. How are you feeling?"

With a slight laugh, she said, "Well, let's put it this way—my two sisters, Kate and Jessica, are getting married this Saturday out at the ranch. I'm their maid of honor. I could *not* stay sick." She pointed to her foot, which sported a white dressing across the top. "I had to get well fast or they'd have disowned me for not showing up for their weddings."

"You look terrific," Jim murmured. "Like nothing ever happened."

She waved her hands and laughed. "*That* was thanks to you and homeopathy. When I got back to the ranch, I had Jessica bath the wound with tincture of Calendula three times a day.'' She patted her injured foot. ''It really speeded up the healing.''

''And that stuff you took? What did you call it? Arnica? What did it do for you?''

She was pleased he remembered the remedy. ''Arnica reduces the swelling and trauma to injured soft tissue.''

He slid the last door shut, his inventory completed. ''That's a remedy we could sure use a lot of around here. We scrape so many people up off the highway that it would really help.''

Rachel watched as he climbed out of the ambulance. There was no wasted motion about Jim Cunningham. He was lithe, like the cougar he was named after. And she liked the sense of steadiness and calmness that emanated from him like a beacon. His Apache blood was obvious in the color of his skin, his dark, cut hair and high cheekbones. What she liked most were his wide, intelligent eyes and his mouth, which was usually crooked in a partial smile. Jim was such an opposite to the warring Cunningham clan he'd been born into. He was like his mother, who had been known for her calm, quiet demeanor. Rachel knew little more about her, except that she'd been always full of laughter, with a twinkle in her eye.

''We're done here,'' Jim said genially, holding out his hand to her. He told himself he was enjoying Rachel too much. He wondered if she was married, but he didn't see a wedding ring on her left hand as he took it into his own. She stepped carefully out of the ambulance to the concrete floor beside him. "And I'm done with my shift." He glanced at his watch. "Noon, exactly." And then he took a huge risk. "If I recall, up at the Flag hospital I offered you lunch. I know a great little establishment called the Muse Restaurant. Best mocha lattes in town. How about it?" His heart pumped hard once, underscoring just how badly he wanted Rachel to say yes.

Jim saw her forest green eyes sparkle with gold as he asked her the question. Did that mean yes or no? He hoped it meant yes and found himself holding his breath, waiting for her answer. As he studied her upturned face, he felt her undeniable warmth and compassion. There was a gentleness around her, a Zenlike quality that reminded him of a quiet pool of water—serene yet very deep and mysterious.

"Actually," Rachel said with a laugh, "I came here to invite *you* to lunch. It was to be a surprise. A way of thanking you for saving my neck."

A powerful sensation moved through Jim, catching him off guard. It was a delicious feeling.

"That's a great idea," he murmured, meaning it. "But I asked first, so you're my guest for lunch. Come on, we'll take my truck. It's parked just outside. I'll bring you back here afterward."

Rachel couldn't resist smiling. He looked boyish as the seriousness in his face, the wrinkle in his brow disappeared in that magical moment. Happiness filled her, making her feel as if she were walking on air. Once again Jim cupped his hand on her elbow to guide her out of the station. She liked the fact that he matched his stride to hers. Normally she was a fast walker, but the injury to her foot had slowed her down.

Jim's truck was a white Dodge Ram with a shiny chrome bumper. It was a big, powerful truck, and there was plenty of Arizona—red mud which stuck to everything—on the lower half of it, probably from driving down the three-mile dirt road to the Cunningham ranch. He opened the door for her and she carefully climbed in.

Rachel was impressed with how clean and neat the interior was, unlike many men's pickups. As she hooked the seat belt, she imagined the orderliness came from him working in the medical field and understanding the necessity of cleanliness. She watched as Jim climbed in, his face wonderfully free of tension. He ran his fingers through his short, dark hair and then strapped himself in.

"Have you thought about the repercussions of being seen out in public with me?" he drawled as he slipped the key into the ignition. The pickup purred to life, the engine making a deep growling sound.

Wrinkling her nose, Rachel said, "You mean the gossip that will spread because a Cunningham and a Donovan broke bread together?"

Grinning, he nodded and eased the truck out of the parking spot next to the redbrick building. "Exactly."

"I was over at Fay Seward's, the saddle maker's,

yesterday, and she was telling me all kinds of gossip she'd heard about us.''

Moving out into the traffic, slow moving because of the recent snow, Jim chuckled. "I'll bet."

Rachel looked out the window. The temperature was in the low thirties, the sky bright blue and filled with nonstop sunlight. She put her dark glasses on and simply enjoyed being near Jim as he drove from the tourist area of Sedona into what was known as West Sedona. "I really missed this place," she whispered.

The crimson rocks of Sedona created some of the most spectacular scenery he'd ever seen. Red sandstone and white limestone alike were capped with a foot of new, sparkling snow from the storm several days before. With the dark green mantle of forest across the top of the Rim, which rose abruptly to tower several thousand feet above Sedona, this was a place for an artist and photographer, he mused.

Glancing over at her, he asked, "Why did you stay away so long?"

Shrugging, Rachel met his inquiring gaze. "Isn't it obvious? Or is it only to me?"

Gripping the steering wheel a little more tightly, he became serious. "We both left when we were kids. Probably for similar reasons. I went into the forest service and became a firefighter. Where did you go? I heard you moved overseas?"

Pain moved through Rachel. She saw an equal amount in Jim's eyes. It surprised her in one way, because the men she had known never allowed much emotion to show. "I moved to England," she said.

"And Jessica went to Canada and Kate became a tumbleweed here in the States."

"Yes."

Jim could feel her vulnerability over the issue. "Sorry, I didn't mean to get so personal." He had no right, but Rachel just seemed to allow him to be himself, and it was much too easy to become intimate with her. Maybe it was because she was in the medical field; she had a doctor's compassion, but more so.

With a wave of her hand, she murmured, "No harm done. I knew when I moved home to try and help save our ranch that there were a lot of buried wounds that needed to be aired and cleaned out and dressed."

"I like your analogy. Yeah, we all have old wounds, don't we?" He pulled into a shopping center with a huge fountain that had been shut off for the winter. Pointing up the walk, he said, "The Muse—a literary café. All the writers and would-be writers come here and hang out. Since you're so intelligent, I thought you might enjoy being with your own kind."

Smiling, Rachel released the seat belt. "How did you know I'm writing a book?"

Jim opened his door. "Are you?"

With a laugh, she said, "Yes, I am." Before she could open her own door, Jim was there to do it. He offered his hand and she willingly took it because the distance to the ground was great and she had no desire to put extra stress on the stitches still in her foot.

"Thank you," she said huskily. How close he was! How very male he was. Rachel found herself wanting to sway those few inches and lean against his tall, strong frame. Jim's shoulders were broad, proudly thrown back. His bearing was dignified and filled with incredible self-confidence.

Unwilling to release her, Jim guided Rachel up the wet concrete steps. "So what are you writing on?" The slight breeze lifted strands of her dark hair from her shoulders, reminding him how thick and silky it was. His fingers itched to thread through those strands once again.

"A book on homeopathy and first aid. I'm almost finished. I already have a publisher for it, here in the States. It will be simultaneously published by an English firm, too."

He opened the door to the restaurant for her. "How about that? I know a famous person."

With a shake of her head; Rachel entered the warm restaurant, which smelled of baking bread. Inhaling the delicious scent, she waited for Jim to catch up with her. "Mmm, homemade bread. Doesn't it smell wonderful?"

He nodded. "Jamie and his partner, Adrian, make everything fresh here on the premises. No canned anything." He guided her around the corner to a table near the window. Each table, covered in white linen, was decorated with fresh, colorful flowers in a vase. The music was soft and New Age. In each corner stood towering green plants. Jim liked the place because it was alive with plants and flowers.

Rachel relinquished her coat to Jim. He placed it on one of several hooks in the corner. The place was packed with noontime clientele. In winter and spring, Sedona was busy with tourists from around the world who wanted to escape harsh winters at home. The snowfall earlier in the week was rare. Sedona got snow perhaps two to four times each winter. And usually, within a day or two, it had melted and been replaced with forty-degree weather in the daytime, thirty-degree temperatures at night.

Sitting down, Jim recognized some of the locals. He saw them watching with undisguised interest. The looks on their face said it all: a Cunningham and Donovan sitting together—peacefully—what a miracle! Frowning, Jim picked up the menu and then looked over at Rachel, who was studying hers.

"They've got great food here. Anything you pick will be good."

Rachel tried to pay attention to the menu. She liked the fact that Jim sat at her elbow and not across from her. It was so easy to like him, to want to get to know him better. She had a million questions to ask him, but knew she had to remain circumspect.

After ordering their lunch, and having steaming bowls of fragrant mocha latte placed in front of them, Rachel began to relax. The atmosphere of the Muse was low-key. Even though there wasn't an empty table, the noise level was low, and she appreciated that. Setting the huge bowl of latte down after taking a sip, she pressed the pink linen napkin briefly to her lips. Settling the napkin back in her lap, she met and held Jim's warm, interested gaze. He wasn't model handsome. His face had lines in it, marks of character from the thirty-some years of his life. His thick, dark brows moved up a bit in inquiry as she studied him.

"I know what you're thinking," he teased. "I'll bet you're remembering this acne-covered teenager from junior high school, aren't you?"

She folded her hands in front of her. "No, not really. I do remember you being terribly shy, though."

"So were you," he said, sipping his own latte. Jim liked the flush that suddenly covered her cheeks. There was such painfully obvious vulnerability to Rachel. How had she been able to keep it? Life usually had a way of knocking the stuffing out of most people, and everyone he knew hid behind a protective mask or wall as a result. Rachel didn't, he sensed. Maybe that was a testament to her obvious confidence.

"I was a wallflower," Rachel conceded with a nervous laugh. "Although I did attend several clubs after school."

"Drama and photography, if my memory serves me."

Her brows rose. "That's right! Boy, what a memory *you* have." She was flabbergasted that Jim would remember such a thing. If he remembered that, what else did he recall? And why would he retain such insignificant details of her life, anyway? Her heart beat a little harder for a moment.

With a shy shrug, Jim sipped more of his latte. "If the truth be told, I had a terrible crush on you back then. But you didn't know it. I was too shy to say anything, much less look you in the eyes." He chuckled over the memory.

Gawking, Rachel tried to recover. "A crush? On me?"

"Ridiculous, huh?"

She saw the pain in his eyes and realized he was waiting for her to make fun of him for such an admittance. Rachel would never do that to anyone. Especially Jim.

"No!" she whispered, touched. "I didn't know...."

"Are you sorry you didn't know?" Damn, why had he asked that? His stomach clenched. Why was it so important that Rachel like him as much as he had always liked her? His hands tightened momentarily around his bowl of latte.

"Never mind," he said, trying to tease her, "you don't have to answer that on the grounds it may incriminate you—or embarrass me."

Rachel felt his tension and saw the worry in his eyes. A scene flashed inside her head; of a little boy cowering, as if waiting to get struck. Sliding her fingers around her warm bowl of latte, she said, "I wish I had known, Jim. That's a beautiful compliment. Thank you."

Unable to look at her, he nervously took a couple of sips of his own. Wiping his mouth with the napkin, he muttered, "The past is the past."

Rachel smiled gently. "Our past follows us like a good friend. I'm sure you know that by now." Looking around, she saw several people staring openly at them with undisguised interest. "Like right now," she mused, "I see several locals watching us like bugs under a microscope." She met and held his gaze. Her lips curved in a grin. "Tell me our pasts aren't present!"

Glancing around, Jim realized Rachel was right. "Well, by tonight your name will be tarnished but good."

"What? Because I'm having lunch with the man who saved my life? I'd say that I'm in the best company in the world, with no apology. Wouldn't you?"

He felt heat in his neck and then in his face. Jim couldn't recall the last time he'd blushed. Rachel's gently spoken words echoed through him like a bell being rung on a very clear day. It was as if she'd reached out and touched him. Her ability to share her feelings openly was affecting him deeply. Taking in a deep breath, he held her warm green gaze, which suddenly glimmered with tears. Tears! The soft parting of her lips was his undoing. Embarrassed, he reached into his back pocket and produced a clean handkerchief.

"Here," he said gruffly, and placed it in her hand.

Dabbing her eyes, Rachel sniffed. "Don't belittle

what you did for me, Jim. I sure won't." She handed it back to him. He could barely meet her eyes, obviously embarrassed by her show of tears and gratitude. "You and I are in the same business in one way," she continued. "We work with sick and injured people. The only difference is your EMT work is immediate, mine is more long-term and certainly not as dramatic."

He refolded the handkerchief and stuffed it back into his rear pocket. "I'm not trying to make little of what we did out there for you, Rachel. It wasn't just me that saved your life. My partner, Larry, and four other firefighters were all working as a team to save you."

"Yes, but it was your experience that made you put that blood-pressure cuff on my leg, inflate it and stop the hemorrhaging from my foot."

He couldn't deny that. "Anyone would have figured that out."

"Maybe," Rachel hedged as she saw him begin to withdraw from her. Why wouldn't Jim take due credit for saving her life? The man had great humility. He never said "I," but rather "we" or "the team," and she found that a remarkable trait rarely seen in males.

Lowering her voice, she added, "And I understand from talking to Kate and Jessica, that you gave me a pint of your blood to stabilize me. Is that so?"

Trying to steel himself against whatever she felt about having his blood in her body, Jim lifted his head. When he met and held her tender gaze, something old and hurting broke loose in his heart. He recalled that look before. Rachel probably had forgotten the incident, but he never had. He had just been coming out of the main doors to go home for the day when he saw that a dog had been hit by a car out in front of the high school. Rachel had flown down the steps of the building, crying out in alarm as the dog was hurled several feet onto the lawn.

Falling to her knees, she had held the injured animal. Jim had joined her, along with a few other concerned students. Even then, Rachel had been a healer. She had torn off a piece of her skirt and pressed it against the dog's wounded shoulder to stop the bleeding. Jim had dropped his books and gone to help her. The dog had had a broken leg as well.

Jim remembered sinking to his knees directly opposite her and asking what he could do to help. The look Rachel was giving him now was the same one he'd seen on her face then. There was such clear compassion, pain and love in her eyes that he recalled freezing momentarily because the energy of it had knocked the breath out of him. Rachel had worn her heart on her sleeve back then, just as she did now. She made no excuses for how she felt and was bravely willing to share her vulnerability.

Shaken, he rasped, "Yeah, I was the only one around with your blood type." He opened his hands and looked at them. "I don't know how you feel about that, but I caught hell from my old man and my brothers about it.'' He glanced up at her. ''But I'm not sorry I did it, Rachel.''

Without thinking, Rachel slid her hand into his. Hers was slightly damp, while his was dry and strong and nurturing. She saw surprise come to his eyes and felt him tense for a moment, then relax.

As his fingers closed over Rachel's, Jim knew tongues would wag for sure now about them holding hands. But hell, nothing had ever felt so right to him. Ever.

''I'm grateful for what you did, Jim,'' Rachel quavered. ''I wouldn't be sitting here now if you hadn't been there to help. I don't know how to repay you. I really don't. If there's a way—''

His fingers tightened around hers. ''I'm going hiking in a couple of weeks, near Boynton Canyon. Come with me?'' The words flew out of his mouth. What the hell was he doing? Jim couldn't help himself, nor did he want to. He saw Rachel's eyes grow tender and her fingers tightened around his.

''Yes, I'd love to do that.''

''Even though,'' he muttered, ''we'll be the gossip of Sedona?''

She laughed a little breathlessly. ''If I cared, really cared about that, I wouldn't be sitting here with you right now, would I?''

A load shifted off his shoulders. Rachel was free in a way that Kate Donovan was not, and the discovery was powerful and galvanizing. Jim very reluctantly released her hand. ''Okay, two weeks. I'm free on Saturday. I'll pack us a winter picnic lunch to boot.''

''Fair enough,'' Rachel murmured, thrilled over the prospect of the hike. ''But I have one more favor to ask of you first, Jim.''

''Name it and it's yours,'' he promised thickly.

Rachel placed her elbows on the table and lowered her voice. ''It's a big favor, Jim, and you don't have to do it if it's asking too much of you.''

Scowling, he saw the sudden worry and seriousness on her face. ''What is it?''

Moistening her lips, Rachel picked up her purse from the floor and opened it. Taking out a thick, white envelope, she handed it to him. ''Read it, please.''

Mystified, Jim eased the envelope open. It was a wedding invitation—to Kate and Jessica's double wedding, which would be held on Saturday. He could feel the tension in Rachel. His head spun with questions and few answers. Putting the envelope aside, he held her steady gaze.

''You're serious about this…invitation?''

''Very.''

''Look,'' he began uneasily, holding up his hands, ''Kate isn't real comfortable with me being around. I understand why and—''

''Kate was the one who suggested it.''

Jim stared at her. ''What?''

Rachel looked down at the tablecloth for a moment. ''Jim,'' she began unsteadily, her voice strained, ''I've heard why you came back here, back to Sedona. You want to try and straighten out a lot of family troubles between yourself, your father and two brothers. Kate didn't trust you at first because of the past, the feud between our families…actually, between our fathers, not us for the most part.'' She looked up and held his dark, shadowed gaze. ''Kate doesn't trust a whole lot of people. Her life experiences make her a little more paranoid than me or Jessica, but that's okay, too. Yesterday she brought this invitation to me and told me to give it to you. She said that because you'd saved my life, she and Jessica wanted you there. That this was a celebration of life—and love—and that you deserved to be with us.''

He saw the earnestness in Rachel's eyes. ''How do you feel about it? Having the enemy in your midst?''

''You were never my enemy, Jim. None of you were. Kelly had his battles with your father. Not with me, not with my sisters. Your brothers are another thing. They aren't invited.'' Her voice grew husky. ''I *want* you to be there. I like Kate's changing attitude toward you. It's a start in healing this wound that festers among us. I know you'll probably feel uncomfortable, but by showing up, it's a start, even if only symbolically, don't you think? A positive one?''

In that moment, Jim wished they were anywhere but out in a public place. The tears in Rachel's eyes made them shine and sparkle like dark emeralds. He wanted to whisper her name, slide his hands through that thick mass of hair, angle her head just a little and kiss her until she melted into his being, into his heart. Despite her background, Rachel was so fresh, so alive, so brave about being herself and sharing her feelings, that it allowed him the same privilege within himself.

He wanted to take her hand and hold it, but he couldn't. He saw the locals watching them like proverbial hawks now. Jim didn't wish gossip upon Rachel or any of the Donovan sisters. God knew, they had suffered enough of it through the years.

One corner of his mouth tugged upward. ''I'll be there,'' he promised her huskily.

Chapter Five

"**W**here you goin' all duded up?" Bo Cunningham drawled as he leaned languidly against the open door to Jim's bedroom.

Jim glanced over at his brother. Bo was tall and lean, much like their father. His dark good looks had always brought him a lot of attention from women. In high school, Bo had been keenly competitive with Jim. Whatever Jim undertook, Bo did too. The rivalry hadn't stopped and there was always tension, like a razor, between them.

"Going to a wedding," he said.

He knotted his tie and snugged it into place against his throat. In all his years of traveling around the U.S. as a Hotshot, he'd never had much call for wearing a suit. But after having lunch with Rachel, he'd gone to Flagstaff and bought one. Jim had known that when his two brothers saw him in a suit, they'd be sure to make fun of him. Uniform of the day around the Bar C was jeans, a long-sleeved shirt and a cowboy hat. He would wear his dark brown Stetson to the wedding, however. The color of his hat would nearly match the raw umber tone of his suit. A new white shirt and dark green tie completed his ensemble.

Bo's full lips curled a little. "I usually know of most weddin's takin' place around here. Only one I know of today is the Donovan sisters."

Inwardly, Jim tried to steel himself against the inevitable. "That's the one," he murmured, picking up his brush and moving it one last time across his short, dark hair. It was nearly 1:00 p.m. and the wedding was scheduled for 2:00. He had to hurry.

"You workin' at bein' a traitor to this family?"

Bo's chilling question made him freeze. Slowly turning, he saw that his brother was no longer leaning against his bedroom door, but standing tensely. The stormy look on his face was what Jim expected.

Picking up his hat, Jim stepped toward him. "Save your garbage for somebody who believes it, Bo" Then he moved past him and down the hall. Since Jim had come home, Bo had acted like a little bantam rooster, crowing and strutting because their father was planning in leaving Bo and Chet the ranch—and not Jim. Frank Cunningham had disowned his youngest son the day he'd left home years before. As Jim walked into the main living area, he realized he'd never regretted that decision. What he did regret was Bo trying at every turn to get their father to throw him off the property now.

As Jim settled his hat on his head, he saw his father positioned near the heavy cedar door that he had to walk through to get to his pickup. The look on his father's face wasn't pleasant, and Jim realized that Bo, an inveterate gossip, had already told him everything.

"Where you goin', son?"

Jim halted in front of his father's wheelchair. As he studied his father's eyes, he realized the old man was angry and upset, but not out of control. He must have remembered his meds today. For that, Jim breathed an inner sigh of relief.

"I'm going to a wedding," he said quietly. "Kate and Jessica Donovan are getting married. It's a double wedding."

His father's brows dipped ominously. "Who invited you?"

"Kate did." Jim felt his gut twist. He could see his father's rage begin to mount, from the flash of light in his bloodshot eyes to the way he set his mouth into that thin, hard line.

"You could've turned down the invitation."

"I didn't want to." Jim felt his adrenaline start to pump. He couldn't help feeling threatened and scared—sort of like the little boy who used to cower in front of his larger-than-life father. When Frank Cunningham went around shouting and yelling, his booming voice sounded like thunder itself. Jim knew that by coming back to the ranch he would go through a lot of the conditioned patterns he had when he was a child and that he had to work through and dissolve them. He was a man now, not a little boy. He struggled to remain mature in his reactions with his father and not melt into a quivering mass of fear like he had when he was young.

"You had a choice," Frank growled.

"Yes." Jim sighed. "I did."

"You're doin' this on purpose. Bo said you were."

Jim looked to his right. He saw Bo amble slowly out of the hallway, a gleeful look in his eyes. His brother *wanted* this confrontation. Bo took every opportunity to make things tense between Jim and his father in hopes that Jim would be banned forever from the ranch and their lives. Jim knew Bo was worried that Frank would change his will and give Jim his share of the ranch. The joke was Jim would never take it. Not on the terms that Frank would extract from him. No, he wouldn't play those dark family games anymore. Girding himself against his father's well-known temper, Jim looked down into his angry eyes.

"What I do, Father, is my business. I'm not going to this wedding to hurt you in any way. But if that's what they want you to believe, and you want to believe it, then I can't change your mind."

"They're *Donovan's!*" Frank roared as he gripped the arms of his wheelchair, his knuckles turning white. His breathing became harsh and swift.

"Damn you, Jim! You just don't get it, do you, boy? They're our enemies!"

Jim's eyes narrowed. "No, they're not our enemies! You and I have had this argument before. I'm not going to have it again. They're decent people. I'm not treating them any differently than I'd treat you or a stranger on the street."

"Damn you to hell," Frank snarled, suddenly leaning back and glaring up at him. "If I wasn't imprisoned in this damned chair, I'd take a strap to you! I'd stop you from going over there!"

"Come on, Pa," Bo coaxed, sauntering over and patting him sympathetically on the shoulder. "Jim's a turncoat. He's showin' his true colors, that's all. Come on, lemme take you to town. We'll go over to the bar and have a drink of whiskey and drown our troubles together over this."

Glaring at Bo, Jim snapped, "He's diabetic! You know he can't drink liquor."

Bo grinned smugly. "You're forcing him to drink. It's not my fault."

Breathing hard, Jim looked down at his father, a pleading expression in his eyes. Before Frank became diabetic, he'd been a hard drinker. Jim was sure he was an alcoholic, but he never said so. Now Jim centered his anger on Bo. His brother knew a drink would make his father's blood sugar leap off the scale, that it could damage him in many ways and potentially shorten his life. Jim knew that Bo hated his father, but he never showed it, never confronted him on anything. Instead, Bo used passive-

aggressive ways of getting what he wanted. This
wasn't the first time his brother had poured Frank a
drink or two. And Bo didn't really care what it did
to his father's health. His only interest was getting
control of the ranch once Frank died.

Even his father knew alcohol wasn't good for his
condition. But Jim wasn't about to launch into the
reasons why he shouldn't drink. Placing his hand on
the doorknob, he rasped, "You're grown men.
You're responsible for whatever you decide to do."

The wedding was taking place at the main ranch
house. The sky was sunny and the sky a deep, almost startling blue. As Jim drove up and parked his
pickup on the graveled driveway, he counted more
than thirty other vehicles. Glancing at his watch, he
saw that it was 2:10 p.m. He was late, dammit. With
his stomach still in knots from his confrontation with
his father, he gathered up the wedding gifts and hurried to the porch of the ranch house. There were
garlands of evergreen with pine cones, scattered
with silver, red and gold glitter, framing the door,
showing Jim that the place had been decorated with
a woman's touch.

Gently opening the door, he saw Jessica and Kate
standing with their respective mates near the huge
red-pink-and-white flagstone fireplace. Rachel was
there, too. Reverend Thomas O'Malley was presid-
ing and sonorously reading from his text. Walking
as quietly as he could, Jim felt the stares of a number
of people in the gathered group as he placed the

wrapped gifts on a table at the back of the huge room.

Taking off his hat, he remained at the rear of the crowd that had formed a U around the two beautiful brides and their obviously nervous grooms. Looking up, he saw similar pine boughs and cones hung across each of the thick timbers that supported the ceiling of the main room. The place was light and pretty compared to the darkness of his father's home. Light and dark. Jim shut his eyes for a moment and tried to get a hold on his tangled, jumbled emotions.

When he opened his eyes, he moved a few feet to the left to get a better look at the wedding party. His heart opened up fiercely as he felt the draw of Rachel's natural beauty.

Both brides wore white. Kate had on a long, traditional wedding gown of what looked to Jim like satin, and a gossamer veil on her hair. Tiny pearl buttons decorated each of her wrists and the scoop neck of her dress. Kate had never looked prettier, with her face flushed, her eyes sparkling, her entire attention focused on Sam McGuire, who stood tall and dark at her side. In their expressions, Jim could see their love for one another, and it eased some of his own internal pain.

Jessica wore a tailored white wool suit, decorated with a corsage of several orchids. In her hair was a ringlet of orchids woven with greenery, making her look like a fairy. Jim smiled a little. Jessica had always reminded him of some ethereal being, someone not quite of this earth, but made more from the stuff of heaven. He eyed Dan Black, dressed in a dark blue suit and tie, standing close beside his wife-to-be. Jim noticed the fierce love in Black's eyes for Jessica. And he saw tears running down Jessica's cheeks as she began to repeat her vows to Dan.

The incredible love between the two couples soothed whatever demons were left in him. Jim listened to Kate's voice quaver as she spoke the words to Sam. McGuire, whose face usually was rock hard and expressionless, was surprisingly readable. The look of tenderness, of open, adoring love for Kate, was there to be seen by everyone at the gathering. Jim's heart ached. He wished he would someday feel that way about a woman. And then his gaze settled on Rachel.

The ache in his heart softened, then went away as he hungrily gazed at her. He felt like a thief, stealing glances at a woman he had no right to even look at twice. How she looked today was a far cry from how she'd looked out at the accident site. She was radiant in a pale pink, long-sleeved dress that brushed her thin ankles. A circlet of orchids similar to Jessica's rested in her dark, thick hair, which had been arranged in a pretty French braid, and she carried a small bouquet of orchids and greenery in her hands. She wore no make-up, which Jim applauded. Rachel didn't need any, he thought, struck once again by her exquisite beauty.

Her lips were softly parted. Tears shone in two paths across her high cheekbones as the men now began to speak their vows to Kate and Jessica. Everything about Rachel was soft and vulnerable, Jim realized. She didn't try to hide behind a wall like Kate did. She was open, like Jessica. But even more so, in a way Jim couldn't yet define. And then something electric and magical happened. Rachel, as if sensing his presence, his gaze burning upon her, lifted her head a little and turned to look toward him. Their eyes met.

In that split second, Jim felt as if a lightning bolt had slammed through him. Rachel's forest green eyes were velvet, and glistening with tears. He saw the sweet curve of her full lips move upward in silent welcome. Suddenly awkward, Jim felt heat crawling up his neck and into his face. Barely nodding in her direction, he tried to return her smile. He saw relief in her face, too. Relief that he'd come? Was it personal or symbolic of the fragile union being forged between their families? he wondered. Jim wished that it was personal. He felt shaken inside as Rachel returned her attention to her sisters, but he felt good, too.

The dark mass of knots in his belly miraculously dissolved beneath Rachel's one, welcoming look. There was such a cleanness to her and he found himself wanting her in every possible way. Yet as soon as that desire was born, a sharp stab of fear followed. She was a Donovan. He was a Cunningham. Did he dare follow his heart? If he did, Jim knew that the hell in his life would quadruple accordingly. His father would be outraged. Bo would

use it as another lever to get him to look unworthy
to Frank. Jim had come home to try and change the
poisonous condition of their heritage. What was
more important—trying to change his family or
wanting to know Rachel much, much better?

There was a whoop and holler when both grooms
kissed their brides, and the party was in full swing
shortly after. Jim recognized everyone at the festive
gathering. He joined in the camaraderie, the joy
around him palpable. The next order of business was
tossing the bridal bouquets. Jim saw Rachel stand at
the rear of the excited group, of about thirty women,
and noticed she wasn't really trying to jockey for a
position to possibly catch one of those beautiful orchid bouquets. Why not?

Both Kate and Jessica threw their bouquets at the
same time. There were shrieks, shouts and a sudden
rush forward as all the women except Rachel tried
to catch them. Ruby Forester, a waitress in her early
forties who worked at the Muse Restaurant, caught
Jessica's. Kate's bouquet was caught by Lannie
Young, who worked at the hardware store in Cottonwood. Both women beamed in triumph and held
up their bouquets.

Remaining at the rear of the crowd, Jim saw two
wedding cakes being rolled out of the kitchen and
into the center of the huge living room. From time
to time he saw Rachel look up, as if searching for
him in the crowd of nearly sixty people. She was
kept busy up front as the cakes were cut, and then

sparkling, nonalcoholic grape juice was passed around in champagne glasses.

After the toast, someone went over to the grand piano in the corner, and began to play a happy tune. The crowd parted so that a dance floor was spontaneously created. A number of people urged Kate and Sam out on the floor, and Jim saw Jessica drag Dan out there, too. Jim felt sorry for the new husbands, who obviously weren't first-rate dancers. But that didn't matter. The infectious joy of the moment filled all of them and soon both brides and grooms were dancing and whirling on the hardwood oak floor, which gleamed beneath them.

Finishing off the last of his grape juice, Jim saw a number of people with camcorders filming the event. Kate and Jessica would have a wonderful memento of one of the happiest days of their lives. He felt good about that. It was time the Donovans had a little luck, a little happiness.

After the song was finished, everyone broke into applause. The room rang with laugher, clapping and shouts of joy. The woman at the piano began another song and soon the dance floor was crowded with other well-wishers. Yes, this was turning into quite a party. Jim grinned and shook a number of people's hands, saying hello to them as he slowly made his way toward the kitchen. He wanted to find Rachel now that her duties as the maid of honor were pretty much over.

The kitchen was a beehive of activity, he discovered as he placed his used glass near the sink. At least seven women were bustling around placing hors d'oeuvres on platters, preparing them to be taken out to serve to the happy crowd in the living room. He spotted Rachel in the thick of things. Through the babble he heard her low, husky voice giving out directions. Her cheeks were flushed a bright pink and she had rolled up the sleeves on her dress to her elbows. The circlet of orchids looked fetching in her hair. The small pearl earrings in her ears, and the single-strand pearl necklace around her throat made her even prettier in his eyes, if that were possible.

Finally, the women paraded out, carrying huge silver platters piled high with all types of food—from meat to fruit to vegetables with dip. Jim stepped to one side and allowed the group to troop by. Suddenly it was quiet in the kitchen. He looked up to see Rachel leaning against the counter, giving him an amused look.

He grinned a little and moved toward her. The pink dress had a mandarin collar and showed off her long, graceful neck to advantage. The dress itself had an empire waistline and made her look deliciously desirable.

"I got here a little late," he said. "I'm sorry."

Pushing a strand of dark hair off her brow, Rachel felt her heart pick up in beat. How handsome and dangerous Jim looked in his new suit. "I'm just glad you came," she whispered, noting the genuine apology in his eyes.

"I am, too." He forced himself not to reach out

and touch her—or kiss her. Right now, Rachel looked so damned inviting that he had to fight himself. "Doesn't look like your foot is bothering you at all."

"No, complete recovery, thanks to you and a little homeopathic magic." She felt giddy. Like a teenager. Rachel tried to warn herself that she shouldn't feel like this toward any man again. The last time she'd felt even close to this kind of feeling for a man, things hadn't ended well between them. Trying to put those memories aside, Rachel lifted her hands and said, "You clean up pretty good, too, I see."

Shyly, Jim touched the lapel of his suit. "Yeah, first suit I've had since...I don't remember when."

"Well," Rachel said huskily, "you look very handsome in it."

Her compliment warmed him as if she had kissed him. Jim found himself wanting to kiss her, to capture that perfect mouth of hers that looked like orchid petals, and feel her melt hotly beneath his exploration. He looked deep into her forest green eyes and saw gold flecks of happiness in them. "I hope by coming in late I didn't upset anything or anyone?"

She eased away from the counter and wiped her hands on a dish towel, suddenly nervous because he was so close to her. Did Jim realize the power he had over her? She didn't think so. He seemed shy and awkward around her, nothing like the charge medic she'd seen at her accident. No, that man had been confident and gentle with her, knowing exactly what to do and when. Here, he seemed tentative and unsure. Rachel laughed at herself as she fluttered nervously around the kitchen, realizing she felt the same way.

"I have to get back out there," she said a little breathlessly. "I need to separate the gifts. They'll be opening them next."

"Need some help?"

Hesitating in the doorway, Rachel laughed a little. "Well, sure.... Come on."

Jim and Rachel took up positions behind the linen-draped tables as the music and dancing continued unabated. He felt better doing something. Occasionally, their hands would touch as they closed over the same brightly wrapped gift, and she would jerk hers away as if burned. Jim didn't know how to interpret her reaction. He was, after all, a dreaded Cunningham. And more than once he'd seen a small knot of people talking, quizzically studying him and then talking some more. Gossip was the lifeblood of any small town, and Sedona was no exception. He sighed. Word of a Cunningham attending the Donovan weddings was sure to be the chief topic at the local barbershop come Monday morning.

Worse, he would have to face his father and brothers tonight at the dinner table. His stomach clenched. Trying to push all that aside, he concentrated on the good feelings Rachel brought up in him. Being the maid of honor, she had to make sure everything ran smoothly. It was her responsibility to see that Kate and Jessica's wedding went off without a hitch. And it looked like everything was going wonderfully. The hors d'oeuvres were placed on another group of tables near the fireplace, where flames were snapping and crackling. Paper plates, pink napkins and plenty of coffee, soda and sparkling grape juice would keep the guests well fed in the hours to come.

It was nearly 5:00 p.m. by the time the crowd began to dissipate little by little. Jim didn't want to go home. He had taken off his coat, rolled up his shirtsleeves and was helping wash dishes out in the kitchen, along with several women. Someone had to do the cleanup. Kate and Sam had gone to Flagstaff an hour earlier, planning to stay at a friend's cabin up in the pine country. Jessica and Dan had retired to their house on the Donovan spread, not wanting to leave the ranch.

Jim had his hands in soapy water when Rachel reappeared. He grinned at her as she came through the doorway. She'd changed from her pink dress into a pair of dark tan wool slacks, a long-sleeved white blouse and a bright, colorful vest of purple, pink and red. Her hair was still up in the French braid, but the circlet of orchids had disappeared. The pearl choker and earrings were gone, too.

She smiled at him as she came up and took over drying dishes from one of the older women. "I can see the look on your face, Mr. Cunningham."

"Oh?" he teased, placing another platter beneath the warm, running water to rinse it off.

"The look on your face says, 'Gosh, you changed out of that pretty dress for these togs.'"

"You're a pretty good mind reader." And she was. Jim wondered if his expression was really that revealing. Or was it Rachel's finely honed observation skills that helped her see through him? Either way, it was disconcerting.

"Thank you," she said lightly, taking the platter from him. Their fingers touched. A soft warmth flowed up her hand, making her heart beat a little harder.

"I'm sorry I didn't get to dance with you," Rachel said in a low voice. There were several other women in the kitchen and she didn't want them to overhear.

Jim had asked her to dance earlier, but she had reluctantly chosen kitchen duties over his invitation. He'd tried not to take her refusal personally—but he had. The Cunningham-Donovan feud still stood between them. He understood that Rachel didn't want to be seen in the arms of her vaunted enemy at such a public function.

"That's okay. You were busy." Jim scrubbed a particularly dirty skillet intently. Just the fact that Rachel was next to him and they were working together like a team made his heart sing.

"I wished I hadn't been," Rachel said, meaning it. She saw surprise flare in his eyes and then, just as quickly, he suppressed his reaction.

"You know how town gossip is," Jim began, rinsing off the iron skillet. "You just got home and you don't need gossip about being caught in the arms of a Cunningham haunting your every step." He handed her the skillet and met her grave gaze.

Pursing her lips, Rachel closed her fingers over his as she took the skillet. She felt a fierce longing build in her. She saw the bleakness in Jim's eyes, and heard the past overwhelming the present feelings between them. She wanted to touch him, and found herself inventing small ways of doing just that. The light in his eyes changed as her fingertips brushed his. For an instant, she saw raw, hungry desire in his eyes. Or had she? It had happened so fast, Rachel wondered if she was making it up.

"That had nothing to do with it, Jim," she said, briskly drying the skillet. "Kate told me you'd come home to try and mend some family problems. She told me how much you've done to try and make that happen. I find it admirable." Grimacing, she set the skillet aside and watched him begin to scrub a huge platter. "I really admire you." And she did.

Jim lifted his chin and glanced across his shoulder at her. There was pleasure in his eyes. Shrugging her shoulders, Rachel said, "I don't know if you'll be successful or not. You have three men who want to keep the vendetta alive between us. And I'm *sure*," she continued huskily, holding his gaze, "that you caught hell today for coming over here."

Chuckling a little, Jim nodded and began to rinse the platter beneath the faucet. "Just a little. But I don't regret it, Rachel. Not one bit."

She stood there assessing the amount of discomfort she heard in his voice. She was a trained homeopath, taught to pay attention to voice tone, facial expressions and body language, and sense on many level what was really being felt over what was being verbally said. Jim was obviously trying to make light of a situation that, in her gut, she knew was a huge roadblock for him.

"Did your father get upset?"

Obviously uncomfortable, Jim handed her the rinsed platter. "A little," he hedged.

"Probably a lot. Has Bo changed since I saw him in school? He used to be real good at manipulating people and situations to his own advantage."

Jim pulled the plug and let the soapy water run out of the sink. "He hasn't changed much," he admitted, sadness in his voice.

"And Chet? Is he still a six-year-old boy in a man's body? And still behaving like one?"

Grinning, Jim nodded. "You're pretty good at pegging people."

Drying the platter, Rachel said, "It comes from being a homeopath for so many years. We're trained to observe, watch and listen on many levels simultaneously."

Jim rinsed off his soapy hands and took the towel she handed him. "Thanks. Well, I'm impressed." He saw her brows lower in thought. "So, what's your prescription for my family, Doctor?"

She smiled a little and put the platter on the table behind them. The other women had left, their duties done, and she and Jim were alone—at last. Rachel leaned against the counter, with no more than a few feet separating them. "When you have three people who want a poisonous situation to continue, who don't want to change, mature or break certain habit patterns, I'd say you're in over your head."

Unable to argue, he hung the cloth up on a nail on the side of the cabinet next to the sink. Slowly rolling his sleeves down, Jim studied her. "I won't disagree with your assessment."

Her heart ached for him. In that moment, Rachel saw a vulnerable little boy with too much responsibility heaped upon his shoulders at too young an age. His mother had died when he was six, as she recalled, leaving three little boys robbed of her nurturing love. Frank Cunningham had lost it after his wife died. Rachel remembered that story. He'd gone on a drinking binge that lasted a week, until he finally got into a fight at a local bar and they threw him in the county jail to cool down. In the meantime, Bo, Chet and Jim had had to run the ranch without their grief-stricken father. Three very young boys had been saddled with traumatic responsibilities well beyond their years or understanding. Rachel felt her heart breaking for all of them.

"Hey," she whispered, "everyone's leaving. I'd love to have some help moving the furniture back into place in the living room. It's going to quiet down now. Do you have time to help me or do you have to go somewhere?"

Jim felt his heart pound hard at the warmth in her voice, the need in her eyes—for his company. Her invitation was genuine. A hunger flowed through him. He ached to kiss Rachel. To steal the goodness of her for himself. Right now he felt impoverished, overwhelmed by the situation with his family, and he knew that by staying, he was only going to make things worse for himself when he did go home. His father expected him for dinner at 6:00 p.m. It was 5:30 now.

As Jim stood there, he felt Rachel's soft hand, so tentative, on his arm. Lifting his head, he held her compassionate gaze. "Yeah, I can stick around to help you. Let me make a phone call first."

Smiling softly, Rachel said, "Good."

Chapter Six

Jim enjoyed the quiet of the evening with Rachel. The fire was warm and cast dancing yellow light out into the living room, where they sat on the sofa together, coffee in hand. It had taken them several hours to get everything back in order and in place. Rachel had fixed them some sandwiches a little while ago—a reward for all their hard work. Now she sat on one end of the sofa, her long legs tucked beneath her, her shoes on the floor, a soft, relaxed look on her face.

Jim sat at the other end, the cup between his square hands. Everything seemed perfect to him—the quiet, the snowflakes gently falling outside, the beauty of a woman he was drawn more and more by the hour, the snap and crackle of the fire, the intimacy of the dimly lit room. Yes, he was happy, he realized—in a way he'd never been before.

Rachel studied Jim's pensive features, profiled against the dark. He had a strong face, yet his sense of humor was wonderful. The kind of face that shouted of his responsible nature. Her stomach still hurt, they had laughed so much while working together. Really, Rachel admitted to herself, he was terribly desirable to her in every way. Rarely had she seen such a gentle nature in a man. Maybe it was because he was an EMT and dealt with people in crisis all the time. He was a far cry from her father, who had always been full of rage. Maybe her new relationship with Jim was a good sign of her health—she was reaching out to a man of peace, not violence.

Pulling herself from her reverie, she said, "Did I ever tell you what made me slam on my brakes up there in the canyon?"

Jim turned and placed his arm across the back of the couch. "No. I think you said it was a cat."

Rachel rolled her eyes. "It wasn't a cougar. When I got home from ER, I asked Jessica to bring me an encyclopedia. I lay there in bed with books surrounding me. I looked under *L* for leopard, and that wasn't what I saw. When I looked under *J* for jaguar…" She gave him a bemused look. "That was what I saw out there, Jim, in the middle of an ice-covered highway that morning—a jaguar." She saw the surprise flare in his eyes. "I thought I was hallucinating, of course, but then something very unusual—strange—happened.''

"Oh?'' Jim replied with a smile. He liked the way her mouth curved into a self-deprecating line. Rachel had no problem poking fun at herself—she was confident enough to do so. As she moved her hand to punctuate her story, he marveled at her effortless grace. She was like a ballet dancer. He wanted to say that she had the grace of a jungle cat—a boneless, rhythmic way of moving that simply entranced him.

"Jessica and Kate came in about an hour later to check on me, and when I showed them the picture in the encyclopedia, well, Jessica went bonkers!'' Rachel chuckled. "She began babbling a mile a minute—you know how Jess can get when she's excited—and she told me the following story, which I've been meaning to share with you.''

Interested, Jim placed his empty coffee cup on the table. The peacefulness that surrounded Rachel was something he'd craved. Any excuse to remain in her company just a few minutes longer he'd take without apology. "Let's hear it. I like stories. I recall Mom always had a story for me at bedtime,'' he said wistfully, remembering those special times.

Sipping her coffee thoughtfully, Rachel decided to give Jim all the details Jessica had filled her in on since the day she'd come home from the hospital. "Awhile back, Morgan Trayhern and his wife, Laura, visited with us. They were trying to put the pieces of their lives back together after being kidnapped by drug lords from South America. An Army Special Forces officer by the name of Mike Houston was asked to come and stay with them and be their "guard dog" while they were here with us. Dr. Ann Parsons, an MD and psychiatrist who worked for Morgan's company, Perseus, also stayed here." Rachel gestured to the north. "They each stayed in one of the houses here at the ranch.

"Jessica made good friends with Mike and Ann while we were here for the week following Kelly's funeral. At the time, I was too busy helping Kate to really get to know them, although we shared a couple of meals with them and I helped Morgan and Laura move into the cabin up in the canyon, where they stayed." She frowned slightly. "One of the things Jessica said was that she confided in Mike. She asked how he, one man, could possibly protect anyone from sneaking up on Morgan and Laura if they wanted to, the ranch was so large. I guess Mike laughed and said that he had a little help. Jessica pressed him on that point, and he said that his mother's people, the Quechua Indians, had certain people within their nation who had a special kind of medicine. 'Medicine,' as you know, means a skill or talent. He said he was born with jaguar medicine."

Laughing, Rachel placed her cup on the coffee table. The intent look in Jim's eyes told her he was fascinated with her story. He wasn't making fun of her or sitting there with disbelief written across his face, so she continued. "Well, this little piece of information really spurred Jessica on to ask more questions. You know how she is." Rachel smiled fondly. "As 'fate' would have it, Jessica's good friend, Moyra, who lived up in Vancouver, was also a member of a Jaguar Clan down in Peru. And, of course, Mike was stationed in Peru as a trainer for Peruvian soldiers who went after the drug lords and stopped cocaine shipments from coming north to the U.S. Jessica couldn't let this little development go, so she really nagged Mike to give her more information.

"Mike told her that he was a member of the Jaguar Clan. He teasingly said that down there, in Peru, they called him the Jaguar god. Of course, this really excited Jessica, who is into paranormal things big-time." Again, Rachel laughed softly. "She told Mike that Moyra had *hinted* that members of the Jaguar Clan possessed certain special 'powers.' Did he? Mike tried to tease her and deflect her, but she just kept coming back and pushing him for answers. Finally, one night, just before she left to go home to Canada, Mike told her that people born with Jaguar Clan blood could do certain things most other people could not. They could heal, for one thing. And when they touched someone they cared about or loved, that person could be saved—regardless of how sick or wounded he or she was. Mike admitted that he'd gotten his nickname out in the jungles fighting cocaine soldiers and drug lords. He told her that one time, one of his men got hit by a bullet and was bleeding to death. Mike placed his hand over the wound and, miraculously, it stopped bleeding. The man lived. Mike's legend grew. They said he could bring the dying back to life.''

Fascinated, Jim rested his elbows on his knees and watched her shadowed features. ''Interesting,'' he murmured.

''I thought so. But here's the really interesting part, Jim.'' She moved to where he was sitting, keeping barely a foot between them. Opening her hands, she whispered. ''Jessica also told me more than once that Moyra had a jaguar spirit guardian. Jessica is very clairvoyant and she can 'see' things most of us can't. She told me that when Carl, her ex-husband, was stalking her, Moyra would know he was nearby. One afternoon, Jessica was taking a walk in the woods when she came to a creek and saw Moyra.'' Rachel shook her head. ''This is going to sound really off-the-wall, Jim.''

He grinned a little. ''Hey, remember my mother was Apache. I was raised with a pretty spiritually based system of beliefs.''

Rachel nodded. ''Well, Jessica swears she saw Moyra standing in the middle of the creek, and then the next moment she saw a jaguar there instead!''

''Moyra turned into a jaguar?''

Rachel shrugged. ''Jessica swears she wasn't seeing things. She watched this jaguar trot off across the meadow and into the woods. Jessica was so stunned and shocked that she ran back to the cabin, scared to death! When Moyra came in a couple hours later, Jessica confronted her on it. Moyra laughed, shrugged it off and said that shape shifting was as natural as breathing to her clan. And wasn't it more important that she and her jaguar guardian be out, protecting Jessica from Carl?''

With a shake of his head, Jim studied Rachel in the firelight. How beautiful she looked! He wanted to kiss her, feel her ripe, soft lips beneath his mouth. Never had he wanted anything more than that, but he placed steely control over that desire. He liked the intimacy that was being established between them. If he was to kiss her, it might destroy that. Instead, he asked, "How does this story dovetail into your seeing that jaguar?"

Rachel laughed a little, embarrassed. "Well, what you didn't tell me was that there was a terrible accident a mile below where I'd crashed!''

He nodded. "That's right, there was. I didn't want to upset you."

Rachel reached out and laid her hand on his arm. She felt his muscle tense beneath her touch. Tingles flowed up her fingers and she absorbed the warmth of his flesh. Reluctantly, she withdrew her hand. The shadows played against his strong face, and she felt the heat of his gaze upon her, making her feel desired. Heat pooled within her, warm and evocative.

Clearing her throat, she went on. "Jessica was the one who put it all together. She thinks that the jaguar was protecting me from becoming a part of that awful wreck down the road. We calculated later that if I hadn't spun out where I did, I could easily have been involved in that fiery wreck where everyone was burned to death.'' Rachel placed her arms around herself. ''I know it sounds crazy, but Jessica thinks the jaguar showed up to stop me from dying.''

''You almost did, anyway,'' Jim said, scowling.

She relaxed her arms and opened her hands. ''I never told you this, Jim. I guess I was afraid to— afraid you'd laugh at me. But I did share it with my sisters. Until you arrived, I kept seeing this jaguar. I saw it circle my car. I thought I was seeing things, of course.'' She frowned. ''Did *you* see any tracks around the car?''

''I wasn't really paying attention,'' he said apologetically. ''All my focus was on you, the stability of the car, and if there were any gas leaks.''

Nodding, Rachel said, ''Of course...''

''Well...'' Jim sighed. ''I don't disbelieve you, Rachel.''

She studied him in the growing silence. ''I thought you might think I was hallucinating. I *had* lost a lot of blood.''

''My mother's people have a deep belief in shapeshifters—people who can turn from human into animal, reptile or insect form, and then change back into a human one again. I remember her sitting me on her knee and telling me stories about those special medicine people.''

''Jessica thinks it was Moyra who came in the form of a jaguar to protect me until you could arrive on scene.'' She laughed a little, embarrassed over her explanation.

Jim smiled thoughtfully. "I think because we're part Indian and raised to know that there is an unseen, invisible world of spirits around us, that it's not really that crazy an explanation. Do you?"

Somberly, Rachel shook her head. "Thanks for not laughing at me about this, Jim. There's no question you helped save my life." She held his dark stare. "If it wasn't for you, I wouldn't be sitting here right now." She eased her hand over his. "I wish there was some way I could truly pay you back for what you did."

His fingers curled around her slender ones, as his heart pounded fiercely in his chest. "You're doing it right now," he rasped, holding her soft, glistening gaze. The fact that Rachel could be so damned open and vulnerable shook Jim. He'd met so few people capable of such honest emotions. Most people, including himself, hid behind protective walls. Like Kate Donovan did, although she was changing, most likely softened because of her love for Sam McGuire.

Rachel liked the tender smile on his mouth. "Now that the weddings are over, I have a big job ahead of me," she admitted in a low voice. "My sisters are counting on me to bring in some desperately needed money to keep the ranch afloat." Looking up, she stared out the window. A few snowflakes twirled by. "If we don't get good snowfall this winter, and spring rains, we're doomed, Jim. There's just no money to keep buying the hay we need to feed the cattle because of the continued drought."

"It's bad for every rancher," he agreed. "How are you going to make money?"

She leaned back on the couch and closed her eyes, feeling content despite her worry. The natural intimacy she felt with Jim was soothing. "I'm going to go into Sedona on Monday to find an office to rent. I'm going to set up my practice as a homeopath."

"If you need patients, I'll be the first to make an appointment."

She opened her eyes and looked at him. He was serious. "I don't see anything wrong with you."

Grinning a little, he said, "Actually, it will be for my father, who has diabetes. Since meeting you, I did a little research on what homeopathy is and how it works. My father refuses to take his meds most of the time, unless I hand them to him morning and night."

"Can't your two brothers help out?" She saw his scowl, the banked anger in his eyes. Automatically, Rachel closed her fingers over his. She enjoyed his closeness, craved it, telling herself that it was all right. Part of her, however, was scared to death.

"Bo and Chet aren't responsible in that way," he muttered, sitting up suddenly. He knew he had to get home. He could almost feel his father's upset that he was still at the Donovan Ranch. Moving his shoulders as if to get rid of the invisible loads he carried, he turned toward Rachel. Their knees met and touched. He released her hand and slid his arm to the back of the couch behind her. The concern in her eyes for his father was genuine. It was refreshing to see that she could still feel compassion for his father, in spite of the feud.

"Your father's diabetes can worsen to a dangerous level if he doesn't consistently take his meds."

"I know that," Jim said wearily.

"You're carrying a lot of loads for your family, aren't you?"

Rachel's quietly spoken words eased some of the pain he felt at the entire situation. "Yes…"

"It's very hard to change three people's minds about life, Jim," she said gently.

One corner of his mouth lifted in a grimace. "I know it sounds impossible, but I have to try."

Feeling his pain and keeping herself from reacting to it the way she wanted to was one of the hardest things Rachel had ever done. In that moment, she saw the exhaustion mirrored in Jim's face, the grief in his darkened eyes.

"You go through hell over there, don't you?"

He shrugged. "Sometimes."

Rachel sat up. "You'll catch a lot of hell being over here for the wedding."

"Yes," he muttered, slowly standing up, unwinding his long, lean frame. It was time to go, because if he didn't, he was going to do the unpardonable: he was going to kiss Rachel senseless. The powerful intimacy that had sprung up between them was throbbing and alive. Jim could feel his control disintegrating moment by moment. If he didn't leave—

Rachel stood up and slipped her shoes back on her feet. "I'll walk you to the door," she said gently. Just the way Jim moved, she could tell he wasn't looking forward to going home. Her heart bled for him. She knew how angry and spiteful Old Man Cunningham could be. As Jim picked up his suit coat and shrugged it across his broad shoulder, Rachel opened the door for him, noticing how boyish he looked despite the suit he wore. He'd taken off the tie a long time ago, his open collar revealing dark hair on his chest.

They stood in the foyer together, a few inches apart. Rachel felt the power of desire flow through her as she looked up into his burning, searching gaze. Automatically, she placed her hand against his chest and leaned upward. In all her life she had never been so bold or honest about her feelings. Maybe it was because she was home, and that gave her a dose of security and confidence she wouldn't have elsewhere. Whatever it was, Rachel followed her heart and pressed her lips to the hard line of his mouth.

She had expected nothing in return from Jim. The kiss was one to assuage the pain she saw banked in his eyes—the worry for his father and the war that was ongoing in his family. Somehow, she wanted to soothe and heal Jim. He had, after all, unselfishly saved her life, giving his blood so that she might live. She told her frightened heart that this was her reason for kissing him.

As Rachel's soft lips touched his mouth, something wild and primal exploded within Jim. He reached out and captured her against him. For an instant, as if in shock, she stiffened. And then, just as quickly, she melted against him like a stream flowing gently against hard rock. Her kiss was unexpected. Beautiful. Necessary. He opened his mouth and melded her lips more fully against his. Framing her face with his hands, he breathed her sweet breath deep into his lungs. The knots in his gut, the worry over what was waiting for him when he got home tonight, miraculously dissolved. She tasted of sweet, honeyed coffee, of the spicy perfume she'd put on earlier for the wedding. Her mouth was pliant, giving and taking. He ran his tongue across her lower lip and felt her tremble like a leaf in a storm beneath his tentative exploration.

How long had it been since he'd had a woman he wanted to love? Too long, his lonely heart cried out. Too long. His craving for her warmth, compassion and care overrode his normal control mechanisms. Hungrily, Jim captured Rachel more fully against him. Her arms slid around his shoulders and he felt good and strong and needed once again. Just caressing the soft firmness of her cheek, his fingers trailing across her temple into the softness of her hairline, made him hot and burning all over. He felt her quiver as he grazed the outside curve of her breast, felt her melting even more into his arms, into his searching mouth as it slid wetly across her giving lips. He was a starving thief and he needed her. Every part and cell of her. His pulse pounded through him, the pain in his lower body building to an excruciating level.

Rachel spun mindlessly, enjoying the texture of his searching mouth as it skimmed and cajoled, his hands framing her face, his hard body pressing her against the door. She felt him trembling, felt his arousal against her lower body, and a sweet, hot ache filled her. It would be so easy to surrender to Jim in all ways. So easy! Her heart, however, was reminding her of the last time she'd given herself away. Fear began to encroach upon her joy. Fear ate away at the hot yearning of her body, her burning need for Jim.

"No..."

Jim heard Rachel whisper the word. Easing away from her lips, which were now wet and soft from his onslaught, he opened his eyes and looked down at her. Though her eyes were barely opened, he saw the need in them. And the fear. Why? Had he hurt her? Instantly, he pulled back. The tears in her eyes stunned him. He *had* hurt her! *Damn!* He felt her hands pressing against his chest, pushing him away. She swayed unsteadily and he cupped her shoulders. Breathing erratically, he held her gently. She lifted her hand to touch her glistening lips. A deep flush covered her cheeks and she refused to looked up at him.

Angry with himself for placing his own selfish needs before hers, he rasped, "I'm sorry, Rachel...."

Still spinning from the power of his kiss, Rachel couldn't find the right words to reply. Her heart had opened and she'd felt the power of her feelings toward Jim. Stunned in the aftermath of his unexpected response, she whispered, "No...." and then she couldn't say anything else. Rocking between the past and the present, she closed her eyes and leaned against the door.

"I shouldn't have done it," Jim said thickly. "I took advantage.... I'm sorry, Rachel...." Then he opened the door and disappeared into the dark, cold night.

Rachel was unable to protest Jim's sudden departure. She could only press her hand against her wildly beating heart and try to catch her breath. One kiss! Just one kiss had made her knees feel like jelly! Her heart had opened up like a flower, greedy for love, and she was left speechless in the wake of his branding kiss. When had *any* man ever made her feel like that? At the sound of the engine of a pickup in the distance, her eyes flew open. She forced herself to go out to the front porch. Wanting to shout at Jim, Rachel realized it was too late. He was already on the road leading away from the ranch, away from her.

She stood on the porch, the light surrounding her, the chill making her wrap her arms around herself. A few snowflakes twirled lazily down out of an ebony sky as she watched Jim drive up and out of the valley, the headlights stabbing the darkness. What had she done? Was she crazy? Sighing raggedly, she turned on her heel and went back into the ranch house.

As she quietly shut the huge oak door, she felt

trembly inside. Her mouth throbbed with the stamp
of Jim's kiss and she could still taste him on her
lips. Moving slowly to the couch, she sat down before she fell down, her knees still weak in the aftermath of that explosive, unexpected joining. Hiding her face in her hands, Rachel wondered what
was wrong with her. She couldn't risk getting involved again. She couldn't stand the possible loss;
remembered how badly things had ended the last
time—all the fears that had kept her from happiness
before threatened to ruin her relationship again. But
Jim was so compelling she ached to have him, explore him and know him on every level. He was so
unlike the rest of his family. He was a decent human
being, a man struggling to do the right thing not only
for himself, but for his misguided, dysfunctional
family. With a sigh, she raised her head and stared
into the bright flames of the fire. Remembering the
hurt in his eyes when she'd stopped the kiss, she
knew he didn't know why she'd called things to a
halt. He probably thought it had to do with him, but
it hadn't. Somehow, Rachel knew she had to see
him, to tell him the truth, so that Jim didn't take the
guilt that wasn't his.

Worriedly, Rachel sat there, knowing that he
would be driving home to a nasty situation. Earlier,
she'd seen the anguish in his eyes over his family.
Taking a pillow, she pressed it against her torso, her
arms wrapped around it. How she ached to have Jim
against her once again! Yet a niggling voice reminded her that he had a dangerous job as an EMT.

He went out on calls with the firefighters. Anything could happen to him, and he could die, just like… Rachel shut off the flow of her thoughts. Oh, why did she have such an overactive imagination? She sighed, wishing she had handled things better between her and Jim. He probably felt bad enough about her pushing him away in the middle of their wonderful, melting kiss. Now he was going to be facing a very angry father because he had been here, on Donovan property. Closing her eyes, Rachel released another ragged sigh, wanting somehow to protect Jim. But there was nothing she could do for him right now. Absolutely nothing.

"Just where the hell have you been?" Frank Cunningham snarled, wheeling his chair into the living room as Jim entered the ranch house at 9:00 p.m.

Trying to quell his ragged emotions, Jim quietly shut the door. He turned and faced his father. The hatred in Frank's eyes slapped at him. Jim stood in silence, his hands at his side, waiting for the tirade he knew was coming. Glancing over at the kitchen entrance, he saw Bo and Chet standing on alert. Bo had a smirk on his face and Chet looked drunker than hell. Inhaling deeply, Jim could smell the odor of whiskey in the air. What had they been doing? Plying their father with liquor all night? Feeding his fury? Playing on his self-righteous belief that Jim had transgressed and committed an unpardonable sin by spending time at the Donovans? Placing a hold on his building anger toward his two manipulative brothers, Jim calmly met his father's furious look.

"You knew where I was. I called you at five-thirty and told you I wouldn't be home for dinner."

Frank glared up at him. His long, weather-beaten fingers opened and closed like claws around the arms of the chair he was imprisoned in. "Damn you, Jim. You know better! I've begged you not to consort with those Donovan girls."

Jim shrugged tensely out of his coat. "They aren't girls, father. They're grown women. Adults." He saw Bo grin a little as he leaned against the door, a glass of liquor in his long fingers. "And you know drinking whiskey isn't good for your diabetes."

"You don't care!" Frank retorted explosively. "I drank because you went over there!"

"That's crap," Jim snarled back. "I'm not responsible for what you do. I'm responsible for myself. You're not going to push that kind of blame on me. Guilt might have worked when we were kids growing up, Father, but it doesn't cut it now." His nostrils quivered as he tried to withhold his anger. He saw his father's face grow stormy and tried to shield himself against what would come next. A part of him was so tired of trying to make things better around here. He'd been home nearly a year, and nothing had changed except that he was the scapegoat for the three of them now—just as he had been as a kid growing up after their mother's death.

"Word games!" Frank declared. He wiped the back of his mouth with a trembling hand. "You aren't one of us. You are deliberately going over to the Donovan place and consorting with them to get at me!''

Jim raised his gaze to Bo. "Who told you that, Father? Did Bo?"

Bo's grin disappeared. He stood up straight, tense.

Frank waved his hand in a cutting motion. "Bo and Chet are my eyes and ears, since I can't get around like I used to. You're sweet on Rachel Donovan, aren't you?"

Bo and Chet were both smiling now. Anger shredded Jim's composure as he held his father's accusing gaze.

"My private life is none of your—or their—business." He turned and walked down the hall toward his bedroom.

"You go out with her," Frank thundered down the hall, "and I'll disown you! Only this time for good, damn you!"

Jim shut the door to his bedroom, his only refuge. In disgust, he hung up his suit coat and looped the tie over the hangar. Breathing hard, he realized his hands were shaking—with fury. It was obvious that Bo and Chet had plied their father with whiskey, nursing all his anger and making him even more furious. Sitting down on the edge of his old brass bed, which creaked with his sudden weight, Jim slipped off his cowboy boots. Beginning at noon tomorrow, he was on duty for the next forty-eight hours. At least he'd be out of here and away from his father's simmering, scalding anger, his constant snipping and glares over his youngest son's latest transgression.

Undressing, Jim went to the bathroom across the hall and took a long, hot shower. He could hear the three men talking in the living room. Without even bothering to try and listen, Jim was sure it was about him. He wanted to say to hell with them, but it wasn't that easy. As he soaped down beneath the hot, massaging streams of water, his heart, his mind, revolved back to Rachel, to the kiss she'd initiated with him. He hadn't expected it. So why had she suddenly pushed him away? He didn't want to think it was because his last name was Cunningham. That would hurt more than anything else. Yet if he tried to see her when he got off duty, his family would damn him because she was a Donovan.

Scrubbing his hair, he wondered how serious Frank was about disowning him. The first time his father had spoken those words to him, when he was eighteen, Jim had felt as if a huge, black hole had opened up and swallowed him. He'd taken his father's words seriously and he'd left for over a decade, attempting to remake his life. Frank had asked him to come home for Christmas—and that was all.

Snorting softly, Jim shut off the shower. He opened the door, grabbed a soft yellow towel and stepped out. He knew Frank would follow through on his threat to kick out of his life—again. This time Jim was really worried, because neither Bo nor Chet would make sure Frank took his meds for his diabetic condition. If Jim wasn't around on a daily basis to see to that, his father's health would seriously decline in a very short time. He didn't want his father to die. But he didn't want to lose Rachel, either.

Rubbing his face, he drew in a ragged breath. Yes, he liked her—one helluva lot. Too much. How did a man stop his heart from feeling? From wanting? Rachel fit every part of him and he knew it. He sensed it. Could he give her up so that his father could live? What the hell was he going to do?

Chapter Seven

"**D**ammit all to hell," Chet shouted as he entered the ranch house. He jerked off his Stetson and slammed the door behind him. Dressed in a sheep-skin coat, red muffler and thick, protective leather gloves, he headed toward his father, who had just wheeled into the living room.

Jim was rubbing his hands in the warmth of the huge, open fireplace at one end of the living room when Chet stormed in. His older brother had a glazed look in his eyes, a two-day beard on his cheeks and an agitated expression on his face.

"Pa, that dammed cougar has killed another of our cows up in the north pasture!" Chet growled, throwing his coat and gloves on the leather couch. "Half of her is missing. She was pregnant, too."

Frank frowned, stopped his wheelchair near the fireplace where Jim was standing. "We've lost a cow every two weeks for the last four months this way," he said, running his long, large-knuckled hands through his thick white hair.

As Jim turned to warm his back, Chet joined them at the fireplace, opening his own cold hands toward the flames. Chet's eyes were red and Jim could smell liquor on his breath. His brother was drinking like Frank used to drink before contracting diabetes, he realized with concern. Jim sighed. The last three days, since he'd come back from the Donovan wedding party, things had been tense around the house. He was glad his forty-eight hours of duty had begun shortly thereafter, keeping him on call for two days with the ambulance and allowing him to eat and sleep at the fire station down at Sedona. Luckily, things had been quiet, and he'd been able to settle down from the last major confrontation with his father.

"Have you seen the spoor, Chet?" Jim asked.

"Well, shore I have!" he said, wiping his running nose with the back of his flannel sleeve. "Got spoor all over the place. There's about a foot of snow up there. The tracks are good this time."

"We need to get a hunting party together," Frank growled at them. "I'm tired of losing a beef every other week to this cat."

"Humph, we're losin' two of 'em, Pa. That cat's smart—picks on two for one."

"You were always good at hunting cougar,"

Frank said, looking up at Jim. ''Why don't you drive up there and see what you can find out? Arrange a hunting party?''

Jim was relieved to have something to do outside the house. Usually he rode fence line, did repairs and helped out wherever he could with ranching duties. His father had ten wranglers who did most of the hard work, but Jim always looked for ways to stay out of the house when he was home between his bouts of duty at the fire station.

''Okay. How's the road back into that north pasture, Chet?''

''Pretty solid,'' he answered, rubbing his hands briskly. ''The temps was around twenty degrees out there midday. Colder than hell. No snow, but cold. We need the snow for the water or we're going to have drought again,'' he muttered, his brows moving downward.

''I'll get out of my uniform and go check on it,'' Jim told his father.

With a brisk nod, Frank added, ''You find that son of a bitch, you shoot it on sight, you hear me? I don't want any of that hearts and flower stuff you try to pull.''

Jim ignored the cutting jab as he walked down the darkened hall to his bedroom. Moving his shoulders, he felt the tension in them ease a little. In his bedroom, he quickly shed his firefighter's uniform and climbed into a pair of thermal underwear, a well-worn set of Levi's, a dark blue flannel shirt and thick socks. As he sat on the bed, pulling on his cowboy boots, his mind—and if he were honest, his heart—drifted back to Rachel and that sweet, sweet kiss he'd shared with her. It had been three days since then.

He'd wanted to call her, but he hadn't. He was a coward. The way she'd pulled away from him, the fear in her eyes, had told him she didn't like what they'd shared. He felt rebuffed and hurt. Anyone would. She was a beautiful, desirable woman, and Jim was sure that now that she was home for good, every available male in Sedona would soon be tripping over themselves to ask her out. Shrugging into his sheepskin coat, he picked up the black Stetson that hung on one of the bedposts, and settled it on his head.

As he walked out into the living room, he saw Chet and his father talking. In another corner of the room was a huge, fifteen-foot-tall Christmas tree. It would be another lonely Christmas for the four of them. As he headed out the door, gloves in hand, he thought about Christmas over at the Donovan Ranch. In years past, they'd invited in the homeless and fed them a turkey dinner with all the trimmings. Odula, their mother, had coordinated such plans with the agencies around the county, and her big-heartedness was still remembered. Now her daughters were carrying on in her footsteps. Rachel had mentioned that her sisters would be coming back on Christmas Eve to help in the kitchen and to make that celebration happen once again.

Settling into the Dodge pickup, Jim looked

around. The sky was a heavy, gunmetal gray, hanging low over the Rim country. It looked like it might snow. He hoped it would. Arizona high country desperately needed a huge snow this winter to fill the reservoirs so that the city of Phoenix would have enough water for the coming year. Hell, they needed groundwater to fill the aquifer below Sedona or they would lose thousands of head of cattle this spring. His father would have to sell some of his herd off cheap—probably at a loss—so that the cattle wouldn't die of starvation out on the desert range.

Driving over a cattle guard, Jim noticed the white snow lying like a clean blanket across the red, sandy desert and clay soil. He enjoyed his time out here alone. Off to his left, he saw a couple of wranglers on horseback in another pasture, moving a number of cows. His thoughts wandered as he drove and soon Rachel's soft face danced before his mind's eyes. His hands tightened momentarily on the wheel. More than anything, Jim wanted to see Rachel again. He could use Christmas as an excuse to drop over and see her, apologize in person for kissing her unexpectedly. Though he knew he'd been out of line, his mouth tingled in memory of her lips skimming his. She'd been warm, soft and hungry. So why had she suddenly pushed away? Was it him? Was it the fact that he was a Cunningham? Jim thought so.

Ten miles down the winding, snow-smattered road, Jim saw the carcass in the distance. Braking, he eased up next to the partially eaten cow. The wind was blowing in fierce gusts down off the Rim and he pulled his hat down a little more tightly as he stepped out and walked around the front of the truck.

As he leaned down, he saw that the cow's throat was mangled, and he scowled, realizing the cat had killed the cow by grabbing her throat and suffocating her. There was evidence of a struggle, but little blood in the snow around her. Putting his hand on her, he found that she was frozen solid. The kill had to have occurred last night.

Easing up to his full height, he moved carefully around the carcass and found the spoor. Leaning down, his eyes narrowing, he studied them intently. The tracks moved north, back up the two-thousand-foot-high limestone and sandstone cliff above him. Somewhere up there the cat made his home.

Studying the carcass once again, Jim realized that though the cat had gutted her and eaten his fill, almost ninety percent of the animal was left intact and unmolested. That gave him an idea. Getting to his feet, he went back to the pickup, opened the door and picked up the mike on his radio to call the foreman, Randy Parker.

"Get a couple of the boys out here," Jim ordered when Randy answered, "to pick up this cow carcass. Put it in the back of a pickup and bring it to the homestead. When it gets there, let me know."

"Sure thing," Randy answered promptly.

Satisfied, Jim replaced the mike on the console. He smiled a little to himself. Yes, his plan would work—he hoped. Soon enough, he'd know if it was going to.

Rachel was in the kitchen, up to her wrists in mashed potatoes, when she heard a heavy knock at the front door. Expecting no one, she frowned. "I'm coming!" she called out, quickly rinsing her hands, grabbing a towel and running through the living room. It was December 23, and she had been working for three days solid preparing all the dishes for the homeless people's Christmas feast. Her sisters would be home tomorrow, to help with warming and serving the meal for thirty people the following day.

When she opened the door, her eyes widened enormously. "Jim!"

He stood there, hat in hand, a sheepish look on his face. "Hi, Rachel."

Stunned, she felt color race up her throat and into her face. How handsome he looked. His face was flushed, too, but more than likely it was from being outdoors in this freezing cold weather. "Hi...." she whispered. The memory of his meltingly hot kiss, which was never far from her heart or mind, burned through her. She saw his eyes narrow on her and she felt like he was looking through her.

"Come in, it's cold out there," she said apologetically, moving to one side.

"Uh...in a minute." He pointed to his truck, parked near the porch. "Listen, we had a cow killed last night by a cat. Ninety percent of it is still good meat. It's frozen and clean. I had some of our hands bring it down in a pickup. I brought it here, thinking that you might be able to use the meat for your meal for the homeless on Christmas Day.''

His thoughtfulness touched her. ''That's wonderful! I mean, I'm sorry a cougar killed your cow...but what a great idea.''

Grinning a little, and relieved that she wasn't going to slam the door in his face, he nervously moved his felt hat between his gloved fingers. ''Good. Look, I know you have a slaughter-freezing-and-packing area in that building over there. I'm not the world's best at carving and cutting, but with a couple of sharp knives, I can get the steaks, the roasts and things like that, in a couple of hours for you.''

Rachel smiled a little. ''Since we don't have any other hands around, I'd have to ask you to do it.'' She looked at him intently. ''Are you *sure* you want to do that? It's an awful lot of work.''

Shrugging, Jim said, ''Want the truth?''

She saw the wry lift of one corner of his mouth. Joy surged through her. She was happy to see Jim again, thrilled that her display the other night hadn't chased him away permanently. ''Always the truth,'' she answered softly.

Looking down at his muddy boots for a moment, Jim rasped, ''I was looking for a way to get out of the house. My old man is on the warpath again and I didn't want to be under the same roof.'' He took a deep breath and then met and held her compassionate gaze. ''More important, I wanted to come over here and apologize to you in person, and I had to find an excuse to do it.''

Fierce heat flowed through Rachel. She saw the uncertainty in Jim's eyes and heard the sorrow in his voice. Pressing her hand against her heart, which pounded with happiness at his appearance, she stepped out onto the porch. The wind was cold and sharp.

''No,'' she whispered unsteadily, ''you don't need to apologize for anything, Jim. It's me. I mean...when we kissed. It wasn't your fault.'' She looked away, her voice becoming low. ''It was me...my past....''

Stymied, Jim knew this wasn't the time or place to question her response. Still, relief flooded through him. ''I thought I'd overstepped my bounds with you,'' he said. ''I wanted to come over and apologize.''

Reaching out, Rachel gripped his lower arm, finding the thick sheepskin of his coat soft and warm. ''I've got some ghosts from my past that still haunt me, Jim.''

The desire to step forward and simply gather her slender form against him was nearly his undoing. His arm tingled where she'd briefly touched him. But when he saw her nervousness, he held himself in check understood it. Managing a lopsided, boyish smile, he said, ''Fair enough. Ghosts I can handle.''

''I wish I could,'' Rachel said, rolling her eyes. ''I'm not doing so well at it.''

Settling his hat back on his head, he turned and

pointed toward a building near the barn. "How about I get started on this carcass? I'll wrap the meat in butcher paper and put it in your freezer."

She nodded. "Fine. I'm up to my elbows in about thirty gallons of mashed potatoes right now, or I'd come over to help you."

He held up his hand. "Tell you what." Looking at the watch on his dark-haired wrist, he said, "How about if I get done in time for dinner, I take you out to a restaurant? You're probably tired of cooking at this point and you deserve a break."

Thrilled, Rachel smiled. "I'd love that, Jim. What a wonderful idea! And I can fill you in on my new office, which I rented today!"

He saw the flush of happiness on her face. It made him feel good, and he smiled shyly. "Okay," he rasped, "it's a date. It's going to take me about four hours to carve up that beef." By then, it would be 7:00 p.m.

"That's about how much time I'll need to finish up in the kitchen." Rachel turned. "I've got sweet potatoes baking right now. Fifty of them! And then I've got to mash them up, mix in the brown sugar, top them with marshmallows and let them bake a little more."

"You're making me hungry!" he teased with a grin. How young Rachel looked at that moment. Not like a thirty-year-old homeopath, but like the girl with thick, long braids he remembered from junior high. Her eyes danced with gold flecks and he absorbed her happiness into his heart. The fact that

Rachel would go to dinner with him made him feel like he was walking on air. "I'll come over here when I'm done?"

Rachel nodded. "Yes, and I'm sure you'll want to shower before we go."

"I'm going to have to." Now he was sorry he hadn't brought a change of clothes.

"Sam McGuire didn't take all his shirts with him on his honeymoon. I'll bet he'd let you borrow a clean one," she hinted with a broadening smile.

"I'm not going to fight a good idea," Jim said. He turned and made his way off the porch. He didn't even feel the cold wind and snow as he headed back to his truck. Rachel was going to have dinner with him. Never had he expected that. The words, the invitation, had just slipped spontaneously out of his mouth. Suddenly, all the weight he carried on his shoulders disappeared. By 7:00 p.m. he was going to be with Rachel in an intimate, quiet place. Never had he looked forward to anything more than that. And Jim didn't give a damn what the locals might think

Jim took Rachel to the Sun and Moon Restaurant. He liked this place because it was quiet, the service was unobtrusive and the huge, black-and-white leather booths surrounded them like a mother's embrace. They sat in a corner booth; no one could see them and the sense of privacy made him relax.

Rachel sat next to him, less than twelve inches away, in a simple burgundy velvet dress that hung to her ankles. It sported a scoop neck and formfitting long sleeves, and she wore a simple amethyst pendant and matching earrings. Her hair, thick and slightly curly, hung well below her shoulders, framing her face and accenting her full lips and glorious, forest green eyes.

Jim had taken a hot shower and borrowed one of Sam's white, long-sleeved work shirts. Jim had wanted to shave but couldn't, so knew he had a dark shadow on his face. Rachel didn't seem to care about that, however.

After the waitress gave them glasses of water and cups of mocha latte, she left so they could look over the menu.

"That burgundy dress looks good on you," Jim said, complimenting Rachel.

She touched the sleeve of her nubby velvet dress. "Thanks. It's warm and I feel very feminine in this. I bought it over in England many years ago. It's like a good friend. I can't bear to part with it." She liked the burning look in his eyes—it made her feel desirable. But she was scared, too, though. Jim was being every bit the gentleman. She hungered for his quiet, steady male energy. His quick wit always engaged her more serious side and he never failed to make her laugh.

"I'm glad we have this time with each other," he told her as he laid the menu aside. "I'd like to hear about your years over in England. What you did. What it was like to live in a foreign country."

She smiled a little and sipped the frothy mocha

latte, which was topped with whipped cream and cinnamon sprinkles. "First I want to hear how we came by this gift of beef you brought us." She set her cup aside.

Jim opened his hands. "It's the strangest thing, Rachel. For the last four months, about once every two weeks, a cat's been coming down off the Rim and killing one of the cows. My father's upset about it and he wants me to put together a hunting party and kill it."

"This isn't the first time we've had a cougar kill stock," Rachel said.

"That's true." He frowned and glanced at her. Even in the shadows, nothing could mar Rachel's beauty. He saw Odula's face in hers, those wide-set eyes, the broadness of her cheekbones. "But I'm not sure it's a cougar."

"What?"

Shaking his head, Jim muttered, "I saw the spoor for myself earlier today. We finally got enough snow up there so we had some good imprints of the cat's paws." He held up his hand. "I know cougar." Smiling slighty, he said, "My friends call me Cougar. I got that name when I was a teenager because I tracked down one of the largest cougars in the state. He had been killing off our stock for nearly a year before my father let me track him for days on end up in the Rim country." Scowling, he continued, "I didn't like killing him. In fact, after I did it, I swore I'd never kill another one. He was a magnificent animal."

"I saw the other night that you wear a leather thong around your neck," Rachel noted, gesturing toward the open collar of his shirt, which revealed not only the thong, but strands of the dark hair of his upper chest.

Jim pulled up the thong, revealing a huge cougar claw set in a sterling silver cap and a small medicine bag. "Yeah, my father had me take one of the claws to a Navajo silversmith. He said I should wear it. My mother's uncle, who used to come and visit us as kids, was a full-blood Apache medicine man. He told me that the spirit of that cougar now lived in me."

"Makes sense."

"Maybe to those of us who are part Indian," he agreed.

Rachel smiled and gazed at the fearsome claw. It was a good inch in length. She shivered as she thought of the power of such a cougar. "How old were you when you hunted that cougar?"

"Fifteen. And I was scared." Jim chuckled as he closed his hands around the latte. "Scared spitless, actually. My father sent me out alone with a 30.06 rifle, my horse and five days' worth of food. He told me to find the cougar and kill it."

"Your father had a lot of faith in you."

"Back then," Jim said wistfully. "Maybe too much." He gave her a wry look. "If I had a fifteen-year-old kid, I wouldn't be sending him out into the Rim country by himself. I'd want to be there with him, to protect him."

"Maybe your father knew you could handle the situation?"

Shrugging painfully, Jim sipped the latte. "Maybe." He wanted to get off the topic of his sordid past. "That spoor I saw today?"

"Yes?"

"I'm sure it wasn't a cougar's."

Rachel stared at him, her cup halfway to her lips. "What then?"

"I don't know *what* it is, but I know it's not what my father thinks. I took some photos of the spoor, measured it and faxed copies of everything to a friend of mine who works for the fish and game department. He'll make some inquiries and maybe I can find out what it really is."

Setting the cup down, Rachel stared at him. "This is going to sound silly, but I had a dream the other night after we…kissed.…"

"At least it wasn't a nightmare."

She smiled a little nervously. "No…it wasn't, Jim. It never would be." She saw the strain in his features diminish a little.

"What about this dream you had?"

"Being part Indian, you know how we put great stock in our dreams?"

"Sure," he murmured. "My uncle Bradford taught all of us boys the power of dreams and dreaming." Jim held her gaze. Reaching out, he slipped his hand over hers, to soothe her nervousness. "So, tell me about this dream you had."

Rachel sighed. His hand was warm and strong.

"My mother, Odula, was a great dreamer. Like your uncle, she taught us that dreaming was very important. That our dreams were symbols trying to talk to us. Of course," she whispered, amused, "the big trick was figuring out what the dream symbology meant."

"No kidding," Jim chortled. He liked the fact that Rachel was allowing him to hold her hand. He didn't care who saw them. And he didn't care what gossip got back to his father. For the first time, Jim felt hopeful that his father wouldn't disown him again. Frank Cunningham was too old, too frail and in poor health. Jim was hoping that time had healed some of the old wounds between them and that his father would accept that Rachel was a very necessary part of his life.

"Well," Rachel said tentatively, "I was riding up in the Rim country on horseback. I was alone. I was looking for something—someone...I'm not sure. It was a winter day, and it was cold and I was freezing. I was in this red sandstone canyon. As we rode to the end of it, it turned out to be a box canyon. I was really disappointed and I felt fear. A lot of fear. I was looking around for something. My horse was nervous, too. Then I heard this noise. My horse jumped sideways, dumping me in the snow. When I got to my feet, the horse was galloping off into the distance. I felt this incredible power surround me, like invisible arms embracing me. I looked up..." she held his intense gaze "...and you won't believe what I saw."

"Try me. I'm open to anything."

"That same jaguar that caused me to wreck the car, Jim." Leaning back, Rachel felt his fingers tighten slightly around her hand. "The jaguar was there, no more than twenty feet away from me. Only this time, I realized a lot more. I knew the jaguar was a she, not a he. And I saw that she was in front of a cave, which she had made into a lair. She was just standing there and looking at me. I was scared, but I didn't feel like she was going to attack me or anything."

"Interesting," Jim murmured. "Then what happened?" Noting the awe in Rachel's eyes as she spoke, he knew her story was more than just a dream; he sensed it.

"I felt as if I were in some sort of silent communication with her. I *felt* it here, in my heart. I know how strange that sounds, but I sensed no danger while I was with her. I could feel her thoughts, her emotions. It was weird."

"Sort of like…" he searched for the right words "…mental telepathy?"

"Why, yes!" Rachel stared at him. "Have you been dreaming about this jaguar, too?"

He grinned a little and shook his head. "No, but when I finally met and confronted that big male cougar, we stared at one another for a long moment before I fired the gun and killed him. I *felt* him. I felt his thoughts and emotions. It was strange. Unsettling. After I shot him, I sank to my knees and I cried. I felt terrible about killing him. I knew I'd done something very wrong. Looking back on it, if I had it to do all over again, I wouldn't have killed him. I'd have let him escape.''

''But then your father, who's famous for his hunting parties, would have gotten a bunch of men together and hunted him down and treed him with dogs.'' Rachel shook her head. ''No, Jim, you gave him an honorable death compared to what your father would have done. He'd have wounded the cat, and then, when the cougar dropped from the tree, he'd have let his hounds tear him apart.'' Grimly, she saw the pain in Jim's eyes and she tightened her fingers around his hand. ''Mom always said that if we prayed for the spirit of the animal, and asked for it to be released over the rainbow bridge, that made things right.''

He snorted softly. ''I did that. I went over to the cougar, held him in my skinny arms and cried my heart out. He was a magnificent animal, Rachel. He knew I was going to kill him and he just stood there looking at me with those big yellow eyes. I swear to this day that I felt embraced by this powerful sense of love from him. I *felt* it.''

''Interesting,'' she murmured, ''because in my dream about this jaguar, I felt embraced by her love, too.''

''Was that the end of your dream?''

''No,'' she said. ''I saw the jaguar begin to change.''

''Change?''

Rachel pulled her hand from his. She didn't want

to, but she saw the waitress was taking an order at the next table and knew she'd soon come to take theirs. "Change as in shape shifting. You told me last time we spoke that you knew something about that."

"A little. My uncle, the Apache medicine man, said that he was a shape-shifter. He said that he could change from a man into a hawk and fly anywhere he wanted, that he could see things all over the world."

"The Navajo have their skin-walkers," Rachel said in agreement, "sorcerers who change into coyotes and stalk the poor Navajo who are caught out after dark."

"That's the nasty side of shape shifting," Jim said. "My uncle was a good man, and he said he used this power and ability to help heal people."

"My mother told us many stories of shape-shifters among her people, too. But this jaguar, Jim, changed into a woman!" Her voice lowered with awe. "She was an incredibly beautiful woman. Her skin was a golden color. She had long black hair and these incredible green eyes. You know how when leaves come out on a tree in early spring they're that pale green color?"

He nodded. "Sure."

"Her eyes were like that. And what's even more strange, she wore Army camouflage pants, black military boots, an olive green, sleeveless T-shirt. Across her shoulders were bandoliers of ammunition. I kid you not! Isn't that a wild dream?"

He agreed. "Did she say anything to you?"

"Not verbally, no. She stood there and I could see her black boots shifting and changing back into the feet of the jaguar. She was almost like an apparition. I was so stunned by her powerful presence that I just stood there, too, my mouth hanging open." Rachel laughed. "I felt her looking *through* me. I felt as if she were looking for someone. But it wasn't me. I could feel her probing me mentally. This woman was very powerful, Jim. I'm sure she was a medicine woman. Maybe from South America. Then I saw her change back into the jaguar. And she was gone!" She snapped her fingers. "Just like that. Into thin air."

"What happened next?"

"I woke up." Rachel sighed. "I got up, made myself some hot tea and sat out in the living room next to the fireplace, trying to feel my way through the dream. You had kissed me hours before. I was wondering if my dream was somehow linked to that, to you."

Shrugging, Jim murmured, "I don't know. Maybe my friend at the fish and game department will shed some light on that spoor print. Maybe it's from a jaguar." He gauged her steadily. "Maybe what you saw on the highway that day was real, and not a hallucination."

Rachel gave a little laugh. "It looked pretty physical and real to me. *If* it is a jaguar, what are you going to do?"

Grimly, Jim said, "Number one, I'm not going to

kill it. Number two, I'll enlist the help of the fish and game department to track the cat, locate its lair and then lay a trap to harmlessly capture it. Then they can take the cat out of the area, like they do the black bears that get too close to civilization.''

Rachel felt happiness over his decision. ''That's wonderful. If it is a jaguar, it would be a crying shame to shoot her.''

He couldn't agree more. The waitress came to their table then, and once they gave her their orders, Jim folded his hands in front of him and caught Rachel's sparkling gaze. Gathering up his courage, he asked, ''Could you use another hand on Christmas Day to help feed the homeless? Things are pretty tense around home. I'll spend Christmas morning with my father and brothers, but around noon, I want to be elsewhere.''

''You don't have to work at the fire department?'' Rachel's heart picked up in beat. More than anything, she'd love to have Jim's company. Kate would have Sam at her side, and Jessica would be working with Dan. It would be wonderful to have Jim with her. She knew Kate was settling her differences with Jim, so it wouldn't cause a lot of tension among them. Never had Rachel wanted anything more than to spend Christmas with Jim.

''I have the next three days off,'' he said. He saw hope burning brightly in Rachel's eyes. The genuine happiness in her expression made him feel strong and very sure of himself. ''So, you can stand for me to be underfoot for part of Christmas Day?''

Clapping her hands enthusiastically, Rachel whispered, "Oh, yes. I'd love to have you with us!"

Moving the cup of latte in his hands, Jim nodded. "Good," he rasped. He didn't add that he'd catch hell for this decision. His father would explode in a rage. Bo and Chet would both ride him mercilessly about it. Well, Jim didn't care. All his life, he'd try to follow his heart and not his head. His heart had led him into wildfire fighting for nearly ten years. And then it had led him home, into a cauldron of boiling strife with his family. Now it whispered that with Rachel was where he longed to be.

As he saw the gold flecks in her eyes, he wanted to kiss her again—only this time he wanted to kiss her senseless and lose himself completely in her. She was a woman of the earth, no question. He was glad they shared a Native American background. They spoke the same language about the invisible realms, the world of spirit and the unseen. Jim never believed in accidents; he felt that everything, no matter what it was, had a purpose, a reason for happening. And the best thing in his life was occurring right now.

A powerful emotion moved through him, rocking him to the core. Could it be love? Studying Rachel as she delicately sipped her latte, her slender fingers wrapped around the cup, he smiled to himself. There was no doubt he loved her. The real question was did she love him? Could she? Or would she never be able to because she was a Donovan and he a Cunningham? Would Rachel always push him away, because of all the old baggage and scars between their two families?

Jim had no answers. Only questions that ate at him, gnawed away at the burgeoning love he felt toward Rachel. He knew he had to take it a day at a time with her. He had to let her adjust to her new life here in Sedona. He had to use that Apache patience of his and slow down. Let her set the pace so she would be comfortable with him. Only then, Jim hoped, over time, she would grow to love him, and want him in her life as much as he wanted her.

Chapter Eight

Rachel tried to appear unaffected by the fact that Jim Cunningham was in the kitchen of their home on Christmas Day. Both Kate and Jessica kept grinning hugely with those Cheshirelike smiles they always gave her when they knew something she didn't. Jim had arrived promptly at noon and set to work in the kitchen with the two men while the Donovan sisters served the sumptuous meal to thirty homeless people in their huge living room.

Christmas music played softly in the background and there was a roaring blaze in the fireplace. The tall timbers were wreathed in fresh pine boughs, and the noise of people laughing, talking and sharing filled the air. Rachel had never felt so happy as she passed from one table to another with coffeepot in hand, refilling cups. Among the people who had come were several families with children. Kate and Sam had gone to stores in Flagstaff and asked for donations of presents for the children. They'd spent part of their honeymoon collecting the gifts and then wrapping them.

Each child had a gift beside his or her plate. Each family would receive a sizable portion of Jim's beef to take back to the shelter where they were living. Jessica and Dan had worked with the various county agencies to see that those who had nowhere to go would have a roof over their head for the winter. Yes, this was what Christmas was *really* all about. And it was a tradition their generous, loving mother had started. It brought tears to Rachel's eyes to know that Odula's spirit still flowed strongly through them. Like their mother, the three daughters felt this was the way to gift humanity during this very special season.

The delight on the children's faces always touched Rachel deeply. For some odd reason, whenever she looked at a tiny baby in the arms of its mother, she thought of Jim. She felt a warm feeling in her lower body, and the errant, surprising thought of what it might be like to have Jim's baby flowed deliciously through her. With that thought, Rachel almost stumbled and fell on a rug that had been rolled to one side. She felt her face suffuse with heat. When she went back to the kitchen to refill her coffee urn, she avoided the look that Jim gave her as he busily carved up one of the many turkeys. Dan was spooning up mash potatoes, gravy and stuffing onto each plate that was passed down the line. Sam added cranberries, Waldorf salad and candied yams topped with browned marshmallows.

Rachel wished for some quiet time alone with Jim. When he'd arrived, they were already in full swing with the start of the dinner. The kiss they'd shared, the intimacy of their last meal together, all came back to her. She found herself wanting to kiss him again. And again. Oh, how she wished her past would disappear! If she could somehow move it aside.... There was no question she desired Jim. And she knew she wanted to pursue some kind of relationship with him. But fear was stopping her. And it was giving him mixed signals. Sighing, Rachel looked forward to the evening, when things would quiet down and they would at last be alone. She had her own house at the ranch, and she could invite Jim over for coffee later and they could talk.

"Heck of a day," Jim said, sipping coffee at Rachel's kitchen table. Her house, which had been built many years ago by Kelly Donovan, was smaller than the other two he'd built for his daughters, but it was intimate and Jim liked that. Although Rachel had only recently moved into it, he could see her feminine touches to the pale pink kitchen. There were some pots on the windowsill above the sink where she had planted some parsley, chives and basil. The table was covered with a creamy lace cloth—from England, she'd told him.

"Wasn't it though?" Rachel moved from the stove, bringing her coffee with her. She felt nervous and ruffled as she looked at Jim. How handsome he was in his dark brown slacks, white cowboy shirt and bolo tie made of a cougar's head with a turquoise inset for the eye. His sleeves were rolled up from all the kitchen duty, the dark hair on his arms bringing out the deep gold color of his weathered skin.

"When you came in at noon, you looked pretty stressed out," Rachel said, sitting down. Their elbows nearly touched at the oval table. She liked sitting close to him.

With a shrug, Jim nodded. "Family squabble just before I left," he muttered.

"Your father didn't want you to come over here, right?" She saw the shadowy pain in his eyes as he avoided her direct look.

"Yeah, you could say that." Jim sipped his coffee grimly.

"And you have dark shadows under your eyes."

He grinned a little and looked at her. "You don't miss much, do you?"

"I'm trained to observe," Rachel teased. Placing her hands around the fine, bone china cup, she lost her smile. "Why do you stay at your father's house if it's so hard on you?"

Pain serrated Jim. His brows dipped. "I don't know anymore," he rasped. "I thought I could help make a difference, turn the family around, but no one wants to change. They want me to change into one of them and I'm not going to do it.''

"In homeopathy, it's known as an obstacle to cure,'' Rachel said. "They don't want to change their dysfunctional way of living because it suits their purposes to stay that way.'' She gave Jim a tender look. "You wanted to be healthy, not dysfunctional, so you left as soon as you could and you stayed away until just recently. I've treated thousands of people over the years and I know from experience that if they don't want to leave the job, the spouse or the family that is causing them to remain sick or unhealthy, there's little I, a homeopathic remedy or anything else can do about it.''

"Sort of like the old saying you can lead a horse to water but you can't make her drink?''

"Yes,'' Rachel replied with a sigh, trying to give him a smile. Jim looked exhausted. She had seen that look before when a person was tired to the bones with a struggle they were losing, not winning. She opened her hands tentatively. "So, what are your options? Could you move out and maybe see your father, whom you're worried about, from time to time?''

Rearing back on two legs of the chair, Jim gazed over at her. The lamp above the table softly lit Rachel's features. He was hungry for her compassion, her understanding of the circumstances that had him caught like a vise. He valued her insights, which were wise and deep. "I've been thinking about that,'' he admitted reluctantly. ''Only, who will make sure my father takes his meds twice daily?''

''How long has your father had diabetes?''

''Ten years.''

''And how did he survive that long without you being there to make sure he took his meds?''

Wryly, he studied her in the ensuing silence. ''Touché.''

''Could you find a house to rent in Sedona?''

''Maybe,'' he said. ''I'll just have to see how it goes.''

''What was the fight about before you left to come to our ranch?''

His mouth quirked. ''Chet's all up in arms about this cat that killed the beef. He's whipping up Bo and my father into forming a hunting party tomorrow to go track the cat, tree it and kill it. I argued not to do that, to call the fish and game department and work with them to trap the cat and take it somewhere else, into a less-populated area.''

Rachel felt sudden fear grip her heart. ''And what did they decide?''

Easing the chair down on all four legs, Jim muttered, ''They're going out tomorrow morning to hunt the cat down and kill it.''

She gasped. ''No!''

''I'm with you on this.'' Again, he studied her. ''After hearing your dream, and talking more to Jessica today, I'm convinced it's a jaguar up there on the Rim, not a cougar, Rachel. Jessica's sure that it's a shape-shifter. She's worried that it's Moyra, her friend, coming to check on her, on the family.'' Shrugging, he eased out of the chair and stood up, coffee cup in hand. ''I don't know if I believe her or not, but it really doesn't matter. I don't care if it's a cougar or a jaguar—I don't want to see it treed and killed.'' Leaning his hip against the counter, he asked, ''Want to come with me tomorrow to track the cat? I've got the day off. I called Bob Granby, my friend from the fish and game department, and told him I was going to ride out early tomorrow, get a jump on my brothers' plan, and try to find the cat first. I'll be carrying a walkie-talkie with me. Bob promised that if I could locate the cat, he'd meet us, establish jurisdiction and make my family stop the hunt. Then we could lay out bait to lure the cat into a humane device.''

Her heartbeat soared. ''Yes, I'd love to go with you.'' Then she laughed a little. ''I haven't thrown a leg over a horse in a long time, but that's okay. You know, Sam and Dan are good trackers, too. They could help.''

Jim shook his head. ''No. If my brothers saw them, they'd probably open fire on them. Besides, this is on Cunningham land and they don't want them trespassing. I can't risk a confrontation, Rachel.''

''What about me? What if they see me with you?''

''That's a little different. They don't get riled with a woman. They will with a man, though. Some of

the Old West ethics are still alive and well in them.''
He smiled briefly.

"Just tell me your plans,'' she said, "and I'll
come with you.''

"If you can pack us a lunch and dinner, I hope
to be able to track the cat and locate it by no later
than tomorrow afternoon. We'll have a two-hour
head start on their hunting party. If we could use
Donovan horses, that would keep what I'm doing a
secret.''

Rachel felt her stomach knot a little. "What will
your brothers do if they find out you've beat them
to the punch on this?''

"Scream bloody blue murder, but that's all.'' Jim
chuckled. "They've had enough tangles with the
law of late. Neither of them wants to see the inside
of a county jail again for a long time. Once they
know I'm working for the fish and game department,
they'll slink off.''

Sighing, Rachel nodded. "Okay, I'll let Kate
know. I'm sure Sam will make sure we've got two
excellent trail and hunting horses. I'll pack our
food.''

Jim nodded, then looked at his watch. It was
nearly midnight. "I need to get going,'' he said reluctantly, not wanting to leave. Setting the coffee
cup on the table, he reached into his back pocket
and brought out a small, wrapped gift. "It's not
much, but I wanted to give you something for
Christmas.''

Touched, Rachel took the gift, thrilling as their

fingers met. "Why, thank you! I didn't expect anything...." She removed the bright red ribbon and the gold foil wrapping.

Jim felt nervous. Settling his hands on his hips, he watched the joy cross Rachel's face. Her eyes, her beautiful forest green eyes, sparkled. It made him feel good. Better than he'd felt all day. Would Rachel like his gift? He hadn't had much time to find something in Sedona that he thought she might want. He hoped she'd like it at least.

Rachel gasped as the paper fell away. Inside were two combs for her hair. They were made of tortoise shell, and each one had twelve tiny, rounded beads of turquoise across the top. Sliding her fingers over them, she saw they were obviously well crafted.

"These are beautiful," she whispered, as she gazed up at his shadowed, worried features. "I've never seen anything like them...."

Shyly, Jim murmured, "I have a Navajo silversmith friend, and I went over to his house yesterday. You have such beautiful hair," he continued, gesturing toward her head. "And I knew he was working on a new design with hair combs." He smiled a little as he saw that she truly did treasure his gift. "When I saw these, I knew they belonged to you."

Without a word, Rachel got up and threw her arms around his neck, pressing herself to him. "Thank you," she quavered near his ear. She felt Jim tense for a moment, as if surprised, and then his arms flowed around her, holding her tightly, his hand sliding up her spine. Heat flared in her and she lifted her face from his shoulder to look up at him. His eyes were hooded and burning—with desire. Breathless and scared, Rachel felt the old fear coming up. She didn't care. She was in the arms of a man who was strong and good and caring. Although his gift was small, it was thoughtful and it touched her like little else could.

Closing her eyes, Rachel knew he was going to kiss her. Nothing had ever seemed so right! As her lips parted, she felt the powerful stamp of his mouth settle firmly upon hers and she surrendered completely to him, to his strong, caring arms and to the heat that exploded violently within her. His lips were cajoling and skimmed hers teasingly at first. She felt his moist breath against her cheek. The taste of coffee was present on his lips. His beard scraped her softer skin, sending wild tingles through her. His fingers moved upward, following the line of her torso, barely brushing the curvature of her firm breasts.

More heat built within her and she felt an ache between her thighs. How long had it been since she'd made love? Far too long. Her body screamed out for Jim's continued touch, for his hands to cup her breasts more fully, to touch and tease them. Instead, he slid his hand across her shoulders, up the slender expanse of her neck to frame her face. He angled her jaw slightly so that he could have more contact with her mouth. His tongue trailed a languid pattern of fire across her lower lip. She quivered violently. He groaned. Their breath mingled, hot, wild and swift. Her heart pounded in her breast as his mouth settled firmly over hers. She lost herself in the power of him as a man, in the cajoling tenderness he bestowed upon her, the give and take of his mouth upon hers and the sweet, hot wetness that was created between them.

Slowly, ever so slowly, Jim eased away from her mouth. Rachel wanted to cry out that she wanted more of him, of his touch. The dark gleam in his eyes showed the primal side of him, and she shivered out of need, wondering what it would be like to go all the way with Jim. She felt his barely leashed control, felt it in the tremble of his hands along the sides of her face as he continued to hungrily press her into himself in those fragile moments strung between them.

"If I don't go now," he told her thickly, "I won't leave...." The pain in his lower body attested to his need of Rachel. She was soft, supple and warm in his arms. He saw the drowsy look in her eyes, how much his capturing kiss had affected her. Gently, he ran his hands across her crown and down the long, thick strands of her hair. She swayed unsteadily, and he held her carefully in his arms. It was too soon, his mind shrilled at him. Rachel had to have time to get to know him. And vice versa. He'd learned patience a long time ago when it came to relationships. And more than anything, Jim wanted his relationship with Rachel to develop naturally, and not become a pressure to her. When he saw the question in her gaze, he knew he'd made the right decision.

Despite the desire burning in her eyes, he also saw fear banked in their depths. She was afraid of something. Him? Her past? Maybe a man she had known in England. That thought shattered him more than any other. Yes, he had to back off and find out more about her and what she wanted out of life—and if he figured in her dream at all.

Easing away, he smiled a little. "We're going to be getting up at the crack of dawn to leave. We need to get some sleep." What Jim really wanted was to sleep with Rachel in his arms. But he didn't say that.

"Yes..." Rachel whispered, her voice faint and husky. She wanted Jim to stay, and the words were almost torn from her. But it wouldn't be fair to him—or her. If she was lucky, maybe tomorrow, as they tracked the cat, she could share her fears, her hopes and dreams with him.

The snort of the horses, the jets of white steam coming from their nostrils, were quickly absorbed by the thick pine forest that surrounded them as Rachel rode beside Jim. They had been in the saddle for nearly three hours and the temperature hovered in the low thirties up on the Rim. Bundled up, Rachel had never felt happier. And she knew why. It was because she was with Jim. They had spoken little since he'd started tracking. The spoor was still visible, thanks to the snow that hadn't yet melted off the Rim. Down below on the desert floor, the drifts had already disappeared.

Jim rode slightly ahead on a big black Arabian

gelding. There was a rifle in the leather case along
the right side of his saddle, beneath his leg. Rachel
knew he didn't want to use it, but if the cat attacked,
they had to defend themselves. It was a last resort.
His black Stetson was drawn low across his brow
as he leaned over the horse, looking for spoor. There
weren't many, and Rachel was amazed at how well
he could track on seemingly nothing. Occasionally
he'd point out a tiny broken twig on a bush, a place
where the snow had melted, a part of an imprint left
in the pine needles—rocks that she wouldn't have
seen without Jim's expertise.

Unable to get their heated kiss out of her head,
Rachel waited for the right time to talk to him. Right
now, he needed silence in order to concentrate. They
were two hours ahead of his family's hunting party.
Bo and Chet weren't great at tracking, and Jim
hoped his brothers would lose the trail, anyway.

He held up his hand. "Let's stop here for a bite
to eat." He twisted around in the saddle, resting his
hand on the rump of his gelding. Rachel was beautiful in her dark brown Stetson. She had a red wool
muffler wrapped around her neck, and she wore a
sheepskin jacket, Levi's, boots and thick, protective
gloves. He was glad she'd dressed warmly, even
though the temperature was rising and he was sure
it would get over thirty-two degrees in the bright
sunshine. Dismounting, he dropped the reins on the
gelding, knowing that a ground-tied horse, once the
reins were dropped, would not move.

Coming around, he held out his hands to Rachel,

placing them around her waist and lifting her off the little gray Arabian mare she rode. He saw surprise and then pleasure in her eyes as she settled her own hands trustingly on his upper arms while he gently placed her feet on the ground. It would have been so easy to lean down and take her ripe, parted lips, so easy... Tearing himself out of that mode, Jim released her.

"What have you brought for us to eat?" He took the horses and tied them to a nearby tree. The trail had led them into a huge, jagged canyon of red-and-white rock. Noticing a limestone cave halfway up on one wall, he realized it was a perfect place for a cat to have a lair.

Rachel felt giddy. Jim's unexpected touch was exhilarating to her. Taking off her gloves, she opened up one of the bulging saddlebags. "I know this isn't going to be a surprise to you. Turkey sandwiches?"

Chuckling, Jim grinned and came and stood next to her. "We'll sit over there," he said. There were some black lava rocks free of snow that had dried in the sunlight. "I like turkey."

"I hope so." Rachel laughed softly. She purposely kept her voice low. When tracking, making noise wasn't a good idea.

"Come on," he urged, taking the sandwich wrapped in tinfoil. "Let's rest a bit. Your legs have to be killing you."

Rachel was happy to sit with her back against his on the smooth, rounded surface of the lava boulder. It was a perfect spot, the sunlight lancing down through the fir, spotlighting them with warmth. She removed her hat and muffler and opened up her coat because it was getting warmer. Picking up her sandwich, she found herself starved. Between bites, she said, "My legs feel pretty good. I'm surprised."

"By tonight," he warned wryly, "your legs will be seriously bowed."

She chortled. "That's when I take Arnica for sore muscles."

He grinned and ate with a contentment he'd rarely felt. The turkey tasted good. Rachel had used a seven-grain, homemade brown bread. Slathered with a lot of mayonnaise and a little salt on the turkey, the sandwich tasted wonderful. Savoring in the silence of the forest, the warmth of the sun, the feel of her resting against his back and left shoulder, he smiled.

"This is the good life."

Rachel nodded. "I love the peace of the forest. As a kid, I loved coming up on the Rim with my horse and just hanging out. When I was in junior high and high school, I was in the photography club, so I used to shoot a lot of what I thought were 'artistic' shots up here." She laughed and shook her head. "The club advisor, a teacher, was more than kind about my fledgling efforts."

Smiling, Jim said, "I almost joined the photography club because you were in it."

Her brows arched and she twisted around and caught his amused gaze. "You're kidding me!"

"No," he said, holding up his hand. "Honest, I

had a crush on you for six years. Did you know that?''

Even though he'd already confessed his boyhood crush, his words still stunned her. Maneuvering around so that she sat next to him, their elbows touching, she finished off her sandwich and leaned down to wipe her fingers in the snow and pine needles to clean them off. "I still can't believe you had a crush on me.''

"Why is that so hard to believe? I thought you were the prettiest girl I'd ever seen." And then his smile softened. "You still are, Rachel.''

Her heart thumped at the sincerity she heard in Jim's voice, and the serious look she saw on his face. "Oh," she said in a whisper, "I never knew back then, Jim....''

Chuckling, he took a second sandwich and unwrapped it. "Well, who was going to look at a pimply faced teenager? I wasn't the star running back of the football team like Sam was. I was shy. Not exactly good-looking. More the nerd than the sportshero type." He chuckled again. "You always had suitors who wanted your attention.''

"Well," she began helplessly, "I didn't know...''

He caught and held her gaze. "Let's face it," he said heavily, "back then, as kids, we wouldn't have stood a chance anyway. You were a hated Donovan. If my father had seen me get interested in you, all hell would've broken loose.''

Glumly, Rachel agreed. "He'd have probably

beaten you within an inch of your life. Come to think of it, so would my dad.''

"Yeah, two rogue stallions against one scrawny teenage kid with acne isn't exactly good odds, is it?''

Laughing a little, Rachel offered him some of the corn chips she'd bagged up for them. Munching on the salty treat, she murmured, ''No, that's not good odds. Maybe it's just as well I didn't know, then....''

The silence enveloped them for a full five minutes before either spoke again. Rachel wiped the last of the salt and grease from the chips off on her Levi's. There was something lulling and healing about being in a forest. It made what she wanted to share with Jim a little easier to undertake. Folding her hands against her knees, she drew them up against her.

''When I moved to England, a long time ago, Jim, I went over there to get the very best training possible to become a homeopath. I had no desire to live at the ranch. I knew my mother wanted all of us girls to come home, but none of us could stomach Kelly's drinking habits.'' She shook her head and glanced at Jim. His eyes were dark and understanding. ''I loved my mother so much, but I just couldn't bring myself to come back home after I graduated from four year's training at Sheffield College. I went on to become a member of the Royal Society of Homeopaths and worked with several MDs at a clinic in London. I really loved my work, and how homeopathy, which was a natural medicine, could cure terrible illnesses and chronic diseases.

"I was very good at what I did, and eventually, the administrator at Sheffield College asked me to come back and teach. They offered me not only a teaching position, but said I could write a book on the topic and keep practicing through clinic work at their facility."

"It sounds like a dream come true for you," Jim said.

"Well, it was even more than that," she said ruefully, leaning down and picking up a damp, brown pine needle. Stroking it slowly with her fingertip, she continued, "I met Dr. Anthony Armstrong at the clinic. He was an MD. Over time, we fell in love." She frowned. "Because of my past, my father, I was really leery of marriage. I didn't want to get trapped like my mother had been. Tony was a wonderful homeopath and healer. We had so much in common. But I kept balking at setting a wedding date. This went on for five years." Rachel shook her head. "I guess you could say I was gun-shy."

Jim's heart sank. "You had good reason to be," he answered honestly. "Living with Kelly was enough to make all three of you women gun-shy of marriage and of men in general." And it was. Jim had feared Kelly himself. Nearly anyone with any sense had. The man had been unstable. He'd blow up and rage at the slightest indiscretion, over things that didn't warrant such a violent reaction. As much as Jim tried to imagine what it had been like for

Rachel and her sisters, he could not. What he did see, however, was the damage that it had done to each of them, and he realized for the first time how deeply wounded Rachel had been by it as well.

"I was scared, Jim," she said finally, the words forced out from between her set lips. "Tony was a wonderful friend. We loved homeopathy. We loved helping people get well at the clinic. We had so much in common," she said again.

"But did you love him?"

Rachel closed her eyes. Her lips compressed. "Do you always ask the right question?" She opened her eyes and studied Jim's grave face. His ability to see straight through her, to her core, was unsettling but wonderful. Rachel had never met a man who could see that deep inside her. And she knew her secret vulnerabilities were safe with Jim.

"Not always," Jim murmured, one corner of his mouth lifting slightly, "but I try, and that's what counts." Seeing the fear and grief in Rachel's eyes, he asked gently, "So what happened? Did you eventually marry him?"

Allowing the pine needle to drop, she whispered, "No…I was too scared, Jim. Tony and I—well, we were good friends. I gradually realized I really didn't love him—not like he loved me. Maybe, in my late twenties, I was still gun-shy and wasn't sure about love, or what it was really supposed to be. I had a lot of phone conversations with my mother about that. I just wasn't sure what love was."

Seeing the devastation on Rachel's face, hearing

the apology in her husky voice, he bit back the question that whirled in his head: *And now? Do you know what love is? Do you know that what we have is love?* "Time heals old wounds," he soothed. "I've seen it for myself with my father. When I left at age eighteen, I hated him. It took me ten years to realize a lot of things, and growing up, maturing, really helped."

"Doesn't it?" Rachel laughed softly as she lifted her head and looked up at the bright blue sky. The sunlight filtered delicately down among the fir boughs, dancing over the snow patches and pine needles.

"That's why I came home. Blood is thicker than water. I thought I could help, but I haven't been able to do a damned thing." Ruefully, he held her tender gaze. "The only good thing that's happened out of it is meeting you again."

Her throat tightened with sudden emotion and she felt tears sting the backs of her eyes. Her voice was off-key when she spoke. "When I became conscious in that wreck and saw you, your face, I knew I was going to be okay. I didn't know how, but I knew that. You had such confidence and I could feel your care. You made me feel safe, Jim, in a way I've never felt safe in my life." She tried to smile, but failed. Opening her hands, Rachel pushed on, because if she didn't get the words out, the fear would stop her from ever trying again.

"I know we haven't known each other long, but I feel so good around you. I like your touch, your kindness, the way you treat others. There's nothing not to like about you.'' She laughed shyly. Unable to meet his gaze because she was afraid of what she might see, she went on. ''I'm so afraid to reach out…to—to like you…because of my past. I hurt Tony terribly. I kept the poor guy hanging on for five years thinking that I could remake myself, or let go of my paranoia about marriage, my fear of being trapped by it. I thought it would go away with time, but that didn't happen. I felt horrible about it. That poor man waited in hope for five years for me to get my act together—and I never did.'' Sorrowfully, Rachel turned and met Jim's gaze. It took the last of her courage to do that because he deserved no less than honesty from her.

''Now I've met you. And what I feel here—'' she touched her heart with her hand ''—is so strong and good and clean that I wake up every morning happy, so happy that I'm afraid it's all a dream and will end. That's stupid, I know. I know better than that. It's not a dream.…''

Gently, Jim turned and captured her hands in his. ''Maybe it's a dream that's been there all along, but due to life and circumstances, you couldn't dream it—until now?''

Just the tenderness of his low voice made her vision blur with tears. Rachel hung her head. She felt Jim's hands tighten a little around hers. ''I'm so scared, Jim…of myself, of how I feel about you…of the fact that your family would come unglued if— if I let myself go and allow the feelings I have for you to grow. I'm scared of myself. I wonder if I'll freeze again like I did with Tony. I don't want to hurt anyone. I don't want to make you suffer like I did him.''

"Listen to me," Jim commanded gruffly as he placed his finger beneath Rachel's chin, making her look up at him. Tears beaded her thick, dark lashes and there was such misery in her forest green eyes. "Tony was a big boy. He knew the score. You weren't teenagers. You were adults. And so are we, Rachel." Jim slid his hand across the smooth slope of her cheek. "I know you're scared. Now I know why. That's information that can help us make decisions with each other." He brushed several strands of dark hair away from her delicate ear. "I couldn't give a damn that my last name is Cunningham and yours is Donovan. The feud our fathers and grandfathers waged with one another stops here, with us. We aren't going to fight anymore. It's this generation that has to begin the healing. I know you know that. So does Kate and Jessica. My family doesn't— not yet. And maybe they never will. But I can't live my life for them. I have to live my life the way I think it should go."

Rachel closed her eyes as he stroked her cheek. His hand was roughened from hard work, from the outdoors, and she relished his closeness, his warmth.

"I guess," Jim rasped in a low voice, "I never got over my crush on you, Rachel." He saw her eyes open. "What I felt as an awkward, gawky teenager, I feel right now. When I saw it was you trapped in that car, I almost lost it. I almost panicked. I was so afraid that you were going to die. I didn't want you to leave me.'' He shook his head and placed his hand over hers again. ''When you needed that rare blood type, and I had the same type, I knew something special was going down. I knew it here, in my heart. I was glad to give my blood to you. For me, with my Apache upbringing, I saw it symbolically, as if the blood from our two families was now one, in you.'' He gazed into her green eyes and hoped she understood the depth of what he was trying to share with her.

''In a way, we're already joined. And I want to pursue what we have, Rachel—if you want to. I'm not here to push you or shove you. You need to tell me if I have a chance with you.''

Chapter Nine

Before Rachel could answer, both horses suddenly snorted and started violently. Jim and Rachel jumped to their feet and turned toward the fir tree, where the horses were firmly tied and standing frozen, their attention drawn deeper into the canyon.

Rachel's eyes widened enormously and her heart thudded hard in her chest. There, no more than a hundred feet away on the wall of the canyon next to the cave, stood a huge, stocky jaguar. The cat switched its tail, watching them.

Jim moved in front of her, as if to protect her. She could feel the fine tension in his body, and she gasped. The jaguar was real! Though the cat was a hundred feet above them and unable to leap toward them, her emotions were screaming in fear.

"Don't move," Jim rasped. His eyes narrowed as he slowly turned and fully faced the jaguar. For some reason, he sensed it was a female, just as in Rachel's dream. The cat was positively huge! He'd seen photos and films of jaguars, but never one in the wild. They were a lot stockier than the lithe cougar and weighed a helluva lot more. The cat's gold-and-black fur looked magnificent against the white limestone cliff. Between her jaws was a limp jackrabbit she'd obviously brought back to her lair to enjoy.

The snort of the horses echoed warningly down the canyon walls and Jim automatically put his arm out, as if to stop Rachel from any forward movement. He felt her hand on the back of his shoulder.

Rachel was mesmerized by the stark beauty of the jaguar as the cat lowered her broad, massive head and gently placed the dead rabbit at her feet. Looking down at them as if she were queen of all she surveyed and they mere subjects within her domain.

"She's beautiful!" Rachel whispered excitedly. "Look at her!"

Jim barely nodded. He was concerned she would attack. Fortunately, both horses were trained for hunting and were able to stand their ground rather than tear at their reins to get away—which any horse in its right mind would have done under the present circumstances. He estimated how long it would take to reach his gelding, unsnap the leather scabbard, pull out the rifle, load it and aim it. The odds weren't in his favor.

''She's not going to harm us,'' Rachel whispered. Moving closer to Jim, their bodies nearly touching as she dug her fingers into his broad shoulder. ''This is so odd, Jim. I feel like she's trying to communicate with us. Look at her!''

He couldn't deny what Rachel had voiced. The cat lazily switched her tail, but showed no sign of alarm at being so near to them. Instead, she eased to the ground, the rabbit between her massive front paws. Sniffing the morsel, she raised her head and viewed them again.

''Listen to me, Rachel,'' Jim said in a very low voice, keeping his eyes on the jaguar. ''I want you to slowly back away from me. Mount your horse and, as quietly as you can, *walk* it out of the canyon. Once you get down the hill, take the walkie-talkie you have in the saddlebag and make a call to Bob. Tell him we've located the cat and it's a jaguar. The walkie-talkie won't work up here in the fir trees. You need an open area. It might take you fifteen minutes to ride down this slope to the meadow below. Call him and then wait for him down there. I know he's on 89A waiting for us. He can drive through the Cunningham ranch. Tell him to go to the northernmost pasture. We'll meet him there.''

''What are you going to do?''

''Stay here.''

Alarmed, Rachel asked, ''Why? Why not come with me?''

''Because if she wants to charge someone, I'd rather it be me, not you.'' He reached behind him and his hand found her jean-clad thigh. Patting her gently, he said, "Go on. I'll come down the hill fifteen minutes from now. I just want to give you a head start. The cat isn't going to follow you if she has me here. Besides, she's eating her lunch right now. If she's starving, that rabbit will put a dent in her appetite and she'll be far less likely to think of us as a meal."

Rachel understood his logic. "Okay, I'll do it." Her heart still pounded, but it wasn't fear she felt in jaguar's presence, just a thrilling excitement. He nodded slowly. "I'll see you in about twenty minutes down below in that meadow?"

Compressing her lips, Rachel reached out and squeezed his hand. "Yes," she said. "*You* be careful."

He smiled tensely. "I don't get any sense she's going to attack us."

"Me neither." Rachel released his hand. "She's so beautiful, Jim! And she's the one I saw standing in the middle of 89A. I'd swear it because I remember that black crescent on her forehead. I thought it looked odd, out of place there. It's impossible that two jaguars would have that same identical marking, isn't it?"

"Yeah, they're all marked slightly different," he agreed. "Sort of like fingerprints, you know?" He felt safe enough to turn his head slightly. Rachel's eyes were huge and full of awe as she gazed up on the cliff wall at the cat. Her cheeks were deeply flushed with excitement. Hell, he was excited, too.

"I think this is wonderful!" she gushed in a low voice. "The jaguars are back in Arizona!"

Chuckling a little, Jim said, "Well, *some* people will be thrilled with this discovery and others won't be. Like my family. Now we know who's been eating a beef every two weeks."

Frowning, Rachel sighed. "Thank goodness the fish and game department will capture her and take her someplace where she won't get killed by man."

"I talked to Bob this morning. He said jaguars were not only protected in South and Central America, but that they would be federally protected here if they ever migrated far enough north to cross the border."

"Well," Rachel said, "she certainly has. It's nice to know she can't be shot by your brothers, though they'd probably do it anyway if they had the chance, I'm sorry to say."

Glumly, Jim agreed. "No argument there. Better get going."

She patted his shoulder. "This whole day has been an incredible gift. I'll see you in about twenty minutes." Then she slowly backed away from him.

Jim tensed when the jaguar snapped up her head as Rachel began to move. Would the cat attack? Run away? He watched, awed by the beauty and throbbing power that seemed to emanate from the animal. She was a magnificent beast—so proud and queenly in the way she lifted her head to observe them. As Rachel mounted her horse and walked it out of the canyon, the cat flicked its tail once and then resumed eating her kill.

Recalling the time he'd hunted and trapped the mountain lion up here on the Rim, Jim realized this was a far cry from that traumatic event. Glancing down at his watch, he decided to give Rachel twenty minutes before he mounted up to go back down the slope and join her in the meadow. If the truth be known, he savored this time with the jaguar. He felt privileged and excited. This time he didn't have to kill, as he had with the mountain lion. The memory caused shame to creep through him as he stood there observing the jaguar. After he'd killed the cougar, his father had slapped him on the back, congratulating him heartily. Jim had felt like crying. He'd killed something wild and beautiful and had seen no sense to it.

His Apache mother had given each of her sons an Apache name when they were born. Even though it wasn't on his birth certificate, she'd called him Cougar. He remembered how she had extolled his cougar medicine, and how she made him realize how important it was. Even though he'd only been six years old when she died, her passionate remarks had made a lasting impression on him.

The past unfolded gently before him as he stood there. His mother had always called him Cougar because Jim was a white man's name, she'd told him teasingly. In her eyes and heart, he was like the cougar, and he knew he would learn how to become one because the cougar was the guardian spirit that had come into this life with him. Jim recalled the special ceremony his mother's people had had for him when he was five years old. Since she was Chiricahua, they'd traveled back to that reservation and her people had honored him. The old, crippled medicine man had given him a leather thong with a small beaded pouch attached to it. Inside the pouch was his "medicine."

To this day, Jim wore that medicine bag around his neck. The beading had long ago fallen off and he'd had to change the leather thong yearly. Whether it was crazy or not, Jim had worn that medicine bag from the day it had been placed on him during that ceremony. The medicine man head told him that the fur of a cougar was in the bag, that it was his protector, teacher and guardian. Sighing, Jim looked down at the rapidly melting midday snow. Maybe that was why that mountain lion never charged him when he came upon him that fateful day so long ago. The cat had simply looked at him through wise, yellow eyes and waited. It was as if he knew Jim had to kill him, so he stood there, magnificent and proud, awaiting his fate.

Suddenly Jim felt as if the claw he wore next to his small medicine bag was burning in his chest. Without thinking, Jim rubbed that area of his chest. He wondered if this jaguar sensed his cougar medicine. He knew that the great cats were related to one another. Was that why she chose not to charge him? His Anglo side said that was foolish, but his Apache blood said that he was correct in this assumption. The jaguar saw him as one of them. She would not kill one of her own kind. And then a crazy smile tugged at a corner of Jim's mouth. Rachel must have jaguar medicine, for it was this cat that had saved her from a fiery death at the accident that occurred less than a mile down the road. It was this cat that had leaped into the middle of the highway to stop her.

With a shake of his head, he knew life was more mystical than practical at times. He recalled the dream Rachel had had of the jaguar turning into a warrior woman. Gazing up at the animal, he smiled. There was no question he was being given a second chance. This time he wasn't going to kill. He was going to trap her and have her taken to an area where no Anglo's rifle could rip into her beautiful gold-and-black fur.

Remembering Rachel, he glanced at his watch. To his surprise, fifteen minutes had already flown by! Jim wished he could slow down time and remain here, just watching the jaguar, who had finished her meal and was licking one paw with her long, pink tongue.

Rachel had just reached the snow-covered meadow when to her horror she saw two cowboys emerge from the other end of it. Halting her horse, she realized it was Bo and Chet Cunningham and they had spotted her. Hands tightening on the reins, Rachel was torn by indecision. Should she try and outrun them? Her horse danced nervously beneath her, which wasn't like the animal at all. When she saw the rifles they carried on their saddles and the grim looks on their unshaven faces, she felt leery and decided to stand her ground. When the two men saw her, they spurred their mounts forward, the horses slipping and sliding as they thundered across the small meadow.

"Who the hell are you?" Bo demanded, jerking hard on the reins when he reached her. His horse grunted, opened its mouth to escape the pain of the bit and slid down on its hindquarters momentarily.

Rachel's horse leaped sideways. Steadying the animal, she glared at Bo. The larger of the two brothers, he looked formidable in his black Stetson, sheepskin coat and red bandanna. Danger prickled at Rachel and she put a hand on her horse's neck to keep him calm.

"I'm Rachel Donovan. Your brother—"

"A Donovan!" Chet snarled, pulling up on the other side of her horse.

Suddenly Rachel and her lightweight Arabian were trapped by two beefy thirteen-hundred-pound quarter horses. Bo's eyes turned merciless. "What the hell you doin' on our property, bitch?" he growled. His hand shot out.

Giving a small cry of surprise, Rachel felt his fingers tangle in her long, thick hair. Her scalp radiated with pain as he gave her a yank, nearly unseating her from the saddle. She pulled back on the reins so her gelding wouldn't leap forward.

"Oww!" she cried, "Let me go!"

Breathing savagely, Bo wrapped his fingers a little tighter in her hair. ''You bossy bitch. What the hell you doin' on Cunningham property? You're not welcomed over here.''

She could smell whiskey on his breath as he leaned over, his face inches from hers. Hanging at an angle, with only her legs keeping her aboard her nervous horse, Rachel tried to think. As the pain in her scalp intensified, the feral quality in Bo's eyes sent a sheet of fear through her.

''Let's get 'er down,'' Chet snapped. ''Let's teach her a lesson she won't forget, Bo. A little rape oughta keep her in line, wouldn't ya say?''

Rachel cried out in terror. Without thinking, she raised her hand to slap Bo's away. Knocking her arm away, Bo cursed and balled his right hand into a fist. Before she could protect herself, she saw his fist swing forward. Suddenly the side of her head exploded in stars, light and pain.

She was falling. Semiconscious, she felt the horse bolt from beneath her. Landing on her back, she hit the ground hard, and her breath was torn from her. She saw Chet leap from his horse, his face twisted into a savage grin of confidence as he approached her. She struggled to sit up but he straddled her with his long, powerful legs, slamming her back down into the red mud and snow. She felt his hands like vises on her wrists, pulling them above her head. Screaming and kicking out, she tried to buck him off her body, but he had her securely pinned. Grinning triumphantly at her, he placed his hand on the open throat of her shirt and gave a savage yank. The material ripped with a sickening sound.

"*No!*" Rachel shrieked. "Get off me!" She managed to get one hand free and she struck at Chet. She heard Bo laugh as the blow landed on the side of Chet's head.

"Ride 'er strong, brother. Hold on, I'll dismount and come and help you."

Panic turned to overwhelming terror. Sobbing, Rachel fought on, pummeling Chet's face repeatedly until he lifted his arms to protect himself.

At the same time, she heard Bo give a warning scream.

"Look out! A cougar! There's that cougar comin'!"

As Chet slammed Rachel down to the ground again, her head snapped back. Blood flowed from her nose and as she tried to move, she felt darkness claiming her. Chet dragged himself off her and ran for his horse, which danced nervously next to where she lay in the snow.

Bo cursed and jerked his horse around as the large cat hurtled toward them.

"Son of a bitch!" he yelled to Chet, and he made a grab for his rifle. His horse shied sideways once it caught sight of the charging cat coming directly at him.

Chet gave a cry as he remounted, his horse bucking violently beneath him as he clung to the saddle horn. The animal was wild with fear and trying to run.

Rachel rolled onto her stomach, dazed. The jaguar was charging directly down upon them. For a moment, she thought she was seeing things, but there was no way she could deny the reality of the huge cat's remarkable agility and speed, the massive power in her thick, short body as she made ground-covering strides right at them.

Snow and mud flew in sheets around the cat as she ran. Then suddenly the jaguar growled, and Rachel cried out as the sound reverberated through her entire being.

"Kill it!" Chet screeched, trying to stop his horse. He yanked savagely on one rein, causing his horse to begin to circle. *"Kill it!"* he howled again.

Bo pulled his horse to a standstill and made a grab for his rifle. But before he could clear the weapon from the scabbard, the jaguar leaped directly at him.

Rachel saw the cat's thick back legs flex as she leaped, saw the primal intent in her gold eyes rimmed in black. Everything seemed to move in slow motion. Rachel heard herself gasp and she raised her arms to protect herself from Bo's horse, which was dancing sideways next to her in order to escape the charge. Mud and snow flew everywhere, pelting Rachel as she watched the cat arch gracefully through the air directly at Bo, her huge claws bared like knives pulled from sheaths.

Bo gave a cry of surprise as the jaguar landed on the side of his horse. His mount reared and went over backward, carrying rider and cat with him. As

Rachel rolled out of the way and jumped to her feet, she heard another shout. It was Jim's voice!

Staggering dazedly, Rachel looked toward where Jim was flying down the snow-covered slope at a hard gallop, his face stony with anger. The snarl of the jaguar behind her snagged Rachel's failing attention. Her knees weakened as she turned. To her horror, she saw the jaguar take one vicious swipe at the downed horse and rider. Bo cried out and the horse screamed, its legs flailing wildly as it tried to avoid another attack by the infuriated jaguar.

Within seconds, the jaguar leaped away, taking off toward the timberline at a dead run. Though Bo was on the ground his horse had managed to get to its feet and run away, back toward the ranch. Chet had gotten his horse under control finally, but his hands were shaking so badly he couldn't get his rifle out of its sheath.

Bo leaped to his feet with a curse. He glared as Jim slid his horse to a stop and dismounted. "Get that damn cougar before he gets away!" Bo shouted, pointing toward the forest where the cat had disappeared once again.

Ignoring his brother, Jim ran up to Rachel. When he saw the blood flowing down across her lips and chin, the bruise marks along her throat, her shirt torn and hanging open, rage tunneled up through him. He reached out to steady her and she sagged into his arms with a small, helpless cry. Gripping her hard, he eased her to the ground. Breathing raggedly he glanced up at Bo, who was looking down at his left leg, where one of his leather chaps had been ripped away. The meadow looked like a battlefield. Blood was all over the place.

"Are you all right, Rachel?" Jim asked urgently, touching her head and examining her.

"Y-yes...." Rachel whispered faintly.

"What happened? Did the jaguar—"

"No," she rattled, her voice cracking. "Bo hit me. They saw me, trapped me between their horses. Your brother jerked me by my hair. When he went for my throat to haul me off my horse, I tried to shove his arm away. That's when Bo hit me." Blinking, Rachel held Jim's darkening gaze. "Chet tried to rape me. Bo was coming to help him until the jaguar charged...." Gripping his hand, she rasped, "Jim, that jaguar came out of nowhere. She protected me. I—I...they were going to rape me.... They thought I was alone. They didn't give me a chance to explain why I was on their property. Bo and Chet just attacked."

"Don't move," Jim rasped.

Rachel watched dazedly as Jim leaped to his feet. The attack of the jaguar had left her shaking. Terror still pounded through her and she didn't want Jim to leave. In four strides, he approached Bo, grabbing him by the collar of his sheepskin coat.

"What the hell do you think you were doing?" Jim snarled, yanking Bo so hard that his neck snapped back. He saw his brother's face go stormy.

"Get your hands off me!"

"Not a chance," Jim breathed savagely. Then he

doubled his fist and hit Bo with every ounce of strength he had. Fury pumped through him as he felt Bo's nose crack beneath the power of his assault. His brother crumpled like a rag doll.

Chet yelled at him to stop, but kept his fractious horse at a distance. "You can't hit him!" he shrieked.

Jim hunkered over Bo, who sat up, holding his badly bleeding nose. "You stay down or next time it'll be your jaw," he warned thickly. Bo remained on the ground.

Straightening up, Jim glared at Chet. "Get the hell out of here," he ordered.

"But—"

"Now!" Jim thundered, his voice echoing around the small meadow. Jabbing his finger at Chet, he snarled, "You tell Father that this cat is under federal protection. The fish and game department is going to come in and trap it and take it to another area. If either of you think you're going to kill that jaguar, I'll make sure it doesn't happen. You got that?"

Chet glared at him, trying to hold his dancing horse in place. "Jaguar? You're crazy! That was a cougar. We saw it with our own eyes!"

Blinking in confusion, Jim looked over at Rachel. When he saw her sitting in the snow, packing some of it against the right side of her swollen face and bleeding nose, he wanted to kill Bo for hurting her. Leaning down, he grabbed his brother by his black hair. "You sick son of a bitch," he snarled in his face. "You had no *right* to do that to Rachel—to any woman!'' He saw Bo's face tighten in pain as he gripped his hair hard. ''How does it feel?'' Jim rasped. ''Hurts, doesn't it? You ever think about that before you beat up on someone, Bo?''

''Let go of me!''

''You bastard.'' Jim shoved him back into the snow. ''Now you lay there and don't you move!'' He turned and strode back to Rachel. Leaning down, his hands on her shoulders, he met her tear-filled eyes.

''Hang on,'' he whispered unsteadily, ''I'm calling for help.''

''Just get Bob Granby. I didn't make the call yet, Jim....''

Nodding, he went over to his horse and opened one of his saddlebags. His gaze nailed Bo, who was sitting up, nursing his bloody nose and sulking. Pulling out a small first-aid kit, he went back to Rachel.

''Get my homeopathic first-aid kit,'' she begged. ''I can stop the bleeding and the swelling with it.''

He went to her horse and got the small plastic kit. Kneeling beside her, his hand still shaking with rage, he opened the kit for her. ''I'm sorry,'' he rasped, meaning it. As she opened one of the vials and poured several white pellets into her hand, he felt a desire to kill Bo and Chet for what they'd done to her. Rachel's cheek was swollen and he knew she'd have a black eye soon. Worse, her nose looked puffy, too, and he wondered if it was broken. Setting the kits down, he waited until she put the pellets in her mouth.

"Let me see if your nose is broken," he urged as he placed one hand behind her head. It was so easy, so natural between them. The tension he'd seen in her, the wariness in her eyes fled the moment he touched her. A fierce love for her swept through him. As gently as possible, he examined her fine, thin nose.

"Good," he whispered huskily, trying to smile down at her. "I don't think it's broken."

Rachel shut her eyes. With Jim close, she felt safe. "Did you see what happened?" she quavered.

"Yeah, I saw all of it," he told her grimly. Placing a dressing against her nose, he showed her how to hold it in place. "Stay here. I want to make that call to Bob and a second one to the sheriff."

Eyes widening, Rachel looked up at the grim set of his face. "The sheriff?"

"Damn straight. Bo's going up on assault charges. He's not going to hit you and get away with it," he growled as he rose to his feet.

Rachel closed her eyes once again. Her head, cheek and nose were throbbing. Within minutes, the homeopathic remedy stopped the bleeding and took away most of the pain in her cheekbone area. As she sat there in the wet snow, she began to shiver and realized shock was setting in. Lying down, she closed her eyes and tried to concentrate on taking slow, deep breaths to ward it off. The snort and stomp of nervous horses snagged her consciousness. She heard Jim's low, taut voice on the walkie-talkie,

Chet's high, nervous voice as he talked to Bo in the background.

What had happened? Chet said a cougar had charged them. Yet Rachel had seen the female jaguar. And how had Jim known she was in trouble? He'd come off that mountain at a dangerous rate of speed. It was all so crazy and confusing, she thought, feeling blackness rim her vision. She hoped the homeopathic remedy would pull her out of the shock soon. It should. All she had to do was lie quietly for a few minutes and let it help her body heal itself from the trauma.

More than anything, Rachel wanted to be home. The violence in Bo's eyes had scared her as nothing else ever had. She knew that if the jaguar had not charged him, if Jim hadn't arrived when he did, they would have raped her—simply because she was a Donovan. The thought sickened her. Jim was right—the sheriff must be called. She had no problem laying charges against Bo and Chet. If she had her way, it would be the last time Bo ever cocked his fist at a woman. The last time. Judging from the murderous look in Jim's eyes, he was ready to beat his older brother to a pulp. Rachel had seen the savagery in Jim's face, but she knew he wasn't like his two older brothers. He'd hit Bo just enough to disable him so he couldn't hurt either of them in the meantime. Unlike his brothers, Jim had shown remarkable restraint.

A fierce love welled up through Rachel as she lay there in the cooling snow. Though she felt very cold

and emotionally fragile at the moment, the heat of
the sun upon her felt good. No one had ever hurt
her like this in her life. The shock had gone deep
within her psyche. The last thing Rachel expected
was to be physically attacked. Now all she wanted
to do was get Bob Granby up here with the humane
trap. And then she wanted to go home—and heal.
More than anything, Rachel needed Jim right now,
his arms around her, making a safe place for her in
a world gone suddenly mad.

Chapter Ten

Rachel's head ached as she sat on the edge of the gurney in the emergency room at the Flagstaff Hospital. If it weren't for Jim's presence and soothing stability through a host of X rays and numerous examinations by doctor and nurses who came into her cubical from time to time, her frayed nerves would be completely shot. Luckily, Jim knew everyone in the ER, making it easier for her to tolerate the busy, hectic place.

Rachel closed her eyes and held the ice pack against her badly swollen cheek. She'd found out moments earlier that her cheekbone had sustained a hairline fracture. At least her nose wasn't broken, she thought with a slight smile. Jim's hand rarely left hers. She could tell he was trying to hide his anger and upset from her. Bob Granby from the fish and game department had come out and met them on the Cunningham land about the same time a deputy sheriff, Scott Maitland, had rolled up. Chet and Bo were taken into custody and transported to the Flagstaff jail, awaiting charges.

Rachel was about to speak when the green curtains surrounding her cubical parted. She felt Jim's hand tighten slightly around hers as Deputy Scott Maitland approached the gurney. She knew Maitland was going to ask for a statement. Her head ached so badly that all she wanted to do was crawl off alone to a quiet place and just rest.

Maitland tipped his gray Stetson in her direction. "Ms. Donovan?"

Rachel sat up a little and tried to smile, but wasn't successful. "Yes?"

Apologetically, Maitland looked over at Jim and reached out to shake his hand. "Sorry about this, Jim."

"Thanks, Scott." He looked worriedly at Rachel. "She's in a lot of pain right now and some shock. Can you take her statement later?"

Maitland shook his head. He held a clipboard in his large hands. "I'm afraid not. Your father already has his attorney, Stuart Applebaum, up at the jail demanding bail information for your brothers. We can't do anything until I take your statements."

Rachel removed the ice pack and tried to focus on the very tall, broad-shouldered deputy. The Maitlands owned the third largest cattle ranch in Arizona.

The spread was run by two brothers and two sisters and Scott was the second oldest, about twenty-eight years old. The history of the Maitland dynasty was a long and honorable one that Rachel, who was a history buff, knew well. For her senior thesis, she'd written up the history of cattle ranching for Arizona. She knew from her research that Cathan Maitland had come from Ireland during the Potato Famine in the mid-1800s and claimed acreage up around Flagstaff. He'd then married a woman Comanche warrior, whose raiding parties used to keep the area up in arms, as did the Apache attacks.

As Rachel looked up into Scott's clear gray eyes, she saw some of that Comanche heritage in him, from his thick, short black hair to his high cheekbones and golden skin. He had a kind face, not a stern one, so she relaxed a little, grateful for his gentle demeanor as he walked over and stood in front of her. His mouth was pulled into an apologetic line.

"Looks like you're going to be a raccoon pretty soon," he teased.

Rachel touched her right eye, which she knew was bruised and darkening. "You're right," she said huskily.

"I'll try and make this as painless and fast as possible," he told her. "I think the docs have pretty much wrapped you up and are ready to sign you out of here so you can go home and rest." His eyes sparkled. "I'll see if I can beat their discharge time for you."

"Thanks," Rachel whispered, and placed the ice pack back on her cheek very gently.

"Just tell me in your own words what happened," Maitland urged, "and I'll fill out this report."

Rachel tried to be as clear and specific as possible as she told the story. When she said that she had seen the jaguar, Scott's eyes widened.

"A jaguar?"

"Yes," Rachel murmured. She looked at Jim, who continued to hold her hand as she leaned against his strong, unyielding frame. "Jim saw it, too."

"I did, Scott. A big, beautiful female jaguar."

"I'll be damned," he said, writing it down.

"Why are you acting so surprised?" Jim inquired.

"Well, your brothers swear they were attacked by a cougar." Maitland studied Rachel. "And you're saying you saw a jaguar come running down that hill and attack Bo?"

"I'm positive it was a jaguar," Rachel said.

"Scott, let me break in here and tell you something Rachel doesn't know yet. When she left to head down to the meadow, that female jaguar just sat at the opening to her lair, cleaning off her paws after finishing her jackrabbit. And then suddenly she jumped up, leaped off that ledge and ran right by me." Jim scratched his head. "She stopped about a hundred feet away from me, growled, looked down the mountain and then back at me. As crazy as this sounds, I got the impression I had to hurry—that something was wrong." Grimly, his eyes flashing, he added, "I leaped into the saddle and rode hell-bent-for-leather down that mountain. That jaguar was right in front of me, never more than a hundred yards away. She was running full bore. So were we. When I came out of the woods, I saw my brothers had Rachel down on the ground. That was when the jaguar really sped up. She was like a blur of motion as she ran right for Bo."

"I saw the jaguar leap," Rachel told Scott in a low voice. "I heard her growl and saw her jump. I saw her slash out with her claws at Bo." She frowned. "You saw Bo's chaps, didn't you?"

"Yeah." Scott chuckled. "No way around that. That cat slashed the hell out of them and that's thick cowhide leather." He scratched his jaw in thought. "The only disagreement we've got here is that two witnesses say it was a cougar and you both say it was a jaguar."

"Does it really matter?" Rachel asked grimly.

"No, I guess it doesn't. The fact that Bo assaulted you and Chet threatened you with rape is the real point of this report."

Shivering, Rachel closed her eyes. She felt Jim place his arm around her and draw her against him more tightly. Right now she felt cold and tired, and all she wanted was rest and quiet, not this interrogation.

"Let's try and get this done as soon as possible," Jim urged his friend. "She's getting paler by the moment and I want to get her home so she can rest."

"Sure," Maitland murmured.

* * *

Rachel never thought that being home—her new home on her family ranch—would ever feel so good. But it did. Kate and Jessica had come over as soon as Jim had driven into the homestead. They'd fussed over her like two broody hens. Kate got the fire going in the fireplace out in the living room and Jessica made her some chamomile tea to soothe her jangled nerves. Jim had gotten her two high-potency homeopathic remedies, one for her fracture and the other for her swollen cheek and black eye. She drank the tea and took the remedies. Five minutes later, she was so tired due to the healing effects of the remedies that she dropped off asleep on her bed, covered by the colorful afghan knit by her mother many years before.

Jim moved quietly down the carpeted hall to Rachel's bedroom. The door was open and Kate and Jessica had just left. He'd told them he was going to stay with Rachel for a while just to make sure she was all right. The truth was he didn't want to leave her at all. Torn between going home and facing his infuriated father and remaining with her, he stood poised at the door.

Rachel lay on her right side, her hands beneath the pillow where her dark hair lay like a halo around her head. The colorful afghan wasn't large enough to cover her fully and he was concerned about the coolness in the house. The only heat supply was from the fireplace, and it would take awhile to warm the small adobe home. Moving quietly, he went to the other side of the old brass bed, pulled up a dark pink, cotton goose down bedspread and gently eased it over her. Snugging it gently over her shoulders, he smiled down at Rachel as she slept.

Her golden skin looked washed out, almost pasty. Reaching down, he grazed her left cheek, which was soft and firm beneath his touch. Her lips were slightly parted. She looked so vulnerable. Rage flowed through him as he straightened. His right hand still throbbed and he was sure he'd probably fractured one of his fingers in the process of slugging Bo. Flexing his fingers, Jim felt satisfaction thrum through him. At least Bo was suffering just a little from hurting Rachel. If Jim had his way, his brother was going to suffer a lot more. This was one time that neither his father's lawyer nor his money would dissuade Rachel from putting both his brothers up on charges that would stick. With their past criminal record, they were looking at federal prison time.

Jim needed to get home and he knew it. Leaning over, he cupped her shoulder and placed a light kiss on her unmarred brow.

"Sleep, princess," he whispered. *I love you.* And he did. A lump formed in his throat as he left the bedroom and walked quietly down the hall. Shrugging into his sheepskin coat and settling the black Stetson on his head, he left her house. Outside, the sun was hanging low in the west, the day nearly spent. What a hell of a day it had been. As he drove his pickup down the muddy red road, Jim's thoughts revolved around his love for Rachel. He knew it was too soon to share it with her. Time was needed to cultivate a relationship with her. If he'd had any doubt about his feelings for her, he'd lost them all out there in that meadow.

Working his mouth, Jim drove down 89A toward Sedona. Just before town was the turnoff for the Bar C. His hands tightened on the steering wheel as he wound down Oak Creek Canyon. The world-famous beauty of the tall Douglas firs, the red and white cliffs rising thousands of feet on both sides of the slash of asphalt, did not move him today as they normally did.

Would Rachel allow him to remain in her life after what had happened? Would his Cunningham blood taint her so that she retreated from him, from the love he held for her? He sighed. There would be a trial. And Jim was going to testify with Rachel against his brothers. Everything was so tenuous. So unsure. He felt fear. Fear of losing Rachel before he'd ever had her, before she could know his love for her.

Jim tried to gather his strewn emotions, knowing all hell would break lose once he stepped into the main ranch house when he got home. His father, because he was wheelchair bound, relied on one of them to drive him wherever he wanted to go. Jim was sure Frank was seething with anger and worry over Bo and Chet. But his father ought to be concerned about Rachel, and what they had done to her—and what they would have done had it not been for that jaguar attacking.

Shaking his head as he drove slowly down the dirt road toward home, Jim wondered about the discrepancy in the police report. How could Bo and Chet have seen a cougar when it was a jaguar? What the hell was going on here? No matter, the fish and game expert would see the tracks, would capture the jaguar in a special cage, and that would be proof enough. His brothers were well known for their lies. This was just one more.

"What the hell is going on?" Frank roared as Jim stepped through the door into the living room. He angrily wheeled his chair forward, his face livid.

Quietly shutting the door, Jim took off his hat and coat and hung them on hooks beside it. "Bo and Chet are up on assault charges," he said quietly as he turned and faced his father.

"Applebaum tells me Rachel Donovan is pressing charges. Is that true?"

Allowing his hands to rest tensely on his hips, Jim nodded. "Yes, and she's not going to withdraw them, either. And even if she did," he said in a level tone, holding his father's dark gaze, "I would keep my charges against them, anyway."

"How could you? Dammit!" Frank snarled, balling up his fist and striking the chair arm. "How can you do this to your own family? Blood's thicker than water, Jim. You *know* that! When there's a storm, the family goes through it together. We're supposed to help and protect one another, not—"

"Dammit, Father," he breathed savagely, "Bo hit Rachel. She's got a fractured cheekbone. Not that you care." His nostrils flared and his voice lowered to a growl. "You don't care because she's a Donovan. And you couldn't care less what happens to anyone with that last name." Punching his finger toward his father, he continued, "I happen to love her. And I don't know if she loves me. This situation isn't going to help at all. But whatever happens, I'll tell you one thing—they aren't getting away with it this time. All your money, your influence peddling and the political strings you pull aren't going to make the charges against them go away. Chet and Bo were going to rape her. Did you know that? Is that something you condone?" He straightened, fury in his voice. "Knowing you, you'd condone it because her last name was Donovan."

Stunned, Frank looked up at him. "They said nothing about rape. Applebaum said Bo threw a punch her way because she lashed out at him."

"Yeah, well, it connected, Father. Big-time." Jim pushed his fingers angrily through his short hair and moved over to the fireplace. He felt his father's glare follow him. Jim's stomach was in knots. He was breathing hard. A burning sensation in the middle of his chest told him just how much he wanted to cry with pure rage over this whole fiasco.

Frank slowly turned his wheelchair around.

Scowling at Jim. "What's this you said about loving this woman?"

"Her name is Rachel Donovan, Father. And yes, I love her."

"She love you?" he asked, his voice suddenly weary and old sounding.

Jim pushed his shoulders back to release the terrible tension in them. "I don't know. It's too soon. And too damn much has happened. I'll be lucky if she doesn't tar and feather me with the same brush as Bo and Chet."

"My own son…falling in love with a Donovan…. My God, how could you do this to me, Jim? How?"

Looking into his father's eyes, Jim saw tears in them. That shook him. He'd never seen his father cry—ever. "You know," Jim rasped, "I would hope the tears I see in your eyes are for what Rachel suffered at their hands and not the fact that I love her."

Frank's mouth tightened. "Get out of here. Get out and don't ever come back. You're a turncoat, Jim. I'm ashamed of you. My youngest boy, a boy I'd hoped would someday run the Bar C with his brothers…." He shook his head. His voice cracked with raw emotion. "Just when I need you the most, you turn traitor on me. And you're willing to sell your brothers out, too. How could you? Your own family!"

Fighting back tears, Jim held his father's accusing gaze as a lump formed in his throat. He wanted to scream at the unfairness of it all. Suddenly, he didn't care anymore. "I've spent nearly a year here, trying to straighten out things between you, me, and my brothers," he said thickly, "and it backfired on me. I got warned more times than not that I can't fix three people who'd like to stay the way they are." He headed slowly to his coat and hat. "You can't see anything because you're blinded by hate, Father. The word *Donovan* makes you like a rabid dog. Well," he said, jerking his coat off the hook, "I won't be part and parcel of what you, Bo or Chet want to do. I don't give a damn about this ranch, either, if it means others will suffer in order to claim it." He shrugged on his coat. "You're willing to do anything to get revenge for transgressions that died with Kelly."

His heart hurt in his chest and his voice wobbled dangerously as he jerked open the door. Settling his hat on his head, he rasped unevenly, "I'll be moving out. In the next week, I'll come over and pick up my stuff. I'll be seeing you in court."

"Rachel, you look so sad," Jessica said with a sigh. She touched her sister's shoulder as she headed for the store in Rachel's kitchen. "The homeopathy sure helped get rid of that shiner you had and there's hardly any swelling left on your cheek. But nothing has cheered you up yet." She smiled brightly and poured some tea for both of them. Sunlight lanced through the curtains, flooding the cheery kitchen.

Thanking Jessica for the tea, Rachel squeezed a bit of fresh lemon into it. "I'm okay...really, I am."

Jessica sat down across from her and frowned. "It's been four days now since it happened. You just mope around. Something's wrong. I can feel it around you."

The tart, sweet tea tasted good to Rachel. Gently setting the china cup down on the saucer, she stared at it and said softly, "I wonder why Jim hasn't come by?"

"Ahh," Jessica said with a burgeoning smile, "that's it, isn't it? Why, I didn't know you were sweet on him, Rachel."

Looking up at her youngest sister, Rachel whispered, "I guess what happened out there in the meadow did something to me—ripped something away so I could see or feel more...." Lamely, she opened her hands. "I know he probably thinks I think less of him because of what his two brothers did to me."

"Hmm," Jessica murmured, "I don't sense that." She laughed, pressing her hand to the front of the green plaid, flannel, long-sleeved shirt.

"Your intuition?" Rachel valued Jessica's clairvoyant abilities.

"Maybe Jim hasn't come around because he's busy. You know, with two brothers in jail, someone has to run the Bar C, and he's got a part-time job as an EMT with the Sedona Fire Department. I imagine between the two, it has kept him hopping."

"Always the idealist."

Chortling, Jessica asked, "Do you like the alternative?"

"No," Rachel admitted sadly, sipping her tea. "I think Jim's avoiding me."

"I don't."

There was a knock on the front door. Jessica grinned and quickly stood up, her long blond braids swinging. "Are you expecting anyone?"

"No," Rachel said.

"I'll get it. You stay here."

Rachel was about to protest that she wasn't an invalid—and that Kate and Jessica were doting too much over her—when she heard a man's low, husky voice. *Jim.* Instantly, her heart began to beat hard in her chest and she nearly spilled the contents of her cup as she set it askew on the saucer.

"Look who's here!" Jessica announced breathlessly as she hurried back into the kitchen, her eyes shining with laughter.

Jim took off the baseball cap he wore when he was on EMT duty. He saw Rachel stand, her fingertips resting tentatively on the table, her cheeks flushed a dull red. Would she rebuff him? Tell him to leave? He was unsure as he held her widening eyes.

"Hi," he said with a broken smile. "I just thought I'd drop over and see how you were coming along."

Jessica patted his arm in a motherly fashion. "Believe me, you're just what the doctor ordered, Jim. Listen, I gotta go! Dan is helping me repot several of my orchid girls over in the greenhouse and he needs my guidance." She flashed them both a smile, raised her hand and was gone, like the little whirl-wind she was.

When Jim heard the front door close, he met and held Rachel's assessing, forest green gaze. "I wasn't sure if I should drop over unannounced or not," he began, the cap in his right hand.

"I—I'm glad to see you," she said. "Would you like to have some tea? Jessica just made some a little while ago." The look on his face tore at her. She saw dark smudges beneath his bloodshot eyes and a strain around his mouth. He looked as if he hadn't slept well at all.

"Uh...tea sounds great," and he replied, maneuvering around to the chair and pulling it out. He placed his dark blue cap on the table and said, "I can't stay long." He patted the pager on his belt. "I'm on duty."

Nervously, Rachel went over to the kitchen cabinet and pulled out another cup and saucer. Jim was here. Here! How could she tell him how much she missed his presence in her life? Compressing her lips, she poured him some tea and placed it in front of him.

"Kate brought over some fresh doughnuts that Sam picked up from the bakery this morning. You look a little pasty. Maybe some food might help?"

Jim looked up. "That sounds good," he said. "I'll take a couple if you have them handy." He studied the woman before him. Rachel's hair was combed and hung well below her shoulders, glinting with red-gold highlights. She wore a pale yellow, long-sleeved blouse, tan slacks and dark brown loafers. In his eyes, she'd never looked more beautiful. Her black eye was gone and he saw only the slightest swelling along her right cheekbone. She almost looked as if nothing had happened. But it had.

Thanking her for the chocolate-covered doughnuts, he watched as she sat down next to him after pouring herself more hot tea. He gauged the guarded look on her features.

"How are you surviving?" he asked, munching on a doughnut. For the first time in four days, he found himself hungry. Ravenous, in fact—but even more, he was starved for her company, her voice, her presence.

"Oh, fine…fine…." Rachel waved her hands in a nervous gesture. "But you don't look too good." She avoided his eyes. "I've been worried about you, Jim. About you having to go over to your father's home and live there and take the heat from him about your brothers." She gestured toward his face. "You look like you haven't been sleeping well, either."

With a grimace, he wiped his mouth with a napkin. "A lot's changed since we last were together," he admitted slowly.

"Is your father okay?"

He heard the genuine worry in Rachel's voice. Her insight, her care of others was one of the many things he loved fiercely about her. Putting the cup aside, he laid his arms on the table and held her gaze.

"He had a stroke four days ago."

"Oh, no!" Rachel cried.

Scowling, Jim rasped, "Yeah...."

"And what's his prognosis?"

He shook his head and avoided her eyes. "The docs up in Flag say he's going to make it. His whole right side is paralyzed, though, and he can't talk anymore."

Squeezing her eyes shut, Rachel whispered, "Oh, Jim, I'm so sorry. This is awful." She opened her eyes. "Why didn't you call and tell me about it?"

Shrugging painfully, he put the doughnuts aside. "Honestly?"

"Always," she whispered, reaching out and slipping her fingers into his hand.

"I was afraid after what happened that you wouldn't want to be around me any more...because of my brothers. You know, the Cunningham name and all...."

Rachel felt her heart break. Tears gathered in her eyes. "Oh, Jim, no! Never...not ever would I let how I feel toward you change just because of your last name." She reached out and took his other hand. "Is there anything we can do to help you? Or your father?" She knew Frank Cunningham would be an invalid now, confined to bed unless he went through therapy. And even then, Frank would be bound to a wheelchair for the rest of his life. She saw tears glimmer in Jim's eyes and then he forced them away. His hands felt strong and good on hers.

Without a word, she released his hands, stood up

and came around the table. Moving behind him, she slid her arms around him and pressed her uninjured cheek against his and just held him. She felt so much tension in him, and as she squeezed him gently, he released a ragged sigh. His hands slid across her lower arms, and she closed her eyes.

"I feel so awful for all of you," she whispered brokenly. "I'm sorry all this happened."

The firmness of her flesh made him need her even more. Without a word, Jim eased out of her arms and stood up. Putting the chair aside, he faced Rachel. Tears ran down her cheeks. She was crying for his father, for him and for the whole, ugly situation. Her generosity, her compassion, shook him as nothing else ever could.

"What I need," he said unsteadily as he held out his hand toward Rachel, "is you...just you...."

Chapter Eleven

As Rachel pressed herself to Jim, his arms went around her like steel bands. The air rushed out of her lungs, and she felt his shaven cheek against her own. A shudder went through him as he buried his face in her thick, dark hair. Clinging to her like a man who was dying and could be saved only by her. Her heart opened and she sniffled, the tears coming more and more quickly.

"I'm sorry, so sorry," she sobbed. "I didn't mean to cause this kind of trouble...and your father—"

"Hush," Jim whispered thickly, framing her face with his hands. He was mindful of her fractured right cheekbone, and he barely touched that area of her face. He looked deeply into her dark, pain-filled eyes. Tears beaded on her dark lashes. Her mouth was a tortured line. "This isn't your fault. None of it, princess."

He winced inwardly as he realized he'd allowed his endearment for her slip out. Rachel blinked once, as if assimilating the word. She gulped, her hands caressing the back of his neck and shoulders.

"There's been so much misery between our families," she whispered unsteadily. "I was hoping…oh, how I was hoping things would settle down now that Kelly was gone."

Caressing her uninjured cheek, Jim wiped the tears away with his fingers. "We aren't going to pay the price that those two decided to pay one another, Rachel. We aren't. You and I—" he looked deeply into her eyes, his voice low and fervent "—can have a better life. A happier one if we want it. We can make better decisions than they ever have. We should learn from them, not duplicate their actions."

Closing her eyes, she felt a fine quiver go her. "Not like Chet and Bo," she admitted painfully.

He nodded grimly. "We're nothing like those two. They have to find their own way now. Father is mute. He'll never speak again. He'll never be able to wield the power or call in the chips like he did before his stroke." Caressing her hair, Jim added wearily, "Chet and Bo will go to prison for at least a couple of years. I've talked to the district attorney for Coconino County, and he said that, based upon the evidence and our testimony and their past jail records, the judge won't be lenient. He shouldn't be.''

Numbly, Rachel rested her brow against his chin. She felt the caress of his fingers through her hair and relaxed as he gently massaged her tense neck and shoulders. ''It's all so stupid,'' she said. ''They could have done so many other things with their lives—good things.''

''They made their bed,'' Jim told her harshly, flattening his hands against her supple back, ''now let them lie in it.''

Surrendering to his strength, Rachel flowed against him. She heard Jim groan in utter pleasure. Breathing in his masculine scent, she reveled in his warm, tender embrace. As the moments flowed by, she closed her eyes and simply absorbed his gentle and protective nature.

Pressing a kiss to her hair, Jim finally eased Rachel away just enough to look into her languid eyes. There was a sweet, spicy fragrance to her hair and he inhaled it deeply. Rachel was life. *His* life. He saw the gold flecks in the forest green depths of her eyes, and he fought the urge to lean down and take her delicious, parted lips. Instead, he asked wryly, ''We never got to finish our conversation up on the Rim, do you realize that?''

Heat burned in Rachel's cheeks as she stood in his arms, her hands on his hard biceps. ''You're right…we didn't.''

''What do you think? Am I worth the risk? I know you are.''

Shyly, Rachel searched his serious features. "Yesterday," she whispered, "I thought a lot about you...how long I've known you, and how I hadn't realized you had a crush on me back then."

"My crush on you," Jim told her, moving a strand of hair away from her flushed cheek, "never ended."

Swallowing hard, Rachel nodded. "I began to understand that."

"I'm scared. Are you?"

"Very," Rachel admitted in a strained voice, her fingers digging a little more firmly into his arms. "When Bo dragged me off the horse, I thought I was going to die, Jim. I could see the hatred in both your brothers' eyes and I knew..." She swallowed painfully. Her eyes misted and her voice softened. "I knew I loved you and I didn't have the courage to tell you I did. And I was sorry because I thought I'd never see you again." A sob stuck in her throat, and she felt hot tears spilling down her cheeks again.

Jim held her hard against him and gently rocked her back and forth. "It's okay, princess. I know you love me." He laughed a little shakily. "What a crazy time this is." He kissed her hair and then carefully cupped her face. "I love you, Rachel Donovan. And ten thousand stampeding horses aren't going to stop me from seeing you whenever I can."

His mouth was warm and strong as it settled against her tear-bathed lips. Rachel moaned, but it was a moan of surrender, of need of him. She tasted the sweet tartness of the lemon and sugar on his lips, the scent of juniper around him as he deepened his exploration of her. Her breath became ragged and her heart pounded. The power of his mouth, the searching heat of him surrounded her, drugged her, and she bent like a willow in his arms.

Just then, his beeper went off.

"Damn," he growled, tearing his mouth from hers. Apologetically, he eased Rachel into the nearest chair. "I'm sorry," he said, looking down at the pager. "Larry and I are on duty. It's probably an EMT call."

"The phone's in the living room," Rachel whispered, dizzy from his unexpected, tender kiss. Touching her tingling lower lip, she felt euphoria sweep through her. Just the sound of his steady, low voice as he talked on the phone, was comforting to her. He loved her. The admission was sweet, filled with promise. And filled with terror. But as she sat there remembering the taste and touch of Jim, Rachel realized her terror hadn't won. It was still there, but not as overwhelming as before. Maybe the fact that she had almost died made her realize how good life was with Jim in it.

Jim walked back into the kitchen, his brow knitted. "I've got to go. There's been a multiple accident about a mile down 89A from here."

Rachel nodded and stood up. Her knees felt weak. Before she could speak, he slid his arm around her, drew her against him and captured her parted lips with his mouth. It was a hot, searching, almost desperate kiss. Before she could respond, he released her and rasped, ''I get off tomorrow at noon. I'll bring lunch.''

Then he was gone. Rachel swayed. Touching her lips gently, she felt a stab of fear—only this time she was worried over Jim and the accident scene. She remembered his promise of lunch tomorrow and the thought blanketed her, filling her with warmth. Never had she felt this way before. Her heart throbbed with a joy she'd never known. Love. She was in love with Jim Cunningham.

A little in shock over the realization, Rachel sat down before she fell down. She heard a knock at the front door, and then Kate's voice rang through the house.

''Rachel?''

''In here,'' she called. ''Come on in.''

Kate took off her cowboy hat and ran her fingers through her dark, tangled hair. She grinned as she came into the kitchen.

''I just saw Jim leaving in a hurry. He on call?''

''Yes. There's been a bad accident a mile down from our ranch on 89A. Are Dan and Sam here?''

''Yep,'' she said with a sigh, going over to the kitchen counter and pouring herself a cup of tea. ''It's really nice,'' she murmured, ''that you're home now. I like having an excuse to escape from vetting horses and cattle and to come over here and see you.''

Smiling up at her older sister, Rachel patted the chair next to her own. ''Isn't it great? Come, sit down. You're working too hard, Kate.'' Rachel knew her sister was up well before daybreak everyday, and rarely did she and Sam hit the sack until around midnight. She didn't know how Kate did it. Perhaps she had Kelly's drive and passion for the ranch more than any of the sisters.

Flopping down on the chair, Kate sipped her tea. "Mmm, this hits the spot on a cold day." She crossed her legs. Her cowboy boots were scuffed and dusty. "Did you hear the latest? Sam and I just came in from Sedona."

"No." Rachel rolled her eyes. "I hate town gossip. You know that."

"Mmm, you'll be interested in this," Kate said. She took another gulp of the steaming coffee and sat up. Tapping the table with her finger, she said, "We heard from Deputy Scott Maitland that Bo and Chet are probably going away to do federal prison time."

Rachel nodded. "Yes, Jim just told me the same thing."

"They deserve it," she growled. "If I'd been there, I'd probably have blown their heads off with my rifle, and then I'd never live outside of prison bars again."

Rachel grimaced. "Thank goodness you weren't there, then. You've seen enough of that place."

Kate made a face. "No kidding."

"Did you hear that Jim's father had a stroke? He's up at the Flag hospital recovering."

Shocked, Kate sat up. "No. What happened?"

"I'm not sure. Maybe it was the shock of Bo and Chet being in jail."

"Or you pressing charges," Kate muttered angrily. "I'm surprised that Old Man Cunningham didn't keel over of a stroke a decade ago. He's always blowing his top over some little thing."

"Two of your sons going to prison isn't little," Rachel said softly. "The ranch, from what Jim said, is in his brothers' names."

"Is Old Man Cunningham paralyzed?"

"Yes. He's pretty bad," Rachel murmured worriedly.

"Well," Kate said, pushing several strands of hair away from her flushed cheek, "that means Jim is going to have to assume the running of the Bar C."

Surprised, Rachel bolted upright. She stared at Kate. "What?"

"Sure," she said, leaning back in the chair and sipping her coffee, "someone's got to run it now that the old man can't. Chet and Bo are probably looking at five years in the pen. Maybe they'll get off in two and a half for good behavior. If Jim doesn't quit his job as an EMT and return to the ranch, it will fall apart. Who will be there to pay the bills? Give the wranglers their checks? Or manage the place?" With a shake of her head, Kate said, "Boy, what goes around comes around, doesn't it? Cunningham was trying to put us out of business and look what's happened to him." She brightened a little. "Come to think of it, that trumped-up lawsuit he's got against us will die on the vine, too."

Smiling grimly, she got up and poured herself another cup of tea. "This disaster might be a blessing in disguise. If we can get his lawyer off our backs, we won't have to spend money filing—money we don't have."

Rachel nodded and watched her sister sit back down. She wondered about everything Kate had told her. Would Jim really settle down to ranching life on his father's spread? For the first time, she saw hope for a future with Jim.

The noontime sun streamed into Rachel's small but cozy kitchen as Jim sat sharing the lunch he'd promised with her. He'd stopped at a deli in town and gotten tuna sandwiches, sweet pickles and two thick slices of chocolate cake. Ever since he'd arrived, he'd been longing to take her in his arms again, to finish what they'd only started yesterday. But he could still see a slight swelling along her right cheekbone where it had been fractured. As badly as he wanted to make love to her, he would wait until she was healed. The way she carefully ate told him that moving her jaw caused her pain. Instead, he decided to tell her his news. "I quit my job at the fire department."

"To run the ranch?" Rachel asked, carefully chewing her sandwich and studying the man before her. Jim wore his dark blue uniform, leaving his baseball cap on the side of the table as he ate. He looked exhausted, and Rachel knew it was due to worrying over his father's condition. She was glad he'd come by, though—how she had looked forward to seeing him again!

"Yes," he said, sipping the hot coffee. "I talked to the hospital and they're beginning recovery therapy for my father. He's got all kinds of medical insurance, so it won't be a problem that way, thank God."

Rachel raised her brows. "It's a good thing he has insurance. We have none. Can't afford it."

"Like about one-third of all Americans," Jim agreed somberly.

"When will you bring him home?"

"In about a week, from the looks of it."

"How do you feel about running the Bar C?" she asked tentatively.

"Odd, I guess." He exchanged a warm look with her. "When I left after high school, I figured I'd never be back. When I did come home, Father told me Bo and Chet would take over the ranch after he died."

"How did you feel about that?"

"I didn't care."

"And now?"

He grinned a little. "I still don't." Reaching out, he captured her hand briefly. "I've got my priorities straight. I want a life with the woman who stole my heart when I was a teenager."

She smiled softly at the tenderness that burned in his eyes. "I still can't believe you loved me all those years, Jim. You never said a thing."

"I was a shy kid," he said with a laugh. "And I

had the curse of my father's Donovan-hating on top of it. That was the best reason not to approach you."

Rachel nodded and reluctantly released his hand. "I know," she whispered sadly. Holding his gaze, she asked, "Have you ever wondered what our lives might have been like if our fathers hadn't been carrying on that stupid feud?"

"Yeah," he said fondly, finishing off his second sandwich. Being around Rachel made him famished. "We'd probably have married at eighteen, had a brood of kids and been happy as hell."

Rachel couldn't deny the possible scenario. "And now? What do you want out of life, Jim?"

Somberly, he picked up her hand as she laid her own half-eaten sandwich aside. "You. Just you, princess."

Coloring, she smiled. "That's a beautiful endearment."

"Good, because as an awkward, shy teenager, I used to fantasize that you were a princess from a foreign country—so beautiful and yet untouchable."

Her voice grew strained with tears. "What a positive way to look at it, at the situation." Rachel gently pressed the back of his hand to her left cheek. The coals of desire burned in his eyes and she ached to love Jim. He'd made it clear earlier that, because her cheekbone was fractured, they should wait, and she'd agreed. To even try and kiss him was painful. Waiting was tough, but not impossible for Rachel. She understood on a deeper level that they needed the time to reacquaint themselves with one another, without all the family fireworks and dramatics going on around them.

He eased his hand from hers. "I brought something with me that I've been saving for a long, long time." He grinned sheepishly and dug into the left pocket of his dark blue shirt. "Now," he cautioned her lightly, "you have to keep this in perspective, okay?"

Rachel smiled with him. Jim suddenly was boyish, looking years younger. His eyes sparkled mischievously as he pulled something wrapped in a tissue from his pocket. "Well, sure. What is it, Jim?"

Chuckling, he laid the lump of tissue on the table between them. "I had such a crush on you that I saved my money and I went to Mr. Foglesong's jewelry store and bought you this. I kept dreaming that someday you'd look at me, or give me a smile, and we would meet, and at the right moment, I could give you this." He gestured toward it. "Go ahead, it's yours. A few years late, but it's yours, anyway."

Jim saw Rachel's cheeks flush with pleasure as she carefully unwrapped the tissue on the table. He heard her audible gasp and saw her dark green eyes widen beautifully.

"Now, it's nothing expensive," he warned as she picked up a ring encrusted with colorful gems on a silver band. "It's base metal covered with electroplated silver. The stones are nothing more than cut glass."

Touched beyond words, Rachel gently held the ring encircled with sparkling, colorful "diamonds."

"Back then, every girl wore her boyfriend's ring around her neck on a chain."

He laughed. "Yeah, going steady."

"And you were going to give this to me?" She held it up in a slash of sunlight that crossed the table where they sat. The ring sparkled like a rainbow.

"I wanted to," Jim told her ruefully. "I saved my money and bought it the first year I saw you in junior high."

The realization that Jim had kept this ring through six years of school and never once had she even said hello to him or smiled at him broke her heart. No, he was a Cunningham, and Rachel, like her sisters, had avoided anyone with that name like the plague. She felt deep sadness move through her as she slipped the ring on the fourth finger of her right hand. It fit perfectly. Tears burned in her eyes as she held out her hand for him to inspect.

"How does it look?" she quavered.

Words choked in Jim's throat as he slid his hands around hers. "Nice. But what I'm looking at is beautiful."

Sniffing, Rachel wiped the tears from her eyes with trembling fingers. "This is so sad, Jim. You carried this ring for six years in school hoping I'd say hello to you, or at least look you in the eye. Every time I saw a Cunningham coming, I'd turn the other way and leave. I'm so sorry! I didn't know.... I really didn't know...."

"Hush, princess, it doesn't matter. You came home and so did I, and look what happened." His mouth curved into a gentle smile as he held her tear-filled eyes. "We have a chance to start over, Rachel. That's how I see it." Gripping her hand more firmly, he continued, "Life isn't exactly going to be a lot of fun this next six weeks, but after that, things should settle out a little."

"I know," she agreed. Six weeks. The trial would be coming up in a month and then Chet and Bo would get from the judge what they deserved. It would take six weeks for her fractured cheekbone to heal. And then... Her heart took off at a gallop. Then she could make love to Jim. The thought was hot, melting and full of promise. She ached to have him, love him and join with him in that beautiful oneness.

"I'm sure my brothers will be going to prison," Jim said in a low voice. "And my father is going to take up a lot of my time. I'll have to get used to running the ranch. I was thinking of asking Sam for some help and guidance. He was the manager of the Bar C for a while, and he knows the inner workings of it. He can kind of shadow me until I get into the full swing of things."

Rachel nodded. "I know Sam would do anything to help out. We all will, Jim."

"Do you know how good that is to hear?" he rasped. "No more fighting between the Donovans and the Cunninghams. Now we'll have peace. Isn't that something?"

It was. Rachel sat there in awe over the realization. "I never thought of it in those terms before, but you're right.'' She gave a little laugh. ''Just think, the next time your cattle stray onto our land or vice versa, no nasty phone calls. Just a call saying, 'hey, your cows are straying again.''' She laughed. ''Do you know how *good* that will be?''

''The range war between us is over,'' he said, patting her hand and admiring the ring on her finger once again. It was a child's innocent love that had bought that present for her, but Jim felt his heart swell with pride that Rachel had put it on, nevertheless.

''There's something I want to tell you,'' he said. ''When I left here the other day after Bo and Chet assaulted you, I went home and had it out with my father.'' He frowned. ''It probably contributed to him having a stroke, but I can't be sorry for what I told him.'' He held Rachel's soft green eyes. ''I told him I was in love with you.''

''Oh, dear, Jim.''

''He needed to hear it from me,'' he rasped. ''He didn't like it, but that's life.''

''And he accused you of being a traitor?''

''Yes,'' Jim replied, amazed by her insight. But then, he shouldn't be surprised. She had always been a deep and caring person. ''He said I was being a traitor to the family.''

''What else? I can see it in your eyes.''

Ordinarily, Jim would feel uncomfortable revealing so much of himself, but with Rachel, he felt not only safe in showing those depths within him, but he wanted to. "My father disowned—for the second time."

"No...." Rachel pressed her hand against her heart as she felt and heard the pain in his voice, saw it clearly in his face and eyes. "And then he had that stroke?"

"He had one of the wranglers drive him up to the Flag jail. From what I hear from Scott Maitland, who was there when my father entered into the jail facility, he got into a hell of a fight with the sheriff of Coconino Country, Slade Cameron. That's when he had the stroke. They called 911 and he was taken right over to the hospital from there. Scott told me at the hospital, after I arrived, that my father was demanding that Cameron let my brothers go on bail. The judge had refused them bail, too, and Cameron was backing the judge's decision to the hilt."

Inwardly, Rachel shivered. She knew why the judge had not given them bail. The Cunningham brothers had a notorious history of taking revenge on people who pressed charges against them. That was why they had gotten away without punishment until now—they'd threatened their victims until they dropped the charges. But not this time. Rachel would have kept pressing charges even if they had gotten bail.

"So his anger blew a blood vessel in his brain," Jim told her quietly. "I'm surprised it hadn't happen before this, to tell you the truth."

She nodded and got up. Leaning against the

counter, she studied him in the gathering warmth and silence. "How are you feeling about all this?"

Shrugging, Jim eased out of the chair and came to her side. He slid his arm around her shoulders and guided her into the living room. "Guilty. I can't help but feel that way, but I wasn't going to live a lie with my father, either. He had to know I loved you and that I was going to testify in your defense at Chet and Bo's trial."

She moved with him to the purple-pink-and-cream-colored couch near the fireplace. Sitting down, she leaned against him, contented as never before. "And even though he's disowned you a second time, you're going to stay and run the ranch?"

Jim absorbed the feel of her slender form. How natural, how good it felt to have Rachel in his arms. Outside the picture window, he saw snowflakes twirling down again. The fire crackled pleasantly, and he'd never felt happier—or sadder. "Yes. This disowning thing is a game with my father. I know he meant it, but now it doesn't matter."

Rachel rested her head against his strong, capable shoulder. "And you really want to run the Bar C?"

"Sure." He grinned down at her. "Once a cowboy, always a cowboy."

"An EMT cowboy. And a firefighter."

"All those things," Jim agreed.

"And when Bo and Chet get out of prison, what will you do? Hand the ranch over to them to run?"

Sobering, Jim nodded. He moved his fingers languidly down her shoulder and upper arm. "Yes," he said grimly, "I will."

"He'll never be able to run it," Rachel said worriedly.

"Bo and Chet are the owners, technically. I know they aren't going to want me around when they get out."

"And your father? What will you do? Continue to live there?"

Gently, he turned Rachel around so that she faced him. "When the time's right, I'm going to propose to you. And if you say yes, you'll live over on the Bar C with me. We have several other homes. I'll put my father in one of them and we'll live at the main ranch house. Even though he disowned me, he's going to need me now. And I'm hoping we can mend fences, at least for the sake of his health. When Bo and Chet get out, you and I will leave."

Rachel thrilled to the idea of being Jim's wife. His partner for life. All her previous fears were gone and she knew that was because she was certain of her love for Jim. Heat burned in her cheeks and she held his hopeful gaze. "Kate wants us to live here. In this house, Jim. She already told me we were welcome here in case we got 'serious' about one another."

Grinning, he caressed her hair and followed the sweep of it down her shoulder. "Kate saw us getting together?"

"Kate's not a dumb post."

Chuckling, Jim nodded. "No, I'd never accuse her of being that, ever."

Sliding her hand up his cheek, Rachel felt the sandpaper quality of his skin beneath her palm. She saw Jim's eyes go dark with longing—for her. It was such a delicious feeling to be wanted by him. "Then you wouldn't mind living here and working on the Donovan Ranch instead when the time came?"

"No," he whispered, leaning over and placing a very light kiss on the tip of her nose, "why should I? I'll have you. That's all I'll ever need, princess. Where I live with you doesn't matter at all. It never did."

Sliding into his waiting arms, Rachel closed her eyes and rested her head against Jim's shoulder. A broken sigh escaped her. The next six weeks were going to be a special hell for all of them on many levels. The trial would tear them all apart, she knew. And Jim would be away from her more than with her because he would have to be at the Bar C learning how to manage the huge ranch. And she, well, she had just rented an office in Sedona and there was a lot of pressure on her to get patients and start making money and contributing to paying off that huge debt against the ranch.

"I can hardly wait," Rachel quavered, "for these next six weeks to be done and gone."

Holding her tightly, Jim ran his hand along the line of her graceful back. Pressing a kiss to her hair, he murmured fervently, "I know, princess. Believe me, I know…"

Chapter Twelve

The mid-February sunlight was strong and bright as Rachel sat on her horse, her leg occasionally touching Jim's as the gelding moved to nibble the green grass shoots that surrounded them. The patches of snow here and there on the red clay soil of the Cunningham pasture was strong evidence of the fact that the steady snowfall would break some of the drought conditions that had held everyone captive.

"The cattle are going to eat well," Jim commented as he moved his hat up on his brow and gazed at Rachel. She looked beautiful in Levi's, a long-sleeved white blouse, leather vest and black Stetson cowboy hat. Her hair was caught up in a single braid that lay down the middle of her back.

Nodding, she leaned down and stroked the neck of her black Arabian mare. "For once."

They sat on their horses on a hill that overlooked both Donovan and Cunningham ranch land, a barbed wire fence marking the division line. Down below, on the Donovan side, Kate and Sam were working to repair fence so that their cattle wouldn't wander over onto Cunningham property. At least, Jim thought, this time there was going to be teamwork between the two families, and not angry words followed by violence.

"How's your father?" Rachel asked. Jim's face took on a pained expression. Frank Cunningham had never recovered after the stroke as the doctors had hoped. He was now bedridden, with twenty-four-hour nursing care at the ranch house. Jim divided his duties between managing the huge ranch and trying to help his father, who had given up on living. She knew it was just a matter of time. Frank hadn't been doing well since he'd found out that his two sons were going to prison. Bo got a year and Chet two years.

"Father's little better today," he said, wiping the sweat off his brow. "That's why I came out with the line crew."

"It does you good to get out of that office you've been living in."

Grinning a little, he held Rachel's dancing, lively gaze. "I was going stir-crazy in there, if you want the truth." Jim knew that ever since the trial, which had taken place two weeks earlier, Rachel had been upset and strained. For the first time, he was seeing her more relaxed. Now she had a thriving office filled with patients who wanted natural medicine, like homeopathy, instead of drugs. To say she was a little busy was an understatement. Income from her growing business was helping to pay off some bills on the Donovan Ranch.

"What's the chances of you coming over for dinner tonight?" Rachel asked, her heart beating a little harder. The ache to be with Jim, to share more time with him, never left her. The last six weeks had been a hell for them. They needed a break. She needed him. The stolen kisses, the hot, lingering touches, weren't enough for her anymore.

Frowning, Jim said, "How about a picnic tomorrow? I wanted to go back up on the Rim and explore where they captured that jaguar and took her away." Reaching over, he closed his hand over hers. "Want to come along?"

"I'll provide the lunch?" Rachel asked, thrilling at his strong, steady grip on her hand. The burning hunger in his eyes matched her own feelings. How she hungered to have a few moments alone with Jim! The demands in their lives had kept them apart and she wanted to change that.

"You bet," he murmured with a smile.

"Have you heard from Bob Granby in the fish and game department about how the jaguar is getting along in her new haunt?"

Jim shifted in the saddle, the leather creaking pleasantly beneath him. "Matter of fact, I did. She's been taken over to the White Mountain area and is getting along fine there. He said two more jaguars have been spotted in the mountains north of Tucson, so they are migrating north for sure.''

"I love how things in nature, if they are disturbed, will come back into harmony over time.''

Reluctantly releasing Rachel's hand, Jim nodded. "I like the harmony we're establishing right now between the two ranches.''

"It will last only a year,'' she commented sadly.

He studied her. "Not if you agree to marry me, Rachel.''

Her heart thudded. She stared at Jim. "What?''

He grinned a little. "Well? Will you?''

She saw that boyish grin on his face, his eyes tender with love—for her. Lips parting, she tried to find the words to go along with her feelings.

"Is your stunned look a no or a yes?'' he teased, his grin widening. Over the last six weeks, they had grown incredibly close. Nothing had ever felt so right or so good to Jim. He prayed silently that Rachel wanted marriage as much as he did.

Touching her flaming cheeks, Rachel said, "Let me think about it? I'll give you an answer tomorrow at lunch, okay?''

Nodding, he picked up the reins from the neck of the quarter horse he rode. A part of him felt terror that she'd say no. Another part whispered that Rachel truly needed the time. But that was something he could give her. Leaning over, he curved his hand behind her neck and drew her to him.

"What we have," he told her, his face inches from hers, "is good and beautiful, princess. I'll wait as long as you want me to." He smiled a little, recalling that she had made the other man in her life wait five years and even then she couldn't marry him. Things were different this time around and Jim knew it. Over the last six weeks, he'd watched Rachel's fear dissolve more and more. The fact that he'd loved her since he was a teenager, he was sure, had something to do with it. Leaning over a little more, he crushed her lips to his and tasted sunlight, the clean, fresh air on them. It was so easy to kiss Rachel. And how wonderful it would be to love her fully. Her cheek was healed now, and he didn't have to worry about possibly hurting her when he kissed her hard and swiftly. And he knew she wanted him, too, noting her warm, hot response to his mouth skimming hers.

Easing away, Jim reluctantly released her. There was a delicious cloudiness in Rachel's eyes, and he read it as longing—for him. "I'll meet you at the north pasture at ten tomorrow morning?" he asked huskily.

Rachel felt dizzy with heat, with an aching longing for Jim. Every time he stole a kiss unexpectedly from her, she wanted him just that much more. Touching her lips, she nodded. He look so handsome and confident, sitting astride his bay gelding with that dangerous look glittering in his eyes, one corner of his mouth pulled into a slight, confident smile.

"Yes—tomorrow...."

Rachel found Kate out in the barn, feeding the broodmares for the evening. She helped her older sister finish off the feeding by giving the pregnant Arabian mares a ration of oats. When they were done, Rachel sat down on a bale of hay at one end of the barn. Kate walked up, took off her hat and, wiping her brow with the back of her hand, joined her.

"Thanks for the help."

Rachel nodded. "I need to share something with you, Kate, and I wanted you to hear it from me and not secondhand."

She saw Kate's face go on guard. Rachel smiled a little. "It's good news, Kate."

"Whew. Okay, what is it?" she asked, running her fingers through her hair. "I could use good news."

Wasn't that the truth? Rachel smiled tentatively. "Jim asked me to marry him today." She watched Kate's expression carefully. "I've already told Jessica and Dan. Now I want to tell you and Sam. I'd like to know how you feel about the possibility." Her gut clenched a little as she waited for Kate to speak.

"Jim's a good man," Kate said finally, in a low voice. She picked at some of the alfalfa hay between her legs where she'd straddled the bale. Her brows knitted as she chose her words. "I didn't like him before. But that's because his last name is Cunningham.'' Looking up, she smiled apologetically. ''I'm the last one who should be holding a grudge. The more I saw of Jim in different circumstances, the more I realized that he was genuine. He's not like the others in his family. And he's trying to straighten things out between the two families.''

''If I tell him yes,'' Rachel whispered, a catch in her voice, ''that means I'll be living over there for a while, at least until Bo and Chet come back to claim the ranch.''

''And then,'' Kate said, straightening and moving her shoulders a little, ''you can come home and have your house back if you want.''

''Then you don't mind if I tell Jim yes?''

Kate gave her a silly grin. Leaning over, she hugged Rachel tightly for a moment. ''You love each other! Why should I stand in the way? Jim's a good person. He means to do right by others. He can't help it if he's got rattlesnakes for brothers.''

Grinning, Rachel gripped Kate's long, callused hand. ''Thanks, Kate. Your blessing means everything to me. I—I didn't want to come back here and not be welcomed.''

Tears formed in Kate's eyes and she wiped them away self-consciously. ''Listen, I've committed enough mistakes for the whole family. You've both forgiven me. Why can't I do the same for you and Jim? So, when's the big day?''

''I don't know—yet. Jim and I are going to ride up on the Rim tomorrow morning where we found the jaguar's den. I'm packing a lunch.''

Rising, Kate said, "Great! I'm sure you'll know a lot more when you come down." Holding her hand out to Rachel, she sighed. "Isn't it wonderful? We've all come home from various parts of the world and we're getting our ranch back on its feet. Together."

Rachel released Kate's hand and walked slowly down the aisle with her. She slipped her arm around her sister's slender waist. "Dreams do come true," she agreed. "I hated leaving here when I did. I cried so much that first year I was gone. I was so homesick for Mama, for this wonderful land...."

Sighing, Kate wrapped her arm around Rachel's waist. The gloom of the barn cast long shadows down the aisle as they slowly walked together. "All three of us were. At least we had the guts to come back and work to save our ranch."

"And we're finally coming out from under the bank's thumb!" Rachel laughed, feeling almost giddy about their good fortune. Kate and Sam had sold off half the Herefords for a good price. With the bank loan paid off, they now had a clear shot at keeping the ranch once and for all.

Kate looked down at her, smiling. "Want another piece of good news?"

"Sure? Gosh, two in a row, Katie. I don't know if I can handle it or not!"

She laughed huskily. Patting her abdomen, she said, "I'm pregnant."

Stunned, Rachel released her and turned, her mouth dropping open. "What?"

Coloring prettily, Kate kept her hand across her abdomen. "I just found out this afternoon. Doc Kaldenbaugh said I was two and a half months along. Isn't that wonderful?"

"And Sam? Does he know about it?" Rachel asked, feeling thrilled. She saw the shyness in Kate's face and the joy in it, too.

"Sure, he was with me."

"Oh!" Rachel cried, throwing her arms around Kate and hugging her. "This is so wonderful! I'm gonna be an aunt!"

Kate laughed self-consciously. "Hey, I'm going to need all the help I can get. This mothering role isn't one I know a whole lot about."

Tears trickled down Rachel's cheeks. "Don't worry," she whispered, choking up, "Jessica and I will love being aunts and helping you out. I think among the three of us, we can do the job, don't you?"

Kate grinned mischievously. "You mean Jessica hasn't told you yet?"

"Told me what?"

"She's expecting, too."

Stunned, Rachel stared. "What? When did this all happen? Where was I?"

Chuckling, Kate said, "We both went to Doc Kaldenbaugh today. Seem Jessica is expecting twins. They run in Dan Black's family, you know."

Rachel pressed her hands to her cheeks, dumbfounded. She saw Kate's eyes sparkle with laughter over her reaction.

"So, little sis, you and Jim had better get busy, eh? I'm assuming you want children?"

"More than anything," Rachel said, her voice soft and in awe. "You're *both* pregnant!"

"Yes," Kate gave her a satisfied smile. She turned and shut the barn doors for the night with Rachel's help. "Sam is going to hire a couple more wranglers now that we have some money. Then I can ease off on some of the work I've been doing. He wants me to take it easy." She laughed as she brought the latch down on the door. "I can't exactly see me knitting and crocheting in the house all day, can you?"

Rachel shook her head. "No, but Sam's right— you do need to ease off on some of that hard, physical labor you do on the ranch. I'm sure Jessica could use some help in her flower essence business. You like the greenhouse."

"I was thinking I would help her," Kate said. Patting Rachel on the shoulder, she said, "I'll let Jessica know I told you the big news. When you see Jim tomorrow, and say yes, tell him from me that I'm glad he's going to be a part of our family."

Rachel nodded and gripped her sister's hand for a moment. Kate's blessing made things right. "I will," she whispered. "And thanks for understanding."

"Around here," Kate said, looking up at the bright coverlet of stars in the black night above them, "everything is heart centered, Rachel. I like living out of my heart again. This ranch is our heart, our soul. I'm looking forward to having kids running around again. I'm really looking forward to seeing life and discoveries through their eyes. You know?''

Rachel did know. She lifted her hand. ''Good night, Kate. That baby you're carrying will be one of the most loved children on the face of this earth.'' And it would be. As Rachel made her way through the darkness, broken by patches of light from the sulfur lamps placed here and there around the ranch, she smiled softly. They had suffered so much—each of them, and now life was giving them gifts in return for their courage. Her heart expanded and she longed to see Jim. Rachel could hardly wait for morning to arrive.

''Isn't that wonderful news?'' Rachel asked as she sat on the red-and-white checkered blanket. Jim had spread the picnic blanket out at the mouth to the canyon, beneath an alligator juniper that was probably well over two hundred years old. Above them was the empty lair where the jaguar had once lived.

He munched thoughtfully on an apple. Lying on his side, his cowboy hat hung on a low tree limb, he nodded. ''Twins. Wow. Jessica and Dan are going to be busy.''

Chuckling, Rachel put the last of the chocolate cake and the half-empty bottle of sparkling grape juice back into the saddlebags. ''No kidding.''

''You like the idea of being an aunt?'' Jim asked, slowly easing into a sitting position. He watched as

Rachel put the items away. No matter what she did, there was always grace about her movements. Today she wore her hair loose and free, with dark strands cascading across her pale pink cowboy shirt.

"I love the idea."

He caught her hand. "What do you think about having children?"

His hand was warm and dry as she met and held his tender gaze. "I've always wanted them. And you?"

"They're a natural part of life—and love," he said slowly as he pulled a small box from his pocket. Placing the gray velvet box in the palm of her hand, he whispered, "Open it, Rachel...."

Heart pounding, she smiled tremulously. Rachel knew it was a wedding ring. She loved the idea of him asking to marry her here, in this special canyon the jaguar had come home to. In many ways, the Donovan women were like that jaguar—chased away by a man. And they, too, had finally returned home.

Her fingers trembled as she opened the tiny brass latch. Inside was a gold band. Instead of a diamond, however, there were eight channel-cut stones the same height as the surface of the ring so they wouldn't snag or catch on anything. Each stone was a different color, and as Rachel removed the ring, they sparkled wildly in the sunlight.

"This is so beautiful, Jim," she whispered. Tears stung her eyes as she held it up to him. "It's like this ring." She held up her hand, showing him the "going steady" ring he'd bought so long ago and that she'd faithfully worn since he'd gotten up the courage to give it to her.

Touched, Jim nodded. "Do you like it?"

"Like it?" Rachel stroked the new ring. "I love it...."

"I had it made by a jeweler in Sedona. He's well known for one-of-a-kind pieces. I drew him a picture of the other ring and he said he could do it. Instead of cut glass, though, each of those are gemstones. There's a small emerald, topaz, pink tourmaline, ruby, white moonstone and opal set in it."

Amazed at the simple beauty of the wedding ring, Rachel sighed. "Oh, Jim, this is beyond anything I could imagine."

Wryly, he said, "Can you imagine being my wife?"

Lifting her chin, Rachel met and held his very serious gaze. "Yes, I can."

Satisfaction soared through him. "Let's see if it fits." He took the ring and slid it onto her finger. The fit was perfect. Holding her hand, he added huskily, "You name the date, okay?"

Sniffing, she wiped the tears from her cheeks with her fingers. "My mother's birthday was March 21. I'd love to get married on that day and honor her spirit, honor what she's given the three of us. Is that too soon?"

Grinning, Jim brought her into the circle of his arms. "Too soon?" He pressed a kiss to her hair as she settled against his tall, hard frame. "I was think-ing, like, tomorrow?"

Rachel laughed giddily. "Jim! You don't mean that, do you?"

He leaned down and held Rachel in his arms, tak-ing her mouth gently. She was soft and warm and giving. As her hand slid around his neck, a hot, trembling need poured through him. He skimmed her lips with his and felt her quiver in response. She tasted of sweet cherries and chocolate from the cake she'd just eaten. Running his hands through her thick, unbound hair, he was reminded of the strength that Rachel possessed.

Drawing her onto the blanket, he met her eyes, dazed with joy and need. "I want to love you," he rasped, threading his fingers through her hair as it fell against the blanket like a dark halo. Sunlight filtering through the juniper above them dappled the ground with gold. The breeze was warm and pine scented. Everything was perfect with Rachel beside him. Nothing had ever felt so right to Jim as this moment.

"Yes…" Rachel whispered as she moved her hands to his light blue chambray shirt. She began to unsnap the pearl buttons one at a time until the shirt fell away, exposing his darkly haired chest. Closing her eyes, Rachel spread her hands out across his torso, the thick, wiry hair beneath her palms sending tingles up her limbs. There was such strength to Jim, she realized, as she continued to languidly explore his deep, well-formed body. At the same time, she felt his fingers undoing the buttons on her blouse. Each touch was featherlight, evocative and teasing. Her nipples hardened in anticipation as he moved the material aside, easing it off her shoulders. The sunlight felt warm against her exposed skin as the last of her lingerie was shed.

The first, skimming touch of his work-roughened fingers along her collarbone made her inhale sharply. Opening her eyes, she drowned in his stormy ones. They had always called him Cougar and she could see and feel his desire stalking her now. As he spread his hand outward to follow the curve of her breast, her lashes fluttered closed. Hot, wild tingling sped through her and she moaned as his fingers cupped her flesh.

Moments later, she felt his lips capture one hardened nipple and a cry of pleasure escaped her lips. Instinctively, she arched against him. His naked chest met hers. A galvanizing fire sizzled through her as he suckled her. The heat burned down her to her lower abdomen, an ache building so fiercely between her thighs that she moaned as his hand moved to release the snap on her Levi's. Never had Rachel felt so wanted and desired as now. As he lifted his head, he smiled down at her. His gaze burned through her, straight to her heart, to her soul. This was the man she wanted forever, she realized dazedly.

As he slipped out of his Levi's, after pulling hers from her legs, Rachel felt shaky with need. Her mind wasn't functioning; she was solely captive to her emotions, to the love she felt for Jim as he eased her back down on the blanket. As his strong, sun-darkened body met and flowed against hers, she re-leased a ragged little sigh. Automatically, she pressed herself wantonly against him. His hand ranged down across her hip to her thigh. As she met his mouth, and he plundered her depths hotly, she slid her hand up and over his chest. Their breathing was hot and shallow. Their hearts pounded in fury and need.

The moment his hand slid between her thighs, silently asking her to open to him, she felt his tongue move into her mouth. Where did rapture begin and end? Rachel wasn't sure as his tongue stroked hers at the same time his fingers sought and found the moist opening to her womanhood. Sharp jolts of heat moved up through her. The cry in her throat turned to a moan of utter need. In moments, she felt him move across her, felt his knee guide her thighs open to receive all of him, and she clung to his capturing, cajoling mouth.

She throbbed with desire. She couldn't wait any longer. Thrusting her hips upward, she met him fear-lessly, with equal passion. The moment he plunged into her, she gave a startled cry, but it was one of utter pleasure, not pain. His other hand settled be-neath her hips and he moved rhythmically with her. The ache dissolved into hot honey within her. This warmth of the sunlight on her flesh, his mouth seek-ing and molding, their breath wild and chaotic, all blended into an incredible collage of movement, sound, taste and pleasure. A white-hot explosion occurred deep within her, and Rachel threw back her head with a cry and arched hard against him. Through the haze of sensations she heard him growl like the cougar he really was. His hands were hard on her shoulders as he thrust repeatedly into her, heightening her pleasure as the volcanic release flowed wildly through her. In those moments, the world spun around them. There was only Jim, his powerful embrace, his heart thundering against hers as they clung to one another in that beautiful moment of creation between them.

Languidly, Rachel relaxed in his arms in the aftermath. Barely opening her eyes, she smiled tremulously up at him. His face glistened with perspiration; his eyes were banked with desire and love for her alone. Stretching fully, Rachel lay against his muscular length, his arms around her, holding her close to him.

"I love you," Jim rasped as he kissed her hair, her temple and her flushed cheek. "I always have, sweet woman of mine." And she was his. In every way. Never had Jim felt more powerful, more sure of himself as a man, as now. She was like sweet, hot honey in his arms, her body lithe, warm and trembling. How alive Rachel was! Not only was there such compassion in her, he was lucky to be able to share her passion as well. Moving several damp strands of hair from her brow, he drowned in her forest green eyes, which danced with gold flecks.

Her lips were parted, glistening and well kissed. She had a mouth he wanted to kiss forever.

His words fell softly against her ears. Rachel sighed and closed her eyes, resting her brow against his jaw. Somewhere in the background, she heard the call of a raven far above the canyon where they lay. She felt the dappled sunlight dancing across her sated form. The breeze was like invisible hands drying and softly caressing her. More than anything, she absorbed Jim's love, the protectiveness he naturally accorded her as she lay in his arms. This was a man whose heart, whose morals and values were worth everything to her—and then some. It didn't matter that his last name was Cunningham. By them loving one another, Rachel thought dazedly, still lost in the memory of their lovemaking, a hundred-year-old feud no longer existed between their families.

Moving her hand in a weak motion across his damp chest, she smiled softly. "I love you so much, darling." She looked up into his eyes. "I'm looking forward to spending the rest of my life showing you just how much."

Tenderly, he caught and held her lips beneath his. It was a soft kiss meant to seal her words between them. He felt as if his heart would explode with happiness. Did anyone deserve to feel this happy? He thought not as he wrapped her tightly against him. Chuckling a little, he told her, "Well, maybe as of today, we'll start a new family dynasty. A blend of Cunningham and Donovan blood."

The thought of having Jim's baby made her feel

fulfilled as never before. Rachel laughed a little. "You can't have a feud this way, can you?"

"No," he answered, sighing. So much worry and strain sloughed off of him in that moment as he moved his large hand across her rounded abdomen. Rachel had wide hips and he knew she'd carry a baby easily within her. Their children. The thought brought him a sense of serenity he'd never known before this moment.

As Jim looked down at Rachel, he cupped her cheek and whispered, "I'll love you forever, princess. You and as many children we bring into the world because of the love we hold for one another."

* * * * *

Spence Harrison has to solve the mystery of his past so that he can be free to love the woman who has infiltrated his heart.

The Country Club

For money
or love?

The
Country
Club

SILHOUETTE

Where passion runs deep and love lasts forever

MONTANA GROOMS

Laurie Page   Linda Turner   Allison Leigh

On sale 21st May 2004

*Available at most branches of WHSmith,
Tesco, Martins, Borders, Eason, Sainsbury's
and all good paperback bookshops.*

SILHOUETTE®

SPECIAL EDITION™

presents

Winchester

Brides

By Pamela Toth

**IT TAKES A SPECIAL KIND OF WOMAN TO TAME
THESE IRRESISTIBLE BACHELORS!**

Cattleman's Honour

(May 2004)

Man Behind the Badge

(June 2004)

A Winchester Homecoming

(July 2004)

0404/SH/LC86

SILHOUETTE®
SENSATION™

proudly presents
a brand-new series from

INGRID WEAVER

EAGLE SQUADRON

Elite warriors who live—and love—by
their own code of honour.

EYE OF THE BEHOLDER

March 2004

SEVEN DAYS TO FOREVER

May 2004

AIM FOR THE HEART

August 2004

0304/SH/LC83

SILHOUETTE®

DESIRE™

are proud to introduce

DYNASTIES: THE BARONES

Meet the wealthy Barones—caught in a web of danger, deceit and...desire!

Twelve exciting stories in six 2-in-1 volumes:

0104/SH/LC78